DISSIDENT DRAMAT

To Marian, Róisín and Ian –
with gratefulness, appreciation and love

DISSIDENT DRAMATURGIES

Contemporary Irish Theatre

EAMONN JORDAN
University College Dublin

IRISH ACADEMIC PRESS
DUBLIN • PORTLAND, OR

First published in 2010 by Irish Academic Press

2 Brookside
Dundrum Road
Dublin 14, Ireland

920 NE 58th Avenue, Suite 300
Portland, Oregon,
97213-3786 USA

www.iap.ie

© 2010 Eamonn Jordan

British Library Cataloguing in Publication Data
An entry can be found on request

ISBN 978 0 7165 3013 8 (cloth)
ISBN 978 0 7165 3015 2 (paper)

Library of Congress Cataloging-in-Publication Data
An entry can be found on request

Printed in Great Britain by the MPG Books Group, Bodmin and King's Lynn

Contents

Acknowledgements

First of all, thanks to all the staff at Irish Academic Press who have helped make this book possible. Their work has made this a far better book. I am indebted to the whole team, especially Lisa Hyde, for her encouragement, advice and guidance. Thanks to Hilary Hammond and Guy Holland for editing and proofreading support. I gratefully acknowledge Gallery Press for the kind permission to quote from the work of Marina Carr and Tom Kilroy; Methuen for permission to reproduce extracts from the work of Martin McDonagh and Tom Murphy, Nick Hern Books for permission to quote from the works of Stella Feehily, Marie Jones, Conor McPherson, Mark O'Rowe, Eugene O'Brien and Enda Walsh, amongst others. Thanks to Faber & Faber for permission to quote from the works of Marina Carr, Brian Friel, Tom Kilroy, Martin McDonagh and Frank McGuinness.

Since I began thinking and writing about Irish theatre over the last twenty years, my ideas have been shaped by numerous performances, inspired by many conversations and furthered by the research that I have read. In terms of that scholarship, I am indebted to the monographs, edited collections and writings of Pat Burke, Csilla Bertha, Richard Allen Cave, Enrica Cerquoni, Brenna Clarke Katz, Joe Cleary, David Cregan, Seamus Deane, Gerald Fitzgibbon, Lisa Fitzpatrick, Christopher Fitz-Simon, Joan Fitzpatrick, Imelda Foley, Adrian Frazier, Karen Fricker, Nicholas Grene, Colin Graham, David Grant, Susan Cannon Harris, Sara Keating, Tom Kilroy, Declan Kiberd, Mária Kurdi, Cathy Leeney, Helen Lojek, Joseph Long, Patrick Lonergan, Marianne McDonald, Anna McMullan, Tom Maguire, PJ Matthews, Victor Merriman, Hiroko Mikami, Christopher Morash, Donald Morse, Paul Murphy, Christopher Murray, Riana O'Dwyer, Redmond O'Hanlon, Fintan O'Toole, Anne O'Reilly, Ondřej Pilný, Richard Pine, Lionel Pilkington, Mark Phelan, Catherine Rees, Shaun Richards, Anthony Roche, Brian Singleton, Bernadette Sweeney, Melissa Sihra, Carmen Szabó, Rhona Trench, Mary Trotter, Clare Wallace, Fintan Walsh, Steve Wilmer and Rebecca Wilson. The challenges posed by this scholarship are to be found in most of what I have written. It was Fintan O'Toole's groundbreaking book *Tom*

Murphy: The Politics of Magic that initially inspired my work as a critic. And in terms of performance, directors, designers and actors have inspired this book in a variety of ways.

Teaching has also been a privilege. My ideas and convictions have been shaped by those encounters. My work at Drama Studies Centre, UCD School of English, Drama and Film (1994–99 and 2006–), has benefited from the inspiring colleagues over the years: Enrica Cerquoni, Finola Cronin, Dan Farrelly, Hilary Gow, Andy Hinds, Mary Howard, Karen Jackman, Joseph Long, Emilie Pine, Sara Keating, Marie Kelly, Cathy Leeney, Christopher Murray, Redmond O'Hanlon, Anthony Roche, Carmen Szabó, Kevin Wallace, Ian Walsh, Eric Weitz, Mike Wilock and Marilena Zarouilla.

Undergraduate and Masters students in UCD have always proved to be provocative, particularly those whose minor theses I had the privilege of supervising. Ph.D. students Anne O'Reilly, and more recently Susanne Colleary, Finola Cronin, Michael Maguire, Audrey McNamara, Iris Park Noelia Ruiz and Eva Urban have been a great inspiration, as have all the current Ph.D. students working at the Drama Studies Centre. In UCD School of English, Drama and Film, to my many colleagues, I would like to say thank you, and particular thanks to Andrew Carpenter and Nicholas Daly, and also to the Principal of the College, Mary Daly.

In my three years at IES Dublin, Ashley Taggart, Megan Markey, Siobhan Ni Chonchuir, Regina Fitzpatrick, Joan Gillespie, Darren Kelly, Julie Anne Stevens, Gillian O'Brien, Kevin Rafter, Caroline McSweeney, Diane Richardson, Antoinette Duffy and Cathal Quinn have been inspirational colleagues in very different ways. My work with students at Tisch School of Arts (NYU), Dublin was always a great pleasure and challenge, and thanks to Susanne Bach for making that possible.

I would especially like to thank all my students and colleagues in Social Studies and Performing Arts at the Institute of Technology Sligo, especially Declan Drohan, John Kavanagh, Una Mannion, John Pender and Perry Share, who inspired me by their reflections and insights.

A special thanks to my in-laws, Bridget O'Connell and Stáis Dollard and to Pat and Claire, Kian and especially Finn, all of whom have been a huge inspiration through the latter end of this project.

As always, for Ian, Róisín and Marian, I am perpetually grateful. Thanks to the theatre companies and photographers who allowed me to reproduce their work.

I am very appreciative of funding from the National University of Ireland and the University College Dublin Research Seed Fund towards the preparation and publication costs of this book.

Special thanks to Mairéad Delaney, Archivist, Abbey Theatre, Martina Murphy at An Grianán Theatre, Alena Melichar for help with Ivan Kyncl's archive, Gavin Clarke at the Royal National Theatre, London, Ciaran Deane at Field Day Publications and to the photographers, Simon Annand, Ross Kavanagh, Ivan Kyncl, Paul McCarthy, Stanley Machett, and Keith Pattison for their kind permissions to reproduce images.

Sections of this book were read by Lilian Chambers, Lisa Fitzpatrick, Marian Jordan and Rhona Trench and I thank them for their invaluable advice and guidance. I alone am responsible for any errors. Many editors of journals and books have fed into the process of revising my thoughts over the years. Thanks to Mária Kurdi for a letter of support for this book and much encouragement over the last years.

Versions of these chapters have appeared in an array of publications and the work has been revised and shaped for another purpose. Chapter 2 is built around the following works: 'From Playground to Battleground: Metatheatricality in the Plays of Frank McGuinness' in *Theatre Stuff: Critical Essays on Contemporary Irish Theatre* (Dublin: Carysfort Press, 2000), 194–208, and 'The Metatheatricalisation of Memory in Brian Friel's *Dancing at Lughnasa*' in *Cultural Memory: Essays on European Literature and History*, Rick Caldicott and Anne Fuchs, eds (Bern: Peter Lang, 2003), 129–145; 'Thomas Kilroy's *Double Cross*: Mediatized Realities and Sites of Multiple, Projected Selves' in *Focus: Studies in English Literature*, Winter 2004, 101–115, and 'Menace and Play: Dissipating and Emerging Dramaturgies in Irish Theatre in the 1990s' in *Anachronist*, 13, 2007/8, a piece that also informs some of my conclusions.

Chapter 3 uses four earlier attempts to deal with these issues: 'The Theatrical Representation of Incest in Marina Carr's *On Raftery's Hill*' in *Journal of Applied Social Care,* 3.1, Spring 2001, 138–150, 'From Context to Text: The Construction of Innocence and Sexual Violation in Contemporary Irish Theatre' in *Bullán* (Journal of Irish Literature), Winter 2001, 47–65, 'The De-Privileging of Innocence and the Masquerade of the Damned: Frank McGuinness' *Innocence*' in *The Theatre of Frank McGuinness: Stages of Mutability*, ed. Helen Lojek (Dublin, Carysfort Press, 2002), 50–78, and 'Kicking with Both Feet?: Marie Jones's *A Night in November*', *Irish Review*, 2008.

Chapter 4 is a compression of three articles: 'Unmasking the Myths?: Marina Carr's *By the Bog of Cats* and *On Raftery's Hill*' in *Amid Our Troubles: Irish Versions of Greek Tragedy*, eds Marianne McDonald and Michael Walton (London: Methuen, 2002), 243–262,

'Project Mayhem, an Avenger's Tragedy: Mark O'Rowe's *Howie The Rookie*', *Irish Review,* Spring 2007, and 'Urban Dramas: Any Myth will Do' in Paul Murphy and Melissa Sihra eds, *The Dreaming Body: Contemporary Irish Theatre* (Oxford: Oxford University Press; Gerrards Cross: Colin Smythe, 2009).

Chapter 5 is a revised version of 'Pastoral Exhibits: Narrating Authenticity in Conor McPherson's *The Weir*', *Irish University Review*, Autumn 2004, 351–368, and 'The Native Quarter: Martin McDonagh's West of Ireland Plays' in *Sub-versions: Trans-European Readings of Modern Irish Literature*, edited by Ciaran Ross (Amsterdam: Rodopi, 2009).

The section on *The Pillowman* in chapter 6 is a revised version of 'The Fallacy of Agency in Arthur Miller's *Death of a Salesman* and Martin McDonagh's *The Pillowman*', *Hungarian Journal of English and American Studies*, 2005, 32–50, and 'War on Narrative: Martin McDonagh's *The Pillowman*' in *The Theatre of Martin McDonagh* (Dublin: Carysfort Press, 2006), 174–97. A version of chapter 7 first appeared in 'Monologue and the Erasure of Public Spaces in Irish Theatre' in *The Monologue in Modern Theatre*, edited by Clare Wallace (Prague: Litteraria Pragensia Books, 2006), 125–156.

List of Figures

Thanks to Mairéad Delaney, Archivist, Abbey Theatre Archives, Martina Murphy at An Grianán Theatre, Alena Melichar for help with Ivan Kyncl's archive, Gavin NT, Ciaran Deane at Field Day Publications

Introduction

THE DEMOCRACY DELUSION

From the mid to late 1980s until the end of the millennium and after, Irish society altered radically and it did so at a pace previously unknown and unanticipated, even by those who offered the most fanciful imaginings, optimistic reckonings and projections. This transformation worked its way through almost all echelons, economic, political, social, intellectual and cultural, and it came about thanks to a number of diverse circumstances and improbable situations; namely the impact of European Union membership from 1973 and the structural funding that ensued from it, direct foreign inward investment mainly provided by American multinationals and by companies in key globalized markets like the financial services, technology and pharmaceutical sectors, and benefits accruing from the beginnings of the Peace Process in Northern Ireland from 1994 through to the Good Friday Agreement in 1998 and after.[1]

Equally, general technological advancements, a better educated, young and mobile workforce, the availability of cheap money, a rapid alteration in sexual behaviours, the expansion of drug and club cultures, a progressively more liberal agenda informing legislation, significantly declining unemployment, the repopulation of rural areas, substantially decreased emigration figures, and significant increases in prosperity per capita and social mobility prompted a host of other changes, challenges and opportunities. On the negative side, one would point out the Americanization of Irish culture, the increasing individuation of its citizens, the more frequent lack of generosity and tolerance of the disadvantaged amongst its population, its casual disregard for environmental issues, the de-unionization of a workforce, the spurious consciousness of wealth accumulation, complex and mainly disreputable tax breaks, and most of all, soft touch governmental regulation of all things financial and an uncanny trust in the marketplace and competition to determine cost, worth and value.

In addition, the decline in the influence of the Catholic Church, in part due to sex scandals within the Church, international sporting successes for teams and individuals, the election of two consecutive women presidents, a slackening of the propensity to include Britain in the evaluation or elaboration of Irish identities, benefits from social partnership, and cheaper travel internationally all led to different types of individual and collective mobility, economically, socially and culturally. Economic migrants and asylum seekers changed the intercultural nature of Irish society most substantially: currently migrants make up close to 10 per cent of the population.

The abortion debate led to a referendum in 1983 and the constitution was amended to 'defend the life of the unborn', but a right to travel for an abortion was granted by way of an amendment to the constitution in 1992, following a Supreme Court decision in the X Case. The year 1993 saw the decriminalizing of homosexuality, prompted by the victory of the David Norris case at the European Court of Human Rights in 1988. Divorce was introduced by way of a referendum in 1995. In the Irish Republic a series of tribunals investigated corrupt and illegal business and political practices, namely the Beef Tribunal Enquiry of 1991, the Blood Transfusion enquiry in 1997 into the supply of contaminated blood products and Hepatitis C infections, the McCracken and Moriarty Tribunal investigations into secret payments to politicians (1997), and the Flood/Mahon tribunal investigation into alleged corrupt payments to politicians for planning permissions and land rezoning decisions. All of these investigations showed just how complicit the body politic was, or was perceived to have been, with vested interests and big businesses across a range of sectors.

However, during this period new types of social and economic issues emerged, such as longer working hours and commuting times, increasing costs of child care, phenomenal increases in personal addictions and indebtedness (some would cynically claim as a swapping of government debt for personal debt), relative and perceived disimprovements in health-care service provision despite substantial increases in government spending, and the emergence of dormer towns, places to which people only go home during the working week to sleep. Fundamentally, Ireland became a low tax economy, looking to Boston and not Berlin as the prevailing influence. Consumption patterns also changed with a desire for expensive designer and luxury items increasingly on the agenda and people seeking mortgages at a younger age than previously. So as Ireland moved through a period of accelerated history, delivering what R.F. Foster calls 'history in fast-forward mode, as transformations accumulate in economic practice, in social and religious experience, in cultural achievement and in political relationships, both at home and abroad'.[2] The changes came quick and fast during these compulsive decades, with colossal benefits and significant costs, pointed inequalities and the relative or proportional absence of opportunities for many of the more marginalized social groups. Capital equity rather than social equality was often the main focus of personal ambition and the driver of social mobility.

Of course, the 9/11 disaster led to desperate attempts by America to spend its way out of a crisis, and to cheap money being made available to sustain its economy, which directly resulted in sub-prime lending. Speculative, dubious and illegal financial practices that had become more complex and unreal, through things like securitization and derivatives, the activities of investment banks and hedge funds led to devastating consequences. Effectively, the world had gone from an old traditional model of trading in goods, services and ideas to retailing or trading paper. Also, the US spent trillions of dollars on disastrous wars in Iraq and Afghanistan.

Very recently, Ireland has been regarded as the most globalized country in the world by a number of different measures, which at the time seemed to many an attractive attribute, but the impact and the devastation of that worldwide connectivity and the truer meaning of being a top-rank globalized society came home to roost during the global recession starting in 2007.[3] As I write in early 2009, that general, sweeping overview of changes since the 1980s needs radical updating, reconsideration and revision. The global credit crunch, the collapse of the housing markets in many first-world countries, the disastrous demise of some global investment businesses, a crumbling of shares values and substantial increases in unemployment have already occurred, with more challenges anticipated. Closer to home, recession, deflation and a huge drop in consumer confidence, the near collapse of the Irish banking system, an inability of the banking system to recapitalize from normal sources and a fear to extend credit to customers, a major government budget shortfall in 2008/9 and just as substantial government deficits are anticipated going forward. These factors suggest that many of those local prosperity and wealth gains were driven by spurious speculation as much as by anything else and are now about to recede.

It is a very evident socio/economic shift from an abundance for many to one where there is increasing financial and personal devastation, through the inability to pay taxes and bills and to maintain one's employment, let alone to worry about reduced lifestyle choices and slashed disposable income. The inability of government to contain the economic wildfire, in part is down to Ireland's open economy, but is also due to the inability to imagine alternative scenarios other than growth or to have contingency plans in place. Short-term planning was favoured over long-term strategic considerations. The types of anticipative intelligence and foresight that one requires of governance, policy initiatives and regulation are noticeable by their relative absence. Yet despite the gloom, if the necessary corrections occur through a change in global economies, and through a mix of national policy decisions or ones superimposed by external forces, then a more optimistic perspective is probable. These socio/economic, cultural and political realities shape the worlds in which the plays under consideration were produced, but what might be the nature of that relationship?

'A DRAMATURGY OF CHANGING STATES'

In very general terms, from the 1980s onwards arts funding in Ireland altered significantly, the quality of training and educational opportunities grew, in terms of academic study, performance and arts administration. Some Irish directors and performers trained abroad and this allowed their work to be informed by international best practices. Likewise, the Dublin Theatre Festival, Dublin's Fringe Festival and the Belfast and the Galway Arts Festivals, amongst others, like the Project Arts Centre, offered regular opportunities for writers and theatre makers to engage with diverse ways of creating theatre and to experience different performance competencies, and ways of conceiving novel types of audience interaction. Also, Irish production companies tested their work abroad more frequently.

The work of companies like Druid Theatre Company, Field Day, Rough Magic and the Gate and Abbey Theatres did a good deal to develop new work and promote it internationally. Most substantially, international companies were increasingly willing to perform Irish plays, either in the language/context as written, as adaptations or in translation.[4] The vibrancy and accomplishments, in terms of productions, box office and awards for Sebastian Barry, Marina Carr, Anne Devlin, Brian Friel, Tom Kilroy, Frank McGuinness, Martin McDonagh (Anglo-Irish), Conor McPherson, Tom Murphy, Billy Roche and Enda Walsh are very evident. Companies like Barabbas... the company, Blue Raincoat, Charabanc, Corcadorca, Corn Exchange, Fabulous Beast, Fishamble, Gúna Nua, Loose Canon, Macnas, Prime Cut, Pan-Pan, Performance Corporation, Red Kettle, Tall Tales and Tinderbox made theatre that was often inspiring and at times radically different from the primarily text-based theatre tradition. The task of this book is to focus on some of the new writing that emerged during this period from the 1980s, rather than on devised work.

The type of texts under discussion here clearly evolved, by consolidating, expanding, spring-boarding and rejecting some more traditional approaches to writing for theatre from the late 1950s forward. While the late twentieth-century dramaturgy of Irish theatre must be traced back through Samuel Beckett to William Butler Yeats, Lady Augusta Gregory, Oscar Wilde and in particular John Millington Synge and Sean O'Casey, it is clear that during the late 1950s and early 1960s new and different types of writing emerged; Tom Murphy's *A Whistle in the Dark* (1961) and Brian Friel's *Philadelphia, Here I Come!* (1964) were the plays that most pronounce the emergence of a new approach to writing and performing for Irish theatre. Many argue that these plays were a reaction against the conventional conformism of the writing from the 1930s forward, but current research on this earlier period argues that this was not necessarily an era of stagnation and traditionalism, but rather one of vitality and experimentalism, if one looks beyond the activities of the more conservative producing houses. The plays of the new era from the late 1950s forward were cognisant of developments in Europe and America, were intent on addressing subjects that were under-discussed, and were focused on confronting repression, injustice and the historical and contemporaneous implications of imperialism and colonization.

In fact, it was not until the mid-1980s/early 1990s that such a dominant approach to theatre writing began to shift and modify in any noticeable way. This says as much about the relative stagnancy of Irish society during this period as it does about the rich seam of concerns that were available to these writers.[5] The task I set myself is to foreground the dramaturgical variations and dynamics of plays that exemplify this contemporary period, ever alert to the fallacies of a constructed tradition and the impossibilities of isolating a tradition of writing from what happens internationally. I do so neither to establish an elemental rupture nor to affirm fundamental continuities in dramaturgical practices. Christopher Murray argues that during the 100-year history of the Abbey Theatre, 'In the history itself there is this frequent doubling back, recapitulation, slowing up of pace, followed by surges forward, to be again followed by what looks like recapitulations once more of earlier patterns.'[6] Murray's comment offers a more pragmatic measure of evolving forms.

Obviously, there are no neutral and apolitical spaces, character, incidents or situations, but works of art are seldom position statements. In some ways, the specificity of Ireland's history seems to urge a specific type of reading and response. As Nicholas Grene suggests, 'As long as there has been a distinct Irish drama it has been closely bound up with national politics that the one has often been considered more or less a reflection of the other.'[7] On that basis, it is reasonable to encourage a fundamental affiliation or an essential rapport between text and context. There are many illustrations of those that do.

Fintan O'Toole, for example, claims, with the exception of Sean O'Casey, that Irish theatre before Tom Murphy 'assumes a single unified society, in line with nationalist ideology'. However O'Toole argues, '[T. K.] Whitaker's revolution called into being new class forces, new divisions of urban and rural, new consumer choices, new modes of behaviour, so that "Ireland" itself as a fixed and coherent notion which could underlie the work of a writer ceased to exist.'[8] O'Toole adds: 'It was replaced by a series of divisions, a series of variations on Ireland, a range of individual responses to the problems, not of unity and homogeneity, but of discontinuity, disruption and disunity.'[9] While I can agree with this comment, I cannot go as far as O'Toole when he argues that the achievement of Tom Murphy's work is that it 'forms a kind of inner history of Ireland since the momentous changes which were set in motion in 1959, the fact that it reflects in a more sustained and accurate way the Irish society of those years than does the work of any other writer'.[10] To press home the point he claims that 'Murphy has been able to dramatize an entire society at a time when the theatre has been forced to retreat into the dramatization of individual lives or the lives of a confined strata of society.'[11] No playwright can 'dramatize an entire society', and such burdens should not be on the work or on the making or receiving of theatre.

DO WE HAVE A CONTEXT?

The best plays of the generations of writers since the 1950s would include few realistic plays. That comment does not stop so many critics and spectators in believing with great persistence that Irish theatre is embedded in realism. Indeed one of the main weaknesses of the Irish tradition is its inability to be successful in the modes of realism. Of the plays discussed in this book, very few can be deemed realistic or naturalistic. While the plays may have a realistic grounding, the language, characters, action and form tend to invite a shift in register. The shift of register that Irish plays chase after, even when working within a restrictive form of realism, must be enabled by direction and scenography and atypical approaches to performance. (There is a further disjunction, as a good deal of professional training is given over to acting styles appropriate to the naturalistic tradition in film and theatre performance.)

Hanna Scolnicov's comments, on the early notionally realistic work of Harold Pinter, are applicable to many Irish plays:

> The world of his characters is wholly contained in their words. We understand the words because they resemble the things we say everyday, just as the room in which they move resembles a familiar room. But instead of an imitation of an action, what we get is a disjointed imitation of words imitating words, and objects – objects. The realism of detail produces a hyper-realistic effect without fusing together into a meaningful structure. Although the superficial impression created is of theatrical realism, the disparate elements do not coalesce into a meaningful mimetic structure.[12]

In Irish Theatre, while things may seem familiar, they soon appear 'disjointed', while the language spoken seems real it then drifts elsewhere, and most variables 'do not coalesce into a meaningful mimetic structure'. That absence of things combining together is of vital importance. I think that is a very perceptive way of dealing with the challenges of mimesis. Friel is always more secure when he is shifting away from the confines of realism in work like *Living Quarters* (1977). Likewise Marina Carr in *Portia Coughlan* (1996) shatters the relationship of causality that is fundamental to realism.

Garry Hynes raises a vital issue in relation to realism and verisimilitude: 'There's this issue about Martin [McDonagh] and authenticity – the response that his is not Irish life now and it's not Connemara life. Of course it isn't. It's an artifice. It's not authentic. It's not meant to be. It's a complete creation, and in that sense it's fascinating.'[13] Hynes, in particular, has been very successful as a director in manipulating the idea of 'artifice'. Her longevity and her successes since the mid-1970s are remarkable. Along with Patrick Mason, she has been the most influential director in Irish Theatre for over thirty years. When we trace the most significant premières of new work since the 1970s, the names of Mason and Hynes crop up again and again, and most of the work is not about realism or authenticity, but for both, it is about different modes of representation, scale and register. Another part of their vital contribution is their collaborations with a range of set and lighting designers who provided the appropriate scenographic environments in which to present the work.

History raises other issues in terms of contextualization. The historical figures of Brendan Bracken, Winston Churchill's Minister for Information during World War Two, and William Joyce, a.k.a Lord Haw-Haw, appear in Thomas Kilroy's *Double Cross* (1986). The impact of Bloody Sunday 1972 and the shooting dead of fourteen civilians by the British Army on the streets of Derry impacts on the characters in Frank McGuinness's *Carthaginians* (1988). Marie Jones's *A Night in November* (1994) deals with sectarianism and is informed by the Windsor Park World Cup qualification match in 1993 between Northern Ireland and the Republic of Ireland.[14] Again, real historical backdrops are more inclined to bring questions of authenticity and contextualization to the fore and relegate the notion of fictive elaboration.[15]

Also, there are often some overlapping events in real life with the productions of plays, causing a type of intertextual frisson. Martin McDonagh's *The Pillowman* coincided with the revelations of torture and intimidation in holding cells in Abu Ghraib in 2003, an idea which some critics commented upon, and a production in Istanbul of his *The Lieutenant of Inishmore* corresponded with terrorist bombs in the city in 2003. The production of Frank McGuinness's *Observe the Sons of Ulster Marching Towards the Somme* at the Abbey Theatre had the ceasefires in Northern Ireland as a backdrop in 1994. The American production of this same play in 2001 gave rise to review titles like 'Observe the Sons of America marching towards Iraq'.[16]

Mark O'Rowe's monologue-driven *Howie The Rookie* (1999) brings a different type of complication, and this time in terms of space and locale. The play is set notionally in west Dublin, in a working-class marginal, liminal space of sorts. However, it is not necessarily the Tallaght, Dublin 24, where O'Rowe grew up. In this play O'Rowe blurs the co-ordinates of the space, and explicit references to Dublin are intentionally scattered, something that in turn maps on to the disorientation of the characters. In a recent article, Cathy Leeney reflects on Marc Augé's notion of the 'non-place', 'a space which does not affirm sociological or cultural identities as they have been defined by social and psychological sciences', and this type of approach applies as well to the work of O'Rowe as it does to Anne Devlin, Enda Walsh and many others.[17] The characters in *Howie The Rookie* are displaced and dislodged non-bodies and not precisely located or contextualized by the specific realities of suburban Dublin. Yet, if Dublin is one shadow lingering over the play, the martial arts figure/actor Bruce Lee is the other prevailing spectral presence that provides an alternative popular cultural warrior tradition. And of course what happens to this play when it is performed in Montreal, by actors whose notion of Tallaght is moderately dependent on information they or the dramaturg provide, or in Australia when one of the roles is played by an actor of Aboriginal extraction? If plays are performed in radically different performance contexts, then the contextualization of texts may be notional only, rather than grounded in the specifics of a performance.[18]

So on the one hand, contextual pressures and anomalies are driven by a combination of notional, imaginative and identifiable spaces, the facts of history, authenticity, emotional, psychological, mythical, and political aspects associated with the real, spectator expectations or alignments, and related events mirroring or echoing what happens in a performance. On the other hand, if either the tenets of postmodernism are embraced or the imperatives of contemporary theatre theory are absorbed, the implications are huge, because both perspectives announce the insubstantability of the relationship between text and context. If there is no context being filtered through performance, and no referent beyond the frame of theatrical representation itself, then different types of discussions are necessary about the relationship between texts and realities.

Even when one rejects the implications of the psychological or the sociological, one cannot easily overlook the contextualization imperative, as part of the experiences of performance, as the inclination of the spectator is to relate the work back to their own experiences, or to engage imaginatively with a context different to their own. It has as much to do with modes of perception and construction as it does with cultural training.

Easy contextualization is worse than 'easy sentiment', so it is not a question of whether it is straightforward to find a way of contextualizing theatre, more, it is the understanding of contexts reimagined or imaginary perspectives which can be the springboard for the dramaturgy of the plays that I will consider. Furthermore, performance contextualizations are easier to realize in many ways than textual contextualizations, as there are physical evidence and material details to deal with. Although this book has the word *Irish* in its title, it cannot be simply about nation formation or national identities, its significances, enabling qualities, symbolic associations and connotations, exportability and marketability, or its exclusivities, prior claims, exclusions, limitations, repressions and prejudices. Fundamentally, Ireland does not provide either the coherence or composure of a metanarrative, nor function as the base referent to all the work under discussion, in the way that it might have had in another period of critical writing.

If national identities are to be foregrounded, then national identities are deemed to be 'staged, culturally produced, dynamic, and ... inherently troubled', to use Jen Harvie's perspective.[19] For Harvie, 'UK identities are multiple, mutually contingent, and mutually embedded – simultaneously holding in tension multiple determinants, from affinities with locale, region, and nation to affinities with Europe, global subjectivity, and diasporic communities.'[20] What Harvie says of UK identities applies equally well to Irish ones. My focus is on the dynamics of dramaturgy rather than textualized identities, and while a great deal of the work under consideration was first performed just before or during the period of the Celtic Tiger, it is vital to remember that the work did not necessarily bear much relation to that reality. Playwrights shied away from being topical, or they realized that the dynamics of the lived world did not best serve the stories they wished to tell or the scenarios and images they wished to generate through writing and performance, or the mechanisms of narrative were not appropriate to the circumstances of that society. The texts discussed here put paid to the illusion that if you want to understand the dynamics of the Celtic Tiger period go to the theatre. The best exception to this has to be Declan Hughes's great play *Shiver* (2003). Put bluntly, it is worth keeping in mind as a caution to Enda Walsh's comment that 'Theatre does not come from a real place', or at least most of it does not.[21]

Also as the reach of these playwrights under discussion here works across national boundaries, equally their interests and influences are multiple and varied and not only local, thus their work can be seen in other types of clusters beyond simply national ones; Friel's work on the making of history could be easily linked with Susan-Lori Parks's *The American Play* (1994), McGuinness's history plays with those of Tony Kushner or Bertolt Brecht, O'Rowe and McDonagh can be grouped as Aleks Sierz does with the British In-Yer-Face theatre movement. The work of Enda Walsh is very much at home in German theatre circles. (The collective disposition of many recently formed Irish theatre companies to make their own work could link them in with the radical devising practices of companies of international renown, and so on.) However, I am very interested in the commonalities between the writers under discussion, the shared attractions and repulsions towards the Irish Dream that has shaped writing practices.

Texts of course have both relatively stable and unstable meanings. Both texts and performances work from a series of codes, sequencing, expectations and conventions that audiences are mainly familiar with or potentially tutored to follow, and these help place, position and define the experiences of and responses to performance. Obviously, there are aesthetic, contextual and political dimensions to dramaturgy. However, on the most basic of levels, dramaturgy is first and foremost about composition, emphasizing the 'theory and techniques' of characterization, language, props, time, the use of space, dramatic incidents and actions, and how these things 'are woven together to create the texture of the performance, the performance text',[22] or the potential for multiple performances. Freddie Rokem suggests that:

> Dramaturgical analysis brings together theoretical issues of hermeneutics, text analysis and performance theory with practical, creative work in the theatre. It is a complex, heterogeneous activity connecting research and practice designed to reflect on, as well as to develop and enhance, the creative work in the theatre.[23]

Mary Luckhurst expands on the definition to suggest that dramaturgy ranges from the 'theorization of the dramatic structure and internal logic of play or performance ... to the work of the dramaturg'.[24] Equally for Luckhurst, 'dramaturgy can also refer to external elements relating to staging, the overall artistic concept behind the staging, the politics of performance, and the calculated manipulation of audience response',[25] and by implication she moves things further afield. So, dramaturgy is also a consideration of how drama codes certain values, postulates certain types of arrangements and champions explicitly and implicitly ascendant, burgeoning, reactionary or lingering ideologies. A far more complex understanding would blend all four in a very composite and varying mix.

Propagandist texts set out to limit and indoctrinate, and for the most part these approaches are very blatant. It is when texts are less obvious that it is equally important to query them. Texts are usually as sophisticated as those who exploit or who like to disguise the mechanisms of power, discrimination and inequality, through bias, normalization and unsubstantiated perceptions that promote fears and other responses. For instance, texts can be guilty of the codification of racial, class, sectarian and gender inequalities, or of equally anti-British or anti-American sentiments. Texts may have a bias against wealth (to be wealthy is often a fate worse than that of an informer), or an expressive preference for dysfunctional families and the maintenance of that dysfunction, not relatively functional families looking for viable solutions. Feminist critics have long argued against the patriarchal tradition that seems obsessed with either the idealization or the elimination of the feminine, and postcolonial critics highlight how certain nationalities are confined by stereotypical representations, essentializations, or how characters can only act or speak within restrictive, repressed or unequal frameworks. So, through the seven chapters I use the notion of dramaturgy as offering evidence of textual as well as cultural, gender, geopolitical, and neoliberal networks, patterns and practices of ideology, power, domination, restraint, collusion, subservience and also enablement. I also am cognizant of the socio/political implications of dramaturgy in terms of the construction of spectatorship, citizenship and communities.

The type of analysis I undertake is very specific and focused, and I acknowledge its incompleteness; in a way it is like looking at one major organ of the human body and no more. However, if one were to follow through analytically in a fairly comprehensive fashion on a text like *The Gigli Concert* (1983), *Portia Coughlan* or *The Sons of Ulster*, by evaluating early drafts and the research of the writer, funding applications, preproduction and casting decisions, director journals, production notebooks and visual documentation, detailed rehearsal and performance analysis, published text and versions of same, followed by interviews with directors, designers, administrators and performers, analysis of various performances globally, giving consideration to intertextual, contextual and co-textual framings, and critical and spectator reception, then a full-length book for each text probably would still be partial and deficient. Thus, all analysis is marked by inexhaustibility and incompleteness.

Traditionally and in a very general way, Irish dramaturgy has been based on journey and encounter, belonging and banishment, and on defiance and loss, and framed by deliberations on authenticity. Most of all, they are dramaturgies of restraint or constraint, hindrance and denial, and about the impossibility of home.[26] The opposing force or restraint is also always more external than within, generating irrational forms of violence, both outward and inward in focus. Traditionally, plays were not afraid to raise issues of class and gender representations, but left so many of the female characters adrift of meaning. Issues surrounding relationships like sex and desire were kept in the dark or at best off-stage. The death of children is often the force of connection or disconnection rather than of intimacy and desire.

The persistent negative attitude to wealth was a way of blurring questions about wealth, class and gender inequalities. Bourgeois values are uncritically force-fed in many instances. Dramaturgical solutions to situations and circumstances are more often than not individualized and not collectivized. Aspirations and disablement go hand in hand. At some stages, the 'Irish Play' was, at once about the comfort of stasis, the reluctance to change, and the need to talk and debate without hesitation. Affirmative action lagged well behind the ambitions of language. The distinction between saying something and meaning it, between dreaming it and realizing it, were the comfortable tensions upon which the plays relied. It is the internalization of dominant and repressive values that prohibits action, by diminishing possibility, by giving false and soft targets for challenge, while the deeper structural issues and inequalities are filtered or framed in such a way that they are misunderstood. These give rise to the particulars of Irish comedy and the darkness of its carnivalized consciousness or its tragic/comic dimension. Identity-forming narratives were constructed out of the strictures and constraints of a postcolonial consciousness that is in part based on domination, violence, inclusion and exclusion, objectifications and legitimate grievance. In this instance the Irish dream was distinctly localized by a particular trajectory of history and universalized by the anti-colonial, anti-imperial, anti-authoritarian sensibilities as well as by the perceived lack of agency. Concurrently, myth/dream provided the dramaturgical impetus for plays to evade the trappings of realism and to consolidate something else, primitive, unconscious, that was not so easily articulated.

In this book, in order to deal with this general dramaturgical process, I will highlight six very specific, if restricted, dominant patterns, configurations or constructions that shape the blatant dramaturgy of primarily text-based Irish Theatre. Individual chapters will focus on the relationships between history, memory and metatheatre; the seductive notion of innocence; the significance of myth; the consequences of the pastoral to the framing of Irish theatre; and the implications of storytelling to contemporary dramaturgy. In all of the work produced both locally and abroad, Ireland and a coerced and admired notion of 'Irishness' function in part as a commodity on the global market, but also as something unique in itself. Richard Cave argues as far back as 1906, talking about the Abbey productions of a series of 'IRISH PLAYS' in London, that 'a kind of constellation of specific terms and epithets recurs that steadily defines the company's claim to originality as lying in its concern for a scrupulous authenticity'.[27] Emphasis on exactitude, assurances of consultations with locals were carried out to confirm the configurations of the space and what props were used in order to insinuate authentication. The acting style, equally, had an organic relationship with authenticity. Today, at its worst, Irishness is overdetermined and is a slightly more sophisticated concept than the flat-packed Irish theme pub, easily made to signify whatever you want it to mean; at its best, it is an accomplished and complicated concept, which attracts a range of positive sensibilities and an intuitive set of validations, based on assumptions of warmth, vitality, blatancy and vivacity, and openness. There is also a sense of Irishness as being disruptive and anti-authoritarian, and a force that resists inequality. However, for all of that, Irishness is no more authentic than Scottishness or Indianess. One cannot control the interpretation of another, thus the notions of representation or misrepresentation are futile concepts to bring to bear on the assessment of performance. Neither representation nor misrepresentation is possible when the artifice of performance and the interpretative mechanisms of the individual spectator are brought into consideration. Ultimately, it may be an arbitrary allocation of a label over which nobody can exert control. I will elaborate on this in my conclusion.

ON THE MONEY

In reality, funding for theatre determines the who, what, why, where and the how of practices generally. All of the plays discussed here were premiéred in Ireland or England and were performed with the support of direct or indirect subsidy from either the state and/or sponsorship, and thus are arguably shaped by the imperatives of the state and so become agents of the conservative dominant ethos and thereby incapable of contesting ideology.[28] The interface between funding, commercialization and the marketing of new work is different with each new play. While texts may substantiate dominant ideologies, and while they may reflect a shifting world, the capacities of text and performance to destabilize dominant worldviews, the possibilities of the imagination creating and envisioning anew cannot be so simplistically dismissed.

For Jen Harvie, in the UK, emphasis on the 'creative industries' and on the productivity of the arts prioritizes 'commercial value over social value and fashions culture as marketable commodities rather than as social acts performed by human agents'. She goes on to suggest that:

> [it] also prioritizes the *individual* creative act over *social* cultural activity. The term potentially disempowers people by transforming them from collective audiences and makers into individual and alienated consumers. It celebrated anti-social capitalist commodity fetishism at the expense of social practice.[29]

The approach of Harvie's criticism of UK arts policy is very informative. However, it fails to consider the implications of internationalization of arts practices, and also the spectator is sometimes more than an 'alienated consumer'; there is discernment for many. What she does recognize is the increasing individuation or atomization of social experience, and much of Ireland's arts policy has set out to address that. The funding provision provided by the Arts Council and local councils in Ireland has increased substantially over the last years, and a lot of great work would not have so easily emerged without that support. While the state has a vested interest in the arts, the arts are not simply an élite conspiracy.

I do accept that funding can legitimate certain types of performances and approaches to texts, and while I would never be naïve enough to claim that the state is uninterested in what takes place, what I am proposing to affirm is that the state never legitimates and confines work in a totalizing, all-consuming fashion. Great theatre, if anything, tests ideological affiliations, affirmations and validations. So, my emphasis is very much on a dialectical notion of theatre and performance as on the one hand a passive, reactionary, spurious, inconclusive and inconsequential set of practices and equally, a contestational, interrogative and negotiative arrangement of elusive and dissident energies.

How are the successes of a body of writing measured? By critical and/or commercial triumphs and awards, by the number of international productions or by the quantity and quality of translations into other languages?[30] Possibly the clearest indication of quality is when a text receives a number of distinctive and interpretatively diverse productions over a number of years and enters the repertoire. McGuinness's *The Sons of Ulster*, Stewart Parker's *Northern Star* (1984), Carr's *By the Bog of Cats* (1998), Friel's *Lughnasa, Faith Healer* (1979) or *Translations* (1980) are very good as examples.

My aim is to give some coherence to this book, without being overwhelmed by the anxieties of coverage and fears of exclusion, and without applying the pressures of pure theory, which can be all-consuming, restrictive and monotonous. Further, I am alert to the implications of the frameworks utilized to shape my argument, as much as to the ones that I have on this occasion now brought forward to substantiate what I am saying.

My responses to the plays discussed in this book are utterly shaped by performances I have seen, by readings of these plays prior to and subsequent to performance, by my own reflections, by consideration of critical responses to the work, and of reactions to other work, either with textual or contextual leanings, and by discussions of these plays in the classroom, and by my own lived and imagined experiences. There is a sense of privilege in what is being written about, and how it is written about that simultaneously prioritizes and relegates, includes and excludes, elaborates and suppresses, offers insight and glosses over, and is attentive to anomalies and contradictions.

Choices have to be made about what to include and what to exclude, what is afforded comprehensive coverage and what warrants brief mention. The implications of such choices are various. I must also acknowledge my reluctance to include non-text-based physical theatre for instance, and performances of classic plays, which is new work in a different guise. Further, issues of gender and sexuality, class, race and minority issues are pursued to varying degrees, and most not entirely to my own satisfaction. If my approach was different, there are many plays that would have then become essential, the work of Sebastian Barry, Anne Devlin, Declan Hughes, Tim Loane, Gary Mitchell, Jimmy Murphy, Christina Reid, Stewart Parker, Billy Roche, Ursula Rani Sarma and Michael West spring to mind.

In writing this book, I saw what I was doing as somewhat complementary to what has been already published and about to be published. In a way, that takes away a certain burden of responsibility, in my case for the less than sufficient coverage on Northern Irish playwrights for instance, there is no separationist or partitionist ploy in the decisions made, simply commentators, local and international, have done a great job in providing work that deals with the contemporary Northern Irish plays. Tom Maguire's and Imelda Foley's work are pertinent examples. Contemporary women's writing for the theatre has been considered, for example, in substantial publications by Anne F. O'Reilly (Kelly) and the edited collection by Melissa Sihra, and in forthcoming work by Mária Kurdi, Brenda Liddy and Cathy Leeney. Recent books by Bernadette Sweeney, Patrick Lonergan and Clare Wallace also set out to cover much the same time period as I have, but my approach is appreciably different to all three.

I offer my own perspectives in order to build on and to complement the work of others, without feeling the need to qualify what I say through counter-argument or endnoting, and without the need to differentiate myself explicitly from other approaches. Theatre can be reactionary and debilitating in what it represents and how it represents, but at its best, theatre can lead the way – transgressively, suspiciously, fractiously and duplicitiously, where there is a relentless tension between consensus-forming and dissident dramaturgies. As Garry Hynes notes, 'If we in the theatre are about anything we are about invention. We are about imagining.'[31]

NOTES

1. Northern Ireland saw civil protest, violence, paramilitary murders, internment, hunger strikes, brokered ceasefires, and on 31 August 1994 the IRA committed to a complete cessation of military operations, which was broken by the Canary Wharf bombing in February 1996. The Good Friday Agreement in 1998 looked towards decommissioning and demilitarization, the establishment of the Stormont Assembly and the recent sharing of power between republican Sinn Féin and the Democratic Unionist Party.
2. R.F. Foster *Luck and the Irish: A Brief History of Change, 1970–2000* (Harmondsworth: Penguin, 2007), p.1.
3. Joe Cleary argues that the 'country ceased to be a byword for repression, poverty and sexual starvation and was rebranded instead as an affluently consumerist home of the *craic*'. See *Outrageous Fortune: Capital and Culture in Modern Ireland* (Dublin: Field Day Publications, 2007), p.265.
4. The phenomenon of the Irish play on English stages must be noted from the outset, with new Irish writing frequently being premiéred in London, for instance by the Royal Court, Bush Theatre, Royal Shakespeare Company and Royal National Theatres. And if successful there, a Broadway production was often possible.
5. As early as 1992 Tom Kilroy had identified the demise of the traditional Irish play, sub-dividing it into four categories: the Irish Peasant Play, the Irish Religious Play, the Irish Family Play and the Irish History Play. See Thomas Kilroy, 'A Generation of Playwrights', *Irish University Review* 22–1–2, Spring–Summer 1992, pp.135–41, p.141.
6. Christopher Murray, '"Echoes Down the Corridor": The Abbey Theatre 1904–2004' in *Echoes down the Corridor*, ed. P. Lonergan and R. O'Dwyer (Dublin: Carysfort Press, 2007), p,13.
7. Nicholas Grene, *The Politics of Irish Drama: Plays in Context from Boucicault to Friel* (Cambridge: Cambridge University Press, 1999), p.1.
8. Fintan O'Toole, *Tom Murphy: The Politics of Magic* (Dublin/London: New Island/Nick Hern, 1994, revised edition), p.37.
9. Ibid.
10. Ibid., p.19.
11. Ibid.
12. Hanna Scolnicov, *Woman's Theatrical Space* (Cambridge: Cambridge University Press, 1994), p.137.
13. Garry Hynes in an interview with Cathy Leeney, *Theatre Talk: Voices of Irish Theatre Practitioners*, eds L. Chambers, G. FitzGibbon and E. Jordan (Dublin: Carysfort Press, 2001), p.204.
14. For instance, it could be fabricated characters in notionally historical or contemporary situations or historical figures in imaginary situations; invented characters in conjured situations.
15. Some audience members are inclined to see *The Weir* as capturing their experiences in public houses in rural Ireland in the 1970s forward, and it is substantiated when McPherson outlines the 'origins' of the script in his visits to Jamestown, County Roscommon to see his grandfather and the stories he heard from him. Thus the real meets the imaginative, fabrication coalesces with truth.
16. See Helen Lojek, '*Observe the Sons of Ulster*: Historical Stages' in Lonergan and O'Dwyer (eds), *Echoes down the Corridor*, pp.81–94.
17. Cathy Leeney, 'Hard wired/tender bodies: power, loneliness, the machine and the person in the work of desperate optimists' in '*Performing Ireland*': Australasian Drama Studies Special Issue, eds B. Singleton and A. McMullan, 43, October 2003, pp.76–88, p.78.
18. Also when the original cast members revised their roles for the Peacock production of the O'Rowe play in 2007, the actors were now eight years older, and of course age has a huge bearing on how audiences respond to this particular drama. Youngish characters, bent on destruction in their twenties is one thing, now with the actors in their mid-thirties, the production felt an altogether different piece.
19. Jen Harvie, *Staging the UK* (Manchester: Manchester University Press, 2005), p.3.
20. Ibid., p.7.
21. Enda Walsh in interview with Alex Sierz, www.theatrevoice.com/listen_now/player/?audioID =627 [accessed 30 January 2009]
22. Marco de Marinis, 'Dramaturgy of the Spectator', trans. Paul Dwyer, *Drama Review*, 31–2, Summer 1987, pp. 100–14, p.100 www.links.jstor.org/sici?sici=0012–5962%28198722%

2931%3A2%3C100%3ADOTS%3E2.0.CO%3B2–Z [accessed 7 April 2008]
23. Freddie Rokem, 'Antigone Remembers: Dramaturgical Analysis and Oedipus Tyrannos', *Theatre Research International*, 31–3, pp.260–69, pp.260–61.
24. Mary Luckhurst, *Dramaturgy: A Revolution in Theatre* (Cambridge: Cambridge University Press, 2006), p.10.
25. Ibid.
26. Anne F. O'Reilly maps the relationship between theatre and ritual, connecting sacred space and time with the notions of rites, liminality, transformation and community in *Sacred Play: Soul-Journeys in Contemporary Irish Drama* (Dublin: Carysfort Press, 2004).
27. Richard Cave, 'The Abbey Tours in England' in *Irish Theatre on Tour*, ed. N. Grene and C. Morash (Dublin: Carysfort Press, 2005), pp.9–34, p.15.
28. There has been a big drive towards commercialization with the emphasis on 'hit' and award-winning plays since 1990, beginning with *Dancing at Lughnasa*, *Someone Who'll Watch Over Me* (1992), *The Steward of Christendom* (1995), *The Beauty Queen of Leenane* (1996), *The Weir* (1997), *By the Bog of Cats* (1998), *Stones in His Pockets* (1999) and *The Pillowman*. The presence of marketable stars performing in some of these shows is hugely significant, whether it is David Tennant and Jim Broadbent in the London production of *The Pillowman*, or Jeff Goldblum and Billy Crudup in the New York one, Ralph Fiennes in *Faith Healer* at the Gate Theatre on Broadway, Tom Courtenay in *The Home Place* at the Gate and the West End, Holly Hunter in *By the Bog of Cats* at the San Jose Repertory Theatre and London's West End, or Fiona Shaw in *Woman and Scarecrow* at the Royal Court, for instance. The 2009 production of *Dancing at Lughnasa* at the Old Vic has Andrea Corr, from the pop group The Corrs, playing the role of Chris.
29. Harvie, *Staging the UK*, p.23.
30. An Irish play opening in London, even if it is a fifty-seat auditorium, will draw more comment and newspaper feature pieces than one starting its run in Mullingar.
31. Garry Hynes, 'Accepting the fiction of being "national"', *Irish Times*, 3 May 1993.

1

Dramaturgical Frameworks

According to Cathy Turner and Synne Behrndt, dramaturgy not only 'is a term for the composition itself, it is also a word applied to the *discussion* of composition'.[1] Text-based dramaturgy is both the what and how of theatre-as-text and as-performance and it is concerned with what narratives are being told and how they are being told. Dramaturgy changes as textual practices shift creatively, as cultures and societies alter, because of external influences, because of shifting consciousnesses in how to view realities. Dramatic form regularly antici-pates and determines the expectations of the spectator, in terms of action, characterization, rhythm and of endings in particular. And often the tension between anticipations and expectations and what actually happens is a very useful thing to consider when reflecting on the rela-tionship between text and performance, material and ideological contexts. Dramaturgy is thus concerned with how meanings are embedded in texts and how texts might be orchestrated, manipulated and shaded in per-formance. Shared cultural, material and social practices coexist with the dramaturgical ones. While my main concern is with textual dramaturgy, it is vital to recognize that in all writing there are tendencies, oversights, conformities, expectations of character and anticipated resolutions that justify certain ideological biases, some of which are disguised, some which are more blatant.

Texts may inhibit or hinder agency as well as enabling through suggestivity or by hostility towards the inability of characters to find agency and deny the possibility of change or by characters taking too few risks, or if not achieving change themselves, then modifications and adjustments can be prefigured. The actions of characters may be embedded in psychology, stereotype, myth or in specific function, and the tonal framing of that action can be tragic or comic, ironic or iconic, embryonic or emblematic. However, the levels of agency available to characters are not the only measures, because of given circumstances, and in part, it is an audience's function to respond and challenge the broader dynamics that shape the action of characters. Brechtian dramaturgy is an obvious one to consider here. Either the spectator has that awareness or might be guided towards that discernment by the writing or by the performance. Lionel Pilkington identifies the general ideological conformities 'to the political interests of the state'. However, he continues, theatrical performances are often 'in excess of the meanings proffered by the state', thus 'the political dynamism of Irish theatre lies more in its development and exploration of this excess than in any self-conscious articulation of state policy'.[2] That sense of excess is the hallmark of the types of dissenting dramaturgies I wish to identify.

A KINGDOM FOR AN IDEA

Textual dramaturgy also concerns itself with authorial intentionality and the status of the text. The intentionality of the writer has been an area of deep discussion. Does the writer have any hold on the meaning of a text? Adrian Page reflecting on the work of Roland Barthes suggests: 'We know now that the text is not a line of words realizing a single "theological" meaning (the "message" of the Author-God) but a multi-dimensional space in which a variety of writings, none of them original, blend and clash.'[3] Further, Page reproduces Barthes's well-cited remark: 'To give the text an Author is to impose a limit on that text, to furnish it with a final signified, to close the writing.'[4] (Of course for many who espouse such a consciousness, they are all too willing to credit the director's *mise-en-scène* with such credibility and intent and the critical commentator with a similar acute awareness.)

Likewise, the status of the written text has altered substantially. Within the tradition of writing about Irish theatre and dramaturgy, there are consistent assumptions around the stability of the text and some reflections on the potential of performance to shape the text. However, in the main, more radical takes on that relationship are notable by their absence and the oft-ignored fact that text and performance are reliant on two opposing sign systems.

Traditionally words like the enactment, realization, actualization, blueprint, score and model have been used to articulate that relationship between text and performance. But text has no prior or 'exclusive status' for someone like Patrice Pavis.[5] For Pavis, 'There is no "pre-*mise-en-scène*" already inscribed in the dramatic text', even if one 'always ends up finding a textual indication on which to hang the *mise-en-scène* legitimately'.[6] (And that of course asks the question, can there be an illegitimate *mise-en-scène?*) As Pavis states, the *mise-en-scène* is 'not incidental transcription, representation and explanation of the text'.[7] Likewise, Pavis argues, performance is not 'the actualization, manifestation, or concretization of elements already contained within the text'.[8]

For Pavis, *mise-en-scène* is 'the synchronic confrontation of signifying systems, and it is their interaction, not their history, that is offered to the spectator and that produces meaning',[9] and 'it is an object of knowledge, a network of associations or relationships uniting the different stage materials into signifying systems, created both by the production ... and reception'.[10] Contemporary performances are generated 'without text assuming the role of magnetic pole for the rest of the performance'.[11] While it might be regarded as a weak position when 'Performance appeals to the authority of the text for its interpretation and its very existence',[12] Pavis does not believe that *mise-en-scène* should 'serve' text, and justify itself as a 'correct' or incorrect take,[13] as the philological position suggests that it must justify a 'correct' reading of the text. It assumes that both are conceived of in terms of each other. Text cannot be regarded 'as absolute and immutable reference, fulcrum of the *mise-en-scène* in its entirety'.[14] Regardless, Pavis suggests that one should 'quite naturally reserve a select place for the dramatic text – without however prejudging its status inside the performance: here the text is conceived as being *within* the performance, rather than *above* or *beside* it'.[15]

Pavis argues that a meeting point might be reworkings of texts, where the 'given circumstances' invite a certain perspective, but that the interpretation by a production offers something unforeseen, unanticipated.[16] In the face of such challenges I would argue that the predominant tone of a piece, fidelities to the dominant rhythm of structure and form, say a tragic-comic sensibility, are by necessity observed, therefore the looseness of the relationship between text and performance is not as radical as it might be thought. The sequence of a play's action, the implications of character interactions are substantial in their own right and can be either preserved or discarded, without limiting the role of director or actor to shape the meanings of a performance. A naked actor playing Hamlet is one thing, but erasing Hamlet from *Hamlet* is altogether different.

Generally, most play scripts of course assume the prior role of the director, designers and performers to shape the work. While there is often a collaborative relationship between writer and director, especially with new work, as is the case with many of the plays under consideration in this book, where there is relative artistic and ideological alignment between both parties, a cohesive set of outcomes are probable, but it can be rather different when it is an aggressive arrangement or where the director takes an approach to a text that foregrounds or challenges its ideological leanings and anomalies or superimposes a reading that is not fully borne out by the text. Also, a director may create a performance that unconsciously or intuitively challenges the dominant trajectory of a text, or may refuse to address complex, repressed issues or may suppress aspects of the text. Performances can be framed to invite certain responses; feature pieces in the media, marketing strategies, advertising images, programme notes, lobby displays, interviews and public conversations and the like, plus reviews, but unintentional actions and responses are always part of the equation.

PERFORMANCE AND SPECTATORSHIP

Performance dramaturgy has three distinct types, as Eugenio Barba argues. The first is 'An organic or dynamic *dramaturgy*, which is the composition of the rhythms and dynamisms affecting the spectators on a nervous, sensorial and sensual level'. Secondly there is 'A *narrative dramaturgy*, which interweaves events and characters, informing the spectators on the meaning of what they are watching'. And thirdly there is 'a dramaturgy of changing states' which occurs

> when the entirety of what we show manages to evoke something totally different, similar to when a song develops another sound line through the harmonics. In a performance, this *dramaturgy of changing states* distills or captures hidden significances, which are often involuntary on the part of the actors as well as the director, and are different for every spectator. It gives the performance not only a coherence of its own but also a sense of mystery. The dramaturgy of changing states is the most elusive.[17]

Clearly, Barba's reflections on performance dramaturgy capture some of the elusiveness of performance and the variations and varieties. His comments clearly recognize the cognitive, sensual and emotional partnership that is the performance–audience interface.

In his work on the dramaturgy of spectatorship, Marco de Marinis cites Jerzy Grotowski's comment that the 'ability to guide the spectator's attention' is one of the essential challenges facing the director.[18] The playwright and/or director anticipates a spectator, trusting in his/her 'encyclopedic, intertextual, or ideological'[19] competencies as well as his/her capacity to memorize and be open to emotional and intellectual responses, by being perceptive, skilfully interpretative and aesthetic appreciative. Of course, most audiences can be distracted by all kinds of things; they cannot absorb the totality of the intense interaction that is a live event, they must select what they attend to, and cannot keep track, and are often incapable of bringing together a summative performance perspective as de Marinis suggests.[20] (And of course, equally, the global competencies of a playwright/director or actor must not be assumed.) In many ways audiences are open to dramaturgical, textual, performative and critically interpretative pressures, seduced and initiated by dramatic codes and reliant on familiarity with systems of understanding. Generalist discussions about spectator or spectator-ship are often nullified by gross generalization and absence of proof. The decoding of performance can be shaped by anything from the weather outside and the price of a ticket, the comfortableness of seating arrangements and who is sitting beside you, to familiarity with previous work and to social status, class, gender and ethnicity awarenesses of the spectator. Thus dramaturgy is about establishing the frames of viewing and reception. An ironic sensibility must be codified in particular ways, yet it requires a signalling of the frame in simple, complex or blatant ways. To impose an irony on a play that can cope with it is one thing, to bring to bear an ironic or postmodern frame on something that cannot so easily bear its weight is altogether different. The interpretive possibilities that performance can bring, as well as the nuances and foregrounding that performance can offer, cannot be underestimated. In Frank McGuinness's *Observe the Sons of Ulster Marching Towards the Somme* (1985), part 2 begins with the character Kenneth Pyper peeling an apple, and he cuts himself. We might ask as many questions about the gesture as about the apple itself in terms of signification. Is the gesture intentional or accidental? The moment also hints of Adam and Eve, original sin or sexual temptation, or is there a Snow White motive filtering in? As for the apple in performance, is it green or red, big or small, a fresh or rotten piece of fruit? To isolate these reflections is to sideline the kinaesthetic and proxemic indicators used in per-formance. Thus the amount of reflection and considerations can be a springboard for endless reflection and analysis.

Then, at the end of the scene, Pyper raises his left hand and slashes it with his penknife, Craig flings him a shirt with which to bandage the slashed hand. The shirt suggests some connection to McGuinness's earlier play *The Factory Girls* (1982). The red hand of course symbolizes not only the red hand of Ulster, Pyper's own self-harming tendencies, the self-destructive composition of identities, even tribal identities, but also an awareness of AIDS, blood lust and the homoeroticism of war. And the blood itself, is not real. The first cutting of the hand might be accidental, but it does initiate suggestive sexual innuendo from Pyper. So telling details like the above invite endless consideration.

We can add to reflections on dramaturgy the role of the theatre critic in formalizing critical frameworks, and in positioning the responses of the spectator in advance of seeing a performance. Fintan O'Toole sees in the critical reception of Irish plays in London in the 1960s, and in particular *A Whistle in the Dark* (1961), 'The automatic image, based on no personal knowledge, of the dramatist-as-Irish-thug, the notion that Irish playwrights are primarily personalities and only secondarily dramatists.'[21] Further, O'Toole identifies the 'innate and latent racism' in the critical responses to the play.[22] Analysis of the responses of reviewers to Martin McDonagh's work, for instance, reveal that Irishness is the lens through which violence, psychic and material depravations are to be understood, and not inner-city London where McDonagh grew up. Critics seldom make those types of connections directly back from the work of Mark Ravenhill or Sarah Kane. However, often too much is made of critical responses, as if the critic can either offer the most informed response to a performance, or the opposite, the critic is regarded as a very limited biased spectator who sees the work very narrowly and is ridiculed for it, or whose prejudices are deconstructed in order to make another's analysis substantially more plausible. (Production and reception dramaturgy must take heed of the significance of PR and marketing, event managing and the use of celebrity figures and broadcasters with public profiles to endorse a production.)

When it comes to dramaturgy, one could approach new work from the following perspectives: gender, class, race, religion, ritual, multiculturalism, globalization, diasporic contributions, subaltern studies and emergent companies from migrant communities.[23] To that list one could add the framing of sexual orientations and heteronormativity, queer studies, carnival, space, representations of migrants, corporealities and embodiment, 'utopian'/dystopian performatives, and performance contextualizations, postnationalism, arts policy, international adaptations or the reception of touring performances. I have settled on the ideas of narrative fixations, obsessions with innocence, the repeated pastoralization of place, the challenges provided by the use of mythic templates, the writing tendency to historicize rather than contemporize and the framework of play. I will consider how these approaches work from a textual point of view and then compare the approaches of different writers to the categories I have identified. There are two further

considerations I wish to introduce – some reflections on gender and colonization, both of which frame and sustain my overall argument –
before I return to the specific frameworks I offer in this book.

GENDER

Patriarchy has both prescribed and fictionalized societal, gender, class
and race relations, and it has also, to a considerable extent, fashioned
and fabricated the dramaturgical practices of Irish theatre in terms of
how plays are written, programmed, directed, produced, marketed and
consumed. Moreover, the imaginations of Irish theatre practitioners,
playwrights especially, have been seriously ideologically loaded, not
only in the specific prioritization of primarily male values, references
and aspirations, and in their general scrutiny of and obsession with
masculinity, but also in their consistent relegation and often subjugation
of the feminine. Gendered relationships have been subjected to critical
enquiry in terms of power, authority, the body, space, transgression and
execution of subjectivities.

In the traditional Irish play women were almost always obliged to
substantiate patriarchal rule and were associated with home, otherness
and the land. (Within colonialism, woman is regarded as double colonized.) Feminist critics have argued that most Irish male playwrights
offer their female characters a very limited range of dramaturgical
functions within their dramas and that a narrow range of behaviours
are part of audience expectations.

Anna McMullan contends that in terms of Irish iconography,
'women have been associated both with the homeland, as Mother
Ireland, and with the domestic space, particularly the kitchen. In the
Irish theatrical canon women often figure a lost, damaged or barren
home/land/womb – the Mother in Murphy's *Famine* or Sarah in Friel's
Translations'.[24] Helen Lojek singles out a very specific gender distinction
in McGuinness's work, where

> male artists are typically geographic exiles ... Women artists like
> Eleanor Henryson in *The Bird Sanctuary* and File in *Mutabilitie*
> remain geographically as well as imaginatively in their homes.
> The male artists launch their quests horizontally across the surface
> of the earth; the female artists quest vertically, exploring the
> depths of place and self.[25]

Those binaries that Lojek recognizes are present across a dominant
range of work. Mary Trotter argues that 'Female characters provide the

protagonist with emotional support, a source of conflict, or a sexual interest, but the real attention in the family memory drama centers on the patrilineal relationships.'[26] That notion of 'patrilineal relationships' is very evident in the whole tradition of male writing. Cathy Leeney cogently argues, in her consideration of Teresa Deevy and Marina Carr, that under patriarchy, alienation and exile are the lot of women and these are absorbed often unconsciously and uncritically into Irish dramatic practices: 'The boundaries around Irish women's realities define containment as a form of exile: exile from self-expression, from self-determination.'[27]

I take on board Anne F. O'Reilly's (Kelly's) point that 'the colonization of the female body either as a site for male meaning or carrier of repressed aspects of the cultural unconscious must be addressed by theatre audiences and practitioners'.[28] In more contemporary plays by Ioanna Anderson, Hilary Fannin, Stella Feehily and Elizabeth Kuti, Brian Singleton argues for the move towards the 'de-essentialization of gender, and the new Irish woman in particular: she is taken out of the mythical country kitchen and is reconfigured ... and most importantly, her race and ethnicity are uncoupled from nation and contest the closure inherent in the hegemonic concept of "Irishness".'[29]

Gender, of course, is not simply about the binary categorization of male and female, because within and between both sexes there are multiple and singular expressions of genders with the added issues of power, class, religion, education, sexual orientation, occupation and the choices and circumstances of lives. There is also the issue of ranked relationships within and between genders. That sense of a ranked relationship brings in the consideration of colonization.

COLONIAL DERIVATIVES

A considered overview of this book would point out the relationship between history, imperialism and nation, would single out the split subjectivities of characters and the defiance that seldom becomes confidence, illustrate the frequency with which character articulation fails to lead to action, expose the struggles of identity formation that narrative and monologue fixations seem to suggest, notice the inability to find meaning not in truth, courage or maturation, but in innocence, hint at the inability to be comfortable with material possessions and the body, and demonstrate the sometimes obsessive need for play that is about the contestation and the interrogation of power. Of course, colonization is not Ireland-specific, and for many, Ireland's experience of colonial rule pales into insignificance in the light of what others suffered because of imperialism. Political, cultural, social and economic implications are immediately obvious, while sometimes less obvious are the issues of legislation, socialization, urbanization and emigration, which can be shaped substantially by the colonial encounter. Colonization impacts on modes of knowing, of perceiving and of exchange, interpersonally and collectively. Ireland's general obsession with identity politics has come at the expense of citizenship.

The impact of colonization can sustain itself long after the host country achieves independence. Ireland's period after independence was really a duplication of class and gender hegemonies, with authority passing from British rule to an Irish élite who disguised a fundamental inequality at the core of its value systems, thereby duplicating previous oppression. For Declan Kiberd, 'cultural dependency remained palpable long after the formal withdrawal of the British military: it was less easy to decolonize the mind than the territory'.[30]

METATHEATRICALITY

The metatheatrical meshes regularly with history and memory and the principal plays under discussion are Brian Friel's *Dancing at Lughnasa* (1990), Tom Kilroy's *Double Cross* (1986) and Frank McGuinness's *The Sons of Ulster*, and to a lesser extent Friel's *Translations* (1980). All are exemplary of a specific approach to the metatheatricalization of history, memory and myth.[31] (Equally, work by Sebastian Barry, Stewart Parker, Vincent Woods and Christina Reid could have wholesomely featured in this section.) Fintan O'Toole suggests that major playwrights turn to history plays

> at a time when a society which valued hierarchy, order, tradition, communal values, was being replaced by one which valued freedom, material progress, social mobility, and individualism. At such times, history provides a way of disentangling the contradictions of the present by placing them at a distance. Historical drama is, for these writers, a way of dealing with discontinuity.[32]

While history plays are brought on by 'discontinuity', they also allow a writer to deal, as Christopher Murray notes, with issues of 'power, identity and the national consciousness',[33] and to establish a way of mapping change in the relationship between past and present.

Although history and memory are the obvious drivers of this strand of work, just as important is the energy of artifice or play, which runs the whole gamut from self-conscious performativity to impersonation, from trickery, contrivance or the confidence trick to misrule, from the generation of co-operative narratives to masquerade, parody and burlesque, from mimicry to multiplicity, from drag to re-enactment and from story-telling to play-within-a-play.[34] Play makes room for individual and collective change. Role-playing ensures that identities are not perceived as essentially unchanging, but in process, as they absorb the impulse and impact of play. The 'what if' that role-play demands takes the momentum and rhythm of the play into a different dimension. With role-playing, it is easier to distinguish between accepted, imposed, rejected, misunderstood, residual and emergent versions of identities.

Friel in *Lughnasa* dramatizes the process of memory as play or reinscribed performance, while McGuinness unhinges the reverence of the Battle of the Boyne victory myth through mock play. When the soldiers before going into battle at the Somme re-enact the Battle of the Boyne, they fail to deliver the required result, King James is accidentally victorious, and King William the vanquished: the enactment takes its lead from the less sacrosanct Scarva tradition with Unionism.

Kilroy with *Double Cross* links two individuals from history, the Tipperary-born Brendan Bracken, Minister for Information from 1941 to 1945 in the Churchill government during the Second World War, and the Nazi broadcaster William Joyce (Lord Haw-Haw), of Irish-American origin. What Kilroy succeeds in doing is to show how their disaffections with their own Irish identities lead to their embrace of difference, to the fabrication of identities that at their core are built on self-doubt and disgust. Both characters were played by Stephen Rea in the first production. In *Double Cross* history is the traitor, the force behind the impetus to betray. Because history is over-rehearsed during the mock battle in *The Sons of Ulster*, and because memory is an overworked, manipulated performance in *Lughnasa*, then history and memory mutate into something else. Tom Kilroy's stage direction to *Talbot's Box* (1979) is a fundamentally exemplary one. The stage design is described as 'a primitive, enclosed space, part-prison, part-sanctuary, part-acting space'.[35] That description in fact could be the scenographic template for almost a whole tradition of writing about history, in terms of role, restraint and performance.

INNOCENCE

Innocence is a key term/concept/structure that gets recycled endlessly, and it has a significant, if not the dominant hold over dramaturgy. Innocence takes a variety of forms, from the hope garnered from a new pregnancy or the rescue/survival of a child/innocence to the remembrance of dead children, from the presence of the adult-child or the vulnerable child (not to mention the frequency of imaginary, fake or bizarre offspring) to the destruction of innocence. Innocence can lead to a type of lop-sided consciousness, where accountability is kept at bay, where the means of attesting or interrogating realities are bound up by limited articulation, and by easy, reflexive emotionality.

I use three plays that deal with the structure of innocence in different ways, Carr's *On Raftery's Hill* (2000) is in part about the destruction of innocence through sexual abuse. Marie Jones's *A Night in November* (1994) is an evaluation of sectarianism and possibility, which destabilizes bias not through a quest for truth, but through the naïve journey and transformation of her main character, Kenneth McCallister. Finally, McGuinness's *Innocence* (1986) is about the relationship between religion, sex, creativity, procreation and death. In a general way, I will argue that innocence has been courted and then subsumed into something else by metatheatricality, an argument that can feed indirectly back to my discussions on history, memory and metatheatre. The lost resonance of play is displaced in many instances by a regimented, performative innocence: innocence as artifice. Ultimately, I will argue for an innocence that is neither holy nor foolish, but one that is partly indulgent, playful, transgressive, and partly transformative. The opening part of Paul Mercier's *Kitchen Sink* (1996) is also a return, in part, to a childlike innocence, while plays like Owen McCafferty's award-winning *Mojo Mickybo* (1998), and a lot of the work of Barabbas... the company, especially *Hupnouse* (1999), written for the company by Charlie O'Neill, are sorties into childhood, where poetic innocence is used to express occasional profundities, where the complexity of the adult world is not so much pushed to one side as an insistence on a different, playful type of reality, where an alternative set of values is countenanced. The most obvious use of innocence occurs when play and innocence conspire. Barabbas... the company's production in 1997 of Lennox Robinson's *The Whiteheaded Boy* (1916), where clowning, performativity and actors playing multiple roles, sometimes two characters in the one scene, seemed to be one of the plays that shaped this development.

PASTORAL

Many Irish playwrights have become serial pastoralists, whether it is the blatant anti-pastoral of John B. Keane's *The Field* (1965) or Tom Murphy's *Bailegangaire* (1985), the revisionist, deconstructive pastoral of Tom MacIntyre's *The Great Hunger* (1983, revised 1986), or the recent urban pastorals of Billy Roche's work, *The Cavalcaders* (1996) in particular. Carr's *On Raftery's Hill* can also be seen as a play determined to assault the conventions of the pastoral. Rural spaces/places[36] are regularly regarded as being of fundamental significance, as they are romanticized, naturalized, eroticized, fetishized and mythologized, yet dramaturgically, rustic, almost pastoral framing remains relatively unquestioned and un-interrogated, as it appears normalized and uncontested in many texts and performances. Urban spaces are afforded less consideration.

Commenting on the notion of the west in both Irish and American cultures, Luke Gibbons argues that both 'concern themselves centrally with sites of cultural survival, the sole remaining enclaves of traditional values in a world corrupted by progress and industrialization'.[37] This anti-industrial, anti-progress perspective is a helpful, if incomplete, starting point. Nicholas Grene notes: 'Ireland is always available as a site for pastoral, in its greenness, its littleness, its location as the off-shore-island alternative to the major metropolitan societies of Britain or America.'[38] He articulates the alignment of the pastoral with the 'archaic, traditional and originary', 'wholesome jollity' and 'harmony with nature', and adds it is a space 'marked by quaintness, the charm, the lyrical otherness of Hiberno-English'.[39] Such reflections of course take the analysis into reflections on authenticity, representation, mis-representation, 'whiteness' and 'unrepresentableness'. If one thinks back to the riots that greeted the initial production of John Millington Synge's *The Playboy of the Western World* in 1907, 'That's not the west' was the accusation made against the play. In addition, 'In Ireland, as in America, going west means many things: getting back to rural roots; seeking a final confrontation on the frontier between civilization and wilderness; perhaps even fixing to die', according to Declan Kiberd.[40] That 'final confrontation' is fundamental to my thoughts on the pastoral, as one is obliged to consider the implications of this pastoral consciousness on international and national audiences as well as the sensitivities of critics and commentators to the challenges and complexities of representation.

Martin McDonagh's anti-pastoral, west of Ireland plays, especially *The Leenane Trilogy* and his two Aran Island plays are worth considering in light of these issues. McDonagh's shallow representations are often taken as the exploitative opportunities to stage-manage the Irish pastoral, even when the details of the plays themselves contradict this. I also look very briefly at Marie Jones's *Stones in his Pockets* (1999) and treat it as a subversive, if naïve pastoral representation. Marie Jones queries how Hollywood perceives the pastoral guilelessly and simplistically, yet her superimposition of her own carnivalized inversions of power, out-Hollywoods Hollywood.

I also consider Conor McPherson's *The Weir* (1997), a work that delivers a more complex impression of the rural, pastoral and sanctuary. Through the presence of Valerie, McPherson perverts the pastoral sensibility by telling a story that is a challenge to, even a subversion of the conservative masculinity of the pastoral space. I write this section ever aware of Thomas Kilroy's comment that 'within metropolitan centres there is always a nostalgia for cultures which are untouched, untainted by ennui, the busyness, the crowdedness of the centre'.[41]

MYTH

It is essential to query the use of myths in contemporary Irish drama-turgy. The myths range from classic Greek myths (Medea, Hera and Zeus) to Irish myths (Óisín, Caoineadh Airt Uí Laoghaire, Deirdre of the Sorrows, Táin Bó Cuailgne, Diarmuid and Grainne, and Mad Sweeney), from religious myths of redemption and sacrifice (Faust) to the British redemptive myth of Sir Orfeo, the mythology of Camelot as seen in Billy Roche's *Cavalcaders* and the fairy-tale structure of Shakespeare's *King Lear*, which reverberates through Marina Carr's play *Cordelia Dream* (2008). Popular culture is increasingly influential on the level of myth.

In the older Irish dramatic tradition, many myths are pursued suc-cessfully. John B. Keane's *Sive* (1959) exploits the myth of romantic love, where death is the response when lovers are kept apart, and Keane's *The Field* considers how myth can authorize murder when it comes to the threats of fundamental dispossession (of land, femininity and fertility). Friel's *Translations* is crafted around issues of language dispossession, around cycles of death and rebirth, and considers place and identity myths of origin, rupture and eviction, while *Dancing at Lughnasa* (1990) employs traditional myths of authenticity, community, survival and again of origins. Tom Murphy's *The Gigli Concert* (1983) reworks the Faustian myth, *Conversations on a Homecoming* (1985) builds on myths of collective bonding, belonging and renewal. Fintan O'Toole suggests that Murphy's *Bailegangaire* is 'contained within a timeless mythic structure – that of the nativity play',[42] and further, O'Toole makes an additional connection, noting that the play 'owes its life to the poor man's myth, the folk tale. While myth trades in an heroic world, the folk tale stems from the everyday struggle of ordinary people and constitutes a secret history of the fears and desires of the poor.'[43] Each of these plays reworks myth and expresses what Lisa Fitzpatrick identifies as 'the search for a binding mythology with which to express and unify conceptions of Irish identity for the contemporary stage'.[44]

Myths, according to Richard Kearney, 'were stories people told themselves in order to explain themselves to themselves and to others'.[45] Generally, the traditional interaction of characters in theatre, at its best, leads to encounters that resort to or mirror a mythic cosmos, where conflict has a purpose, where perseverance and courage lead to overcoming odds and where dissent can be validated. Also, myth legitimizes particular behaviours, normalizes certain experiences and expectations, and embraces the symbols and rituals that sustain that register. Richard Kearney suggests that traditional stories or myths 'generally had a sacred ritual function, being recited for a community in order to recall their holy origins and ancestors'.[46] That sacred function tapped into the notion of belonging, and to issues of family, tribe, home and nation. Ireland as nation bore huge symbolic and mythic significance. Ireland has 'fetishized myths of motherland',[47] according to Kearney. Melissa Sihra argues that 'it is important to interrogate the signification of "woman" as idealized trope of nation', for, she continues, 'the social and cultural position of woman has historically been one of symbolic centrality and subjective disavowal as both colonial ideology and nationalist movements promoted feminized concepts of nation, while subordinating women in everyday life'.[48]

Another perspective on the gendering of myth comes from Lisa Fitzpatrick, who argues that in the Irish tradition, masculine resistance is given heroic status through those who died during the revolution of 1916, all the way back to Cúchulain, and likewise the sacrifice of a son is commonplace, but 'nowhere is the sacrifice of a daughter mythologized'.[49] (Marina Carr's *Cordelia Dream* seems like a response to the challenge to mythologize father–daughter relationships and the idea of dysfunctional female sacrifice.)

Also, myth legitimizes history in many ways, whether it is that of injustice or victimhood, or as predestination or rights bestowed by the past. Myths can be a compensatory resource in the face of the carnage of history. The relationship between myth, power and ideology is just as vital and is only implicit in much of the discussion above thus far.

Roland Barthes deals with the specific ideology of myth when, taking a broader perspective on myth, he states:

> Myth does not deny things, on the contrary, its function is to talk about them; simply, it purifies them, it makes them innocent, it gives them a natural and eternal justification, it gives them clarity which is not that of an explanation but that of a statement of fact.[50]

Further, Barthes contends that the bourgeoisie are the guardians of myth as they benefit most from it as myth controls 'all aspects of the law, of morality, of aesthetics, of diplomacy, of household equipment, of Literature, of entertainment'. Within that systematic control, 'The oppressed is nothing, he has only language, that of his emancipation; the oppressor is everything, his language is rich, multiform, supple, with all the possible degrees of dignity at its disposal: he has an exclusive right to metalanguage.' To confirm distinctions, Barthes argues in a similar vein, 'the oppressed *makes* the world, he has only an active, transitive (political) language; the oppressor conserves it, his language is plenary, intransitive, gestural, theatrical: it is Myth. The language of the former aims at transforming, of the latter at eternalizing'.[51] While Barthes is very instructive, his oppressed/oppressor, bourgeois and working-class binaries could do with more subtlety, not to mention a gendering of the argument. However, the overall trajectory of his argument remains substantial. Kearney takes a more open approach, arguing that 'we cannot afford to dispense with the difficult task of determining when myth emancipates and when it incarcerates, that is, when it evolves into a creative symbol and when it degenerates into a mere idol'.[52]

Contemporary playwrights seem to be struggling dramaturgically with both contemporary contexts and how they might exploit, reformulate or reimagine the notion of myth, even when the approach itself exposes the inability to absorb the momentum and deep transactional qualities of myth. Fintan O'Toole identifies the difficulties facing contemporary writing:

> just as it was a century ago, Ireland is a country in search of a national myth. The old epics of nationalist self-assertion and Catholic triumphalism have worn out, and have yet to be replaced. And just as it did a century ago, the theatre is turning to the ancient Irish epics, if not quite for inspiration, then at least for a sense of location.[53]

An earlier generation has the implicit assumption of a depth model provided by myth, in that it had a pattern, resonance and sensibility beyond itself, as it was in touch with something if not sacred, at least elemental. The contemporary playwright is on less solid ground. Increasingly, the encounters between characters seldom if ever appropriate the fundamental dynamics and energies of myth. In that way, sensationalism tends to take root and play an increasing role. Paul Mercier's[54] *Homeland* (2006), set in an urban setting, attempts to piggyback on the Óisín myth. A political fixer-figure, Gerry Newman, returns Óisín-like to Ireland not from the enchanted land of Tír na nÓg but from political exile. He has faced corruption charges and has spilled the beans at a tribunal. He is back in Ireland to solve a final political problem and to redeem himself partly, but unlike Oisín, he survives the return home, perverting the trajectory of the myth. (His Niamh is a prostitute with a blonde wig.) And it is not the Ireland of Christianity, but of interculturalism, post-Celtic Tiger 1.

For O'Toole, 'the difficulty for this whole enterprise is its fundamental ambiguity. On the one hand, the desire to draw on myth suggests that we need it. On the other, we are all now too self-aware not to sense that the difference between mythology and bullshit can be narrow. The absurdity of myth-making is itself at the heart of Mercier's story.'[55] ('I put people in touch with their archetype and then I guide them on their true narrative', the play's central character espouses.) O'Toole sees no life in the myths of old as they are inappropriate as public myths, while at the same time expresses the 'absurdity of myth-making'. Yet implicit is O'Toole's longing for a public myth of socialism, one of shared ownership, equality, community, generosity, freedom and accountability. O'Toole sees it as if 'Mercier is eating his mythic cake while declaring out of the side of his mouth that it is probably junk food. He is simultaneously telling and questioning a story.'[56]

Contrasting Marina Carr's reworking of the Medea myth in *By the Bog of Cats* to Mark O'Rowe's engagement with the myth of the film actor Bruce Lee in *Howie The Rookie* (1999) is a very useful exercise. If Carr successfully latches on to archetype and myth through Medea's murder of a sexual rival and her own children, O'Rowe's work captures the real difficulty in so doing as the resonance and pulse of myth are malformed. The play text of *Howie The Rookie*, published by Nick Hern, carries a blurb describing the script as 'a bizarre feud of honour' and a play 'where the most brutal events take on a mythic significance'. However, the play eludes that space, because the brutality cannot sufficiently resonate. The confrontation has little or nothing to do with 'honour', only 'honour' as a false consciousness of morality, for the central fight is far more about displaced trauma, class isolation and social desensitization, and the self-sacrifice has no consequences of social renewal. The play is all the more complex and better because of the intricate attempt, even calculated failure, to pitch itself at the level of mythic significance.

While not attempting to conflate myth and ideology simplistically, and not endeavouring to regard writers as passive or dormant agents of dominant ideology, I am also looking at how writers use myth to query issues of power, authority, control and freedom, and how myth and narrative can normalize or obscure inequality and injustice, or how playwrights are inhibited in their critique by the inappropriateness of myth or by the inability of myth to be adequately contestational, as they may not be appropriate to the conflicts of contemporary situations and circumstances.

NARRATIVE AND MONOLOGUE

It is necessary to distinguish between the occasional or frequent use of narrative or story-telling as a dramaturgical strategy within the broader structure of a text/performance, versus the more discernable format of the monologue where the actor addresses an audience directly, with characters seldom interacting with each other. The story-telling tradition deals with characters that are inhibited and inhabited by story, enabled and dispossessed of their narratives, personal, collective or national. Kearney suggests that 'Telling stories is as basic to human beings as eating. More so, in fact, for while food makes us live, stories are what make our lives worth living. They are what make our condition *human*.'[57] He adds that 'The art of storytelling ... is what gives us a shareable world.'[58] Both theatre and performance ensembles give additional resonance and framing to this notion of a 'shareable world'.

Further, Ciarán Benson argues that the 'Self' functions primarily as a 'locative system, a means of reference and orientation in worlds of space-time (perceptual worlds) and in worlds of meaning and place-time (cultural worlds). This understanding of self as an ongoing, living process of constant auto-referred locating recognizes the centrality both of the body and of social relations.'[59] The self Benson refers to is substantially a single self, and yet Irish cultural identity formation would also suggest a divided self. More substantially, for Benson, 'We cannot imagine being nowhere ... Being nowhere is quite simply a contradiction in terms ... Self, acts of self-location and locations are inextricably linked and mutually constructive.'[60]

Stories often affirm a will towards life, as individuals journey towards death. Death and loss are ever present, in these stories, as is the loss of time, the terror of aging, requiems for the dead and the shattering of innocence. Further, it is possible to distinguish between overriding individual narratives and counter-narratives, residual or emergent narratives that challenge the stability of a story. If the governing narrative is one of negativity, then the consciousness of either individual or character can only filter experiences predominantly through a negative lens. In contrast, over-optimistic perspectives can seem even, indulgently, sheltered or high-handedly naïve.

Tom Murphy's landmark play *Bailegangaire*, Frank McGuinness's *Someone Who'll Watch Over Me* (1992) and Martin McDonagh's *The Pillowman* (2003) all deal with narrative in very complex ways. In *Someone Who'll Watch Over Me* three western characters are terrorized by their hostage experience in Beirut. In captivity, they tell stories, which range from myth to invented stories, from a version of a children's film to nursery rhymes, from poetry to the re-enactment of a Wimbledon Ladies tennis finals. Through fiction the captives can articulate, with the comfort of distance and irony, their circumstances and make more sense of their predicaments. *Bailegangaire* is the great Irish play about memory, narrative and performance. The horrors of the past are suggested by the story Mommo cannot complete. It is a tale of destructiveness and defiance that is as much a personal as it is a national narrative. *The Pillowman*, while it is set in an eastern European, but unnamed, totalitarian state, belongs substantially to this tradition of story-telling. A writer, Katurian, is interrogated because a series of gruesome murders seem to have an uncanny similarity to some of his own stories. Story-telling is the fascination and fixation, and is potentially redeeming in many instances. All of these three plays have characters interacting in public spaces and use narrative for a variety of purposes.

Brian Friel, in many ways, kick-started the narrative/monologue fixation with *Faith Healer* (1979), a play which relies on four monologues and which offers contradictory and overlapping versions of the lives of its three main characters, Frank Hardy, his partner, Grace, and his business manager, Teddy, as they tour with a performance event that showcases Frank's faith-healing abilities. Each character offers an alternative account of his/her life on the road. The key incidents to the stories of their lives together are heavily disputed. The central themes are that of failed relationships, faith healing, with the faith healer (or artist) as performer or conjurer, and that of memory as both a sustained and deliberate failed performance and a poor rehearsal for the future. The monologue had established itself for a time in the 1990s as the dominant theatrical form, and this was not something unique to Ireland, as writers such as Sarah Kane, Sam Shepard, Eve Ensler, Spalding Gray and Neil LaBute also faced down the challenges of the form. Monologues vary very much in terms of form, from the single-character-direct-audience address type to one-person shows where a single performer enacts a whole series of scenarios, from a testimonial type of theatre to the interlinking of contradictory or supplementary narratives.

I trace the significance of audiences in relation to the notion of *Haltung*, which runs through Bertolt Brecht's vocabulary. The word has various meanings, but late in Brecht's career it meant 'naïvety'.[61] Performance adds not only the layer of theatricality, but also location and dislocation, and just as vitally, the situating of the mobile, expressive actor's body in a defined performance space.

Of course, dramatic character and individuality are completely different things, yet I think we can examine the narrative of characters as indicative of an internal validating and self-constituting system, despite anomalies, contradictions and disjunctions. Additionally, it is vital to view dramatic character more substantially in terms of dramatic function, theatricality, performativity and within the framework of play. On the other hand, we cannot ignore the accumulative theatricality and performativity of identity, as identity is not simply the accretion of experiences, choices, failings, sensations, perceptions, fears, desires and emotionality.

My approach is not attempted in order to give this book a completeness, more it is to manage the similarities, consistencies, anomalies and contradictions as dynamically as possible. Many plays are also in subtle and blatant dialogue with each other, at times it is as if writers are not only revisiting their own work, but rewriting the work of others. There are links and continuities across the sections; sometimes arbitrary and artificial distinctions and divisions are made. Some work could have appeared in different chapters. What makes these plays potentially interesting dramaturgically, are the direct and indirect implications of these dramaturgies for performance nationally and internationally. My emphasis is on the patterns of dramaturgy and what they might suggest and what might need to be considered or subverted in performance. I am less inclined to state where these patterns come from and why they are dominant at specific periods.

NOTES

1. Cathy Turner and Synne Behrndt, *Dramaturgy and Performance* (London: Palgrave, 2007), p.4.
2. Lionel Pilkington, *Theatre and the State in Twentieth-Century Ireland: Cultivating the People* (London and New York: Routledge, 2001), p.223.
3. Adrian Page (ed.), 'Introduction' in *The Death of the Playwright* (Basingstoke: Macmillan, 1992), p.1.
4. Ibid.
5. Patrice Pavis, *Analyzing Performance: Theatre, Dance, and Film*, trans. David Williams (Ann Arbor: University of Michigan Press, 2004), p.205.
6. Ibid., p.206.
7. Patrice Pavis, *Theatre at the Crossroads of Culture*, trans. Loren Kruger (London and New York: Routledge, 1992), p.32.
8. Pavis, *Analyzing Performance*, p.203.
9. Pavis, *Theatre at the Crossroads of Culture*, p.24.
10. Ibid., p.25.
11. Pavis, *Analyzing Performance*, p.206.
12. Ibid., p.204.
13. Ibid., p.205.
14. Ibid., p.204.
15. Ibid., p.199.
16. Ibid., p.205.
17. *Eugenio Barba*, 'The Deep Order Called Turbulence: The Three Faces of Dramaturgy', *Drama Review*, 44–4, Winter 2000, pp.56–66.
18. Marco de Marinis, 'Dramaturgy of the Spectator', trans. Paul Dwyer, *Drama Review*, 31–2, Summer 1987, pp.100–14, p.106. www.links.jstor.org/sici?sici=0012–5962%28198722% 2931%3A2%3C100%3ADOTS%3E2.0.CO%3B2–Z [accessed 7 April 2008]
19. Ibid., p.103.
20. Ibid., p.106.
21. Fintan O'Toole, *Tom Murphy: The Politics of Magic* (Dublin/London: New Island/Nick Hern, 1994, revised edition), p.9.
22. Ibid.
23. As example, Arambe Productions was established in 2004 by Bisi Adigun, the Nigerian Performance Artist, and Olakunle Animashaun's Camino De Orula Productions, established in 2007, had a great success with Athol Fugard's *Sizwe Bansi is Dead* in 2008 at the Project Arts Centre.
24. See 'Unhomely Stages: Women Taking (a) Place in Irish Theatre' in *Druids, Dudes and Beauty Queens: The Changing Face of Irish Theatre*, ed. D. Bolger (Dublin: New Island, 2001), p.72.
25. Helen Lojek, *Contexts for Frank McGuinness's Drama* (Washington, DC: Catholic University of America Press, 2004), p.102.
26. See 'Translating Women into Irish Theatre History' in *A Century of Irish Drama: Widening the Stage*, ed. S. Watt, E. Morgan and S. Mustafa (Bloomington: Indiana University Press, 2000), p.165.
27. Cathy Leeney, 'Ireland's "Exiled" Women Playwrights: Teresa Deevy and Marina Carr' in *The Cambridge Companion to Twentieth-Century Irish Drama*, ed. S. Richards (Cambridge: Cambridge University Press, 2004), pp.150–63.
28. Anne O'Reilly (Kelly), *Sacred Play: Soul Journeys in Contemporary Irish Theatre* (Dublin: Carysfort Press, 2004), p.313.
29. Brian Singleton, 'Sick, Dying, Dead, Dispersed: The Evanescence of Patriarchy in Contemporary Women's Theatre' in *Women in Irish Drama: A Century of Authorship and Representation*, ed. Melissa Sihra (Basingstoke: Palgrave Macmillan, 2007), pp.186–87.
30. Declan Kiberd, *Inventing Ireland: The Literature of the Modern Nation* (London: Vintage, 1996), p.6.
31. All four have both direct and indirect connections with Field Day. The company staged the Kilroy play and *Translations*, turned down the McGuinness play and Friel gave *Lughnasa* to the Abbey, something that appears to have fundamentally damaged the relationship between the actor Stephen Rea and Friel, co-founders of Field Day, and in a way precipitated the slow demise of the company.
32. O'Toole, *Politics of Magic*, p.113.

33. See Christopher Murray, 'The History Play Today' in *Cultural Contexts and Literary Idioms in Contemporary Irish Literature*, ed. M. Kenneally (Gerrards Cross: Colin Smythe, 1998), pp.89–122.
34. Paul Mercier with *Studs* (1989) and Dermot Bolger with *The Lament for Arthur Cleary* (1989) set up very different possibilities for theatre in terms of play/metatheatre. *True Lines* (1993) and *Double Helix* (1995), both devised metatheatrical shows, shaped by John Crowley for Bickerstaffe Theatre Company have had a substantial impact on devising theatre practices in Ireland.
35. Tom Kilroy, *Talbot's Box* (Oldcourt: Gallery Press, 1979), p.9.
36. In Declan Hughes's *Shiver* his character Jenny, when drunk, states 'we've had enough of, Kevin, dead mammies and peeling potatoes and farms and bogs and fucking … all that old tweedy fucking … Seamus Heaney is made of tweed'. See *Shiver* (London: Methuen, 2003), p.43.
37. Luke Gibbons, *Transformations in Irish Culture* (Cork: Cork University Press, 1996), p.23.
38. Nicholas Grene, *The Politics of Irish Drama: Plays in Context from Boucicault to Friel* (Cambridge: Cambridge University Press, 1999), p.212.
39. Ibid., pp.211–14.
40. Declan Kiberd, 'The Real Ireland, Some Think', *New York Times*, 25 April 1999.
41. Thomas Kilroy, 'A Generation of Playwrights', *Irish University Review* 22–1–2, Spring–Summer 1992, pp.135–41, p.141.
42. O'Toole, *Politics of Magic*, p.240.
43. Ibid., p.241.
44. Lisa Fitzpatrick, 'Nation and Myth in the Age of the Celtic Tiger: Muide Éire?' in *Echoes down the Corridor*, ed. P. Lonergan and R. O'Dwyer (Dublin: Carysfort Press, 2006), p.170.
45. Richard Kearney, *On Stories* (London and New York: Routledge, 2002), p.3.
46. Ibid., p.8.
47. Richard Kearney's 'Myth and Motherland' in *Ireland's Field Day* (London: Hutchinson, 1985), p.73.
48. Melissa Sihra, ed., 'Introduction: Figures at the Window' in *Women in Irish Drama: A Century of Authorship and Representation* (Basingstoke: Palgrave Macmillan, 2007), p.1.
49. Fitzpatrick, 'Nation and Myth in the Age of the Celtic Tiger', p.176.
50. Roland Barthes, *A Roland Barthes Reader*, edited and introduced by Susan Sontag (London: Vintage, 1993), p.132.
51. Ibid., p.138.
52. Richard Kearney's 'Myth and Motherland', p.79.
53. Fintan O'Toole, 'Review *Homeland*', *Irish Times*, 20 January 2006; see www.ireland.com/newspaper/features/2006/0120/184438047HM2REVIEWS.html [accessed 15 May 2006]
54. Paul Mercier's work for Passion Machine attempted to deal intelligently with issues of community, class, dispossession, agency and personal motivation. The company performed Mercier's *Drowning* (1985), *Wasters* (1985), *Studs* (1986), *Home* (1988), *Buddleia* (1995), *Kitchensink* (1996), *Native City* (1998), *We Ourselves* (2000) and *Down the Line* (2000).
55. O'Toole, 'Review *Homeland*'.
56. Ibid.
57. Kearney, *On Stories*, p.3.
58. Ibid.
59. Ciarán Benson, *The Cultural Psychology of Self: Place, Morality and Art in Human Worlds* (London and New York: Routledge, 2001), p.4.
60. Ibid., pp.3–4.
61. Peter Brooker, 'Key Words in Brecht's Theory and Practice of Theatre' in P. Thomson and G. Sacks (eds), *The Cambridge Companion to Brecht* (Cambridge: Cambridge University Press, 1994), pp.185–200, p.198.

2

Playing with History and Memory

PERFORMATIVE EPISTEMOLOGIES

To account for the multifarious and compound dramaturgies of Irish theatre, I wish to evaluate some plays that emphasize the complex relationship between memory, history, sometimes myth and metatheatre. First, I want to deal with the history play. Many of the best Irish dramas over the last thirty years have been ones that deal with the past, specifically in contexts that still engage with contemporary perspectives and ideological positions and that challenge biases, inbuilt assumptions and reflexes. That said, all texts have inbuilt codifications of ideological imperatives, have strategies that normalize injustice and inequality, convey obligations and tacit assumptions about what is valued, promoted and marginalized, and prompt certain principles, while leaving others repressed and dismissed. Texts have means of indulging, challenging or of isolating dissent or resistance, through dramatic form, narrative expectations and codifications. At its best, theatre can subvert these dominant ideologies or at least do enough to make the interrogation of these at least feasible, as no text is innocent or free from ideological imperatives. Setting plays in the past and not in the present appears to be a clever way of querying both past and present, yet the tendency to historicize disproportionately, even in a complex way, is regarded by some critics as a ploy to keep the present in relative abeyance.

The principal plays under discussion in this chapter are Brian Friel's *Translations* (1980) and *Dancing at Lughnasa* (1990), Frank McGuinness's *Observe The Sons of Ulster Marching Towards The Somme* (1985) and Tom Kilroy's *Double Cross* (1986). These four plays are regarded as specific types of state-of-the-nation plays by many, but I am increasingly unwilling to agree with this approach. All four dramas are concerned with change, place, home, identities, exile, freedom, repression and authority,[1] and they challenge complex national narratives of simplistic identity formation. Friel in *Translations*

considers the complex interface of tradition, naming, translation, education and language, while *Lughnasa* deals with subsistence living, social
roles and inter-character family dynamics, and also the diverse instincts of
the Mundy sisters in a oppressive patriarchal society in 1930s Ireland.
More than that, however, is the significant way memories persist in
the mind of the play's narrator, Michael, however aspirational, false and
fabricated these recollections might be. Moreover, the process of recollection within the play serves as a metaphor, perhaps, for the way in
which the Irish nation, amongst others, manages to record, dramatize
and negotiate with its past(s), and how it celebrates, passes on, accumulates and inherits the events of a previous era.

Kilroy considers two Irishmen, Brendan Bracken and William Joyce,
who chose to fabricate alternative identities during the Second World
War, Bracken as Winston Churchill's Minister for Information, and
Joyce as a Nazi propagandist, broadcasting across the airwaves of
Britain, inciting citizens against their own government. Joyce, in one of
his broadcasts, accuses Bracken of being a clown and a performer: 'They
like to see you perform, don't you know that? It satisfies their taste in
comedy as a scale, a measurement, politics as entertainment, entertainment as politics.'[2] The character adds: 'In its decadence the imperial
always transposes conquest into circus. The more clownish Irish have
always been willing to step into that ring. And you're the perfect clown
because you believe that life is a matter of taste' (p.45). While
McGuinness's play deals with a portion of the island's history through
loyalist soldiers who fight at the Battle of the Somme during World War
One, it also focuses on loyalist identity formation through the framework of blood sacrifice and destiny tendered by the history/mythology
of the Battle of the Boyne, an event that sanctioned and bizarrely legit-
imized, even into the late 1980s and early 1990s, the activities of loyalist gunmen in Northern Ireland. (Of course, republican paramilitaries
found something equivalent in the 1916 Easter Rising, and this imperative informs the subtext of the play.[3])

Further, many, if not most, of these plays set in the past or fixated
on the past seem to do something with metatheatricality or the idea of
play, and my usage of these interchangeable terms is alert to how play
or metatheatre is present most obviously in play-within-a-play, role-
play, re-enactment, pretence, disguise, mimicry, impersonation and
self-conscious performativity. Additionally, the metatheatrical frame is
a way of elevating the plays from a simplistic representational mode
towards a consciousness of ritual and metaphor. Specifically, for the
first and second generation of postwar playwrights, play often provides

the external framework, where difference is accentuated, possibilities experienced and where identities and fears can be processed. For Richard Schechner, 'Playing, like ritual, is at the heart of performance ... Play is looser, more permissive – forgiving in precisely those areas where ritual is enforcing, flexible where ritual is rigid.'[4] Schechner also outlines how play is both 'indispensable and untrustworthy', as well as 'anarchic' and in need of control, especially by those versed in official culture.

Such play, then, is about the acknowledgement of roles, about the comprehension of pretence and about the expansiveness of identities that are neither fixed nor completely groundless, but are in process. As a disruptive and elastic force, play acknowledges boundaries and demarcations by the very act of transgression that is crucial to so many theatre texts. So much can happen at the borderlands of play, both as an intermediate and intermediary space – where visibility is not good, where depravation unsettles responses, where dynamism evades reflexes and where performativity or role-playing can unsettle or inspire the spectator. By ironizing cultural and political assumptions, by aping inappropriate behaviour, by tinkering with prejudice or by highlighting the inadequacy of certain perceptions, play can distort binary oppositions and undermine stereotypical expectations. Richard Pine, prompted by the writings of Victor Turner, notes that play is 'both innocent and dangerous, both a revel and a risk'.[5] Pine identifies this as the 'if-ness in Friel's work',[6] which is about reflection, scenario imagining, reconfiguring the past, anticipating the future – all risk-taking activities. Friel's *Philadelphia, Here I Come!* (1964) is a useful example of dialogical disruption, where play is a space of exchange and disguise, where co-habiting, surrogate or antithetical realities can feasibly coexist.

In Richard Schechner's words, 'Performances mark identities, bend time, reshape, and adorn the body, and tell stories. Performances – of art, rituals, or ordinary life – are "restored behaviours", "twice-behaved behaviours", performed actions that people train for and rehearse.'[7] The notion of 'restored behaviours' also invites the idea of acquired or anticipative attitudes and behaviours, and this is the acquisitive proficiency that play can offer. Equally, the consistent presence of doubling, and of one-person shows, where an actor plays multiple roles, ensures for Helen Gilbert and Joanne Tompkins that 'Metatheatricality, role doubling exposes the arbitrariness of all roles and foregrounds the illusionistic nature of representation.'[8] The arbitrary nature of roles, duties and responsibilities provokes the idea that change more than stasis is the appropriate perspective.

Marina Jenkyns uses Robert Landy's idea that at the core of performance is the paradox of the 'actor living simultaneously in two realities'.[9] She goes on to say that for Landy, 'taking on a role and taking off a role is a kind of living and dying', one of striving and surrendering, of catalyzing and crystallizing, of display and disguising, of status altering and of lowering, of revelation and duplicity, and one of being and not being. Of course when an actor assumes an alternative role within a performance, then an additional layer of complication is added. Foregrounding the performativity of their characters brings an alertness to the given circumstances, a reflexivity to power, domination and licence, and, of course, tilts reflection towards the viability of difference. Performing emerges as a mode of being, of knowing, of imagining, as a reciprocal exchange with otherness and as a method of embodying creativity, confidence and engagement: it can also function as something intransigent and conservative. Terry Eagleton argues that Oscar Wilde adopts 'a performative rather than a representational epistemology',[10] so it is a 'performative epistemology' that I wish to pursue in relation to these four plays in particular.

In order to trace this postwar dramaturgy and the specifics of metatheatre, the templates provided by an even earlier generation of writers, and in particular how they speculated on confinement, poverty, power, subjectivity, agency and play need to be considered. The basic expectation of drama, deploying Augosto Boal's summary of Lope De Vega's definition, must be 'two human beings, a passion and a platform'.[11] Under this arrangement, between these characters there must be passion, celebration, disharmony, discord, revelry, conviction and danger; circumstances where the characters invest heavily in relationships and/or are provoked on unwanted journeys, leading to clashes of perspective, vision and disposition. Such acute engagement must therefore be hazardous, festive, even relentless, driven by competing passions, with serious loss the ultimate consequence of failure. Great plays more often than not tend to locate themselves at moments of severe transition, disintegration or dismantlement, when the overlap or interfaces between the individual, society and history are in flux. The characters might invest in difference, yet there is still a sense of access to received and shared, or, if not shared, then aspirational moral codes or modes of being. The incisive loss of perceived core values and the emergence of new awarenesses, which are often unwanted, even unwarranted, generate circumstances that help build the dramatic situation.

Drama in this instance becomes at times mythic or ritualistic, or at least sharing the imperatives and inclinations of both. These substantial

texts are layered ones, marked by differences in scale, and are dominated ultimately as much by chaos as either necessity or destiny. The
clarity often associated with great drama is possible, having exposed,
pursued and validated severely restricted choices. A completely pared
down, elemental survival is often the key, with the notion of the
performative self, facing down chaos, inventing worlds and strategies
with which to subsist, rather than prosper.

Irish theatrical stage spaces are often not only singular but also
multiple, with off-stage space vital in establishing the existence of huge
pressures elsewhere – in particular, repressive, oppressive, other worldly,
even surreal forces. There is often a sense of someone looking on, an
individual or an ideology or counter-ideology, which can be intimidating
or voyeuristic on the one hand and seductive, repressive and dominating
on the other. Vanished characters or the absent feminine can exert a
powerful influence on such scenarios. More substantially, the presence
off stage points to another consciousness, another alienating reality or
aspirational reality or fifth province.[12]

It is impossible to ignore the unsettling nature of fabricated identity
in Oscar Wilde's *The Importance of Being Earnest* (1895) and Christy
Mahon's transformation in *The Playboy of the Western World* (1907),
partly prompted by the imaginings of Pegeen Mike, which is driven by a
dark carnivalesque disruptive force, the meshing of the heroic and
unheroic, and guided by the unconscious desire to displace the authority
of the father and the willingness to submit to the new and emerging
order of his new-found infamy in the west. Winnie in Beckett's *Happy
Days* (1961) finds her only solace in the illusion of play, and Krapp in
Krapp's Last Tape (1958) playfully renegotiates with an older version
of self.

Consistently, imitatively and successfully, Irish playwrights have
relied on dismal social situations in order to energize their realities. In
selecting such circumstances, existential choices, primordial struggles
and sibling rivalries were accentuated. Politics provided either the backdrop or the determining governing reality. This struggle is best seen in
the temporary illusion (carnivalesque inversion) of riches in O'Casey's
Juno and the Paycock (1924), where the Boyles, believing that they have
inherited a fortune, surround themselves with the trappings of wealth
and mimic the perceived behaviour of the wealthy. The gap between
the new desperate roles they play and their demeanours and conducts
(desperate in a different way) of act 1 strikes home superbly.[13]

Synge, O'Casey and Beckett, in his early work, manipulated quite
brilliantly the power dynamic, capturing simultaneously the perversity

and the theatricality of power, offsetting it by a huge emphasis on the performative self. In earlier forms of drama the notion of the enemy or oppositional force was clear-cut. Power was apparent and more often than not blatant. The inversion and confrontation of power often took place within the framework of play, with an obvious relationship to the context from which texts emerged.

In the past, choice, or, more accurately, limited choice was one of the keys to most standard dramatic models. We see this also in the early work of Friel and Murphy. Gar O'Donnell in *Philadelphia, Here I Come!* enacts memories, orchestrates fantasies and stage-manages events all to no avail, locked as he is within a cycle that is unbearably restrictive. Within this model, freedom is hard-earned and opportunities are not a recurring phenomenon but are a one-off gamble – the odds of victory are extremely low and postponement means the loss of all possibility. The crossing over from society to the dramatic frame is of course extremely complicated and I make this point again. Here I only wish to deal with the perception of choice (even where illusion might be the most important variable). The dilemma ultimately is how to frame choice, frame opposition and frame confrontation. Defiance might provide a feasible and inarticulate option. Thus, for example, Henrik Ibsen could blur distinctions; his Hedda Gabler is victim and aggressor, bound and yet free to choose, and she is a play-maker (as she manufactures the scenarios, orchestrates the setting), yet is totally fettered to some unknowable and unnamable gendered imperative in the form of patriarchal authority, exemplified by the portrait of her father. Such drama is therefore structured so that no motivation can be attributed with any great certainty: at best choice is not seen as an authoritative selection but as something deficient in conviction and lacking in justification and at worst, as utterly outside the agency of the individual character, as it resides with another authority. If choice is absent, the manner in which the characters conjure the illusion of choice, as in *Waiting for Godot* (1953), can prove to be just as dramatic. Irish theatre has tended to resist notions of coherent subjectivity and has been even complacent about the absence of singular subjectivity thanks, in part, to imperialistic oppression, a repressive education system, religious doctrines and poor circumstances for many of its citizens. Play has therefore been central to the discovery of limitations and to the meshing of identities, and has been a way of generating ruptures and discontinuities.

DANCING AT LUGHNASA: 'PECULIAR VERACITIES'

Brian Friel's *Dancing at Lughnasa* brings together memory and dancing, the sacred and the profane, ritual and transcendence in a brilliantly complicated fashion. Michael is a memory maker, and the play is a dream catcher of sorts. Dance serves as a manifestation of the defiant optimism of the Mundy sisters: 'I want to dance',[14] Agnes states, and memory functions as an expression of buoyancy, even deliverance. The sense of transgressive play is found across a whole range of Friel's works and is here reformulated within the framework of memory.[15] Michael is both narrator and intruder, and he plays with the memory, and at times participates unnaturally in a resuscitated memory as the child, Michael.[16] To be too involved in such processes means often to be without the comfort and confidence that distance brings. How Friel achieves distance from his subject matter is his greatest skill as a playwright. In his plays the emotion is always blatantly painful, but never is it raging; it is expressive only in the determination of the characters to maintain a masked control over it.[17] Play thus complicates flow, expressivity, control and performativity.

In *Lughnasa* Friel emphasizes the memory processes of all the Mundy family, and of Michael, in particular. The family places obsessive weight on memory, as it bestows a level of subjectivity, unconfirmed by other activities in their lives; everything from Father Jack's difficulty in remembering his native tongue all the way to Maggie's memory of the dancing competition that her friend, Bernie O'Donnell and her partner, Curley McDaid, unfairly lost, are mulled over. In *Lughnasa* Michael's memory structure is not so much based on fact as an elaborate combination of fantasy, detail, collaborated evidence, defiance, possibility, reassurance and the impulse towards narrative coherence. Friel captures this quality with the following lines:

> And since there is no lake, my father and I never walked back from it in the rain with our rods across our shoulders. Have I imagined the scene, then? Or is it a composite of two or three different episodes? The point is – I don't think it matters. What matters is that for some reason ... this vivid memory is there in the storehouse of the mind. For some reason the mind has shuffled the pieces of verifiable truth and composed a truth of its own. For me it is a truth. And because I acknowledge its peculiar veracity, it becomes a layer in my subsoil; it becomes part of me; ultimately it becomes me.[18]

If the mind can 'shuffle the pieces', then the shuffling feet, through movement and dance, can trigger something altogether different. Friel can unsettle the verifiability of memory, but unlike Beckett, he cannot divorce memory from eloquence. Mask becomes memory, as mask activates a spirit of deeply harboured energy and a protracted memory of connection, even when, as in *Lughnasa*, such memory is carnivalized and performative. Adam Phillips argues that

> If memories are more like dreams than pieces of reliable documentary evidence, and are disguised representations of forbidden desire, it is as though desire can only be remembered by being successfully forgotten; which in this context means represented by a sufficiently censored dreamable dream, or an often banal replacement-memory. Forgetting, in its versions of disguise, makes desire accessible by making it tolerable.[19]

Michael deliberates on four key formative and 'tolerable' memories: the return of Father Jack from the missions, two close together visits from his father, Gerry Evans, who is normally elsewhere, the presence of a new radio and the memory of his mother and his four aunts dancing. With these seed memories Michael introduces the play, but these close together appearances by his father, whom he sees infrequently anyway, marks the slow demise of Gerry's visits, the return home of his uncle from the missions leads to his death within a year of his home-coming, and although the dance of the Mundy sisters is simultaneously celebratory and defiant, it also becomes the ominous indicator of impending separation.

The gaps between expectation and reality, longing and actualization, and substance and appearance are evident. The early delight at Father Jack's return makes way for the utter shock provoked by his ill-health and unusual religious perspectives, the initial awe in the face of the magic of radio gives way to the sexual tensions and rivalries between the sisters over the partnering of Gerry in dance, the promises of a father to bestow gifts and to ensure his presence in the lives of mother (Chris) and child come to nothing. The heroic homecoming of Jack leads to ostracization and to Kate losing her job, thanks to the hostility of the local parish priest to Father Jack's wayward and unconventional religious practices, in addition the arrival of a new knitting factory leads to an altogether different regime within the household, with Rose and Agnes fleeing to London, only to fall into awful circumstances. Expectation and anticipation deliver nothing. The opposite of what is wished for occurs.

In *Lughnasa* there is of course the central memory that is both written by Friel and defined by Friel, of which Michael claims a type of tentative ownership. The play takes place in what O'Toole calls 'a collapse of past and present into the eternal suspension of memory'.[20] Michael lays claim to a memory moment, the dance sequence, that he himself did not witness, something not many critics have noticed. When the sisters participate in the main dance, Michael is absent. He is playing down the lane. Michael fails, in *Lughnasa,* to acknowledge the contractions of his narrative accounts as Elder Pyper does in *The Sons of Ulster.* Friel does not call an end to Michael's fabrication or his disingenuity: involuntary memory is his Oileán Draíochta [Magic Island] of sorts.

Little can be verified in this drama. The play states that Michael is a 'young man'. Let's say he is 40, at most 50 years old (and both are stretching things), so the memory moment most certainly is not 1990, the date of the first performance. This fact becomes a supplementary frame of mediation. Additionally, act 1 is set on a warm day, 'early in August' and act 2 in 'early September', yet Michael tells us that his father's return visit was a 'couple of weeks' later (p.65). So the play's action moves from early August to early September in just 'three weeks' rather than the expected four, and either way, it contradicts Michael's reference to 'a couple of weeks', which normally suggests two. Time, like memory, exists in an unreliable, suspended, liminal space. Details, like the fact that Gerry, the Welshman, speaks with the 'English accent' (p.43), additionally and intentionally defamiliarize. There are substantially different linguistic, temporal and spatial frames evident, ensuring that space, time, language and dance overlap in a very complicated way. Temporally, there is real, memoried, imagined and ritualistic time in operation, while spatially, real, mythologized, internal, pagan, other-worldly and imagined spaces function simultaneously. In addition there are relationships between off-stage and on-and-off-stage (mimetic/diegetic), Donegal and Ryanga and the imaginary Ballybeg and the Glenties, where the writer's own family, on his mother's side, the MacLoones, were based.

LADIES OF THE DANCE

Through narrative, Michael informs an audience not only what will occur, but, what to expect and what to look out for. He can inform the spectator as to what is to happen to his family and then it materializes in performance. But, although the audience trusts him with the facts, should it still trust his interpretation? Friel urges no. Michael must fail ultimately to determine meaning for the spectator, despite his best efforts. Michael seduces with his tone, and his pleading, and through the way he narrates, deploying key words and seductive rhythms. In his final evocation Michael suggests that 'everybody seems to be floating on those sweet sounds, moving rhythmically, languorously, in complete isolation; responding more to the mood of the music than to its beat' (p.107), whereas in his opening monologue he remembers something somewhat different. He recalls his 'mother and her sisters suddenly catching hands and dancing a spontaneous step-dance and laughing – screaming – like excited school girls' and that 'Marconi's voodoo' deranged 'those kind, sensible women' and transformed 'them into shrieking strangers' (p.8).

During the opening narrative he describes the dancing and atmosphere using words like 'spontaneous', 'laughing', 'screaming', 'excited' and 'deranged'; by the final monologue his depiction relies on words like 'floating', 'rhythmically', 'languorously', 'hushed rhythm' and 'silent hypnotic movement', which offers two contradictory responses. In between, 'grotesque', 'aggressive', 'raucous', 'erratic', 'caricaturing' and 'parodic' are some of the words Friel employs to express the central dance in his stage directions. (Claudia Harris finds that 'these passionate women' are demeaned by his description.[21])

The brilliance of this play lies in the disturbing sense of incongruity established by Michael's contradictory accounts of the dancing, and by Friel's particular stage directions. The playwright is as consciously disruptive and manipulative as Michael attempts to be. Friel complicates his narrator's ownership of memory. Michael's response to the past is utterly unreliable: his summaries are deceptive. Furthermore, in performance something altogether different is added, by the performers, under the director's guidance, and by an audience's expectations of the dance sequence. The consistent problem has been that some directors have run close to Michael's dreamy account and downplayed the essential stage directions prompted by the writer when it comes to the dance. Even when the dancing is aggressive, many audiences become oblivious to Friel's attempts to introduce parody and caricature.

Likewise, there is a subtle difference between the opening and closing tableaux. Characters take up different stage positions. Jack's uniform at the end is utterly different to the one that was seen at the start of the play. In effect, neither tableau can be regarded as a single authentic memory moment; instead both scenes are a collage, superimposed images or a palimpsest. The image of Jack in the first tableau had perhaps more to do with the photo that had fallen from Kate's prayer book than anything else. (Interestingly in the play, Kate is embarrassed by the picture of Jack in a British uniform; in the film version, scripted by Frank McGuinness, such a picture is displayed on the wall of the kitchen.)

So, what prompts Michael's actions? Remember that he was just 7 years old around the time of the seminal incidents. Perhaps it is the traumatic nature of social circumstances and the horror of what was to befall his family? Harrowing details appear from the first narrative onward, often as casual qualifications, as Michael picks his way through the formative experience of the summer of 1936. The narrator attempts to romanticize, to champion and to idealize the energy and exuberance of the Mundy sisters. He finds solace in the past, and everything else is filtered through this memory in order to consolidate meaning in his own life. I have suggested elsewhere that 'In most of Friel's plays the battle cry is "no surrender" to memory; here he plays a different game, as he assiduously invites surrender, tempts an audience in, but defiance is the truer obligation.'[22] Is it that the more brutal the memory the more throw-away it becomes, the more slight the incident the greater the eloquence required and the greater meaning given? Vitally, there is a need to 'forget and a need to prioritize something (a dance sequence) that is, in the overall scheme of things, not entirely substantial. And by so doing, something else is let in'.[23]

Maybe Michael's incapacity to name that pain prompts him instead to celebrate his inability to articulate the substance of the dance that 'owes nothing to fact' and everything to intensity and atmosphere (p.107). That he gets the atmosphere wrong owes much to his need to get the facts wrong. He can try to use language to give a reading of it, he can even suggest that language is unimportant, but all the time words fail, and more importantly the versions of events which he provides are riven with contradiction. In *Living Quarters* (1977) the ledger held by Sir, despite his insistence otherwise, cannot contain all the details. Truth cannot be known, it always remains incomplete; the political implications of this idea are made manifest in *Making History* (1988). Atmosphere becomes fantasy. There is nothing to be restored, nothing to be replayed if, as I have suggested already, the event was never witnessed by Michael in the first place.

MAENAD OR BACCHANTE

Richard Allen Cave notes that the dance and the crazed energy of the women at the moment of dancing 'call to mind the traditional image of the Maenad or Bacchante of classical lore, a woman totally given over to bodily impulse and the sensuality of movement in celebration of the power of the god, Dionysus'.[24] Pine argues that the dance 'belongs to the women, in the sense that a similar action among five men would be inconceivable'.[25] The central dance, as stipulated by the stage directions, is aggressive, self-conscious, transgressive, an attack on a social order that inhibits and controls women and men. The dancing by the Mundy women brings a kind of chaotic disorder that is energizing. By contrast, the dancing of the males is utterly different. Gerry's dance is elegant and formal; Jack's stick dance is pathetic. The recollection is of movement and physicality, and as such, memory has the free structure, rhythm and elusiveness of dance. Commemoration becomes dance, and it becomes both a dance of memory and a ghost dance, as it does in *Observe the Sons of Ulster*, where Elder Pyper states: 'Dance in the deserted temple of the Lord. Dance unto death before the Lord.'[26] Through the spirit of play or dance-play there is release. Likewise, the contradiction and uncertainty that Friel garners from the play's form is not only consistent with the structure of memory, but its fluidity has all the hallmarks of play. We must keep in mind Seamus Heaney's comment that memory in Friel's work is a 'mythological resource rather than a deceptive compensation', therefore play serves as mythic enablement and as a template of possibility.[27] (This comment has particular implications for the later chapter on myth.) Dance-play is the defiance against almost impossible odds. Dancing is the agency of expression for these sisters and memory is the agency of consolation for the young man, who had witnessed his known world almost disintegrate around him.

The Festival of Lughnasa was a yearly event in Ireland, while in Uganda, two harvest festivals were celebrated, 'the Festival of the New Yam' and the other, 'the Festival of the Sweet Casava', both dedicated to the Great Goddess, Obi, to whom sacrifices were offered in order to ensure that the crops would flourish and that the community might communicate with the dead.[28] By drawing on the Ryangan ritualism in the way that Father Jack does, Friel does not attempt to superimpose this ritualistic reality where the secular and the sacred meet, or the pagan world of the back hills at the time of the Lughnasa festivities on to the Mundy's. Neither the dancing nor the pagan can be pastoralized or simplified. As Anna McMullan notes, 'Jack's dance is an enfeebled version of his remembered African rituals, and the killed rooster at the end of the play is like a failed or aborted ritual, an act divorced from its significance.'[29] This sense of ruptured separation haunts the play. Not only do the pagan ceremonies on the back hills result in Sweeney's injuries, but the marital arrangements proposed by Father Jack, whereby the four sisters might be married to one male, could not be managed by the Mundy sisters, as the reality of the tensions between them and

Gerry affirms. Ultimately, it is their defiance with which Michael identifies, not with the energy of the grotesque, of subversion and of caricature.

Many critics see the dancing as a positive feminine gesture and yet
see the act of memory as a masculine negative one. I am not sure why
that should be the case. Claudia Harris suggests that Friel is attempting
'to reconcile his childhood witness of the radio's voodoo possessing
those sensible women and transforming them into screeching strangers
with his current adult acceptance yet continued male incomprehension
of the womanhood expressed in the event'.[30]

The association of woman with such disturbing energy that is non-
rational and bodily-based has been confronted by a number of critics.
As Harris observes:

> The actors need not only the freedom of an actual space on the
> stage, but also the imaginative license to exploit the brief removal
> of the unconscious patriarchal filter that normally controls their
> lives. Friel reproduces the distinctly male perception that society
> has of the women and that the women to a large extent have of
> themselves.[31]

For me, Michael is not reauthorizing or reworking the memory, instead
he is trying to place it. He is not attempting to deny the reality of the
sisters, but the fact that he misreads it can be put down to a number of
things. How this can be viewed as a form of repressive, patriarchal
domination and masculine omnipotence at the expense of women is
difficult to concede. It is not so much a tribute as a statement or
acknowledgement of substantial loss, eased somewhat from a blatant
rage and despair. Soft-focus productions of the play distort this and
make it a tribute.

The characters can have little impact on their situation. Social, political, religious and economic forces have a momentum all of their own.
Life did not grant the women a level of freedom or of subjectivity, nor
did it grant most men much else. As a child, Michael has little control
over his environment, as an adult he has little more. The one thing he
has is some ownership over his memory, but it is not a vengeful, disturbing one. His distorting owes less to misogyny and far more to trauma and
his own sense of powerlessness. While an audience empathizes with
Michael's pain and recognizes how he displaces his trauma, it still
should be alert to the sleight-of-hand, to the clever appropriations of
memory by him. Gar in *Philadelphia, Here I Come!* states that a recollection was 'just the memory; and even now, even so soon, it is being

distilled of all its coarseness; and what's left is going to be precious, precious gold'.[32] It is as if Michael has been flouring, frosting and fostering the memory for too long. But it is misguided to expect survivors to be more mature, perceptive and knowing. Michael is a survivor of painful experiences, but pain offers no guarantee of humanity.

Michael's efforts to romanticize or idealize the dance are not important. What is vital are the dependency and despondency he displays in latching on to it, and the desperation of an individual troubled by painful memories about a family where choices were severely limited, a family that did the best it could under harsh circumstances. Clearly memory is linked with a sense of communal belonging that is at times nostalgic, yet the most considerable ingredient of the play is the sense of active community established by the sisters. They fought, disagreed, contained and sustained antagonisms, compromised, co-operated and cared. There is humanity in their judgements of one another, a leniency even in the most vicious put down or accusation. The survival instinct is to play with memory. Hugh reminds us in *Translations* that 'To remember everything is a form of madness.'[33] Heaney argues that 'it is because of the authenticity of the transition from narrative presentation to reverie and narcotic dream-life at the end of *Lughnasa* that we can respect Michael's entrancement as an adequate response to "evidence"',[34] and he quotes Carl Gustav Jung, who states that 'In the end the only events in my life worth telling are those when the imperishable world irrupted into the transitory one.'[35] O'Toole suggests something akin to Jung, claiming that 'if nothing can really change, then nothing can really die'.[36] Yet Friel's play dramatizes how the perishable world erupts into an intransitory one, a perishable world that was narrated to Michael as part of the family memory, given that he did not witness the key moment of dance. The play is not as much about the preservation of the past and a denial of history's impetus, as a marking of the process of adjustment and realignment within the trauma of ritualized memory.

Friel offers in *Lughnasa* a revised and fabricated memory in the form of anecdotal narrative. Artifice and a carnivalized consciousness are delivered by the presence of the back hills and by the Ryangan narratives expressed by Father Jack. If identity is performative, then memory is equally performative. Friel metatheatricalizes the memory reflex by offering a desecrated ritual of re-enactment. Wild, wayward, errant, delicate and elaborate memory is willed on by a repetition compulsion that is dangerous as well as consolatory. The Mundy sisters' collective dance becomes a primitive rite, an alternative, condensed and reductive

Lughnasa, a temporary aberration from more dominant social realities. Into that mix we can add the recreational voyeurism of non-participation and non-witnessing.

Memory evolves, accumulates and erodes; it is organic and unfixed. Michael is nurtured and sustained by memory, but he cannot call the shots. Michael's memory is a leap of fate in the face of the decline of faith in formal or pagan belief systems. The narrator, as yet, unlike Jack's and Gerry's exchange of hats, which required both gestural and symbolic distancing from the possessions, can only bring 'perhaps' and 'maybe' as the significant distancing needed to move on from the prolongation of the memory of summer 1936. In terms of archetype and collective personifications, George Steiner, quoting Jung, argues that faced with these figures, the mind '"remembers"', it 'knows that it has been here before', for it 'is precisely this *déjà vu* within formula and executive originality which makes our experience of great art and poetry a homecoming to new remembrance'.[37] This is what Friel is after. Memory shares the values of metatheatricality; it shares the function and elaboration, impetus, substance and tenacity of dance play.

The dancing takes a variety of forms, becoming memory's mirror. Traditional reel, step-dance, graceful formal waltzing and a series of grotesque, caricatured, disfigured and dishevelled shuffled movements, enacted by everyone from Rosie to Father Jack, act as apt descriptions of memory. Traditional rhythms, locked into defiance, abandonment and sad surrender, romanticized step-dancing of belonging and togetherness, and the swish and the swirl of the waltz materialize as strands and shards of memory, that then conspire further to coexist as a carnivalized memory of excess, exaggeration, intoxication and gracelessness. Dance is a perverse exemplary moment of union and yet it is the co-celebration of imminent collapse. Memory is an explosive miracle of continuity and the ripening, miraculous reconstitution of the impossible. For all his charm, Gerry is a fraud; despite its magnetism, memory proves to be a charismatic charade, yet its strengths are never dismissed for all of that.

SPLIT SPECULARITY

Thus, as narrator, Michael attempts to articulate a gap between 'what seemed to be and what was, of things changing too quickly before my eyes, of becoming what they ought not to be' (p.8). This is the gap into which the play falls, between what may have been, what was, what is and what ought to be; between the real and the ideal, between the real and the imagined. Memory cannot be entirely truthful; it can only, at best, be warped by time, emotion, desire, repetition and by the frailty of fact. The memory literally is a false one, yet psychologically and culturally, a fabled truth. Thus the drama is about the impossibility of fully accessing, resuscitating, processing or purging memory. But through the intervention and impetus of play, an altogether different energy is let in. To disassociate, to invert, to displace are the keys to what Friel does. After all, when Michael summarizes through narrative intervention much is glossed over, so much is pushed away and so little penetrates the control he possesses. The distinction between pain and pleasure has been blurred by so many contemporary writers; here Friel substitutes one for the other. The pain of loss is displaced by the pleasure of positive memory.

Metatheatre implies a play-within-a-play format as I suggested at the start, and here Friel delivers a memory-within-a-memory or a memory collage. For Gilbert and Tompkins, within a postcolonial context 'A play-within-a-play disperses the centre of visual focus to at least two locations so that the viewer's gaze is both split *and* multiplied' and that '[P]lays-within-a-play demonstrate a split specularity that forms a location of difference; the two object sites of the gaze can never be identical.'[38] Likewise the memory-within-a-memory, framed as *Lughnasa* is by two dissimilar tableaux, and peppered by contradictory narratives, confirms the activity of the dispersal variable and multiplicity of focus that Friel was after. The dialogical structure in *Lughnasa*, similar to the one proposed by the Russian critic Mikhail Bakhtin, ensures not only a polyphonic or double-voiced consciousness, or a double take on reality, but a doubling of image. Somehow life imitates memory and memory imitates life. For Adam Phillips, 'a child can only find his game (and the new self that plays it) by first acknowledging the mother's absence'.[39] Michael still fails to do so. The sisters' (mother proliferation, in a different way) absence is a realization of Michael's own dread of death and fear of not being remembered.

DOUBLE CROSS: DOPPELGÄNGER EFFECT

Stephen Rea played both Bracken and Joyce in the first production of *Double Cross* for Field Day. In order to process the notion of partial doubleness (doubleness is just the default setting), mirroring, demonic duplicity, haunting and symbiosis within the context of Ireland's colonial experience at the hands of the British, Kilroy draws, first of all, on complex staging strategies, a video screen and a radio. A flexible performance space is the foremost requirement; there are shifts from scene to scene, with little attempt to establish quasi-realistic or authentic environments, in the conventional sense. The initial stage direction brings together a notional realistic stage space, which is 'dominated by an Adam fireplace' (p.17), with an alternative type of staging that utilizes a 'hanging washing line' with 'larger than life figures, cut-out cardboard representations of Churchill, King George V and Sir Oswald Mosley', effigies that will be flipped over later when they become 'Dr Goebbels, Hitler and Mosley, again'. A rostrum downstage right represents a range of different locations, and upstage is the video/film screen (p.17). So the stage space is composite and multifunctionally artificial. Other theatrical touches used to suggest the shifting of location include the use of music, the dropping of Tory party streamers and a Union Jack, and the deployment of sounds to suggest bombing raids and such like. The production was initially designed to tour mainly non-conventional theatre venues in Ireland, as was company policy.

More importantly, there are demands placed on actors to shift in and out of roles, to interrogate, exposit, imitate, infer and to step forward and address the audience. Two actors, one male and one female, play an array of characters with utterly distinguishable traits, postures and accents. However, greatest demand is placed on the central actor, who is obliged to play both Bracken and Joyce as protagonists/antagonists in each other's stories, for when Bracken is present on stage, Joyce is brought into being over the airwaves or on the video screen and vice versa. The actor's transformation from one character to the other takes place on stage, visible to an audience in such a way that the mutation exposes the play's metatheatrical inclinations.

The media devices function as filtering, mediating realities, but they also act as liminal, threshold ones, accommodating a type of hybrid reality through the fact that the characters operate in a heterotopic space. While the spectator's exposure to the media elements is intermittent, they remain omnipresent and coercive even when actively non-communicative. It is not a play that is simply using multimedia as an elaborating strategy, but is a play that uses different media in order to comment on the nature of role, identity and performance, where identity is one that is constructed through colonial and ideological interpellations, cultural broadcasts and political imperatives as much as through experience, choices and personal actions.

Although act 1 is called the Bracken Play and act 2 the Joyce Play, they are not discrete, independent units, for the drama is not simply about the dialogue between two parallel acts or the dialogical tension between both. By almost superimposing or mapping, palimpsest-like one act on another, there is persistent cross-contamination, engagement or contact between both characters and the worlds they immediately inhabit, Britain and Germany, and by default, Ireland. All these staging facets ensure the creation of a truly complex, complicated and accomplished *mise-en-scène*.

Bracken was the son of a Fenian revolutionary and Joyce was born in America to an Irish father and English mother but moved back to live in Galway at an early age. Both fled to England in order to find some purpose in their lives at a time when Ireland gained its independence, both embraced politics and both 'fabricated ultra-English identities' (p.20). Joyce ended up as a 'naturalized German citizen of the Third Reich', having 'wanted to be English but had to settle on being German' (p.52). Bracken tried to disguise all traces of his past by fabricating one that nobody truly believed in, but a past that he assumed would give satisfactory credence to his manufactured identity.

Beaverbrook claims that 'anyone can be British ... All you need is a modest command of the language and a total commitment to a handful of symbols, some of which are pretty ludicrous' (p.75). If it were so easy, why did they fail, in different ways? The play interrogates the possibility as to whether or not 'Patriotism and treason may be fuelled by the same hunger' (p.28). So the quest for authentic purpose and their embrace of Britishness in both of their lives is governed fundamentally, perhaps, by the grammars of performance and masquerades of inauthenticity.

Kilroy introduces the Faber edition of the play with the claim that 'To base one's identity, exclusively, upon a mystical sense of place rather than in personal character where it properly resides seems to me a dangerous absurdity' (pp.6–7). But place will define a person if one cannot lay claim to the ownership of that space or where the space within which one lives does not guarantee fundamental freedoms. In a broader context, Gilbert and Tompkins suggest that

> split or fragmentary subjectivity reflects the many and often competing elements that define post-colonial identity, whereas attempts to achieve a subjective 'wholeness' may merely replicate the limited significations of the coloniser/colonised binary through which imperialism maintains control over the apparently unruly and uncivilised 'masses'.[40]

They go on to argue that 'split subjectivity can be viewed ... as potentially enabling rather than as disempowering'.[41] However, the native within the imperialist project must face down his/her internalization of oppression, otherwise what is oppressed can turn into repression or into all kinds of displacement, avoidance and imitative strategies to accommodate or to make sense of subjugation. Split, fractured, decentred subjectivities result in identities that over-invest in performance and style, and less in substance. Clearly, there is an obligation to destabilize the remit of nation in the shaping of identities, while at the same time to embrace the restraint and inadequacy that nationhood formalizes as if to generate a vertigo of self. Perversely, from the innate self-destructiveness of the characters, dramatic creative synergies emerge, so in that sense 'split subjectivity' can be empowering. Christopher Murray reads the play with specific reference to Northern Ireland:

> Joyce's self-destruction shows the 'serpent of history' can indeed bite off its own head in pursuit of an unattainable ideal. The application to internecine strife in Northern Ireland may be inferred. It is a colonial issue: an investigation of the meaning(s) of loyalty. In Northern Ireland one person's loyalty is another's treason. Doubleness is built into the political system.[42]

While both Bracken and Joyce have a vile opinion of each other, both have a gift for language, for invention, misinformation, disinformation, for pretence and disguise. Both display a compulsion to perform and each has a capacity to test the credibility of others to their limits. The relationship between both of the main characters is one of literal false connection, but the symbolic connection the 'principle of circularity' (p.34) that is mentioned in the play is vital. While Nicholas Grene argues that each character is 'constantly confronted by his screen simulacrum, his hated and despised double',[43] for me, the characterizations are more to do with juxtapositions, superimpositions, displacements and fragments, for the characters echo and upstage each other. The notion of double only gets one so far. The spectator gets what effectively is, instead of a play-within-a-play format, a character-within-a-character. The interconnection between Bracken and Joyce benefits from the incongruity of theatrical modes of performance, the Comedy of Manners style of act 1 uneasily resides with act 2, which bears a serious Brechtian influence. So the spectator experiences the meshing of acts, blended performance styles and the layering of characters. To witness a single performer doing both the Bracken and Joyce roles is to regard, perhaps, performance as virtuosity and cultural ventriloquism as pathology. The form of the play, its staging and its multimedia elements all conspire to deliver such potential reflections.

LONDON CALLING

The opening stage image has Bracken attempting to tune into a Joyce broadcast. In this way the radio is used to allow in the disembodied voice of Joyce, while at the same time we get a sense of Bracken's repulsive, compulsive fascination with him. Bracken then goes on to provide a commentary on the broadcast. Joyce's right of reply comes when he accuses Bracken of being a 'specimen of outrageous masquerade' (p.17) and of being a 'poseur and parasite' (p.18). Later Joyce deems him a 'trickster' (p.19). On the other hand, Bracken regards Joyce as 'traitor' (p.19).

Once the action of the play is set, once the possibility of different voices coalescing and disagreeing is established and once the conventions of the drama are articulated to an audience, then there is less use of the video screen; when re-utilized, it is always at key moments of transition and tension. In his review Fintan O'Toole argues that 'the use of film becomes repetitious and undramatic'.[44] (The original production was directed by Jim Sheridan, who went on to direct *My Left Foot* (1989), *In the Name of the Father* (1993) and *In America* (2003).) When an audience witnesses Bracken on the phone, we get a different Brendan each time he communicates. He may either be terrorized by the absence of self or he may well be perversely enabled by it.

When it comes to sex, Bracken again displays a fluctuating ambivalence. Popsie appears before him 'dressed as boy scout' (p.25) and is ready to perform, as Bracken needs 'costuming to become sexually' aroused (p.25). Even on the level of sexual fantasy there is much insecurity and the suggestion of paedophilic fantasies, which cannot equate with paedophilic desire. Popsie's personal explanation is that the reason behind his sexual dysfunction is because he is a 'twisted little Irish puritan' (p.27). Is it better to perceive the Irish as puritanical and sexually repressed by religious doctrine or its opposite, rampantly sexual? Within imperial thinking there is no middle ground for the native. Additionally, Popsie's claim that Bracken can 'conceal nothing' from her (p.27) seems to be an attempt to position herself in a superior and perhaps culturally arrogant situation.

Beaverbook reveals to Bracken that he has pieced together his true/real Templemore, County Tipperary upbringing, but this background is not the one used to introduce him to the Paddington constituency meeting, where the claim is that Bracken is of 'British-Irish stock, was born in Bedfordshire, the son of a distinguished officer in the Indian Army', educated at 'Sedbergh and an Oxford graduate' (p.33). Between the denial for origins and the fabrication of origins lies one of the fundamental tensions within Bracken.

Bracken's brother Peter is another psychic shadow. Sometimes Peter is 'high up in the Admiralty, in charge of vast tea plantations in Ceylon, while at the same time conducting a lucrative business in the City', according to Popsie (p.40), or at other times his brother is 'terribly well connected with the Frogs ... Import-export' (p.23). To the Warden on the rooftop Peter has 'died in action. The RAF. Died splendidly. One of "Stuffy" Dowding's chaps' (p.42). Bracken easily changes the story to say his brother is a 'traitor' when the Warden pushes him for details.

CAREFUL CONSONANTS

However, while most of society disbelieves Bracken, but has the good manners not to question his inconsistencies, and his fantasies, at least not to his face, behind his back they 'smile' at 'Poor Brendan'(p.40). 'Smile' is the appropriate word, for it is not the coarse laughter of defiance, not the laughter of participation or shared irreverence, and not the laughter of ironic self-recognition of themselves as fabricators, moreover, it is the laughter of the refined and the distinguished against a 'red haired golliwog' who wears 'indifferent suits' (p.31), as Castlerosse perceives Bracken's dress sense to be. Bracken's relative uncouthness and his inability to fit in come to the fore, and, despite all of his performative intelligence and despite his business acumen – for he was running five newspapers by the age of 30 – he still participates not as an insider, but as an outsider. Popsie claims that she has 'never known anyone to use the English language quite in the same way' that Bracken does (p.29), and she additionally remarks: 'Well, it's rather as if one were speaking to someone who was discovering the words as he went along. It's aboriginal' (p.30). Made explicit here is the arrogance of the élite, watching someone attempting to belong, yet unable to dismiss fully either his energy, commitment or his successes for that matter. He is kept external, indifferently other, through the arrogant dismissal of his routines and his fabrications. Bracken is both exposed and captivated by language, but he also is enslaved by that language precisely because he functions abnormally and inappropriately within it by the measure of the imperial centre. His thoughts are assembled with a structuring that does not benefit from either familiarity or cultural absorption, in other words, he is without the apprenticeship of tradition or class. He ruptures the syntax despite attempts to be in control. (Joyce asks: 'Are all the careful consonants out of control[?]' (p.46), as it is Joyce who understands his linguistic vulnerability.)

Bracken's play at being British ultimately fails on many levels. Beaverbook notes that Bracken overstates and tries too hard. Bracken quotes Edmund Burke (an Irishman) that to be British is 'To be bred in a place of estimation, to see nothing low or sordid from one's infancy – to be habituated in the pursuit of honour and duty' (p.37). Such a false consciousness is obvious: it is naïve and almost politically innocent and grossly insulting. Likewise, Bracken's disdain for Mahatma Gandhi is telling, rejecting his primitiveness, his political protests and his requests for independence, seeing Gandhi and his people as opposite to Burke's ancient ideal. As Mária Kurdi notes, 'Bracken's misinterpretation of the Burkean legacy and its self-destructive consequences warn against acts that privatize meanings and turn identity into hollow fictions, disregarding its complexity.'[45] For Bracken, people like Gandhi know nothing of 'law' or of 'grace', of culture or of 'cultivated living'. Instead it is their smell, their 'obscene rituals', ultimately their 'animalism' that most offends (p.37). In these admissions Kilroy patterns out the notion of the subaltern and the manner in which binary opposites function to establish systems of superiority and subjugation, but as Homi Bhabha points out through his theorized concept of ambivalence, the oppressor is never omnipotent and the victim is not without the opportunity to resist or reply.[46]

Through attempts to belong, what is lost in the transition and what does the native surrender? He/she may well be merely mimicking an identity that does not belong to him or her, for the terms of participation are weighted too heavily in favour of the colonized, who turns colonization 'into circus'. You may perform the role, but one is seldom if ever allowed to inhabit the role. The disjunction is too overwhelming and not possible to override. Discrimination might be one thing, but the imperial force wields power often with a ruthlessness that is unrefined, crude, coarse, indifferent and indiscriminate. The denial of this fact is something that the play confronts again and again.

Bracken claims not to be anti-Semitic, but does not want Britain invaded by the 'riff-raff of Russia, the refuse of the dens of the East' (p.34). There is little difference between this and the purity of race that Hitler and his cohorts were after. For Joyce, it is the 'Bolshevik Jew of Russia and Capitalist Jew of Wall Street' (p.48) who is 'our evil otherness, the fault in our nature which we must root out' (p.47). Mosley wanted all Jews to be transported to Madagascar. Both imperialism and fascism are in very close alignment in how they demonize otherness.

Towards the end of act 1 the actor must change from playing Bracken to Joyce; it is the presence of the radio that seems to initiate the transformation. The stage direction interestingly indicates that 'the voice of Joyce [is] calling to Bracken across the airwaves', and although

Bracken 'switches off the wireless; the voice continues. He rushes off but the voice follows him' (p.44). This sense of being pursued by a disembodied voice is striking and only the presence of the radio can achieve it. From here we move into Joyce's broadcast and now it is specifically directed towards Bracken again. Joyce is in stern accusatory flow, and his prominence switches from a radio voice to a presence on the video screen, in order to suggest a type of omnipresence.

Two cast members flip over the initial cardboard figures and Bracken disrobes, flipping over, so to speak, to reveal a fascist black shirt and tie. He loses his wig and reveals a cropped hair. Declan Kiberd, in his analysis of Algernon and his fantasy friend Bunbury in Oscar Wilde's *The Importance of Being Earnest*, points out the type of 'off-loading' involved in the notion of the fantasy friend, who also may be an enemy in that he/she is guardian of the repressed. Another male character, Jack, in the Wilde play invents his fictive brother called Ernest. Algernon and Jack must kill off Bunbury and Ernest respectively, for according to Kiberd:

> Many characters in literature have sought to murder their double in order to do away with guilt (as England had tried to annihilate Irish culture), but have found that it is not so easily repressed, since it may also contain man's utopian self (those redemptive qualities found by [Matthew] Arnold in Ireland). Bunbury is Algy's double, embodying in a single fiction all that is most creative and most corrupt in his creator.[47]

Kiberd goes on to suggest that 'No sooner is the double denied than it becomes man's fate.'[48] Joyce now regards Bracken as being at 'one' with himself (p.43). While Joyce does not become Bracken's fate in the literal sense, he does turn into him in a manner of speaking.

Act 2 opens with a compendium of radio broadcasts that alerts the audience to the state of the British nation as the war progresses. The spectator experiences the physical presence of Joyce, with Bracken disembodied on the radio, and towards the play's end, on the video screen. Bracken is trying to unravel the propaganda of Joyce's broadcasts that pretend to come from inside Britain. Apart from great boasts and the announcement of impending attacks, Joyce is altogether more subtle when he suggests little things, such as local clocks are not working entirely accurately. Additionally, by pinpointing some of the British public's private transgressions, he treats these as acts of civic disobedience. Propaganda, as Joyce recognizes, must confirm at some level 'people's desires' or anxieties (p.54).

The play then switches to Berlin; Joyce broadcasts during an air-raid, where he is but one of many transmitting from a 'factory of voices' (p.52). During the city bombardment Joyce is in full flow and is violent, aggressive, even apocalyptic, reflecting on his childhood and his father and on how he, himself, betrayed the Irish Nationalist cause. People were murdered, at least this is the implication, for after he had provided information to the British forces he witnessed blood being washed out the back of a lorry (p.57).

ANOTHER REICH

Act 2 also gives us the world of Joyce and his partner, Margaret, who has an affair with the German native, Erich. Erich also happens to be learning English. Margaret and Erich play 'out some impossible but perfectly delightful romance' (p.63), or at least this is how she herself sees it. However, Margaret and Joyce's affiliation has an even darker underbelly than the Bracken/Popsie one. The affair results in a divorce and the remarriage of Joyce and Margaret. The end of the war is announced by Bracken on the video screen and with the collapse of the Third Reich, the Joyces flee with false papers, passports and identities. Again the notion of a fabricated, bogus self is to the fore. Joyce is captured, or as Joyce puts it, he is 'shot by a Jew pretending to be a Briton' (p.72). The irony is obvious. Joyce's detention comes about only after bouts of what Margaret says he calls his 'Irish roulette' (p.70). Bracken tempted fate by speaking to British soldiers, seeing if they would identify him.

The physical move to a prison location is achieved by Joyce removing his trench-coat and replacing it with a 1940s 'prison jacket' (p.72). With Joyce in prison, Bracken is again on the video screen summarizing and making the legal case for the prosecution. Joyce was tried for treason. The play points out that behind the treason reflex, more often than not, lies an 'inappropriate reverence' for the country one betrays (p.73). For Hiroko Mikami, 'Joyce has chosen ... what he sees as the inner essence of Englishness: its racial purity, something akin to the mythical Aryan ideal ... The irony is, of course, that Joyce became obsessed with the purity of a race to which he did not actually belong.'[49]

In terms of staging, the final moments are astonishing. Initially, Joyce is on stage alone, then Bracken materializes on the video screen and it appears 'as if he were behind bars or a grille of iron' (p.78). Bracken is incarcerated symbolically, whereas Joyce is about to face execution. The next stage direction is vital. Although we have both characters visible on stage, all the lines 'may be spoken by the actor on stage, with closed eyes' (p.78). So you have the actor on stage now voicing two different opinions in two different voices, while the face of Bracken appears on the screen without speaking. The exchange becomes an imaginary meeting between the two characters, Joyce and Bracken. Bracken's reason for being there is because he is searching for his 'brother', his double, his symbolic other, whom, like his father, has the face of a 'condemned' person (p.78).

The silent video presence complicates an audience's response to this meeting. Previously, the video screen had been used as a way of integrating debate between them and as a way of establishing conflicting perspectives, now it becomes like something from a Beckett play, with the actor on stage playing two roles and the haunting presence of the face on the screen. Towards the final moments of the play 'lights go down on the faces of Bracken and Joyce' and the final speech is left to the Lady Journalist who recollects the trial and the presence of the young fascists in the gallery driven by exclusion, poverty, desire and a need for change. In those young men both Bracken and Joyce are resurrected. The fundamental irony in the play is that the victory in war will deteriorate ultimately the reach and resolve of the British Empire.

At the height of his powers up to half of the population of Britain used to listen to Joyce's broadcasts, and as for Bracken, his substantial role as Minister for Information was central to the wartime propaganda, as a way of controlling and motivating citizens. There is the claim within the play itself that the British achieve 'more captives with our dictionaries than with our regiments' (p.21). Erich learns English and does it badly (ironically regarding W.B. Yeats as English). The visibility of Erich's Anglo-philia is apparent, while Joyce's is less obvious.

Kilroy in 1986 sets serious questions for national and international audiences. Some of the play's weaknesses become apparent, as many of them grow out of the need to be strenuously political, almost pamphlet-like. And while the play is accomplished theatrically, it is over-reliant on the process and distancing of theatre rather than on the encounter and physicality of engagement. One could also claim that the metatheatrical through destabilizing possibilities can formulate and formulize some future through gesture, simulation, impersonation, through the thoroughness and dexterity of performance. Imitation is a form of self-defence, but also is a form of preservation, and it is this factor which is not teased out enough by Kilroy.

Colonial strategy is to confuse one's status, to have visible hierarchies and invisible ones, but there is no passport to the comfort of sanctuary of that inner reality that is Britishness. Mimicking the imperialist power will not get you there, even if you gain access to government departments. At the Tory rally the rehearsed refrain 'Bracken for Britain' is delivered (p.33), not that Bracken is British: one can be for 'it' but still never of 'it'.

As Kilroy states in his introduction to the Gallery edition of the play in 1994: 'What interested me was not so much nationalism as source of self-improvement ... but nationalism as a dark burden, a source of trauma and debilitation. It was inevitable then, I suppose, that I should end up writing about a fascist.'[50] Eight years on from the play's first performance, Kilroy is aligning nationalism and fascism, but in previous statements he was suggesting that the absence of, or a seriously restricted, national identity led to a type of fascism.

The flipping of the iconic leaders suggests not only interchangeablity but also how close both sides were to each other. The possible alliance between Mosley's fascists and Churchill's Conservatives to oppose Ramsay McDonald's Labour party is intriguing. The notional common enemy, politically and socially and economically, was those deemed 'other'. On the one hand, the twisted logic of fascist ideology was just an extension of British imperialist practices toward natives and those outside the frame, and fascism's belief in supposed purity was just a more savage form of nationalism. The victim of imperialism internalizes negativity. For some, they believe that the oppressor can be overcome by mimicking it, even inhabiting it. But the hierarchy and oppression implicit in such manoeuvrings must be recognized. The play posits the unnaturalness of fascism, yet suggests how an imperial experience might naturalize it, if a nation offers only negative impressions of the self. If postmodernism stretches for the abolition of self, then postcolonialism rejects the notion of a diabolic and atrophied self and pushes for something more solid and the shedding of oppressive internalizations. Although both Joyce and Bracken are performers, both share an unconscious mutiny against a concept of Irishness, yet there is a real lack of ironic self-awareness by either character, despite their own self-consciously structured metatheatricalities.

Anthony Roche wonders whether 'there is a stable enduring identity behind all the protean impersonations'.[51] They, Bracken and Joyce, operate in the abject shadow of each other. Double-crossing suggests the endurance of cheating, dishonesty and also liminality, where the only stable ingredient is performance, which is seldom if ever neutral.

Joyce accuses Bracken in one of his broadcasts, of being a clown and a performer:

> They like to see you perform, don't you know that? It satisfies their taste in comedy as a scale, a measurement, politics as entertainment, entertainment as politics. In its decadence the imperial always transposes conquest into circus. The more clownish Irish have always been willing to step into that ring. And you're the perfect clown because you believe that life is a matter of taste. (p.45)

TRANSLATIONS: 'SWEET SMELL'

Brian Friel's *Translations* has been regarded by many as a classic ever since its first production. The play tells the story of how a group of British Royal Engineers arrive in Baile Beag (Ballybeg) in 1833 to make an Ordnance Survey map, where they will not only map the territory but also transcribe or 'transliterate the local Gaelic place names and Anglicize them', as Declan Kiberd suggests.[52] The soldiers are ably assisted by Owen, the son of the local hedge school teacher, Hugh. Owen's brother, Manus, works with his father. Manus is in love with Maire, but she falls for Yolland, an English soldier, who ends up missing and is presumed dead by the end of the play.

The map-making process promises more accurate land valuation and more equitable taxes. Kiberd claims that 'to write all new names into a book represents the colonizer's benign assumption that to name a thing is to assert one's power over it and that the written tradition of the occupier will henceforth enjoy the primacy over the oral memory of the natives'.[53] Interlinked with the issues of map-making is the displacement of the hedge school system of education, which while haphazard, improvisatory and lest we forget, illegal until the 1829 Catholic Emancipation Act, was also substantial in its contribution to the education of the indigenous population. The national school system came into being in 1832 and the language of instruction was to be English. Finally, as the play is set in 1830s, there is a constant fear of blight and the failure of the potato crop. Thus Irish Famine is anticipated as an even greater disaster to come.

The play has been challenged by some academics as to the historical accuracy of Friel's drama, and he is often accused of bad politics in how he represents the situation and what he excludes. For instance, the renaming of place names was carried out with a greater degree of subtlety than Friel seems to allow for. At that time, experts in their fields were consulted for the task, and secondly, the force that carried out the map-making process was unarmed, unlike the army in Friel's work. Some critics take the play to task for melding Irish and classical cultures too simplistically and some also see the play as unsophisticated in its attempts to mark the cultural transition or substantial capitulation of the Irish language communities, captured in the shift from owning, living, working, celebrating, travelling, communicating, thinking, recording, remembering and imagining in Gaelic to English.

On first consideration, *Translations* does not fall so easily within the remit of this chapter, but although a metatheatrical consciousness is not as dominant as it is in the other plays discussed here in this chapter, this Friel play does rely on metatheatricality in many ways. The play is written as if the indigenous Irish characters are speaking Gaelic and the soldier/occupiers communicate in English; whereas in performance, the Irish characters all speak in Hiberno-English. So both groups are speaking different versions of the same root language, they cannot communicate directly to each other without the assistance of a translator. From the point of view of the spectator, he or she experiences the play with the knowledge of this linguistic divide, but has access to the notional Gaelic through Hiberno-English. And for most audiences, if the play was performed, even in Ireland, with a mixture of Gaelic and English, they would not be able to follow, without the support of sur-titles. When the play is translated into other languages, all kinds of interesting and complex issues are raised, especially in Europe, with its tradition of shifting borders and communities finding themselves within new national boundaries, which has obvious implications for citizenship and directly or indirectly for language. Christopher Murray notes that when an *Taidhbhearc*, 'Ireland's national Gaelic theatre in Galway, wanted to stage the play half in Gaelic and half in English Friel refused permission, saying it had to be entirely in one language. It is only in that way that the irony of lack of unity of culture is emphasized.'[54]

So the play's metatheatrical convention is thus a language within a language (*Lughnasa*'s convention is a memory within a memory, *Double Cross*'s character within a character and *The Sons of Ulster*'s a history within a history.) The language gap, then, is overridden by the dramatic device and it gives rise to all kinds of humour and anomalies, particularly when Owen translates the speeches of Captain Lancey and especially during the love scene between Lieutenant Yolland and Maire.

The nature of translation and the role of the interpreter are blatantly visible. Early in the play Captain Lancey's lengthy explanations of the process of map-making and the benefits of the procedure are abbreviated initially by Owen, but Owen does stress the benefits and financial savings the community will experience because of the Ordnance Survey. Towards the end of the play, Owen has to translate the more malign threats of Lancey, that if Yolland, the missing soldier is not found within twenty-four hours, Lancey will kill all the local livestock, and another twenty-four hours later he will begin evicting and levelling certain holdings. The articulations of Lancey and his mode of communicating have shifted considerably.

The love scene is wonderfully playful, when the two lovers, Maire and Yolland cannot communicate with each other through language or a shared vocabulary, but connect intimately on the level of sounds, fragments, emotions and physicality. There is enough in the text for their desire for each other to shine through in well-performed productions. Prompted by Edward Said, Kiberd notes that no orientalist text is without a love interest, for 'a ritual infatuation' on the part of some 'wayward son' with some 'mysterious woman of the native tribe ... The woman, like the colony, is a mystery to be penetrated'.[55]

The antic intelligence that is often the hallmark of Friel's work is visible in multiple ways in this work, especially in Jimmy Jack, the child prodigy's attitude to classical culture and his love for the goddess Athene, and the trickster and subversive nature of Doalty. The self-conscious performativity of Hugh is also significant throughout, as is the willingness of the locals to appreciate attempts to mimic his behaviour. Friel in his writing at the time has said of this play that 'the play has to do with language and only language'.[56] It is tantamount to saying that while the British soldiers claim their activities are about map-making, the ominous reality of their existence is about violation, threat and punishment if they do not get their way. Map-making may bring economic rewards in the form of reduced taxes, but it is a colonial activity. To separate the activity of map-making from politics cannot be done; likewise, language cannot be divorced from its political and social realities. Indeed, Friel confirms the former and the play itself, not his diary records, confirm the latter.

Naming is a ritualistic act, it is also paramount to identity, and it is of course a political act, one of authority, power and control. Of the Irish, the Donnelly twins are named in very specific terms, nobody spells out their political and violent activities, but everyone hints with definite assurance. Language is about expression and ownership, and about values and about how one perceives oneself in language. Without access to the intricacies of a mother-tongue, most people would struggle with expression, and one could not explain with a depth or a nuance, or unless one was very proficient in another language. (Sarah struggles to name herself in her own tongue, at the start and by the end of the play, Lancey's intimidatory approach leaves her tongue tied again.)

ROLAND/YOLLAND

The map-making scene is key to an understanding of the play. Owen displays the industry of the efficient colonizer, is practical and keen to keep things on track, seeing the inevitability of the task and not noting the historical and cultural implications. Change is inevitable for Owen. Yolland is willing to stall the process in favour of accuracy, wishing to unearth the local truths, secrets, the traces of memory and meaning in everything. Nostalgia is his lot. Yolland wants to retain 'Bun na hAbhann' and feels 'Burnfoot' is both imprecise and erroneous.

Owen is a go-between and go-for and he misreads his role almost throughout. His is another Bracken figure. Owen likes his new-found role and his unwillingness to put the soldiers straight as to his proper name just confirms it. It is not so much their inability to pronounce his name, as is their careless inability to get his name right in the first place that makes the naming of him as Roland so pointed. Initially, Owen sees himself as progressive, modern, as the play evolves he is reinscribed as 'other', the native guide/interpreter who cannot be trusted. He cannot be two things; he cannot be within two tribes or within two languages by the play's end, as he is forever between both. Close to the end of the play Manus is offered employment as a hedge schoolteacher off the main island, at a location furthest from the reach of English law, and he agrees to take the work as he is a suspect in the disappearance of Yolland. Hugh is willing to settle for compromise and to apply for the new teaching job in his locality, only to find that he is out of favour. He is another who has misjudged the landscape of raw fact.

The places translated by Owen into English now become the locations that Captain Lancey promises to destroy. Destruction supersedes naming in the order of things. In this instance, naming does not fundamentally structure meaning; violence does. Naming, thus, is an eviction, not of sorts, but an eviction full stop. Hugh is pragmatic. He regards the Irish language as a syntax 'opulent with tomorrows' and a language 'full of mythologies of fantasy and hope and self-deception'. And in the here and now, in the present, 'we must learn those new names ... we must learn to make them our own. We must make them our new home' (p.444). Maire, by the play's end, realizes that she needs English if she is to emigrate and survive in America. Hugh promises to teach her. The play ends on a moment of hesitation. Hugh is not capable of citing his extract from *The Aeneid*. The failure to remember is a collapse of sorts, but perhaps it is part of the letting go of a cultural fantasy of connection. The diligence of the material world will eat into the traditional society, the rupture between place and name will wreak its own havoc, and the impending doom that the famine will bring about will force a different type of monstrous carnage.

OBSERVE THE SONS OF ULSTER MARCHING TOWARDS THE SOMME: RHYMING COUPLETS

The Sons of Ulster opens with the Elder Pyper, the only survivor of eight soldiers, reflecting back on the carnage that was the Battle of the Somme. Pyper is haunted by those who have died, for they refuse to leave him in peace because he misrepresents their actions and betrays their values. The tension between tribal acts of remembrance and false testimony is vital. Part 2 is set in an army barracks when the recruits first get to know each other, and part 4 is set just before the soldiers go into battle. Part 3 marks the temporary home-comings of the soldiers in pairs, and four locations are discernable on stage with mini-scenes, cinema-like, with cross-cutting and fading from one to the other, until eventually all four spaces are visible and simultaneously active and a cacophony of distinct voices and sensations coalesce. They are eight Ulster soldiers fighting against the German army (who supposedly learn Gaelic out of malicious intent) fighting for their tribe and fighting for the union between Ulster and Britain. The Somme battle led to countless loss of lives, with many in Ulster left grieving lost ones.

As war plays go, there is considerable tension on stage throughout. The writing is inspired as much by the poetry of the war poets as it is by Bertolt Brecht's *Mother Courage* (1939) or, in terms of form, by Tennessee Williams's *The Glass Menagerie* (1945). The play is equally about paramilitaries in the 1980s, both loyalist and republican, who perversely and delusionally re-enact the sacrificial imperatives of the Somme and of the Easter Rising. More crucial still is the fact that the victory of King William over King James at the Boyne is regarded as the mythic moment that consolidated a loyalist sense of destiny. That McGuinness has his soldiers re-enact the Battle of the Boyne, filtered through the loyalist Scarva tradition (his mock-battle of Scarva) and permits a novel ending to such a battle, where the traditional outcome is reversed, says as much about the imperiousness of history as it does about the imperatives of his dramaturgy to destabilize and to unsettle expectations.

The history play offers that possibility and more besides. Lionel Pilkington suggests that 'written in the wake of a hostile unionist reaction to the New Ireland Forum, McGuinness's play was an attempt to engage positively with the loyalist ideology of Ulster Protestantism ... And may be read as a counterweight to Friel's earlier *Translations*, from which Protestant/Unionist culture is entirely absent'.[57] In addition, as Anthony Roche argues, McGuinness not only managed to confront his own values, but 'to raise unsettling questions about the extent to which Catholic Nationalism has exclusively appropriated the concept of "Irishness" in this century'.[58]

As the play progresses, the soldiers begin to understand the devastation of war, the true substance of their actions and the overwhelming fact that theirs is a blood sacrifice that is driven not by loyalty but by a 'blood lust' (p.100). To see that in one's self and to acknowledge that about one's activities is a huge step for the soldiers to take. All of the soldiers realize that the perspective offered by the apparently half-crazed Pyper at their first meeting together was in fact more or less correct. Regardless, they find solace in the bonds of a smaller community, without cutting their bonds to the larger tribal unit. Their position is more critically astute. What they do discover is that their tribal bond is more problematic and more complicated than they initially perceived to be the case. They had taken ideas and attitudes on board uncritically and had handed away any responsibility for evaluation of situations and circumstances. Such may be the prerogative of younger men and such may be the reality of the uninitiated.

In *The Sons of Ulster* there are numerous incidents of metatheatricality. There are two Pypers, elder and younger, and they bear little relation to one another. Pyper is artist-as-performer in the way that Dido is in *Carthaginians* (1988). The central part of the play is the 'true' memory of the event, which the Elder Pyper, upon his return from the war, tries to distort. Therefore in this way the drama is a history within a history as much as it is a play within a play, given that the drama takes place effectively within Elder Pyper's mind. Additionally, the character Pyper is self-consciously theatrical throughout the play. Pyper is the teller of stories that are unconvincing, surreal and intent on disturbing the minds of the other soldiers. During part 2 he pretends to be an army officer, takes on Craig's name, assaults Anderson through the use of guile and pretence and finally histrionically cuts his hand with a knife to call attention to the symbolism of the red hand of Ulster. Pyper's outsider status is added to by the fact he is from a different class to the others and because of his homosexuality.

The majority of the soldiers initially enact the tribal role expected of them, one that is governed by myth and by definite tribal and ideological expectations. The tribal mask is taken as a given by the soldiers and it is superimposed in a way that does not encourage personal self-knowledge. Beneath such a burden of the collective little individuality is tolerated.

The tribal mask is one that protects, disguises and distorts and it bluntly relegates scepticism, provisionality and critical thinking. Pyper is the initial opponent of this tribal disposition, but by the play's end he wears it in a way that is too self-conscious. As his colleagues remind him, he is trying too hard to belong. His is a performance that is forced, unnatural and uncomfortable for the others to witness. It is not grounded in that the consciousness is new and somewhat unfamiliar and unrooted, given Pyper's earlier utter rejection of tribal belonging and connection.

During Pyper's opening monologue in *The Sons of Ulster* there is another perverted, attempted performance by Pyper, who endeavours to address a multiple audience, that of his dead colleagues, God, his tribe, himself and a theatre audience. Out of his confusion and deceptions something else seeps through. The obligation is that the memory must be replayed in all its complication. No collective agreement must be reached by either historian or tribal representative as to the reason why the soldiers died. Sense cannot be made of their deaths, political purpose must not be solely sought in their actions and simplistic reductions and assumptions are deemed implausible. Motivation cannot be assigned to them adequately. Pyper's ghosts oblige him to remember and the memory is re-enacted for the benefit of Pyper and of the spectator.

If re-enactment of memory is central, then the more serious and disturbing re-enactment is that of unquestioned tribal sacrifice, a deep and profound obligation and loyalty that can only be explained not by love or affiliation, but by hate. The soldiers' experience of recruitment and war leads to an increased tolerance amongst themselves and of themselves, but there is little shift in their prejudice towards Irish nationalism.

DOING THE BOYNE

Regardless of their fear and regardless of the urgency of death awaiting them, the soldiers are never allowed to become heroic role models by the playwright, as their courage is well noted, even seen as laudable. They go to their deaths with some advancement in their knowledge, but no essential truth emerges, life is not validated, and no forgiveness is sought. Fear does not prompt in them integrity or an abundant generosity, but there is a slight shift in perspective. Certainly, the soldiers die almost in vain, certainly they willingly sacrifice themselves for a cause, but little that is heroic is sourced in their actions and nothing inspiring is to be deduced from their exploits. Having experienced the very limited and depleted resourcefulness of the soldiers before the questions of myth, history, or/and tribe, the spectator is urged to ask hard questions about his or her own attitudes.

The soldiers are, in themselves, on the one hand strong, brave and kind, and on the other they are immature, blind and brutal men. McGuinness never allows sentiment to enter into the equation; thereby no easy responses to the play are possible. The soldiers establish a community of sorts, a community whose bond is about friendship, connection and support but is also about violence, sadism, threat and corruption.

Their bond is neither heroic nor simplistic. This is best exemplified in their last great attempt to consolidate the tribal bond through the re-enactment of the Battle of the Boyne, or more correctly the Battle of Scarva, which is a traditional loyalist re-enactment of the Boyne, done on a scale and in a way that is less solemn and less reverential than other celebrations of the Boyne victory, William of Orange's defeat of James II. Roles are doled out, an accompanying commentary initiated and the mock battle of Scarva begins.

During the mock battle Anderson's commentary on the action is biblically inspired, playful and ironic, and his self-confidence is initially prompted by historical inevitability. What stands out is that Anderson's usage of a rhetorical language is no longer appropriate to the situation or to a contemporary consciousness. All effort is placed on continuity and not on change. Anderson warns before the horseplay begins: 'you know the result, keep to the result' (p.82). The idea of history as perpetual replay is challenged. When the wrong result is reached, Millen reads it as 'Not the best of signs' and no more than that (p.84). Nothing can prepare them for the 'real thing' (p.84). Through the fall of William, history is disturbed, discontinuities are accessed and old complacencies are rattled.

The soldiers re-enact the Boyne fight in order to calm them prior to battle and to position their sacrifice within a religious and historical context. With the fall of the half-Catholic Crawford, playing William, the alternative result destabilizes all certainties. If they cannot get it right during a bit of conscious and premeditated play, how can they hope to in the battle before them? History over-heats and is over-rehearsed. There is no calm and no luxury of success hanging over them. Nobody watches over them.

Instead of consolation and assurance, they are left with a profound uncertainty. Nothing could really comfort them, knowing that they face death, but what is remarkable is how little resistance they display to the wrong result, when James emerges victorious. Only Anderson castigates Pyper for the fall. Pyper is not the conscious perpetuator of the fall. Earlier Pyper had offered a critique of war, without a critical distance. It is only when the soldiers re-enact the Battle of the Boyne that things really begin to fall disturbingly into place. It is through the endeavour of play that they become more conscious and that they can consolidate a bond of more considerable depth. But this is a bond that is futile in the face of death.

The victory of the Protestant William of Orange at the Battle of the Boyne over the Catholic King James was the precedent and the religious justification for almost all that followed in an Ulster loyalist consciousness. This is a myth of destiny and the mock battle suggests that some provisionality, or some uncertainty, must also be included in the way we view, receive, propagate and perpetuate history.

The spectator must above all else recognize that the Battle of the Somme cost close to a million lives if British, French or German troops are counted. Indeed the pained playfulness of their diversionary game exacerbates this traumatic awareness. Pyper will not be left alone until he can accept one truth and renegotiate with the facts of the past. The spectator, like Pyper, must be capable of differentiating and embracing the distinction between perception and fact and distinguish between the need to give coherence and shape to a painful experience or point of view, which happens to be a loyalist one, and the downright lies of those who put the heroic actions of many to ill use, especially those who uncritically attempt to perpetuate a cycle of sacrifice, based on a battle long fought and set in a world and system of values that has no longer any basis in actuality. Continuity must not be the stuff of myth and history; instead discontinuity, provisionality and rupture are the necessary prerequisites.

As such, play engenders alertness to performance variables that fundamentally destabilize or postpone responses. If the pleasure of play is in its possibilities, then the terror of play must be the threat of becoming locked into a role, imprisoned in a stereotype or turned into stone, as Pyper perceives himself to be in *The Sons of Ulster*. The malleability of play is turned rigid by grand, dysfunctional imperatives and master narratives, over which the individual cannot exercise any control. Play gives rise to a liminal consciousness that disturbs as much as it distorts, that provokes as much as it perverts, that restates dissent as much as it resists secure points of view. The notion of play confronts rigidity, unsettles lazy thinking and mobilizes possibility, principally through the way in which role-playing provides distance, opportunism and an access to an alternative temporary reality, that can be safe and simultaneously energizing.

If play corrupts in some way, then play within the carnivalesque frame doubly corrupts by offsetting excess against absence, desire against repression and abstinence. Moreover, the persistence of play generates dialogical tensions between opposites, destabilizes gender, class, tribal, historical or economic hierarchies and ultimately unsettles fixed meanings. This is achieved by deploying temporary inversions and the subversions of hierarchical authority. This gesture is fundamentally political. A closing stage direction suggests that both Pypers, elder and younger, move towards each other –'Pyper reaches towards himself' (p.197). However, McGuinness claims that:

> When the two Pypers meet at the end of the play, I do not think it is a closure. I think the play is one long cycle. Pyper is almost doomed to repeat it, telling the story, seeing the story ... That is really what the end of the play is about, that the dance will start again. The play will repeat itself again. It will have to be performed again, again and again.[59]

So, McGuinness opposes endings where the two Pypers embrace, which happened in a number of productions. He suggests: 'you cannot really call it a closure in the play because it has not stopped. The sense of betrayal, the sense of loss has not stopped'.[60] Through play anxieties are worked through, blockages negotiated with and adjustments and change prioritized. Memory, history and myth prove to be the playground and the battleground, the hindrance and the hope.

The dramas in this chapter are dramas about loss and the performance of loss.[61] Play is the dialectical force that energizes the dramas in this chapter by the substantiation of firm, conflicting oppositions and by the establishment of divergent points of view; all of these plays are alert to the overlap between memory, history, fantasy, and narrative and use play for a 'seditious purpose'.[62] Declan Kiberd notes that colonial rule operates through patterned cycles of 'coercion and conciliation'.[63] He attaches to this the notion of the imperial power using the host country as a form of laboratory. Conspiracy, plotting and stage-managed violence must be added as other ingredients, from the sides of imperialism and the host country. This explains in part the experimental conspiracy of play that haunts an Irish consciousness. Gerry Smyth presses for the idea of a third space, prompted by the work of Homi Bhabha. Bhabha sees within the scenario the importance of 'displacement', 'performativity' and the 'mocking spirit of mask and image'.[64] This confirms the significance of the trickster within the Irish tradition. The presence of ghosts, resurrections and divided subjectivities are all hallmarks of a theatre practice that does not conform easily to a single theatrical reality. Smyth emphasizes a 'politics of displacement' in a way that 'their givenness, authenticity and originality' are always held to question.[65]

Gilbert and Tompkins argue that the shape-shifting 'trickster is an ideal character through which to present the theatricalized body of the post-colonial subject'.[66] In Irish theatre the trickster takes many forms, from the traveller figures in Keane's *Sive* (1959) to the character Cactus in Gina Moxley's *Danti-Dan* (1995)[67] and from the scarecrow figure in Marina Carr's *Woman and Scarecrow* (2005), to Bracken, Joyce, Pyper, Dido and the Satyr-like figure, The Equivocator, in McGuinness's *Speaking like Magpies* (2005). Further, 'the trickster's androgyny breaks down binary figurations of gender and thus *defers*, rather than *defers to*, gender-based authority systems'.[68] However, Anna McMullan in her analysis of *Double Cross* points out in this play women 'by revealing or confronting duplicity, have the moral advantage', but 'the transformative potential of the mask eludes them. They are constant fall guys to the player princes.'[69] In *Double Cross* this is an accurate assessment. Popsie's sexual performance is more for Bracken and less for herself.

The 'transformative potential of the mask' is potentially available to Pyper and many women characters in McGuinness's other work. The renowned dance sequence in *Lughnasa* seems to give the women the 'transformative potential' temporarily. In *Translations* change offers initial potential, only for the reality of power to display itself. By the end the drunken Hugh and Jimmy Jack attempt to restore normality through a recitation/performance, which fails.

The plays in this chapter constantly rely on, to use Homi Bhabha's phrase, 'the menace of mimicry' to challenge power and authority.[70] Impersonation undermines and questions the status of power structures, suggesting either a challenge to these modes of authority or indicating that power is transitory, reversible and can be challenged. The notion of fixed and immutable structures is destabilized by the concept of contestational play. So we can link play and performance to notions of confronting oppression, destabilizing politics and to the challenging of authority, with an alertness to instability, incompleteness and unrepresentableness.

NOTES

1. Vincent Woods with *At the Black Pig's Dyke* (1993) represents another superb attempt to bring together the linguistic richness and a vicious, hostile dramatic situation, energized by the distance and rawness of history and by the dynamics of play.
2. Thomas Kilroy, *Double Cross* (London: Faber, 1986), p.45. (Hereafter, all further references to the text will be given in parentheses within the text.)
3. Equally, Michael West's exceptional *Dublin by Lamplight* (2004) could be part of this chapter.
4. Richard Schechner, *Performance Studies: An Introduction* (London and New York: Routledge, second edition, 2002), p.89.
5. Richard Pine, *The Diviner: The Art of Brian Friel* (Dublin: University College Dublin Press, 1998), p.269.
6. Ibid.
7. Schechner, *Performance Studies*, p.28.
8. Helen Gilbert and Joanne Tompkins, *Post-colonial Drama: Theory, Practice, Politics* (London: Routledge, 1996), p.34.
9. Marina Jenkyns, *The Play's The Thing: Exploring Text in Drama and Therapy* (London and New York: Routledge, 1996), p.10.
10. Quoted by Margaret Llewellyn Jones, *Contemporary Irish Drama and Cultural Identity* (Bristol: Intellect, 2002), p.115.
11. Augosto Boal, *The Rainbow of Desire* (London: Routledge, 1995), p.38.
12. See Carmen Szabó's excellent analysis of the Crane Bag/Field Day projects and in particular the notion of a fifth province in *'Clearing the Ground': The Field Day Theatre Company and the Construction of Irish Identities* (Newcastle: Cambridge Scholars Publishing, 2007), pp.1–7.
13. Certainly, plays like John B. Keane's *Sive* (1959) and *Big Maggie* (1969), and Hugh Leonard's *Da* (1973) evaluate how deprivation shapes consciousness. Christina Reid in *Joyriders* (1986) goes a step further by emphasizing the additional political apathy that sponsors her dramatic reality. More recently Dermot Bolger's attempts to map socio/economic disadvantage in a modern setting have been striking and unsettling in *The Lament for Arthur Cleary* (1989) and in *One Last White Horse* (1991).
14. Brian Friel, *Dancing at Lughnasa* in *Plays Two* (London: Faber & Faber, 1999), p.24. (Hereafter, all further references to the text will be given in parentheses within the text.)
15. Friel's story-tellers tend to be voyeurs, sometimes partaking in the action, but usually they are only at the fringes; seldom are they totally immersed in the situation.
16. The male characters in *Lughnasa*, according to Anthony Roche, are 'moved to the margins and rendered deliberately unreal'. See *Contemporary Irish Drama: From Beckett to McGuinness* (Dublin: Gill & Macmillan, 1994), p.285.
17. For Christopher Murray, 'it is as if masque, in the Jacobean sense, were overlaid by anti-masque, and a dissonance expressed'. See '"Recording Tremors": Friel's *Dancing at Lughnasa* and the Uses of Tradition' in *Brian Friel: A Casebook*, ed. W. Kerwin (New York and London: Garland, 1997), p.31.
18. Brian Friel, 'Self-Portrait', *Aquarius*, 5, 1972, p.18.
19. Adam Phillips, *On Flirtation* (London: Faber & Faber, 1994), p.24.
20. Fintan O'Toole, 'Marking Time: From *Making History* to *Dancing at Lughnasa*' in *The Achievement of Brian Friel*, ed. A. Peacock (Gerrards Cross: Colin Smythe, 1993), p.203.
21. Claudia, W. Harris, 'The Engendered Space: Performing Friel's Women from Cass McGuire to Molly Sweeney' in Kerwin (ed.), *Brian Friel: A Casebook*, p.48.
22. Eamonn Jordan, 'Introduction' in *Theatre Stuff: Critical Essays on Contemporary Irish Theatre* (Dublin: Carysfort Press, 2000), p.xlv.
23. Ibid., p.xliv.
24. Richard Allen Cave, 'Questing for Ritual and Ceremony in a Godforsaken World: *Dancing at Lughnasa* and *Wonderful Tennessee*', *Hungarian Journal of English and American Studies*, 5-1, 1999, pp.109–27.

25. Pine, *The Diviner*, p.277.
26. Frank McGuinness, *Observe the Sons of Ulster Marching Towards the Somme* in *Plays 1* (London: Faber & Faber, 1996), p.100. (All further references will be given in parentheses within the text.)
27. Seamus Heaney, 'For Liberation: Brian Friel and the Use of Memory' in Peacock (ed.), *Achievement of Brian Friel*, p.232.
28. Gerald Fitzgibbon's work brings together discussions on Dionysus, the Maenads and Lughnasa rituals, based on Máire MacNeill's book, *The Festival of Lughnasa*, and James Frazer's accounts from *The Golden Bough* of Midsummer fires. See 'Interpreting Between Privacies: Brian Friel and the Boundaries of Language', *Hungarian Journal of English and American Studies*, 5–1, 1999, pp.71–84.
29. Anna McMullan, 'Gender, Authority and the Body in *Dancing at Lughnasa*', *Irish University Review*, 29–1, Spring 1999, p.95.
30. Harris, 'Engendered Space', pp. 44–45.
31. Ibid., p.45.
32. Brian Friel, *Philadelphia, Here I Come!* in *Selected Plays* (London: Faber & Faber, 1984), p.77.
33. Brian Friel, *Translations* in *Plays One* (London: Faber & Faber 1984), p. 445. (Hereafter all further references to the text will be given in parentheses within the text.)
34. Heaney, 'For Libertion', p.235.
35. Ibid., p.236.
36. O'Toole, 'Marking Time', p.204.
37. George Steiner, *Antigones: The Antigone Myth in Western Literature, Art and Thought* (Oxford: Oxford University Press, 1984), p.126.
38. Gilbert and Tompkins, *Post-colonial Drama*, p.250.
39. Adam Phillips, *Darwin's Worms* (London: Faber & Faber, 1999), p.126.
40. Gilbert and Tompkins, *Post-colonial Drama*, p.231.
41. Ibid.
42. Christopher Murray, *Twentieth-century Irish Drama: Mirror up to Nation* (Manchester: Manchester University Press, 1997), p.218.
43. Nicholas Grene, 'Person and Persona', *Irish University Review: A Journal of Irish Studies*, 32–1, Spring/Summer 2002, pp.70–82, p.76.
44. J. Furay and R. O'Hanlon (eds), *Critical Moments: Fintan O'Toole on Modern Irish Theatre* (Dublin: Carysfort Press, 2003), p.52.
45. Mária Kurdi, *Codes and Masks: Aspects of Identity in Contemporary Irish Plays in an Intercultural Context* (Berne: Peter Lang, 2000), p.117.
46. Ania Loomba, *Colonialism/Postcolonialism* (London: Routledge, 1998), p.105.
47. Declan Kiberd, *Inventing Ireland: The Literature of the Modern Nation* (London: Vintage, 1996), p.42.
48. Ibid.
49. Hiroko Mikami, 'Kilroy's Vision of Doubleness', *Irish University Review: A Journal of Irish Studies*, 32–1, Spring/Summer 2002, pp.100–09, p.104.
50. Thomas Kilroy, *Double Cross* (Ashbourne, Co. Meath: Gallery, 1994), p.15.
51. Roche, *Contemporary Irish Drama*, p.207.
52. Kiberd, *Inventing Ireland*, p.620.
53. Ibid.
54. Christopher Murray, 'Palimpsest: Two Languages as One in Translations' in *Brian Friel's Dramatic Artistry: 'The Work has Value'*, ed. D. Morse, C. Bertha and M. Kurdi (Dublin: Carysfort Press, 2006), p.103.
55. Kiberd, *Inventing Ireland*, p.620.
56. Brian Friel, 'Extracts from a Sporadic Diary' in *Ireland and the Arts: A Special Issue of Literary Review*, ed. Tim Pat Coogan (London: Namara, 1985), p.58, cited by Murray in 'Palimpsest', p.95.
57. Lionel Pilkington, *Theatre and the State in Twentieth-century Ireland: Cultivating the People* (London and New York: Routledge, 2001), p.221.
58. Anthony Roche, *Contemporary Irish Drama*, p.266.
59. Mária Kurdi, 'An Interview with Frank McGuinness', *Nua: Studies in Contemporary Irish Writing*, 4–1–2, 2003, pp.113–32, p.116.
60. Ibid.
61. The traditional victory against the odds is taken out of the political arena and reimagined on

the rugby pitch in the case of John Breen's *Alone it Stands* (1999), a drama that marks Munster's famous victory over the New Zealand All-Blacks in 1978, when amateur minnows toppled what was regarded as the greatest team in the world at that time. (Yet the fact that most of the metatheatrical-style plays rely on male characters and male actors is worth noting. The success of the masculine within the limits of the play contrasts with the increasing ineffectualness of the masculine socially.) Six actors play over thirty parts, sometimes across gender. This play is revived regularly to this very day, drawing huge audiences.

62. Gilbert and Tompkins, *Post-colonial Drama*, p.1.
63. Kiberd, *Inventing Ireland*, p.43.
64. Homi Bhabha cited by Gerry Smyth – *Decolonisation and Criticism: The Construction of Irish Literature* (London: Pluto Press, 1998), p.21.
65. Smyth, *Decolonisation and Criticism*, p.22.
66. Gilbert and Tompkins, *Post-colonial Drama*, p.235.
67. See Mária Kurdi '"Teenagers", "Gender Trouble" and Trickster Aesthetics in Gina Moxley's *Danti Dan*', *ABEI Journal* 4, 2002, pp. 67–82.
68. Gilbert and Tompkins, *Post-colonial Drama*, p.235.
69. Anna McMullan, 'Masculinity and Masquerade in Thomas Kilroy's *Double Cross* and *The Secret Fall of Constance Wilde*', *Irish University Review: A Journal of Irish Studies*, 32–1, Spring/Summer 2002, pp.126–36, p.132.
70. Homi Bhabha quoted by Jenny Sharpe in 'Figures of Colonial Resistance' in *Post-colonial Studies Reader*, ed. B. Ashcroft, G. Griffiths and H. Tiffin (London: Routledge, 1995), p.100.

3

The Seduction of Innocence

THE PHANTOM MENACE

While there are many dominant tropes in contemporary Irish theatre, none recurs as frequently perhaps as the concept of innocence. Of course, this prompts one to try to determine what is the meaning of innocence, how is it represented and how is it utilized from a dramaturgical point of view? The notion of innocence must be additionally seen in the context of Irish history in its totality; if the British dominated Ireland partly through the regimentation of binary oppositions, namely civilized–uncivilized, rational–emotional, ordered–disordered, then the Irish responded by fundamentally undermining their power by opposing evil and innocence, the evil empire and the unjustly subjugated native. Innocence thus has a colonial and postcolonial perspective. For example, in McGuinness's *Carthaginians* (1988) those that died on Bloody Sunday garner the label of innocence: 'The innocent dead. There's thirteen dead in Derry.'[1]

The image of a globalized Ireland maintains an affiliation with the naïve, backward, otherworldly or wayward innocence, in addition to the negative stereotypes of drinking and violence. A pastoralization of innocence is often expected. In that way, the chapter has serious links with the chapter on the pastoral and Irish drama. Fintan O'Toole reflects on the years between 1922 and 1958 as the childhood of the Irish state. And part of the myth of Ireland was its golden age, before colonization. Part of the fantasy of conservative ideology was a return to an age of Gaelic civilization, one that was free and innocent – where Ireland would 'return to the childhood innocence of its once and future Arcadia'.[2] To do so the rhetoric of the state prompted the notion of an 'ideal innocence, an innocence which would make Ireland a beacon to the world, the centre of a spiritual empire, which, at the most messianic heights of the rhetoric, might save Christian civilization'.[3] Add to this the extended childhoods of the Irish population, who neither married early nor could afford to leave their homes.

In general terms, innocence is associated with purity, virtuousness and with qualities of childishness and simplicity, and is seen as something without sophistication. In terms of religion, it is a state of being without sin, and its opposites can be the experiences of feeling a sense of guilt, evil and damnation. In a legal sense, the presumption of innocence is fundamental to law, but the burden of proof is only beyond reasonable doubt, therefore, being found innocent or guilty is no absolute proof of accountability. On another level, innocence is associated with other-worldliness, with simplicity, naïvety, with an absence of cunning, deviousness, artifice and of being non-threatening towards others. Again, innocence can be associated with a lack of understanding or blissful ignorance. Also, innocence in adults is associated with harmlessness, with blamelessness and with an absence of responsibility for actions done.

The harm done to the innocent or the violation of innocence are interrogated on a regular basis in Irish theatre. It could be argued that many writers of this generation are drawn towards not so much the politics of innocence, as towards an innocent politics, achieved by romanticizing or sentimentalizing a structure of innocence. On the other hand, it is possible to articulate an alternative perspective and to claim that by working with the concept of innocence the possibility of a radical dramaturgy becomes possible. In this chapter I will reflect on three particular strands to this notion, firstly the destruction of innocence[4] through death, violation, sexual abuse, rape and incest. I will very quickly trace the over-reliance on dead children to generate meaning and then argue that Marina Carr with *On Raftery's Hill* (2000) intriguingly takes all casual sentiment and almost all defiance out of violation. Secondly, I will consider how Frank McGuinness contests the concept of innocence in his under-acknowledged great play *Innocence*, where the tensions between the opposing concepts of innocence and damnation have strong religious, sexual and, more importantly, political overtones. Finally, I will contemplate how Marie Jones disputes the conventions of reconciliation through the utilization of a naïve character in *A Night in November* (1994) in a way that challenges expectations around radical intervention in what are/were the sectarian entrenchments of the Northern Irish Troubles from the 1960s forward, somehow delivering the perverse optimism of innocence. I will also argue that in the face of cynicism there is room for that.

WOULD YOU DIE FOR ME!

So many plays seem to use the specific absence/presence of a dead child to inform both the atmosphere of a play, to shape the dynamics of relationships and as a way of giving heightened expression to extreme and intense emotions of grief, loss and permanence. This is countered by the number of Irish plays that use the imminent arrival of a new child to celebrate possibility and to ratify change. In the following list of plays the energy and sensibility of dead children overshadow the atmosphere; Carr's *Portia Coughlan* (1996), *On Raftery's Hill* and *Ariel* (2002), Sebastian Barry's *Steward of Christendom* (1995), *Our Lady of Sligo* (1997) and *The Pride of Parnell Street* (2007), Frank McGuinness's *Baglady* (1985), Brian Friel's *Faith Healer* (1979) and *Translations* (1980), Hugh Leonard's *Love in the Title* (1999), Conor McPherson's *The Weir* (1997) and Mark O'Rowe's *Howie The Rookie* (1999). The list could go on and on.

O'Rowe ends his plays *Crestfall* (2003) and *Terminus* (2007) with the triumphant survival or birth of a child, and for some, it reeks of a naïve type of dramaturgy. Tom Murphy's *Bailegangaire* (1985) has both dead children and the hope offered by Dolly's pregnancy. Likewise in McGuinness's *Mutabilitie* (1997), the File's child dies in violent and suspicious circumstances, and another, an English child, son of the Spenser family, is found wandering through the forest and is adopted by the Irish. Also, the ghost of both a young boy who hanged himself in a Ballymun flat, a young girl dying from Cystic Fibrosis and a baby girl who died soon after she was born haunts Dermot Bolger's play *The Passion of Jerome* (1999). The main character, endowed with stigmata after a cocaine trip, is unable to save the girl through healing, but he is capable of freeing the ghost of the young boy through his own suffering. The validation of release comes through pain. But it is the death of his own child that really haunts the work, as if the trauma of the death divides husband and wife and as if all other divisions between the couple have been filtered through the trauma of the event; the dead child gives both cause and meaning to their inability to relate. The tension between the privileging of innocence and the fantasy of innocence is formidable in this play, despite a host of smaller failings.

AGE OF INNOCENCE/AGE OF ICE

Since the mid-1980s especially, people have been shocked by stories in the public domain of abuse against children and vulnerable adults. Neglect, victimization, starvation, emotional violation, sexual assault and other horrors of all sorts, including torture, burning, cutting, fingernail extraction and sadism unsettled many. The activities of predatorial, serial abusers and rapists have been reported and details of child prostitution and paedophile rings have also hit the headlines. In terms of sexual abuse, on the one hand, the scale of the problem at times took on epidemic proportions and it also became something to be paranoid about, while, on the other hand, the attempts to downplay the incidence of abuse, through both subtle and uncouth means, was fraught with shortcomings.

Revelations were numerous; from the incidents of date rape to false allegations of assault/abuse, from the Kilkenny incest inquiry to the McColgan family investigation, from the activities of paedophile priests such as Brendan Smyth (1994) and Sean Fortune (1999) to the X-Case (1992), where a teenage rape victim was given the freedom to travel by the Supreme Court to Britain for an abortion, on the basis that her life was at risk, including the risk of suicide, something which previous amendments to the constitution had attempted to outlaw.

However, it was not just individuals, but institutionally structured violation which needed to be considered, lest we forget that patriarchy and power structures often create the rationalization and justification of abusive positions, of its dominance and of its need to control, and the means to cover up violation and to silence victims. In addition, structural inequities within social hierarchies facilitate or normalize violation on some level. Mary Raftery's *States of Fear* (RTE 1999) revealed the full horrors of systematic and institutional abuse in homes and care institutions run by the clergy. The failing of care institutions like the Goldenbridge Home for children, investigations into sexual abuse at both Madonna and Trudder Houses and the horrors of the Magdalene Laundries and of some Industrial Schools, including Artane and St Joseph's Letterfrack, all came to light and gave rise to huge anger, disbelief and sometimes denial.

More recently the Ferns Report (2005), which investigated claims of clerical abuse in the diocese of Ferns, found all kinds of structural and institutional inadequacies when it came to the reporting of and responding to allegations of abuse. It amounted to an absence of due care and very sinister cover-ups by senior clergy, apart from the fact that such abuse was a criminal matter. The Residential Institutions Redress Board (2002) was established to provide compensation for those who were the victims of acts of omission abuse and violation in state-run institutions. The Ryan Report (2009) confirmed the brutality of many who ran state institutions. Violation was often systematic, and church, state, the medical and legal professions colluded to keep victims silent, isolated and denied them justice.

Abuse, in whatever form, is a highly emotive subject that gives rise to a whole host of fears, anxieties, denials, reflexive value judgements, accusations and blame. Regardless, the need of a nation to return to the realities of an injurious past previously denied and a new willingness to monitor the present in order to protect the vulnerable, the innocent and the marginalized has been very much in evidence. Increasingly, children began to be given a status previously withheld from them.[5] The establishment of child-lines, the banning of corporal punishment and the introduction of Stay Safe-type programmes in schools have led to other adjustments and awarenesses. In tandem, child safety legislation, child protection policies and registers, discussions on professional best practice in dealing with allegations, mandatory reporting and other preventative strategies have been in circulation for some time.

The recent case in Roscommon (2009), where a mother was found guilty of neglect, two counts of incest and two of sexual abuse, and was sentenced to seven years, suggests that it has not gone away and that old failings around reportage and investigation have not been resolved. The pressure on and resignation of the Bishop of Cloyne, John Magee, from his post for his mishandling of allegations of child sex abuse in his diocese is a continuing reminder of institutional incompetence and complicity.[6] The bishop was effectively forced into the surrendering of his diocesan administrative duties, but he has still managed to retain his title.

In the face of such revelations of violation, how would Irish playwrights respond to such welcome revelations?[7] Throughout the 1990s many plays dealt with institutional violation and sexual abuse. Patricia Burke Brogan in *Eclipsed* (1992) follows the lives of the 'Penitent' women trapped in the Magdalene laundries, incorrectly held against their will for what were deemed to be crimes of an immoral sexual nature, having babies out of wedlock. Bernard Farrell in *Last Apache Re-Union* (1993) traces how bullying and sexual teasing had led to the suicide of the victim. Frank McGuinness's *Baglady* (1985) deals with the hurt of the single female character and cannot be taken beyond the frame of her suffering at the hands of her father. *Baglady* combines within its monologue format, story-telling, snatches of narrative, symbol and deceptions to reveal the hidden story of his Baglady character, who had been raped by her father and who later gives birth to a child that is taken away from her and drowned by him. Again the physical action is removed from the stage. Baglady's body stores the memory and it helps her to relate the sexual assault narrative as she communicates with and through her body, in the face of pressure to repress and to reject the notion that she was in any way complicit in her own violation. Innocence is un-housed, and the communication with her body is anything but child's play.

Conor McPherson's early monologues, such as *Rum and Vodka* (1992) and *The Good Thief* (1994), are driven by gruesome details of excessive violence. In the former play a man has sex with his wife while she sleeps. After the event he realizes that he could be charged with rape. McPherson's *This Lime Tree Bower* (1995) has a woman raped off-stage, something that signals the death of innocence for the character Joe, and the rape of a young woman in Gary Mitchell's *A Little World of Our Own* (1997) leads to tension amongst a loyalist working-class community and, it ultimately, results in death. In McPherson's *The Weir* one of the characters tells of a burial and the appearance of a strange figure, who insists that a coffin is going down the wrong grave and that it should instead be placed in a grave with a dead child. Later the character learns of the fact that the person to whom he spoke looked uncannily like the person who died, as he later saw the photo in the paper – this man was a suspected paedophile.

Anne Hartigan's play *Jersey Lillies* (1996) accounts for abuse of women forced to work as prostitutes for the German Army during the Second World War. Tom Kilroy in *The Secret Fall of Constance Wilde* (1997) sketches the destructive patterns in Constance's relationship with Oscar all the way back to her sexual violation by her father. The father in this instance is represented by a gigantic puppet figure that is pulled around the stage by actors wearing masks.

Alex Johnston in *Deep Space* (1998) has a rape impacting on his drama, and in *Melonfarmer* (1997) Johnston offers an attempted rape scene in a car, but the implications of this are not followed through dramatically. Declan Hughes in his play *Twenty Grand* (1998) hints at a sexual relationship between a father and daughter, but takes it no further than that. Mark O'Rowe's *Howie The Rookie*, *Made in China* (2001) and *Terminus* detail the threat or the actuality of same-sex male rape. (McGuinness and Carr in *Mutabilitie* and *Portia Coughlan*, respectively, have dealt with the theme of consensual incest.) Gerard Mannix Flynn's *James X* (2003) is a testimony of the brutality and violation that Flynn's character James O'Neill experienced at the hands of agents of church and state, which is rooted in Flynn's own testimony to the High Court in his claim for compensation against the state. (More consideration will be given to this play later in chapter 7.)

What stands out most of all is the fact that these playwrights use a variety of forms in order to capture such details. Moreover, many use narrative rather than character interaction or keep violation off stage, as a way of addressing issues. However, Marina Carr's play *On Raftery's Hill* is the most forceful and sustained evaluation of the complex issues surrounding innocence, victimhood, sexual violation and defiance. Carr places rape centre stage.

ON *RAFTERY'S HILL*: TELLING TALES

Carr tackles the issue of the Raftery family crippled by intergenerational sexual violation. Sorrel Raftery is a young woman living with her sister (Dinah), grandmother (Shalome), brother (Ded) and her father (Red). Sorrel is engaged to Dara Mood and just prior to her wedding her father rapes her. This happens towards the end of the first act and the remainder of the play deals with the consequences, implications and fall-out from the attack. As the drama emerges it is discovered that Dinah is not Sorrel's sister, but is in fact her mother. Red and his then 12-year-old daughter were brought together by Dinah's own mother. Carr grapples with the issues of power, sexuality, secrecy, shame, dysfunction, inferiority, indignity and addiction at the core of sexual abuse. She works with many of the issues and implications of abuse for her characters and for broader society. Is the abuser regarded as mentally ill, morally reprehensible and/or a criminal? In what ways does abuse impact on a victim? Can we distinguish between sexual and psychological gratification? She confirms how family victims of violation can be antagonistic towards each other and seldom allies, and how the victims of abuse through processes of internalization and identification can brutally accommodate themselves to dysfunctionality. Tantamount, of course, is that the social environment in which this play operates is symptomatic of wider structural abuses against women in particular.

Carr deploys a strained, non-naturalistic lyricism to move the play from the notional real on to not so much a surreal consciousness, but a grotesque impressionistic one, informed in part by Greek myth, which will be explored briefly in a later chapter. The direction of Garry Hynes and the stage design by Tony Walton for the first production by Druid Theatre Company at Town Hall Theatre, Galway, gave emphasis to this shift in register, through a combination of dark green and black colours and a bizarre, blackened staircase that reflected the peculiar nature of the household's affiliations. The setting reflects the squalid and dysfunctional psychological conditions of the household and the off-stage space littered with the rotting carcasses of dead farm animals, on the 300-acre farm, serves as a symbolic reminder of decay, mutilation and destruction.

Late in the first act Red's attempt to attract the attention of Dinah, who is in her bedroom, is sublimely represented by Carr. He sings and offers to bring her up a whiskey, and is annoyed by her rejection. Their exchanges are remarkably candid, brutal and full of a knowingness and familiarity that one might expect from disgruntled partners in a long-term sexual relationship, but not that of father and daughter. The exchange between Dinah and Red ends with Dinah telling him not to touch Sorrel. The warning dramatically signals what is to come.

When the young couple return to the house, Red is upstairs but over-hears their conversation. Carr allows the young lovers their innocence and passion and grants them a casual and comfortable freedom. Red's ageing, his fear of his own imminent death as announced by Sorrel, his jealousy of their intimacy and his distaste for the young adults being in charge of their own lives all means that Red is overwhelmed by antago-nism and fears for the future. Carr monitors superbly his frightful rage, his interrogation techniques, how his unconscious desires emerge, and the manner in which he begins to permit himself to become more and more dominant and violent against his daughter.

Previously in the play, Sorrel was not capable of gutting a hare. Now Red begins to demonstrate the activity. Producing a knife and holding Sorrel down, he cuts away her clothing, without nicking the flesh. He then rapes her on the kitchen table. Nobody in the house intervenes, despite Sorrel's pleas for help. Red's justification for his assault is that his daughter has betrayed him by talking badly about him, that he has been 'too soft on' her and because she has been 'prancin round like the Virgin Mary'.[8]

Sorrel's disturbance in response to the rape is unsettling for the other family members.[9] Her violation elicits a regressive, introverted, disassoci-ated response from her. She bathes all the time, barely eats, cries con-stantly and her dress sense changes from being reasonably contemporary and youthful during the first act to baggy, loose-fitting clothing that swamps her body. Sorrel challenges her objectification through her distress. On top of this, she rightly accuses Dinah of being her mother. Later, Dinah openly challenges Red for his assault, but he denies the extent of his wrongdoing. He even goes so far as to accuse Dinah of being jealous of the physical contact that took place between himself and Sorrel. To wrap things up, Red seeks an apology from Sorrel and Dinah encour-ages them to make up, as if it has been some small fracas or fall-out.

Carr dramatizes not only the horrors of incest but also captures a cycle of violation that complicates somewhat the relationship between victim and aggressor, as it is confirmed during the final moments of the play that Red himself is the child of an incestuous relationship between his mother and his grandfather. Moreover, it was hinted at, in the Druid production at least, in the manner in which Red followed Shalome up to her room, with his head unusually close to her buttocks, that Red and Shalome, his mother, may also have shared the same bed. While it is impossible to tabulate the statistics surrounding intergenerational abuse, many studies suggest 'as few as one-third of people who were abused as children become adults who abuse their children'.[10] Thankfully, two-thirds resist the perpetuation of the cycle. Furthermore, individual pathology is not just a distinct problem, but is something that is symptomatic of wider social issues.[11]

Dinah's continuing relationship with Red raises all sorts of uneasy questions. Dinah's ultimate numbed, distraught ambivalence, if you can call it that, is the brilliant feature of the play. To Carr's credit, abuse is not aligned simplistically with poverty. Susan Janko highlights the facts that 'Although child abuse and neglect are present in all ethnic groups and across socio-economic levels, reports of abuse and neglect occur predominantly in families of low socio-economic status.'[12]

The long-term impact of sexual abuse depends on a whole host of factors, from the type of the abuse (consensual, non-consensual, penetrative, non-penetrative), to the degree of coercive violence involved, from the frequency of the abuse to the prior relationship with the abusive person, from the way the child has been 'groomed' for the assault to the ability of the abuser to admit fully his/her crime, from the age of the abused person to the relationship that individual has or had with the abusive person, and from the support provided to the victim after the termination of the event to the individual personality of the victim of abuse.[13] John Briere identifies seven categories of abuse-related problems: 'post-traumatic stress, cognitive distortions, altered emotionality, dissociation, impaired self-reference, disturbed relatedness, and avoidance'.[14] Carr seems to touch on all of these very successfully. Dinah has been a victim for twenty-seven years; Sorrel has only been assaulted once and that bare fact raises huge questions. Christopher Bagley and Kathleen King in their work on victimology, a term which not only applies to abuse but covers responses to different situations, disasters and problems, claim that 'the components of victimization which are relevant are universal rejection, victim-precipitation, learned helplessness, attribution and locus of control, disaster syndrome, traumatic infantilism, and traumatic bonding'.[15] Carr generates many of these concepts in her play with brilliant deliberation, and in particular picks up on the 'learned helplessness' and 'traumatic infantilism' quite brilliantly through the figure of Ded and the madness of Shalome.

In the face of assault, children or young adults remain silent for a number of reasons, including anxiety over the loss of a parent who might be imprisoned, terror of retribution, fear of shaming others and damaging the reputation of the family. Dinah tells Sorrel that Red 'knew how to build up a child's heart ... never forgeh him for thah' (p.40). If they build you up, they can also most certainly take it away.

Incest is not only in evidence within this household. Dara reveals that the father of Sarah Brophy's still-born baby is her own father, who only raped her once. Sarah dies and her father ends up in a mental hospital in Ballinasloe. That, however, is not the fate of the Rafterys. Brilliantly, Carr captures the complexity of Dinah's emotions. Dinah, having suffered twenty-seven years of abuse, is enraged by the fact that nobody protected her and that Sorrel showed no thanks for the care and safe-keeping provided up to that point by Dinah, for such care and protection may have come at Dinah's personal expense. Sorrel distinguishes between the rape of a child and contrary intimacies in the dark of night shared by Dinah and Red, wondering how the 'relationship' continues occasionally into the present and queries how violation becomes a curious comfort? Dinah cannot fully explain it without drawing on the world of children's games: 'Ud's just like children playin in a field ah some awful game, before rules was made' (p.56). She is a perverse partner in a relationship that carries an unbearable cost. Sorrel accuses her: 'Innocent as a lamb, aren't ya' (p.56).

After the rape, Red implicitly hopes to buy Sorrel's silence by presenting Dara with the deeds to fifty acres and a cheque for twenty grand. Dara refuses it. After a brief stand-off between Dara and Red, Sorrel and Dara's exchange is fraught with tension. Sorrel defends her father and takes on his opinions. She calls Dara's family 'scrubbers', just as her father had done previously (p.53). Sorrel expresses confusion, and she also drives Dara away.

Ded, the only son, is utterly marginalized, as he lives in the cowshed and eats his food with dirty hands. Dehumanization has been his way of protecting himself. Carr's stage directions describe him as 'long haired, bearded, filthy: cow dung all over his clothes' and a little later she adds that he is 'beaten to the scut' (p.13). Dinah remarks to him: 'I allas knew wan of us wouldn't make ud' (p.15). In her eyes, he is the broken one and she is the one who has survived the ordeal. Shalome in

On Raftery's Hill had critics citing similarities to Federico García Lorca's mad grandmother in *The House of Bernarda Alba* (1945). Her fantasy is to go home to Daddy in 'Kinneygar' (Moscow), which is an unrealizable fantasy of the highest order. She is infantilized through ageing and madness and Ded through intimidation.[16] Ded tells Sorrel that if 'you were to remove him (Red), ya wouldn't know me' (p.38). Red has not interfered with Ded. Ded states that he is 'no girl to be played wud' (p.38). (This gives the meaning of play an altogether different resonance and also links in with Dinah's earlier quoted comment that it is like 'children playin in a field ah some awful game'.) Sorrel's response is savage: 'I don't think Daddy's choosy. He just wants to bate us all inta the dirt' (p.38). Ded wants to call the guards, but because of his participation in the delivery of Dinah's child, Sorrel, he feels implicated by association. Red forced him to participate and Ded's derangement may have been either caused or exacerbated by the experience.

STRAW DOGS

Isaac, a neighbour, accuses Red of hunting unfairly, after he shot a hare and he then went into the lair and 'strangled the leverets', an action so symbolic of the way he deals with his own family (p.19). When Red interrogates Ded he tells him to 'stop blinkin will ya. You're noh a hare a'ya' (p.26). While confronting Sorrell Dinah accuses her as follows:

> You'll go off and marry Dara Mood and I'll be left wud thah wan racin round like a march hare in her nightdress and Ded atin hees dinner like a dog at the duur and Daddy blusterin and butcherin all the small helpless creatures a the fields. (p.18)

If the animal world is used to capture an essential vulnerability, it is also called upon to highlight savagery and a universe in chaos, where it is the survival of the fittest and where innocence has little or no part. I will pick up on this idea further in the chapter on myth. Carr urges the spectator not to draw on the animal world as some sort of way of justifying what the spectator witnesses on stage, and not to accommodate talk of repression as an unjustified limitation of the natural impulses of the unconscious or Id.

INNOCENCE: 'LAVINS A CHRISTIAN DACENCY'

When in 1986 McGuinness turned in *Innocence* to the great Italian post-Renaissance painter Michelangelo Merisi Caravaggio, the obvious question, even on a cursory level, was what really had the figure of Caravaggio to offer to an Irish playwright? What possible moral, political, cultural and historical differentials, parallels or symmetries might be available between a late twentieth-century Ireland and an Italy of the early 1600s? Is it too simple to think Italy and think Catholic, in the same way that many think of the Irish Republic as being predominantly consumed by Catholic issues?

Looking at the play one realizes very soon that something altogether more subtle is being expressed. On a broader scale, the deliberate use of Irish rather than Italian accents in the production of the play at the Gate Theatre is significant, as is the refusal to confine the play to any one historical period – an objective achieved by the use of anomalies and anachronisms in stage and costume designs, which ensured that the audience was forced to confront its own social and religious realities, through direct parallels with things that were becoming increasingly and actively highlighted by the media at that time, in terms of paedophilia, institutional neglect and violation and corruption by some members of religious orders.[17]

The scope of the play, the breadth of the focus, the dialogue between the two acts, the use of dramatic compression and the blending of fantasy, reality, dream and trauma in order to express something of Caravaggio's personal and artistic struggles and dilemmas, the complex melding of symbols and fragments from Caravaggio's paintings, as well as what the play does to the concept of subjectivity make it the great work that it is. In effect, the persona of Caravaggio and the backdrop of the social, religious and political order of the play fuse to create a dynamic chemistry.[18]

From the outset it is obvious that one needs to distinguish between McGuinness's fictive character and the life of the artist Caravaggio.[19] *Innocence* is set on the day Caravaggio murders Ranuccio Tomassoni, but McGuinness's text shies well away from any type of documentary factuality, a death that is rumoured to have come about over a dispute during a court tennis match. McGuinness's Caravaggio is an angry protestor and subverter of norms, yet he is also a servant of the church, fretful about his allegiance to the institution and convinced of his own damnation, something that is brought about by the internalizing of church teaching on sexuality, as much as anything else. The work is anti-institutional, yet to say that the work is just anti-Catholic is to simplify it.

In this play the darkness of the painter is made obvious, as are his endeavours to articulate, to interpret, to sense and to see things not so much as they are, not as what they might be – in an aspirational sense – but from an eschewed, distraughtfully angular perspective. The painter is renowned for what is called a type of 'cellar-raking light'. The paintings are noted for instances of intensity, of death or near death moments, or the terrorized responses of those looking on, and set in spaces where heaven and earth meet. There is a symbolic connection of the physical and the metaphysical. Examples of these extremes would be in *The Sacrifice of Isaac*, a held or stalled instant at the moment of intended sacrifice, *The Crucifixion of St Peter*, with its near death moment or the after death moment in *The Deposition* or in *Judith Beheading Holofernes*, an instance of destruction, trauma and of pain. Other images of the moment of death occur in *The Death of the Virgin*, *The Crucifixion of St Andrew*, *Salome with the Head of St John the Baptist* and *David and Goliath*.

Although the work of Caravaggio provides intertextual and contextual springboards, *Innocence* is a play that questions beyond the frame through which the artist/writer imagines; one must ask *what* are the conventions and governing forms, *what* is representation, *what* are the implications of creative output(especially if the imagination is ideologically conditioned and if spectators' responses are culturally loaded)? The Gate Theatre's audiences' responses to the play's first Irish production, directed by Patrick Mason and designed by Joe Vanek, were very mixed, with some protesting at what they saw as sacrilegious. (Caravaggio tells his brother that he has been 'up the arses of more priests',[20] and this would strike home even closer in a modern production of this play. It is not that sexuality is an issue, more it is the hypocrisy and the pretence of celibacy to which many take offence.)

ROUGH TRADE

Raymond Williams's oft used idea of a 'structure of feeling' can be reconfigured here as a structure of innocence. It is a structure of thought, an insistence on something that crops up in this play in a variety of guises, initially in the form of binary oppositions – disease and cleanliness, good and evil, and damnation and salvation. Any hierarchial arrangement between innocence and damnation is contested. There is a certain dispossession of innocence. In such a way, the play politicizes the concept of innocence.

The Catholic religion has institutionalized innocence in the form of the Virgin Mary, a person uncorrupted, pure, unsullied, unmarked in a way by human frailty or sin. Sin corrupts. Sin can also damn. Children have always been associated, biblically speaking, with innocence (the slaughter of the innocent), yet the ramifications of such violation become profoundly blatant in this play. Within that grid, McGuinness exploits the role of art in society, the rage, compassion, dismissal, savagery, tenderness of the individual artist, the practice of patronage in various guises, the controlling brutality of some religious figures and the exploitation, both economic and sexual, of the poor. (While Lucio and Antonio, the 'Rough Trade', are not children, their dependence on selling their bodies for material sustenance must be noted.) Through these things McGuinness somehow challenges the conventions of a society that at that time of the play's first production in Ireland, outlawed homosexuality, queried the indulgences of wealth, the capacity of an individual to buy and sell, to be bought and sold. He also challenges the violence implicit in constitutional conservatism, social discrimination (gay bashing and here noticeably its converse), and just as importantly the centrality of violence both to history and to Irish history in particular.

Hiroko Mikami claims that 'It seems that McGuinness holds the view that to be an artist one must also possess a kind of deep innocence at one's core',[21] and she argues also for the notion of 'innocence at creativity's core'.[22] That perspective is probably a bit too positive. McGuinness of course can be seen as the source of that prompting. Of Caravaggio's work, McGuinness states that what lingers is 'some wonderful power that is innocent and strong'.[23] But the detail of the play doesn't testify completely to that.[24] In McGuinness's work innocence is often seen as a stable and insatiable configuration, where a notional uncorrupted defiance may lay hold. (His soldiers in *Observe the Sons of Ulster* believed that their battle was between the elect and the damned.)

In the McGuinness drama innocence and damnation are propositioned as polar opposite positions, only to be eschewed, within the interconnected frameworks of religion, sexuality, creativity and violence. The first part of the play is called 'life' the second 'death', but in 'life' death is found and in 'death' life is found, so in damnation innocence can prosper, in ugliness beauty can reign. This is not a play about art alone, this is not a play only about the creativity and destruction of the artist and this is not a play just about institutional violation: it is a play about how individual agency can be articulated and achieved, within destitution and poverty.

Caravaggio feels himself to be damned, even if he mockingly can tell Lucio and Antonio that he is 'a saint' (p.230). Regardless, he can envision beauty and salvation in the guise of others, who are rejected, labelled and cast aside by society and who live on the fringes, in squalor and with little dignity. The play takes its inspiration from Caravaggio's central placing of the socially dispossessed in his paintings/stagings. He used beggars, vagabonds, prostitutes and thieves, even the dead as models. If Christian doctrine is to be believed, these are the ones that will receive heavenly salvation, and they are the ones that receive the provisional salvation of the artist, who transposes them from one reality to another, who moulds the negative into something positive. Is poverty an intolerable price to pay for salvation? Poverty cannot be the price of salvation. There is an obviously huge political agenda, both explicit and implicit, in the paintings of Caravaggio. In his own time people rejected his humanizing of the saints – clued in, unconsciously perhaps, to some deeper transgression. By using the lowly, Caravaggio was in fact painting their potential salvation, yet the church perhaps only gave lip service to that reality in the way that it treated those who were in poor circumstances. In this play the Cardinal indulges in excess, unwilling to share his food and his surplus with others. Instead, poverty was acceptable, through irresponsibility and the absence of community. This is not to deny the genuine charity of the church down through the ages.

In order to represent the vision and in order to make the images or paintings of Caravaggio's work realizable, McGuinness/Mason/Vanek resorted to a specific type of staging, particularly in the creation of the opening and closing stage images and more importantly as ways of theatricalizing the spiritual and socio/economic reality of the world of Caravaggio by connecting up light and dark, vision and destruction, salvation and damnation, all of which is ultimately prompted by the consciousness of the living dead.

In the programme note to the play, speaking of Caravaggio and Lena, McGuinness states that 'the woman he honoured must have been a match for him, and being Caravaggio, it must have been a queer match. So I began to paint, to play.'[25] The linking of painting and play is vital. The opening tableau of the play shows Caravaggio sleeping in Lena's hovel, experiencing a nightmare. It is a collaged event, including the characters of the Cardinal, Lena and Caravaggio's sister and brother, and involves the assembling of some not so random fragments from the paintings of Caravaggio. Specific objects like a skull, a red cloak and the horse emerge, and these recur with some regularity across the work of the Italian painter.

Worth pursuing just a little are the mobile and the transformative qualities of the cloak, for instance. In the first moments of the play the cloak is used to symbolize a horse, and then it adjusts when Lena caresses it as if it were a child. When the dream sequence ends the action is back in the real world. Towards the end of the play, Lena, taking it from the bag of booty, lays claim to it. Soon after, she places it around Antonio's body in a reconstruction of Caravaggio's painting of *St John the Baptist*. Such repeated prominence releases an elaborate irony – given that such a cloak had been used to such intertextual effect in many of Caravaggio's greatest paintings themselves.[26] McGuinness also calls attention to the feigned, grotesque theatricality of Caravaggio's later paintings.[27] He also manages his own type of subversive dramaturgy. Early on in the play it is revealed that Lena has previously modelled for Caravaggio. 'Caravaggio: I gathered the earth's fruit and the tree's leaf and I plant them in your face for your face is a bowl full of life, full of Lena' (p.218). Lena's face, McGuinness hints, was the inspiration for Caravaggio's paintings either in *The Boy with the Bowl of Fruit*, the still life *The Bowl of Fruit* or the bowl of fruit in the later painting, *The Supper at Emmaus*. Her face serves as inspiration, yet the licence of the inspiration is to detail death and decay. The ordinary is transformed into the eternal and the damned, but from the earliest stages of the play we know not to take Caravaggio too seriously. We can see this trajectory happening early on, when having commented on the beauty of Lena's face as detailed above, he goes on to blow his nose in his hands.

The Whore (Anna), Antonio and Lucio also modelled for Caravaggio. What has he done to them or for them? The Whore, it is suggested, appears in *Death of the Virgin*. (An often claimed, but unproven fact is that Caravaggio painted *The Death of the Virgin* using the dead and bloated body of a prostitute who had drowned herself in a river.)[28] Antonio, it is suggested, is portrayed as the character in *The Boy with the Bowl of Fruit*. Lucio recalls how Caravaggio dressed him up as a tree – as homoeroticized subject/object – squeezing grapes all over him and calling him Bacchus (p.225).[29] The relationship between Caravaggio and Lena opens up the specific issues of homosexuality from the start. As Lena roughly masturbates Caravaggio, the phrase 'the hand of God' is given an altogether new meaning (p.210). There are attempts by many of the characters in the play to make strong associations with the darkness and Caravaggio's sexuality. While there is a strong sense that Caravaggio's inability to accept his sexuality leads to dysfunctionality on a certain level, I think the darkness has as much if not more to do with the Jungian concept of shadow. Innocence is corruption's shadow and vice versa.[30]

As an artist, Caravaggio has little choice but to embrace the patronage of the church. As a dependent on such a structure, he also functions
as a pimp for the Cardinal. Is the concept of patronage totally akin to
an act of prostitution, or is that too simplistic? Does hunger move people outside the frame of morality? While the sexuality of the two male
prostitutes is somewhat confused, their anger in having to sell their
bodies is also made apparent to an audience. Caravaggio provides the
Cardinal with the two young men as a 'gift' (p.237), but it is anything
but a gift. The capacity to buy lives, to purchase sex, to turn or tran-
substantiate humans into objects, is the ultimate expression of power.

The first act ends with two acts of destruction, deeds that articulate
the hostility towards the Cardinal's exploitation: Caravaggio destroys
the paintings and tapestries on the walls and Antonio and Lucio steal a
bag of booty from the Cardinal's palace. The desecration of the
Cardinal's dwelling leads to the death of the man that Caravaggio kills.
That night the artist must stare down the ghosts who haunt him and
through the dream/nightmare Caravaggio finds some solace, but never
enough to grant him absolution. The drama, at first sight, appears to
work within a dialectical model, with act 1 and act 2, life and death,
predominantly reality and dream, relating to each other or acting as
flip-sides of each other. Such neatness collapses on closer inspection, as
such distinctions are run into the ground, through inversion and
licence, through perverse juxtaposition and through a deeply unset-
tlingly reflection on living.

His sister, Caterina is the first figure to appear during the dream
sequence. Caterina tells of her death during childbirth and how she
was sacrificed to save the life of her son. Her rage is against the world.
In effect, McGuinness brings the play within a dream consciousness in
order to deliver a state of reversibility, proliferation and licence, where
the main subversive force is taken from the rejection of negativity and
by the preparation of a space for creativity and living, all of which
takes place within a structure where life and death co-mingle and the
terrors of both are reconciled. In the dream Caravaggio dries the flesh
of the Whore who had drowned, cleanses the face of Antonio and he
kisses life back into Lucio. Having done so, he invites his dream figures, as aspects of himself, to play. There is an exchange of performative, transactional healing that builds on the concept of animal play
introduced in the first act. Caravaggio can awaken from the dream of
death and return back to the living. Life not death has the ultimate
pulling power.

Through the deployment of animal imagery McGuinness broadens the perspective of meaning and violence within the play. Animal imagery often represents the deepest representation of repression and transference. The inhabiting of the animal space is often a way of getting in touch with more elemental forces, archetypal energies that can hint at immobility or its counter-force and thus formulate change. Various types of animals appear regularly in the paintings – a lizard is present in *The Boy Bitten by Lizard*, one of the pictures of *St John the Baptist* includes a ram, and *The Conversion of St Paul* has a white horse. The animals in the paintings earth the artist's vision along with calling attention to sensuous and sexual energies, which the Catholic religion finds almost impossible to accept as healthy, even within the frame of the sacrament of marriage.

In the play itself a horse appears in the opening dream sequence and later on Caravaggio claims that a horse had kicked him, almost blinding him. But the horse is also a symbol of power and oppression, and its association with blindness links the horse with the fear of castration. (See Peter Shaffer's play *Equus* (1973) for its use of symbolism, McGuinness's *The Factory Girls* (1982) for the emphasis on the story of the girl in the comic *Bunty* who escapes on a horse, and *Observe the Sons of Ulster* for the mock battle of the Boyne/Scarva and the horse-play therein.) Wounded by animals, overcoming the animal, energized by the elemental energy of the animal, becoming the animal, all seem to be part of the metatheatrical process that McGuinness has in mind. The goal of this message of transgression is to 'live'.

In the dream sequence the Cardinal appears in rags, as the Cardinal and his servant have reversed places. In a similar vein, and earlier on in the play, McGuinness allows Lucio and Antonio to perform a mock ceremony of transubstantiation, something that surely disturbs the reverence usually paid to the religious act.

> Lucio: This is my body.
> Antonio: This is my blood.
> Lucio: Turn me into bread, God.
> Antonio: Me into wine.
> Lucio: Give us a miracle. Antonio: Give us a man. (p.222)

In Caravaggio's work there is no idealization of saints. Previously in artistic work, saintly figures were portrayed with eyes towards heaven only, seldom towards the things of the world. The corruption of the material world was the burden. Caravaggio painted the saints and grounded them in this material reality, a reality that must be recognized and fought over. So McGuinness, by inverting ritual, by ensuring the secularization of religious ritual and by disconcerting language from its rational transparency through carnivalized play, ensures that images of order are subverted from within. As such, carnival and reconciliation are co-joined.

The play ends with the physical absence of Caravaggio, but his spirit survives through his paintings. In the final sequence of the play Lena dreams that she stood in a beautiful room with Caravaggio's pictures on the walls and that the painter had found peace. Lena laughs because she realizes that Caravaggio was looking down from above, having found salvation in heaven. 'Lena: I knew then somehow we'd won, we turned the world upside down, the goat and The Whore, the queer and his woman' (p.284).[31] Lena is enabled, in order to articulate and to emphasize the appropriations that the production of the play also took. She takes the chalice, cross, bowl and cloak from the bag of church booty, and both secularizes and redistributes its images and symbols. Lena demands that Antonio strip naked so that he can pose for her interpretation of Caravaggio's painting *John the Baptist*. The cycle is complete; the gift is passed on. The fluidity of space, matches the fluidity of self, the multiplicity of selves and tendency of Caravaggio to use the same models across a range of paintings highlights his subversive intent and also the concept of proliferation. Here, the visionary, aspirational beauty of the artist springs from the same individual that can brutally murder; the artist that can deploy his brush to generate elegance is the same one that can shape death with a knife.

MEDUSA V. BACCHUS

Innocence plays with the nature of art, conventions and symbols of Catholicism, deconstructing or inverting associated meaning, indirectly breaching the conventions and assumptions of a belief system of religion and of a society that divides rich and poor. It is just as simplistic to argue that the painter exploited his models, as it is to place a substantial value on the act of ritual cleansing in the dream sequence. In this play the central tensions between creativity and destruction, expression and chaos, damnation and salvation, death and life, and body and soul hit home in the most outrageous and frightening manner.

In a world of power, authority and violation, not to mention poverty and prostitution, is innocence an unratifiable quantity and is innocence the greatest stroke that ideology and religion can pull? Lena states: 'I was mad about Our Lady when I was a girl. Christ, would you believe that? I used to imagine I was her daughter and Jesus was a right pup who tormented me. The innocence of it' (p.209). In addition, the Whore ironically narrates a vision of Jesus Christ who honours her by giving her a message. Anna's message during her vision is that the Pope is without sin; that he is a saint, but the corruption of the church is from the top down, given the Cardinal's remorseless exploitation of the needy.

Instead of goodness and virtue, we get corruption, hidden behind the veil of innocence. Within the frame of the play the church through its patronage also exploits the artist, who needs the commissions to survive. Moreover, the ability of the church to damn becomes the strongest force in the shaping of Caravaggio's consciousness. Sin brings the destruction of innocence: sin brings damnation. The capacity of the powerful to name, accuse, implicate and to damn is questioned and the intentions behind such gestures are exposed.

When Lucio and Antonio are with the Cardinal, Caravaggio pounces on Antonio and holds a knife to his throat. Caravaggio asks: 'Has the big, bad wolf put the fear of God into your innocent souls?' (p.241) Here the Cardinal sees things in animal terms; Caravaggio is the wolf, the two male prostitutes are called mockingly perhaps 'innocent souls', but the fluidity and the multiple meanings of the terms 'innocent' and 'animals' become increasingly apparent.[32] Earlier in the play the Cardinal had called Lucio and Antonio 'poor lambs' (p.241). Biblically speaking, lambs were associated with innocence and are used by Carr in *On Raftery's Hill*. On one level the two men are innocent, yet on another they have no access to innocence, given the degree of corruption that surrounds them, given their participation in the corruption and exploitation, yet the economic reality of their existence ensures that they cannot rely on any value system that confirms innocence. Corruption and compromise are the order of the day. Caravaggio pleads to his models that he is 'innocent of all' they throw at him (p.277). The artist expresses that even the wildest animal is 'innocent at heart', but, although Caravaggio has a 'way with animals', the human may be animal by way of instinct, but ultimately less easily animal by way of reason (p.235).

Innocence marks not so much innocence destroyed as innocence as a site incapable of significant demarcations. In addition, the abuse of privilege in the play also serves as a metaphor for damage caused by structured and institutionalized violation. Dragon, steed, lizard, hare, eagle, hound, lion and unicorn are called upon, again as a sort of false benediction, as the unicorn is asked to 'preserve the species', 'protect the species' (p.280), rather than as a request for a deity to and to watch over individuals. Through a belief in redemption, in the sacrifice of Christ and a consecration of the institutionalization of innocence, through the figure of the Virgin Mary, the Catholic Church shapes attitudes to damnation and redemption.

The work of Caravaggio resides between the torment of Medusa and the calm, poised excesses of Bacchus. Caravaggio's artistic gift is to reframe, to shift perspective, to reimagine. With these things comes possibility. If the Cardinal can bring Caravaggio's brother back into his life, then the dream space, created by Lena (feminine), brings back his sister from the dead. Caravaggio is a mischief maker who misappropriates the icons and symbols of the ruling order. Dream play takes us into the underworld of the mind, and prostitution and poverty take an audience beyond the notions of art and artefact. Artifice gets us to the arena of performance and fluidity, artificiality to the world of codifications, improbable social discourse and etiquette, but both deliver perspectives on corruption. Beneath the reality of art resides dishonesty, beneath the reality of creativity resides destruction and beneath life there is death.

Ultimately the ambivalence of laughter generates misrule and protest and further complicates the concept of innocence. Laughter is defiance and the freeing energy here in this play: it is the laughter of the body and the physical release of laughter, not a holy laughter, but a mirth without any degree of transcendence. Through laughter, innocence proves to be unstable, unruly, as a profane, anarchic innocence is released. All borders and distinctions are transgressed. Art is neither ideologically neutral nor innocent. Metamorphosis, metatheatricality and mutation combine. As such, laughter as much as innocence is the gateway, through the 'rough trade' of reality and the rough trade of art and through, as a consequence, the centring of the dispossessed and the masquerade of the damned. This is what makes innocence so 'radical', unlike the way that innocence is naïvely appropriated as a way of calibrating meaning which is at the core of so much of contemporary Irish dramaturgy. Like Carr, McGuinness connects innocence and play. Marie Jones does the same in a very different way.

A NIGHT IN NOVEMBER: SUBSTANCE ABUSE

When it comes to the relationship between theatre and reality, and, in particular, theatre and Northern Ireland, there are many complex expectations, sensitivities, entrenchments, imperatives and responses to both writing and performances, especially since the late 1960s with the start of the 'Troubles'.[33] Dealing with such an obviously arduous time in history, the strategies of playwrights were manifold, with many trying to find ways of engaging with intransigence, the tribulations and injustices, while at the same time attempting to maintain some tangential distance from the conflict, at least in terms of representation, or more accurately, the impulses and imperatives to represent. Stewart Parker stated:

> The raw material of drama is over-abundant here, easy pickings. Domestic bickering, street wit, tension in the shadows, patrolling soldiers, a fight, an explosion, a shot, a tragic death: another Ulster Play written. What statement has it made? That the situation is grim, that Catholics and Protestants hate each other, that it's all shocking and terribly sad, but that the human spirit is remarkably resilient for all that. Such a play certainly reflects aspects of life here. But it fails to reflect adequately upon them.[34]

Along these lines as outlined by Parker, most felt the need to confront the interfaces between violence, politics, sectarianism, class, community and gender to different extents and in very different ways. (And that is not to say that these are the only variables contemplated or worthy of consideration.) Despite the fear of nakedly polemical approaches, many playwrights were willing to attest and display openly their own idiosyncratic appraisals, but beneath the surface of the writing thinly disguised ideological leanings and sectarian allegiances are almost always evident. Despite this 'over-abundance', playwrights were under intense pressure to deal with all of the above, knowing that their work would be put under a degree of scrutiny that most other writers internationally did not have to face, and feared the simplistic labelling and ghettoizing of their work.

In terms of dramatic form, there were very different approaches pursued.[35] To name but a few, Anne Devlin's *Ourselves Alone* (1985), Christina Reid's *Joyriders* (1986) and later Gary Mitchell's[36] *A Little World of our Own* (1997) and *Tearing the Loom* (1998), and Stuart Carolan's *Defender of the Faith* (2004) are scripts, in the main, that are unquestionably committed to methodologies grounded in verisimilitude, thereby revealing the rivalries, hostilities, fears and distrusts of characters. Furthermore, these plays use backdrops, which, in either relatively contemporary or historic settings, demonstrate the horrors of conflict, the suspicions, misgivings, violence, intimidation, betrayal, suffering, paranoia and hegemonic intransigence of notionally warring factions. In this type of work there are connections between the perceived and acknowledged depth of the crisis and the disharmonies of incompatibilities and the intensity of representations, and between the casualness and inevitability of destructive cycles and the tragedies of lost innocence.

Other playwrights in their dramatizations of the 'Troubles' use history and myth as a way of veering away from the obligations to be factually accurate and the direct, often overwhelming imperatives of authenticity. Frank McGuinness's *Observe the Sons of Ulster Marching Towards the Somme* is an obvious one, and his *Carthaginians*, which deals somewhat tangentially with the events of Bloody Sunday, 28 January 1972, and the trauma and responses that such an atrocity illicited, partly uses the prism of Carthage and Roman Imperialism to reconstitute an inspired response to that event and how it might be grieved. Further, part of the inclination to avoid direct comment and engagement can be seen in the spate of adaptations of Greek tragedies in the 1980s–90s – and it was not just a Northern Irish Field Day phenomenon – by writers who wished to inform their work by allegory, metaphor and myth, as a way of articulating indirectly and otherwise, evocations, correspondences and resonances with the contemporary circumstances. Additionally, writing by Stewart Parker with *Pentecost* (1987) and Anne Devlin's with *After Easter* (1994) chose the registers of vision and imagining as ways of generating transience and mobility, within conditions of violence and embedded sectarianism.

Marie Jones's work has been of a slightly different order from much of the above. Initially she was a performer, who went on to be one of the co-founders of Charabanc Theatre Company (1983). Afterwards she established herself as a writer for that collective. What her plays seem to do is to find parallel, transformative and transitional spaces within which to assess and test novel ideas and new arrangements, however difficult they are to realize in reality. It is a body of work markedly animated by the notion of play and the subversions that play facilitates. Key to this framework is how laughter functions as a form of defiance against oppression and suffering, how it can contest grievance and can rebuff the need to see trauma as the only prism through which everything can be refracted. Jones filters critically through her work many of the ideological biases and crass class and sectarian assumptions upon which prejudices are built, and yet for many, of course, she displays her own motivations, convictions and prejudices through what she writes and shapes for performance.

A Night in November was first produced on 8 August 1994 by DubbelJoint Productions at Belfast Institute of Further Education, directed by Pam Brighton and performed by Dan Gordon. This one-man show is centred around 34-year-old Kenneth McCallister, a dole clerk. The performer plays a whole host of characters with whom Kenneth comes into contact, from family members, service users at work and fellow employees, to football supporters, friends and young kids on the street.[37] The first performance used a single backdrop that was 'a representation of a football crowd', a 'rostra which has three levels representing the terrace', painted in 'red, white and blue' which later flips over to 'green, white and orange'.[38] Robert Ballagh originally designed the set.

THE EAR WHISPERER

The play's governing impetus is provided by Kenneth's experiences at a football match – based on a real event – a game between Northern Ireland and the Republic of Ireland on 17 November 1993, upon whose result was dependent the participation of the Republic's team in the 1994 World Cup in America. On that evening a 1–1 draw was enough to see the Republic's team through, yet the match itself was marred by great controversy. Although the Republic's supporters were barred from attending the match in Windsor Park, some did get their hands on tickets. However, it was the vocalized enmity of many of the Northern Irish supporters towards the Republic's team which drew much attention. Hostile receptions on sporting occasions are nothing new and street battles between rival fans and/or police forces can occur. Most commentators on football acknowledge that insensitive chants, sectarian and racially motivated slurs were part and parcel of many football games in the 1990s. However, evidence from that particular evening from journalists' accounts, testimonies from those there and the confirmation provided by television broadcasts show how fanatical and extreme the hostilities were. Sectarian and race antagonisms were given almost free reign. (Yet it is at a time in history noted for behind-the-scenes activities that were building towards an emergent peace process and were about to be made public.)

The Republic's team comprised players who were Irish-born, those of Irish descent but raised in the United Kingdom, and some with questionable ancestral links, and even one footballer who had played for Northern Ireland as a youth, Alan Kernaghan. According to Ernie, Kenneth's father-in-law, many were playing for Ireland because they were not good enough for England, mercenary players, with no affiliation to the Irish Republic. International football was their only motivation: 'Fenian dirty bastards ... Mercenary Fenian blood ... Papish bastards' (p.70).

However, it is the use of the phrase 'Trick or Treat' on this occasion which triggers much of Kenneth's soul searching. It is an expression normally associated with Halloween, but is given a new register and significance by the massacre, weeks previously, at the Rising Sun Bar, Greysteel, County Derry,[39] when loyalist paramilitaries entered a pub and uttered that phrase before shooting dead seven of the public house's customers. 'Greysteel Seven, Ireland nil' went the chant (p.71). In any context, let alone that of a football match, such slogans are utterly inappropriate and in extreme bad taste, delivered to cause deepest offence.

The heightened nature of the abuse, Kenneth's embarrassment at the singing and chanting, his desire to protect a thinly disguised Republican Irish supporter from the angered crowds by whispering the words of 'The Sash my Father Wore' in his ear, so that he can pretend to sing along and belong, all lead towards a mode of self-reflection that is made poignant, comically naïve and fundamentally performative. Of course, Jones is working with the facts of real events and fictionalizes them through her character. She does not find a character who shouted abuse and remained unchanged by the events of the evening, instead, she finds a character who is embarrassed by the vitriol and sectarianism of his own father-in-law, and who sees, in his own wife, his acquaintances and in himself analogous, if more inhibited and mannered versions of the same visceral antagonisms.

Kenneth begins to query his own prejudices and his participation in the passive and active perpetuation of biased sectarianism in his dealings with those deemed 'dirty Taigs' (p.71), Fenian, Irish and other. He assumes that his Catholic client has too many dependants, is inherently lazy, unwilling to work and is sponging off the state. Kenneth is more subtle in his encounters with his line superior, Jerry, a Catholic who cannot, unlike Kenneth, secure a golf club membership. (In his circle of acquaintances, Kenneth's admission to the golf club is celebrated by all and sundry.)

Having been asked by Jerry for a lift home, Kenneth is obliged for the first time in his life to go into West Belfast or 'bandit country' (p.81), as he calls it. For too long he has equated this area with 'deprivation and filth, and graffiti and too many kids and not enough soap' (pp.82–83). He is prompted to make sense of the life of Jerry, who lives in a substantially sized home, bigger than Kenneth's own. The home has an untidy garden, with kids' toys strewn about. Inside there is a note from Jerry's wife saying that she decided to take the kids to the cinema and that he could cater for himself that evening, a change of plans which does not displease him. Inevitably, we get the clichés of opposing home lives, those of Kenneth and Debrah, and Jerry and his partner, the former ordered, responsible, tidy, cold, calculated, passionless, without warmth or freedom, the latter's ('as other') regarded for its 'wonderful unpredictability' (p.83), its disorderly waywardness, which is regardless full of implicit expressions of spontaneous love. (A fundamental part of Kenneth's journey is reflection, based on fanciful, false binaries. In a way, many people initially measure difference through broad-stroke contrasts and differences. It is the easiest way of so doing.)

The match in Windsor Park, his new golf club membership and all that it gives a free rein to, his trip into 'bandit territory' and the information about the death of his childhood friend Norman Dawson, a celebrated paramilitary, are all the events which force Kenneth to contest his own circumstances and political allegiances.

In many ways, Kenneth is a naïve character set loose on the world of sectarianism, attempting to make sense of or appease its causes, justifications and prejudices. (It is better perhaps than some ex-paramilitary, with a Degree/Ph.D. in Literature, attempting to do the same thing and querying his previous acts of terror. Sometimes, over-awareness can lead to all types of obfuscations.) Kenneth, initially, moves from someone who thinks critically but is unable to say it in public, to someone who finds the courage to challenge conventions. There are a number of moments when he knows what he wishes to say but declines to say them, until one evening when some friends are over for a party, when he unleashes his hostility towards his community's passive aggressive participation in sectarianism. Acts of terror consolidate the status quo which they hold dear. He implies that not enough is done to isolate, restrain or condemn paramilitary activities. Mere lip service or resignation at the ineffectualness of protest is not enough. Kenneth is a sort of innocent or someone who wishes to define for himself a circle of innocence.

OLÉ OLÉ

Kenneth's public outburst isolates him, but he bears the glow of the outsider, the truth teller, and juvenile rebel, and, as an expression of his new-found liberation, he plans to travel to New York to support the Irish football team. In this action there is curiosity, a need for freedom, a desire to take risks and to be defiant, an unconscious, perhaps, necessity to mimic his colleague Jerry, who, along with his wife, will go into debt and not upgrade their car, in order to make a once in a lifetime journey to New York to support the Irish Republic's team in the World Cup.

Kenneth travels to Dublin,[40] takes a flight to New York and watches the match between Italy and Ireland in Eamon Doran's Bar. Along the way he gets trapped in the elation and emotion surrounding both the journey and the event itself. Ireland's victory on that occasion is greeted with intense pride and euphoria, however soon afterwards reports filter through of another shooting, this time by the UVF in Loughinisland, County Down. So the events on the field are always made problematic by events off it, as jubilation is displaced by devastation. Having made the journey, and having temporarily overhauled his life, the play does not give us the aftermath of Kenneth going back home to explain why in order to pay for the trip, he spent his golf membership fees, cashed in the meagre shares he inherited and sold his precious golf clubs. The writer places such potential reflections with an audience.[41] However, the connection between the personal and the political and the sentiment of the piece and the implicit dramaturgical imperatives need further teasing out.

In terms of gender, Debrah is the stereotype of the nagging, cold and henpecking partner. In Kenneth's imitation of his wife, the mimicry is often performed as a heightened, exaggerated, falsetto berating of him by her. Debrah's needs are displaced by these restrictive, shrill and hectoring enunciations. But what is a woman playwright doing representing a female character in such a way? Across this play and also in *Stones in his Pockets*, her two most recognized plays, Jones seems to empower her male characters through the facility of play, yet almost in each instance, the female characters are exceptionally unrounded and negatively imagined; Debrah and Pauline in *A Night in November* and Aisling, the shrill, third Assistant Director, and the exploitative American star actress Caroline Giovanni in *Stones in his Pockets*.[42] Imelda Foley argues that characters like Debrah become 'endorsers and custodians of the patriarchal world that has imprisoned them, the female versions of the colonised who have become the colonisers'.[43] In a more general observation on Northern Irish dramaturgy, Christopher Morash, notes that the 'obligatory off-stage riot claims its sacrificial female victim'.[44] While Debrah is not that type of casualty, femininity it could be argued is the sacrificial victim in this piece, as indeed many have argued of sectarianism.

KICKING WITH BOTH FEET

In terms of politics, David Grant argues that this play is written from 'an explicitly Protestant, post-Ceasefire perspective'.[45] Tom Maguire argues that Jones would be seen by many to have a 'close identification with a working-class nationalist community'.[46] Maguire thus sees the play as a 'public repudiation of the politics of her background'.[47] Clearly, there are very obviously implicit and explicit criticisms of the loyalist and unionist communities' behaviours in terms of class, gender and politics. There are very palpable issues around the 'uniformity' and 'standard regulation' loyalism that Jones allows her character to suggest (p.81). This type of one-size-fits-all loyalism is not enough; far more subtlety is necessary. Maguire notes that a 'negative figuration of loyalism has a long tradition on the stage'.[48] Within the play, loyalism is deemed dour, bigoted, entrenched, self-possessed and unwilling to surrender. Pauline's comment on the Downing Street Declaration[49] is pertinent: 'it smacks of sell-out to me and our politicians will never allow that to happen so it's a pointless exercise' (p.91).

Kenneth moves from seeing Catholics/Nationalists as 'low life at its lowest and all this meant second class, filth, scum and hatred' (p.84) towards perceiving them as altogether more quixotic.[50] He admires the enthusiasm and inventiveness of the Irish supporters in New York, who make pleadingly impressive phone calls looking at the last minute to find places to stay; he thinks highly of the generosity of the Irish football supporters, and he appreciates the raunchiness of the Irish women supporters: 'Girls, this is Kenneth, he prefers ating ice cream to shaggin', is how one of these females introduces him (p.105). There is a deep sense of awe provided by this moment of football victory, of collective belonging and perhaps an artificial hysteria induced by mass gatherings. All of the above seems to smack of the old cliché of losing oneself in another tribe, going native so to speak, and with that the naïvety and unsuspecting danger that the boundary crossing and the encounters may unleash. (Brian Friel captures this impressively with his Yolland character in *Translations*.) It prompts Brian Logan to state 'Jones's critical intelligence accedes to affectionate nationalism.'[51] Foley rightly points out that 'Catholicism is represented as liberation, joy and fluidity, all the concepts which Anne Devlin will portray as being denied within that culture.'[52] Fintan O'Toole finds that the drama rehashes all the old stereotypes and clichés of Catholics and the Southern Irish, while wanting to make virtues of their apparent laxness, vivacity and vices, claiming: 'It is equally insulting to both sides, the only difference being that it insults the identity of Protestants and the intelligence of Catholics.'[53]

TEENAGE KICKS

Clearly, within the play Nationalist/Republican politics are not framed within the same set of negative parameters as Loyalist/Unionist ones. Jerry just gets on with things, and he simply refuses to recognise the presence of the British soldiers in his area. Nothing else is really said by this character on the politics of Northern Ireland. From the play we get a sense of some of the things the Loyalist community has to alter or forfeit. But we don't ever get a sense of what the Nationalist/ Republican community has to put on the negotiating table. In addition, the paramilitary murders mentioned in the play all flow from the loyalist side – Greysteel and Loughinisland. The Greysteel murders were claimed to be in retaliation for those on the Shankill Road carried out by the Provisional IRA. The fact that no Republican atrocities are singled out by the play might be seen as a dangerous ploy, a serious misrepresentation at best, and a divisive strategy at worst.

International audiences less familiar with the complexity of the situation may be swayed by the simplistic sentiment of the piece, but not by the dialectical ramifications of sectarian politics pushing for some sort of end game. Hard bargaining won through to deliver the current situation of governance, and sentiment, it could be argued, counted for little. (Recent documents released by the British Army suggest that the inevitable 'end state' was a military/paramilitary stalemate that drove people to the negotiating table and on to a peace process.)[54]

By the play's end Kenneth turns his back on hundreds of years of tradition and declares himself to be no longer Protestant, Northern Irish and British, but a 'Protestant Man … an Irish Man' (p.108). For someone who hadn't previously crossed the border before taking the flight from Dublin to New York, for someone who regarded Southern Ireland a 'Foreign Country' (p.66), this proves to be a very big change in mindset. It is worth speculating if this shift is too big, too naïve and too forced from dramaturgical or ideological points of views, particularly as Kenneth declares 'I absolve myself … I am free of them' (p.108). Maguire argues that with Kenneth's final remarks there is the simplistic conjoining of 'the apparently antithetical ideas of Irish and Protestant'.[55] ('Apparently' is the apposite term.) By so doing, Maguire asserts 'Individual integrity substitutes for social justice and political equality.'[56] Joe Cleary argues 'Marxian reservations about domestic tragedy have centred on two objections: first, that the genre has typically rehearsed a humanist worldview in which specifically middle-class interests are mystified as universal human values, and, second, that it almost invariably privileges the private over the public sphere as the basis of human value.'[57] Jones can be confronted indirectly from a Marxist and from an equality point of view. Yet, María Kurdi places the play within the terrain of journey and encounters with other, and thus sees Kenneth's journey as one of reconciliation and less immediately bound up with politics.[58]

THE BELFAST SYNDROME

Further, on such incidents of transformation and letting go, in relation to Tim Loane's *Caught Red Handed* (2002), Mark Phelan argues that the play is not 'dependent on doubled identities, but on the removal of one of them'.[59] Phelan further suggests that this play and Jones's are based 'upon the politics of absorption rather than inclusion, of negation rather than negotiation'.[60] (The Stockholm Syndrome– now reconstituted as the Belfast one – the true mark of transformation seems to be with those who surrender one perspective and identify with a previously rival one.) Clearly, critics have contested the apparent sleights of hand, the objectifications/ romanticizations of woman and nationalism, and the implicit sundering or surrendering of the link between unionism and Britain. Morash argues that the specifics of the Northern Irish theatre tradition make it impossible to represent true conflict, because the motivations and the apparent mindlessness are 'unrepresentable'.[61] Further, he argues 'while the Irish tradition provided playwrights with a model that all too readily accommodated the conflict, the dark logic of terror remained, for the most part, beyond the glare of the stage lights'.[62]

In the glare of this 'dark logic', can the dramaturgy of this play be defended? It might be argued in the face of an intractable and relatively inflexible social reality, that a redemptive fantasy is far more opportune, even if commitment gives way to naïvety. That way, a successful change of circumstances are not grounded out inch by inch, compromise by compromise, and negotiation by negotiation, but is achieved through flights of fancy. (Jones does the same in *Stones in his Pockets*, where Jake and Charlie write a movie script and are successful, thereby the extras become stars and the stars extras in some carnivalesque-type Hollywood-inspired inversion (despite it being the imperial enemy), whereby a team of put upon almost no hopers overcome the odds and are victorious.) Can fantasy be the ground upon which accusations of misogyny and sectarianism may be downplayed?

Maybe not everything dramatically has to be about intractability, analytical interrogation of causes and grievances, or about head-on collisions between immovable forces and irresistible objects. Perhaps, insubstantiality is a fundamental component of letting go, as it is partially about playing with the idea, unsettling it from its embeddedness, mobilizing it, and unleashing it under the radar of conscious vigilance. In some ways it is about enablement through sleight of hand – a bit like letting the air out of armbands little by little until eventually a child is swimming with no support, by allowing them to trust in a buoyancy that is not theirs, when in fact it is. Ashley Taggart argues 'For many in this society, upholding tradition can be a life-or-death matter, and the inability to obtain lasting peace, a real amnesty, is very much an inability to create the necessary amnesia.'[63]

MAN CHILD

While this play is a coyly subversive piece of theatre, entrenched within its own political ambitions, the play is still far more than Marie's and Kenneth's big (bogus) adventure. There is no political or sectarian correctness in Jones's representations. There is a huge difficulty in attempting to address both tribal perspectives with balance and impartiality. Moreover, she opts for a classic everyman figure who has no real serious crimes against his name. For many, Kenneth is a dubious endorsement of change. Despite all of the perceived limitations, it is the variable of performance that rattles many of the contesting and disregarding perspectives on the play. On the two occasions I have seen the play, the role of the actors, Dan Gordon and Marty Maguire, in their representation of multiple characters generate different faces, postures, gestures and tones. Such animation undermines the contention that the play represents a simplistically pejorative version of loyalism only. The concept of play is about dissonance, transience, about the space in between, when awarenesses are both heightened and multiple and where the hold of reality is conceded somewhat and its rudimentary values contested. The acuteness of transitional, liminal space may well be the best way to mobilize an 'amnesty', side by side with 'truth and reconciliation'. The approach needs to be multiple, double-jointed and flexible for each to play off each other. Jones offers nothing as ornate as a 'fifth province of the imagination', as Field Day espoused, no purification of the past and the anticipation of wholeness. Of course, to use a football analogy, changing one's preferred/dominant foot is not the same as kicking with both feet. Regardless, Jones offers a prefiguration of agency, out of innocence. Part of the *Oxford English Dictionary*'s definition of innocence is a 'freedom from cunning or artifice; guilelessness, artlessness, simplicity: hence, want of knowledge or sense'. Jones exploits each of these terms for her own ends. Artifice is the ultimate coup.

BORN AGAIN

Innocence can be a fantasy space or pipe dream that enables as well as disables, chasing it down can be a delusion, rejecting it can be a crime, and puncturing of its possibilities destructive. A nation consumed by its innocence is afraid of its shadow, guilt, its capacity to destroy or violate, and is also tempted by the naïvety that it brings to identity formation and the self-focus and self-absorption it prefigures, without tellingly linking it up to anything beyond the self. Innocence can provide no enabling function, but a disabling one, when it is restrictive, inhibitive and manipulative innocence is a fallacy.

There is nothing original about innocence as it is fractured and incoherent and always catalyzes into something else, in such a way that meaning is constantly postponed. However, if innocence is regarded as performative, for them, the term implodes. Thus, innocence is a high-risk business. In McGuinness's *Innocence*, the quest for innocence is made problematic within the frame of this play, for neither a naturalized, pastoralized innocence nor a redeemable religious innocence is accessible. Innocence cannot embrace the compromises, violence, rage, destructiveness, vengeance and pettiness of living without losing its fortitude. In *A Night in November* the naïve character as notionally innocent is a defining counter to the impossibility of truth and reconciliation, of absolution, of making the soul clean. Rape and the death of children are pain validators. Sexual violation seems to be one of the best ways of calibrating innocence. Carr in *On Raftery's Hill* reinvigorates the pain–pleasure dialectic in a way that is urgent, by focusing on the exploitation and violation of innocence in terms of intergenerational compulsion that is beyond morality and personal choice. Innocence both belongs to the beholder and belies the beholder. Innocence cannot be compulsory. Innocence must be deferred and non-consensual.

NOTES

1. Frank McGuinness, *Carthaginians* in *Plays 1* (London: Faber & Faber, 1996), p.352.
2. Fintan O'Toole, *Tom Murphy: The Politics of Magic* (Dublin/London: New Island/Nick Hern, 1994, revised edition), p.94.
3. Ibid.
4. The historical abuse of children is well documented, ranging from murder, assault and victimization to mutilation and sacrifice. See Jean Renvoize, *Innocence Destroyed: A Study of Child Sexual Abuse* (London: Routledge, 1993), pp.29–33.
5. Ibid.
6. Henry McDonald ,'Bishop steps down after accusations of child abuse inaction,' *Observer*, 8 March 2009, www.guardian.co.uk/world/2009/mar/08/child-abuse-catholicism-john-magee [accessed 10 March 2009]
7. Howard Brenton with *Romans in Britain* (1980) includes a rape scene that symbolically connects imperialism and violation. Mark Ravenhill's *Shopping and F***ing* (1996) has a scene where the employer forces a potential employee to go topless before him and a young rent boy pays another male to simulate rape with a fork, in an attempt to re-enact/deal with his own torturous sexual violations, that involved a knife, at the hands of his own father, in such a way that play/simulation becomes the more extreme form of violation. There is little bleaker than Sarah Kane's work, especially *Blasted* (1995) (which brings in rape and cannibalism) and *Crave* (1998) (which incorporates details of a father who sexually assaults his own child (character A) and who also facilitates his own child's sexual violation with her grandfather in a lay-by) push the boat out further.
8. Marina Carr, *On Raftery's Hill* (Oldcastle: Gallery Press, 2000), p.35. (Hereafter, all further references will be placed in parentheses within the body of the text.)
9. 'Depression', 'anxiety', 'hypervigilance', 'dissociation', 'disengagement', 'detachment/ numbing', 'observation', 'amnesia', 'multiple personality disorder', 'impaired self-reference' are all responses to abuse. See John Briere, *Child Abuse Trauma: Theory and Treatment of the Lasting Effects* (London: Sage Publications, 1992), pp.23–45.
10. Susan Janko, *Vulnerable Children, Vulnerable Families: The Social Construction of Child Abuse* (New York: Teacher's College Press, Columbia University, 1994), p.50.
11. Some commentators/therapists try to dismiss as unhelpful the victim–evil binary structure, because it does not cater sufficiently for rehabilitation of the abuser, especially when the abuser has been a victim him/herself previously, but if one cannot insist on the validation of victimization, what can one agree on?
12. Janko, *Vulnerable Children*, p.6.
13. The impact of abuse has a number of dependent factors, including the 'duration and frequency of the abuse', 'multiple perpetrators', 'presence of penetration intercourse', 'physically forced sexual contact', 'abuse at an earlier age', 'molestation by a perpetrator substantially older than the victim', 'concurrent physical abuse', 'abuse involving more bizarre features', 'the victim's immediate sense of personal responsibility for the molestation' and 'victim feelings of powerlessness, betrayal, and/or stigma at the time of the abuse'. See Briere, *Child Abuse Trauma*, pp.5–6.
14. Ibid., pp.xvii–xviii.
15. Christopher Bagley, and Kathleen King, *Child Abuse: The Search for Healing* (London and New York: Tavistock/Routledge, 1990), pp.106–07.
16. Carr's characters are so attuned to their own destructiveness in *Portia Coughlan* and *By the Bog of Cats*. Portia Coughlan in the former and Hester Swane in the latter are so traumatized by past events, Portia by the death of her twin and Hester by the abandonment by her mother, that it might be said that they are women/children, confined by a worldview, locked into a moral rationality that is not appropriate to the adult world. Hester dies with the words 'Mam – Mam –' – the same final words were spoken by young Josie, as she was killed by Hester (p.80). Sebastian Barry's *The Steward of Christendom* (1995) has Thomas Dunne as the play's central character. He lives his final years in a mental institution. The play opens with the words, 'Da, Da, Ma, Ma' (p.72), and ends with a story that involves 'the mercy of fathers' (p.133). (The ghost of his dead son also visits Dunne.) JPW in *The Gigli Concert* (1983), motivated by drugs, vodka and magic, delivers the parodic line 'Mama! Mama! Don't leave me in this dark' (p.39), as he tests the limits of possibility. Innocence as a redemptive consciousness is never far away.
17. Joe Vanek suggests that the play *Innocence* was marked 'by a refusal to be frozen by anachro-

nism – *Innocence* did not belong to a specific period' as the design 'incorporated Victorian fires, fifties chairs and a lot of modern junk' into an 'ostensibly Renaissance setting, thus ensuring that the play was seen not merely as a museum piece'. 'In Conversation with Derek West', *Theatre Ireland*, 29, Autumn 1992, p.26.

18. Caravaggio's 'revolutionary technique of tenebrism, or dramatic, selective illumination of form out of deep shadow, became a hallmark of Baroque painting. Scorning the traditional idealized interpretation of religious subjects, he took his models from the streets and painted them realistically'. Source: www.kfki.hu/~arthp/bio/c/caravagg/biograph.html

19. McGuinness states in his 'Introduction' to *Plays 1*: 'I pieced together a fiction of his life based on a reading of the clues I imagined he'd left in his paintings ... I tried to make him a poet and in his poetry would be his painting. I used the city of Derry as my model for the Rome of his day' (p.xi).

20. Frank McGuinness, *Innocence* in *Plays 1*, p.247. (Hereafter, all further references to this play will be placed in parentheses within the body of the text.)

21. Hiroko Mikami, *Frank McGuinness and his Theatre of Paradox* (Gerrards Cross: Colin Smythe, 2002), p.54.

22. Ibid., p.55.

23. BBC interview, 1 May 1987, quoted ibid., p.70.

24. Speaking of the 1980s, McGuinness argues: 'It is irony that destroys our claims to innocence. It is time to face experience. The poet William Blake wrote songs of innocence and experience. Is he a model for the writer in contemporary Ireland? Do we need a visionary radical with the propensity for seeing angels? No, so the time is not right for another De Valera ... Innocent? We're in it, up to our necks.' Frank McGuinness, 'I am not confident for my country's future', *Irish Times*, 25 December 1989, p.8.

25. Program Note, quoted by Mikami, *McGuinness and his Theatre of Paradox*, p.59.

26. The red cloak appears in *The Crucifixion of St Peter, Judith Beheading Holofernes, Supper at Emmaus, The Deposition, Rest on Flight to Egypt, The Taking of Christ, Madonna del Rosario* and *The Death of the Virgin*. Both the horse and the cloak appear in *The Conversion on the Way to Damascus*, and in *St Jerome* the skull and cloak appear.

27. See Derek Jarman, *Caravaggio* (London: Thames & Hudson, 1986). Jarman's film uses some of the techniques to reframe the works of Caravaggio that McGuinness also utilizes.

28. 'The Death of the Virgin was refused by the Carmelites because of the indignity of the Virgin's plebeian features, bared legs, and swollen belly'. Source: www.kfki.hu/~arthp/bio/c/caravagg/biograph.html

29. In the painting *St John the Baptist* the Youth with the Ram serves as a homoerotic image, as does the naked child Jesus standing on the snake in *Madonna with the Serpent*.

30. Emmanuel Cooper notes that Caravaggio in the painting *The Conversion of St Paul* 'used an image of physical and earthly passion, posing him [Paul] in the physical position of the receptive partner in homosexual love making'. *The Sexual Perspective: Homosexuality and Art in the Last 100 Years in the West* (London: Routledge & Keegan Paul, 1986), pp.20–21.

31. Tom Murphy deploys a similar image of inversion with the goat inheriting the kingdom of God in *The Sanctuary Lamp* (Dublin: Gallery Press, 1984), p.72.

32. The play can be partially read as a reworking of William Blake's poems the *Auguries of Innocence* and *Songs of Innocence* ('For he hears the lamb's innocent call').

33. Internationally, many commentators wish to map a direct relationship between most Irish plays and what was and is perceived to be the Northern crisis, loosely labelled 'The Troubles'. So even a play such as Martin McDonagh's *The Lonesome West* (1997) seems to have encouraged readings and responses as if it was about tensions between rival ageing brothers in the West of Ireland, and as a comment on a process of peace and reconciliation between two rival factions. In one sense the grasp for metaphor and myth over more realistic-type representations is central to that inclination.

34. Stewart Parker, *Dramatis Personae* (Belfast: John Malone Memorial Committee, 1986), pp.18–19, cited by *Marilyn Richtarik*, 'Across the Water: Northern Irish Drama in London', *South Carolina Review*, 2001, www.clemson.edu/caah/cedp/Ireland%20PDFs/Richtarik.pdf [accessed 2/7/07]

35. Christopher Murray identifies three particular dramatic templates used by Northern Irish playwrights: 'The O'Casey model', which captures the social and political interface; 'The Romeo and Juliet typos', the mixed-marriage type of drama; and 'The theatre of Hope', plays that wished to represent mobility and change. See *Twentieth-century Irish Drama: Mirror up to Nation* (Manchester: Manchester University Press, 1997), pp.189–94.

36. Mitchell himself recently experienced death threats from the loyalist community in which he grew up, and had to go into hiding.

37. Paul Mercier's *Kitchen Sink* (1996) opens with two adult actors pretending to be children playing on a building site. Owen McCafferty's *Mojo Mickybo* (1998) relies on two actors to recreate the world of children and from the bias of the child. The blurring of the adult/child becomes all the more problematic within the frame of metatheatricality, especially in Donal O'Kelly's *Catalpa* (1996), or John Breen's *Alone it Stands* (1999). However, the predominance of masculine characters in a large group of plays that benefit from metatheatricality suggests that within these, the victory of ineffectual masculinity may be problematically indulgent.

38. Marie Jones, *Stones in his Pockets* and *A Night in November* (London: Nick Hern, 2000), p.63. (Hereafter all further references will be placed in parentheses within the body of the text.)

39. The Greysteel massacre happened on 30 October 1993. Three members of the UFF killed seven people, claiming that it was a 'revenge killing' for what the PIRA did with their bomb on the Shankill Road, which left nine dead plus the bomber.

40. Kenneth had never travelled south of the border: 'We were taught to be afraid, to be afraid of the black magic, the dark evil, the mysterious jiggery Popery that'll brainwash us' (96).

41. And beyond the experience of the play, as this New York production at Douglas Fairbanks Theatre attempted to do. 'The power and emotion created in this play has also spilled out into the streets, thanks to a mural outside the theatre ... describing events in Northern Ireland over the past century, painted by Northern Irish political muralists Danny Devenny and Marty Lyons.' See Mary Trotter, Performance Review (14 November 1998), *Theatre Journal*, 51–3, 1999, pp.336–39, www.muse.jhu.edu/journals/theatre_journal/v051/51.3trotter.html [accessed 2/7/07]

42. It could be argued that there is a fear about women having the transformative possibility of the mask, as McMullan points out in a comment cited in chapter 2, or the belief that masculinity has a greater affiliation with play, something which her earlier work with Charabanc would contest.

43. Imelda Foley, *The Girls in the Big Picture: Gender in Contemporary Ulster Theatre* (Belfast: Blackstaff Press, 2003), p.50.

44. Christopher Morash, *A History of Irish Theatre 1601–2000* (Cambridge: Cambridge University Press, 2002), p.263.

45. David Grant 'Breaking the Circle, Transcending the Taboo' in *The Power of Laughter: Comedy and Contemporary Irish Theatre*, ed. Eric Weitz (Dublin: Carysfort Press, 2004), p.45.

46. Tom Maguire, *Making Theatre in Northern Ireland: Through and Beyond the Troubles* (Exeter: University of Exeter Press, 2006), p.140.

47. Ibid., p.139.

48. Ibid., p.154.

49. The Downing Street Declaration (15 December 1993) affirmed the right to 'self-determination' for Northern Ireland, and the right that the solution to the troubles would be an all-island one, made space for paramilitaries to enter talks. An IRA ceasefire followed on 31 August 1994, and on 13 October the Combined Loyalist Military Command followed suit.

50. As children, their play went from cowboys and Indians to UDA and Special Branch men interrogating and killing Fenians (p.85). This is an example of how early sectarian divisions are fostered and uncritically internalized.

51. Brian Logan, *Guardian*, Saturday 13 July 2002, www.arts.guardian.co.uk/print/0,4460636 –110430,00.html [accessed 1/7/2007]

52. Foley, *Girls in the Big Picture*, p.51.

53. Fintan O'Toole, 'A Night in November', *Irish Times*, 5 December 1995, reproduced in *Critical Moments*, ed. Julian Furay and Redmond O'Hanlon (Dublin: Carysfort Press, 2003), pp.157–59.

54. See Gerry Moriarty, 'British Army paper illustrates respect for IRA', *Irish Times*, Saturday 8 July 2007.

55. Maguire, *Making Theatre in Northern Ireland*, p.142.

56. Ibid.

57. Joe Cleary, 'Domestic Troubles: Tragedy and the Northern Ireland Conflict', *South Atlantic Quarterly*, 98–3, 1999, pp.501–37, p.505, www.muse.jhu.edu/journals/south_atlanticquarterly/ v098/98.3cleary.html [accessed 12/7/07]

58. Mária Kurdi, 'Spatializing the Renewal of Female Subjectivity in Marie Jones's *Women on the Verge of HRT*' in *Echoes Down the Corridor: Irish Theatre – Past, Present, and Future*, P. Lonergan and R. O'Dwyer (eds) (Dublin: Carysfort Press, 2007), pp.118–19.
59. Mark Phelan, 'The Fantasy of Post-Nationalism in Northern Irish Theatre: *Caught Red Handed* Transplanting the Planter', *Performing Ireland*, B. Singleton and A. McMullan (eds), *Australasian Drama Studies Special Issue*, 43, October 2003 pp.89–107, p.102.
60. Ibid., p.103.
61. Morash, *History of Irish Theatre*, p.246.
62. Ibid.
63. Ashley Taggart, 'Theatre of War? Contemporary drama in Northern Ireland' in E. Jordan (ed.), *Theatre Stuff: Critical Essays on Contemporary Irish Theatre* (Dublin: Carysfort Press, 2000), pp.67–83, pp.77–78.

'Always the Real Thing':
Contesting the Pastoral

'THAT'S NOT THE WEST'

In recent years the Irish plays that were either most often performed or in receipt of awards were plays about the West of Ireland, from Martin McDonagh's Leenane trilogy, especially, *The Lonesome West* (1997) and *The Beauty Queen of Leenane* (1996) is set in Leenane, County Galway in the mid-west. Kerry, in the south-west, provides the backdrop for Marie Jones's *Stones in his Pockets* (1999) and the not defined 'Northwest Leitrim or Sligo' area (the 'or' has its own significance) is the location for Conor McPherson's *The Weir* (1997). From the earlier generation of Irish writers, Brian Friel's *Dancing at Lughnasa* (1990) is set in Friel's imaginative composite locale, 'Ballybeg', of County Donegal, again in the north-west, and it is also the setting for almost all of his plays. *Lughnasa* has been hugely successful internationally. (The responses of audiences to productions of *Lughnasa* where the pastoral is foregrounded makes it a play equally worth considering in this chapter, although I have chosen to structure my response to *Lughnasa* on a different approach.)

To group these west of Ireland dramas in any totalizing fashion would be incorrect, as they are all so radically different. But what all four writers provide are competing, commodified and marketable versions of pastoral Ireland, as different forms of Ireland's 'west', from north-west to south-west, are shepherded in and there is both a surrender to and sundering of these pastoral idylls.

Terry Gifford calls attention to Roger Sales's claims that the pastoral represents 'refuge, reflection, rescue, requiem, and reconstruction'.[1] According to Gifford, Sales's view is that the pastoral 'is essentially escapist in seeking refuge in the country and often also in the past: that it is a selective "reflection" on past country life in which old settled values are "rescued" by the text; and that all this functions as a simplified "reconstruction" of what is, in fact, a more complex reality'.[2]

My aspiration is to test Sales's five categories and to propose that the pastoral can be less limiting and conservative, and indeed more challenging and original than suggested by Sales, especially when applied to west of Ireland plays.

In general terms, Mária Kurdi suggests that Ireland's west is 'a geographical and historical unit as well as a cultural construct'.[3] Elizabeth Butler-Cullingford reminds us that the pastoral exists across the range of Irish literature:

> Even though de Valera's ideal of frugal self-sufficiency was the product of wartime necessity, it resonates ideologically with the image of Yeats raising his beans and gathering honey in a 'small cabin' on an isolated island. Seamus Heaney has also dug into the rich peat of the Irish pastoral although (like de Valera but unlike Yeats) his roots have real earth on them.[4]

Across the media and culture, the west of Ireland is romanticized, particularly Connemara, equally by those who live and do not live there. Its rugged landscape, the perceived, relative sterility of its soil, its isolation, its strange combination of intensity and waywardness, its eternal longing, the consolations of nature and the sanctuary of the landscape are pitted against the cruelty of the natural environment and the sea, its sense of danger, its subsistence and its perceived lack of sexual intimacy between characters not in relationships and with no real prospects of one, if they so desire. Shaun Richards identifies the function of the west of Ireland as being 'the cornerstone of the Literary Revival'.[5] And for contemporary audiences, it is the 'cornerstone' of something at least as fanciful.

Contemporary productions of Irish plays, in general, devise a certain type of 'west' and international and metropolitan audiences construct a notion of this locale that has little relation to how people live in non-urban Irish settings. In general terms, the 'west' embodies a consciousness that is driven by a feel for the authentic, for a recourse to a grounded sense of identity that is harmonious and not fractured. Moreover, it is an idea of the 'west' that needs to be performed, but performance does not necessarily make it inauthentic. As Colin Graham points out, Adorno in *The Jargon of Authenticity* offers a critique of authenticity as 'a jargonized ideology travestying what it represents',[6] which 'hinges on disrupting the edges of its claims to wholeness and organicism, and its ability to become a self-sufficient ideology and way of speaking'.[7] In many ways it is the insufficiency of the pastoral, despite its wholesomeness, that is made problematic in contemporary Irish theatre.

THE COLONIZER'S TRAJECTORY

The other question is this: should the pastoral, in terms of Ireland, be also given a postcolonial context? On the one hand, in colonial narratives there is the romanticization of the native, in terms of naïve innocence and, on the other, there is the violent indiscipline of the self-same group that warrants rigorous and oppressive control. Fundamentally, the absence of authenticity on a fully civilized level is in part the justification for imperialism, which of course disguises the economic and political dimensions behind subjugation, repression, stereotype and bias. In the face of such objectivizing of transactions between the imperial power and the host nation, Graham sees the quest for authenticity as being part of the cultural revival of the late nineteenth century and the revolutionary, recuperative endeavour that is built around it.[8] Graham suggests that while authenticity may play 'a key role in Irish culture, the function of authenticity in colonial and postcolonial terms in an Irish context will not, because of its liminality, follow the coloniser's trajectory'.[9] Gareth Griffiths similarly argues that 'for Homi Bhabha ... the possibility of subaltern speech exists principally and crucially when its mediation through mimicry and parody of the dominant discourse subverts and menaces the authority within which it necessarily comes into being'.[10] Graham quotes David Lloyd, who suggests that 'it is the inauthenticity of the colonized culture, its falling short of the concept of the human that legitimates the colonial project'.[11]

However, the colonial past allowed the Irish nation to be more comfortable with the vagaries of modernism and industrialization. Gibbons argues that because of its fraught history, 'Irish society did not have to await the twentieth century to undergo the shock of modernity: disintegration and fragmentation were already part of its history so that, in a crucial but not always welcome sense, Irish culture experienced modernity before its time.'[12] This is a clear upgrading and complication of an older binary postcolonial model. Endless postcolonial readings can be misconceived, as the issues are not so much the 'subaltern', with the baggage of dominance, repression and dehumanization, more, a key problem is 'sub-pastoral' identity, where marginality, acceptance and indulgence go hand in hand with submissiveness. What may well be missing is an internalized subordination or masochism. Indeed, a more defined sense of an existential, if incomprehensible and displaced self may be perceived. A curious superiority is to be found in the position of the sub-pastoral character, because it is laced with perceived authenticity.

JAMESTOWN – SLIGO/LEITRIM

The Weir is set in a pub, in 'Northwest Leitrim or Sligo' (p.2), but is not specifically located and is 'inspired by places McPherson visited with his grandfather, whose death, according to the playwright, cast an influential shadow over the play's creation', according to Scott T. Cummings.[13] His grandfather lived in Jamestown, County Roscommon. (Interestingly, pastoral spaces are often without specific dimensions, remaining ill-defined, being no space and every space simultaneously.) The pub functions symbolically as a fantasy and communal locus and as a narrative space, where inebriation offers a sense of relaxation and gives a certain type of licence. The stage direction states that 'This bar is part of a house and the house is part of a farm.'[14] In John B. Keane's *The Field* the pub setting is a location where children play and domestic violence occurs; it is a place of auction, crooked deals, false alibis and interrogation. Both pub spaces in the dramas of Keane and McPherson are noted for their isolation, strangeness and simultaneity of function and for the potential for violation. Likewise, in *The Weir* time merges: historical time is layered on real time and mythic time runs concurrent with naturalistic time.

The intimate stage design for the Royal Court production of *The Weir* was created to satisfy, in part, the quest for authenticity. Many reviewers connected with the voyeuristic experience for the audiences, as if being let in on a secret way of life. (The whiff of peat is equally important.) Can the play establish the concept of authentic space or, more vitally, authentic time? *The Weir* interrogates such concepts, however contaminated and contagious they may be, by considering the implications of the way narrative forms identity. McPherson also maps the pastoralization of space and how the pastoral is summoned into being through narrative. The liminality of the pastoral, to use Graham's definition, ensures the contestation of dominant ideologies, in terms of the urban–rural and class divides. The pastoral does not dispute a disintegrated reality, rather it affirms a retrospective positioning and the fantastical tenacity of the 'life lie', as Henrik Ibsen called it.

It is as if simplicity confirms authenticity because it gives access to certain ways of being, modes of understanding and structures of integrity. Yet the sleight-of-hand, of course, is that such simplicity is almost always marked down as inauthentic, because the pastoral lives remain relatively unlived, relatively unsullied by the compromises of first-world capitalism and thus not matured or hardened by the vagaries of such living. The fact that many of the characters in the above named Irish pastorals can structure their lives primarily around single narratives rather than multiple narrative formations is a similar marker against complex living. Simplicity as a sign of authenticity is false, principally because of the absence of complexity.

SNUG IN A PUB

The characters who gather together in *The Weir* are two pub customers, Jim and Jack, the proprietor, Brendan, a businessman, Finbar, who now lives close by but not in the immediate vicinity, as he once did, and Valerie, who has moved from the city to find some consolation after the death of her daughter and the collapse of her marriage. The locals are the 'natives' whom Finbar will bring Valerie to meet (p.5). The term 'natives' has the whiff of the oriental and the macabre; they are outside the values of dominant culture. The males happen to be primarily non-threatening and non-predatorial. They rile each other, knowing what buttons to press, but they also protect each other. When it is Jim's round, they decline a drink, making it a cheap round for him, and it can be performed with such subtlety that the exchange can be inoffensive.

Jack lives alone. Jim looks after his ageing mother. Brendan does not share his life with anyone. Finbar lives with his wife, but we do not learn much about her during the course of the evening. Valerie, the new arrival, intends to live alone. The pub space is not generally accessible, culturally, psychologically, or symbolically to women. Coincidentally, the ladies' toilet is broken. From the interactions of the characters, the specific dimensions of the pastoral are multiple. *The Weir* offers a world where one's own labour has meaning and relevance and where an act of kindness has communal ramifications. Truths are not sought in the minutiae or in any complex analysis of detail, but in the overview and in dated structures of comprehension. The pastoral is a space where defiance of the larger world order can be articulated, with sentiment but without indulgence. The fetishistic vantage point of the pastoral is consistent with its unpredictability, but is tied in to the relatively regular cycle of the seasons and the rhythms of the natural world, with the harmony and affirmation that these offer. All of these combine to generate a sense of authenticity.

The pastoral is also the space where life questions can be asked, without seeming a threat. Brendan says that Jack is urging him to 'sell the top field' (p.4). Jack remarks that he will persist with the questioning: 'Jack ... I'll keep at you though ... A young fella like you' (p.7). Brendan enquires of Jim: 'Do you think you'll do anything?' (p.9) – if anything happens to Jim's mother, will he sell the place and move elsewhere?

Later Jim asks of Brendan: 'You still wouldn't think about clearing one of the fields for a few caravans?' (p.11). This is one of the key markers of the pastoral. It provides relatively free-speaking, communal spaces where burdens can be shared, questions asked with concern and personal issues are within the public domain.

In terms of the pastoral the rural is more important than the urban, the natural world matters more than the industrial one, and community matters more than individuality. The pastoral landscape of *The Weir* reinscribes community and it also foregrounds dependency, even if the characters are marked by their aloneness.[15] Co-dependency is thus the validating feature and is seen as consolatory. It is a reactionary but also convenient and conventional fallacy. Such interdependence is also, indirectly and implicitly, critical of the audience's own subscription to dominant ideological social formations, given the demise of the extended family and the emergence of the more narrowly focused nuclear or blended family and the increasing individuation of societal arrangements. Jack: 'You know, there's company, all round. Bit of community all spread around the place' (p.28). Later he reaffirms the same sentiment: 'There's a lot to be said for the company. And that ... you know ... someone there' (p.45). It could also be cogently argued that community and connection are the fundamental fantasies of first-world capitalism.

The fact that the pub is not there necessarily to make profit is underlined. It is a space where the landlord is one of the 'boys', where customers can serve themselves and can be trusted to put the price of a drink in the till, and where the exact amount is not required to pay for a drink. At the end of the night Jim is given a free 'small bottle of whiskey' to take home with him (p.42). This is neither an Irish theme pub on any famously named international high street or boulevard, nor is it a Celtic Tiger business venture; this is something different. The gombeen man, chancer, hard-nosed money-man, Finbar, is the opposite of these values. He says to Brendan: 'I wouldn't say that you see too many twenties [pound notes] in here' (p.17). This shows arrogance and absence of generosity. Further details follow: 'Finbar: ... I went to town to seek my fortune. And they all stayed out here on the bog picking their holes' (p.13). In reality, Finbar sought his fortune not in hard work, but in Big Finbar's will. So success is not hard-earned. Dramaturgically speaking, it makes it easy for audiences to take an instant dislike to him. Jack states that Finbar would 'peel a banana in his pocket' (p.17). Not only is he wealthy, he is mean. The tension is as much between local and foreign as it is between capitalism and communal benevolence.

BLOWING IN THE WIND

To be intimate one needs to be local and also one is obliged to live at a level of subsistence, financially, socially and emotionally speaking. 'Blow-ins' is how the Walsh family members are regarded (p.24). The Danes or Norwegians, who are seasonal visitors, are lazily labelled 'Germans', who are accused of sitting around 'playing all old sixties songs on their guitars. And they don't even know the words' (p.49). (As such we get a sense of a high disregard for outsiders, who seek the *faux* authentic feel, believing themselves to be acting like locals.) When the non-Irish nationals are present in the pub, Jack and Jim sit around like a 'couple of old grannies' and later the phrase 'auld ones' (p.49) is used by Brendan to describe their unsettled demeanours. They are any-thing but warm, hospitable and friendly, as the tourist guidebooks would have it, in having to share their space. It must be noted that their unease is seen primarily in feminine terms. Valerie, as a city person, faces resistance, both as a woman and as a blow-in.

Another dominant trope within the frame of the pastoral is sexuality. Sex, within the pastoral context, is seldom about promiscuity or intima-cy, but abstinence, interpersonally at any rate. Brendan is annoyed that Finbar may have sexual interests in Valerie. 'Brendan: The dirty bastard. I don't want him using in here for that sort of carry on. A married man like him' (p.6). Those who defy the limits placed on sex are seen as aberrations: 'Conor Boland. He's over the other side of Carrick there. Has about fifteen fucking kids. Dirty bollocks' (p.49). Within the pastoral, as Nicholas Grene argues, there is an obvious emphasis on the 'persistent celibacy or late marriage amongst the men', while women are situated as 'edgily desired' sex objects 'in a heavily repressed society'.[16] The sexually repressed is not the key, but one component part of the pastoral, and it would be foolish to think otherwise, as some critics would have it. The characters can be curmudgeonly, but also sociable, caring and giving. Thus, generosity and the understanding of and empa-thy for another's loss may be the ultimate markers of something labelled 'authenticity'. Bourgeois culture consistently rediscovers carnival,[17] and it does likewise with pastoral, as this mode offers a fundamental return to a rootedness.

ROYAL COURTED

When McPherson was commissioned to write a new play by the Royal Court's artistic director, Stephen Daldry, the agreement between the writer and the theatre stipulated that the new play must not be another monologue. *The Weir* is what McPherson delivered.[18] From the apparent naturalistic tradition of Irish theatre, McPherson, inspired most of all by Friel's *Faith Healer* (1979), allowed in a rival sensibility, ensuring that story-telling spaces are liminal ones, between the conscious and the unconscious, between reality and dream life. However, the links between story-telling, the ghost story, memory and the past, and between identity and narrative formation, within the frame of the pastoral, are the facets of *The Weir* that most interest me. By means of memory, something additional is allowed to enter the frame. Truths and trust link up in a way that ensures that communication is intimate and deliberate, particularly through the form of narrative. Here all the characters, apart from Brendan, tell a story. Brendan through his lack of narrative desire is perhaps the most grounded character.[19]

In a play so inhibited and immobile in terms of space and movement, narrative offers consolation, through the framework of otherness and through the manipulation of absence. In Murphy's *Bailegangaire* (1985) Mommo constructs meaning through traditional story-telling. An audience can be drawn in by the spell of the story, can begin to generate imaginative worlds, and can construct a reality based on the details provided by the teller. In Frank McGuinness's *Someone Who'll Watch Over Me* (1992), the characters alter through the faculty of story-telling. They grow by embracing each other's stories and by psychologically absorbing the testimony and resistance at the core of another's narrative. The absence of a reluctance to tell is vital.

FRIGHT VICTIMS

Personal stories emerge as the individual begins to assemble the sensations and memories of trauma or pleasure. Stories or experiences set to memory, shaped as narrative, are ways inside a private world. They give access to a level of spirit or internal realities that normal interactions do not make available. In Ireland, people tend to exchange stories more than they involve themselves in discussion or debate. Dialogue often takes the form of narrative. Sometimes people exchange/inhibit the same conversations/narratives again and again, even with the same people. In *The Weir* each character has some dominant memory or remembrance narrative that provides a sense of where he/she has come from and of the events and circumstances that have shaped each of them.

Each character has his/her own internal narrative rhythm that is made external through narrative activity. So, the characters trace themselves through narratives and locate themselves too by marshalling the narratives of others. Throughout the play's action, individual characters are placed by and placed within narratives, as the narrator is simultaneously inside and outside the role. A personal story can become an individual's fixation, a way of constructing a sense of self. The story can also be a way of seducing the listener into a way of thinking and is a means of postponing judgement and of seeking acceptance. If a narrative breaks down or if one can no longer make sense of the world through one's own narrative, then problems emerge. Personal narratives can also use differing distancing features. One can disguise the personal relevance of a story by filtering it through different temporal or spatial frames, or one can displace oneself from the centre of such narratives. One can also, as the characters do in this play, strain individual concerns through imaginative narratives or narratives like personal stories, heresay and ghost stories.

From the point of view of the spectator, does one listen for the flaws and contradictions in the story being told or will the entry point be simply acceptance? Or might one interrogate the clues that point to something else (for often beneath what is said or hurried over, something altogether different is happening)? The relative coherence of the story does not necessarily presuppose a coherent subjectivity, because there is no 'aboriginal or "true" self to which we can return for guidance', according to Ciarán Benson.[20]

Benson deploys Antonio Damasio's framework of 'proto-self, core self and autobiographical self'. The first two are 'largely under the automatic control of the brain in its body', and the final category, 'while dependent on the constantly self-renewing foundations of the proto-self and the core self', is still 'significantly a matter of learning'.[21] Autonarratives duly enable and inhibit. In them we are also operating within the specificity of play and its efficacy. Play adds to articulation by making it sensual and also by sensationalizing memory formation. There is also the reformulation of the performative self through narrative delivery. Narratives are driven partly by the requirements of a form that demands the delivery of a story with impact. The narrative imperative is to ensure that the teller is most alive because between the narrator and audience a form of community is negotiated. The concept of play is in a way not so much about ratifying an older sense of being; rather, its looseness is its primary insistence, releasing both the predatoriality and the territoriality of identity. Identity is fabricated thus as much out of the narrative structure as it is out of the variables of performance.

It is the agreed, shared ritual of narrative exchange that offers, in part, the consolation of the pastoral. Then there is also the national narrative; Ireland as a nation has primarily structured its narrative on defiance, misfortune, hard luck, missed opportunity, and disaster. Giving coherence to the story comes at the expense of the chaos. While it is difficult to let go of the past, it is something that cannot be changed, but one can challenge its meaning and the significance given to it. It has to be said that international audiences, in particular, enjoy such a traumatic burden when articulated emotively in theatres by characters from nations other than their own or by circumstances that are unusually isolated and/or past tense.

Jack's story centres on Maura Nealon. She was a bit of a trickster and enjoyed scaring people. His story is a response to the sounds and noises of the natural world as if these confirmed the presence of the supernatural. The wind is like 'someone singing', according to Jack (p.21). Bridie, Maura's mother, disbelieved initially her daughter's responses to the strange happenings and eerie sensations. Then she too heard lowdown knocks on the door that shook her. The local priest is asked to come round to pray. It is revealed that the 'house had been built on a fairy road' along which the fairies would progress to 'bathe' (p.22). The noise returned to the house when the Weir was being built, according to Maura. Dead birds were the only other sign of unnatural disturbance. Valerie, on her first night in the neighbourhood, learns that her recently purchased house may be haunted, whatever that happens to mean.

Finbar's narrative is next and, rather than diminish the threat implicit in local folklore, his own is again about the supernatural. Niamh Walsh has an experience after consulting an Ouija board. Her parents pick her up from a friend's house. Once back home there was the presence of a ghostly woman on the staircase. A priest was called again. Later the same night, the family received a telephone call, announcing the death of a previous neighbour, an old woman who used to baby-sit the girls when they were young. As he had been called upon to offer assistance to the Walsh family, Finbar ended the evening by staying up all night, as he was unable to face the staircase.[22] While Jack's story does not involve him personally, Finbar manages to place himself indirectly within the narrative. The events affected him enough to force him to give up cigarettes and to move away from the locality soon afterwards.

Jim's story becomes more personal again. Despite being sick with the flu, he had responded to a request from (another) priest in a distant parish to open a grave. While Jim worked alone, a stranger arrived and told that he was digging the 'wrong grave' (p.32). The stranger pointed out an alternative resting place for the dead male, a place where a recently deceased young girl had been buried. Later in a newspaper Jack saw a photo of the deceased man, who was the 'spit of your man' he had 'met in the graveyard' (p.32–33). This person was a 'Pervert' who had abused children (p.33).[23]

Finbar wants to put a halt to things: 'We've had enough of them old stories, they're only an old cod' (p.37). Dominic Strinati discusses Tzvetan Todorov's distinction between three forms of horror: 'the uncanny', 'the marvellous' and 'the fantastic'.[24] With the 'uncanny' the supernatural 'can be explained by rational explanation or logic', for what initially is inexplicable, by the end falls within the framework of knowledge. Thus resolution is realizable. With the 'marvellous', 'seemingly irrational or incomprehensible events can only be explained by accepting, for the purposes and duration of the film or story, the existence of another level of reality', namely, the supernatural. Finally, 'the fantastic' where inexplicable and supernatural events are 'attributable neither to rational explanations, as with the uncanny, nor to an altered level of existence, as with the marvellous', and as a consequence, a degree of 'hesitation' emerges, a hesitation that could be read as excess or lack in equal measure.[25] One of the strengths of *The Weir* is that it works within all three categories.

DEATH POOL

The males may have used the form of the supernatural narrative against Valerie, both consciously and unconsciously. She is, in a sense, an intruder upon the male preserve, just like the non-Irish nationals. But from such a position of subtle weakness, Valerie brings something radical to the action. Unlike the narratives of the men, Valerie's story is of a different order. Married to Daniel and with a good job in Dublin City University, her world is turned upside down when her daughter, Niamh, is drowned in a swimming pool accident. As a young girl, Niamh had anxieties: 'Valerie: ... But at night ... there were people at the window, there were people in the attic, there was someone coming up the stairs. There were children knocking, in the walls. And there was always a man standing across the road whom she'd see' (p.38). In addition, Niamh feared abandonment.

Valerie calmed her by inviting her to phone her if she was ever at all worried. After the child's death, Valerie received a phone call. 'Valerie: I couldn't hear what they were saying. And then I heard Niamh' (p.39). Niamh wanted to be collected and brought home. 'Valerie: ... I mean, I wasn't sure whether this was a dream or her leaving us had been a dream' (p.39). It is intimated that Valerie's hold on reality is suspect. Finbar is most unnerved by the revelation, but Brendan supports Valerie's convictions. Explanations are offered by all for the supernatural elements in the previous stories. The supernatural is thus naturalized. Jim was suffering from flu and had been drinking when he had his experience; Maura Nealon was a heavy drinker and therefore she is not to be trusted; the Walshes were 'fucking headbangers', and Finbar's own experience is excused by the fact that he got 'the wind put up' him that night (p.41).

As Finbar departs, he asks that they go easy on Valerie. Jack intervenes telling Finbar to stop 'being an old woman' and declaring that she will be grand (p.42). When Jim leaves, he remarks that the dead child, Niamh, is 'a little innocent' (that word again) and he promises to pray for her (p.42). Valerie's narrative leads to the most intimate story, delivered by Jack. Once in love, Jack's girlfriend went to work in Dublin. The relationship stalled. One day he was told that she was about to get married. He turned up for the celebration as an invited guest. Upset by the occasion, he left the church 'like a little boy' and went to a bar, where the barman made him a sandwich (p.46). Jack nearly started to cry, so moved was he by the act of charity. His former girlfriend has become a ghost. 'Jack: ... there's not one morning I don't wake up with her name in the room' (p.47). Although he says 'at least' it wasn't 'a ghostly story', it, in fact, is. He is haunted by his failure to be more responsive and responsible by turning down an opportunity that would have required compromise and acceptance. Instead he felt it better to hold out, but for what?

Maturation may be about the acceptance of death at a deep level. Of course, the tradition of singing a song and telling a story also overlaps with something else – wake rituals. The play is in a way a wake for Valerie's dead daughter and other lost things. The characters might be seen to be enacting a wake ritual through ghost stories. The play thus works on one level as a pastoral elegy. Further, for Julia Kristeva, death is a site of abjection. People avoid corpses and the talk of death in order to live. Conversely, people tell stories in order to accommodate the ideas of death in a distancing fashion. Sue Vice cites Kristeva's notion that 'the corpse, most sickening of wastes, is a border that has encroached upon everything', it is 'death infecting life'.[26] Death is containable within the pastoral. But the sense of order associated with the pastoral landscape and the cohesion imposed by the play's form promise one thing and deliver something else. It appears as if the pastoral offers containment, but it does not. Jack states that they will 'all be ghosts soon enough', adding that all of them will 'be sitting here. Sipping whiskey all night with Maura Nealon' (p.47). In the pastoral, loss, or a communal acknowledgement of it, to put it more accurately, is ultimately the key ingredient. In the lived world, loss has less and less currency or value.

Although Valerie's company is regarded as 'inspiring', Jack wonders if the rural escape is the best place for her, a location where stories of ghosts will have 'all her worst fears confirmed' (p.47). Jack apologizes, knowing what they attempted to do to her. Brendan ends up giving Valerie a lift home. Before she leaves, Jack holds her jacket 'for her to put it on' (p.48), a gesture which confirms the chivalrous values of the pastoral. The men will disconcert Valerie greatly and attempt to drive her away through fear, but they still will hold up a coat, open a door and buy her a drink. They project on to her their incomprehension and their anxieties. The centring of Valerie's trauma, within her own story, in a way that the male figures could not achieve within their own narratives, is significant, as is the symbolic situating of the feminine at the core of the psychic space itself. It has frequently been noted that in some Irish plays women serve only a symbolic function, and little or nothing beyond that. In general, for Lynda Henderson, women in Tom Murphy's plays, for example, 'play supporting roles of literal catering, managing, conniving', but they have no access to the 'metaphysical debate'.[27] Anne F. Kelly argues that women in Murphy are partly there to 'carry meanings that the male characters cannot reach. They are the necessary complement, the anima to the male animus – not subjects in their own right.'[28] Does Valerie have access to the 'metaphysical debate' or the supernatural debate, or is her function just an enabling one? I think she enters the 'metaphysical debate' in a very confrontational way, and I will explain why a little later.

Although women are often at the centre of the stories told by men, they are still the suppressed aspect in many ways. On one level it would be easy to argue that the function of the women in *The Weir* is to offer absolution and to tolerate the foibles and idiosyncrasies of the males. Although Valerie is new in the locality, by the end of the evening she offers to help Brendan to tidy up, something that can be read in a number of ways, namely as acceptance, domestication and as an expression of sexual interest. She also helps find his misplaced keys. Almost all of the men are defined in restrictive terms by their relationships with women. Jack's girlfriend abandons him, Jim's is concerned for his ageing mother, and Brendan feels constrained by his sisters and by the absence of a woman in his life. There is a deep sense of abandonment that the male characters shy away from but which becomes apparent in their monologues.

Valerie's attractiveness is seen in very unusual terms. Jack says that Finbar will be in 'sniffing around Valerie every night anyway' (p.50). And he extends the idea to say that Finbar will be 'like a fly on a big pile of shite' (p.50). The inappropriateness of this comment is realized and apologized for. But it is interesting none the less to speculate how audiences respond to the lapse into bad manners. Is it what they expected all the time? Behind the veneer of casual good manners, the pastoral is replete with such clumsy inarticulateness. Only the story-telling, which is frequently rehearsed, is fluent, while all else is fragile and almost inexpressive. The tolerant woman, in the form of Valerie, accepts the vagaries of the ageing, mainly single men. Brendan had just earlier mentioned listening to the Danish sing while he 'picked' his 'hole' (p.49). Tolerance is part of what is widely expected from the feminine within the context of the pastoral.

For the characters, the pleasure of fear, the arousal surrounding the feeling of being scared, the comfort that such sensations are generated in a public arena, and the satisfaction garnered from individual contributions to the process of multiple story-telling and co-dependency release all kinds of complex sensations. Nothing seems inflected, exaggerated or convoluted in Valerie's story. While she relies on the form of narrative, which requires continuity and cause and effect, what she adds is the voice of reality. Her pain is apparently real and the ongoing trauma acute. But is that to align woman with the reality principle, the calling back from fantasy? If so, it has to be acknowledged that feminist critics have grave difficulties with such practices. Does she find a subjective position, and/or does she articulate a narrative from her own interior reality? Or does she make her story up?[29] If she makes it up, then hers is the most exploitative endeavour of them all, not only playing the male characters at their own game, but also beating them. This is not to say that Valerie usurps the narrative process and so undermines the male characters. I simply propose it as a possible reading against the urgency of definitive interpretations of written texts themselves. If we look at things more closely, it could be argued that she mimics their narrative forms, subversively, coincidentally or otherwise.

MAMET TASK

Certain details are common to Valerie's story and those told earlier by the male characters. What initially prompted my idea is that Valerie's daughter's name is Niamh, the same name as the Walsh girl who dabbled with the Ouija board. Then, further similarities, without denying other obvious dissimilarities, become apparent. Some of the connections are very similar; others require some licence. Regardless, they are worth identifying. For instance, Finbar is disturbed by Mrs Walsh's knock. Maura Nealon heard knocking low down, like a child's knock, in Jack's story, and in Valerie's story 'there were children knocking in the walls' (p.38). Likewise, Valerie's Niamh fears a 'man standing across the road' (p.38), which echoes the pervert in the graveyard in Jim's story. There is a blanket placed around Niamh Walsh and Valerie's daughter, after the accident in the swimming pool, is wrapped in a towel. Maura Nealon's house had been vacant for five years and Valerie went back to work five years after Niamh's birth. Valerie's husband 'teaches engineering, at DCU' (p.37), the construction of the Weir is one early topic of conversation. And there is more. A doctor sedates in Valerie's story, as in the story about Niamh Walsh's family. The pervert in Jim's story wanted to get into the grave with the young girl, while Valerie wanted to lift her daughter out of 'the coffin' (p.39). Valerie gets a phone call from her child after her death, and, similarly, phone calls are central to the Walsh family story. Niamh Walsh phoned her mother and asked her to 'come and collect her' (p.25), while Valerie's Niamh asks her mother to 'come and get her' (p.39). Notionally, the Ouija board in Niamh Walsh's story becomes the telephone line in Valerie's tale, as both are the medium of communication between the living and the dead: 'If she's out there?' (p.40) Valerie exclaims, hoping to find ways of making contact with the dead. Also, Valerie's daughter dies in a swimming pool accident, while, coincidentally, the house she has bought is on a path along which the fairies supposedly travel in order to bathe.

Additionally, David Mamet, the writer who inspires McPherson, constantly utilizes the confidence trick in both his film and theatre work. Jack accuses Finbar of fabricating a local history: 'Jack: "The history of the place". You were probably making it all up on the spot, were you' (p.18). Before Brendan's sisters get to the home-place, earlier on that day, they have a meal in the nearest town in order to 'get their story straight' (p.5). So the play suggests fabrication as a key ingredient of local history and the agreeing on a specific narrative as a form of bargaining. Likewise, in the preface to *St Nicholas* and *The Weir*, McPherson talks about inventing a story about being attacked by a seagull to amuse his friends:

> Christmas for most of us can be very busy. Catching up with friends in pubs for nights on end … I decided to break the ice by telling each new person I met a big lie … The first thing people

would say after I'd said this was, 'Is that true?' Because although they didn't believe me, we live in a world where we don't expect complete strangers to lie to us. Not in pubs at any rate. But it's nice in theatre.[30]

There is mischief not only in McPherson inventing stories, but also in his inclusion of such a narrative in a preface to a play about story-telling and public houses.

Almost all the fears, terrors and anxieties mentioned by others previously in their narratives re-emerge, intentionally or not, in Valerie's story. As a woman, she had become the figure for male projections. They wished to frighten her in order to actualize their own fears and to keep them, perhaps, within the realm of the feminine. Fear arousal marks also the process or the potential for sexual arousal, and that cannot be discounted. Valerie's story has at its core a girl-child's death, a mother's grief, and male incomprehension of that grief. She centralizes a female, a tragic victim, at the core of her story. Valerie is no 'fright victim', and, perhaps, we can begin to see her as a fright aggressor.[31] Whether or not Valerie's grief is actual or aggressively performative does not need to be decided upon definitively, but in order to circulate as many potential meanings for a play in performance, I think it needs to be considered, given the notoriously unstable nature of meaning within dramatic texts themselves. If gender and racial concerns can be foregrounded or diminished through production choices in relation to any text, then why not the female contestation of the theatrical space in terms of a play like this? I believe there has been ample evidence expressed here to support this view.

Within the pastoral, characters may be confined by a sense of space, imprisoned by narrative and inhibited in part by community, yet immobility is a comfort rather than a state of severe or extreme anxiety. Is there something wrong with stability, with less complex encounters, when the individual spirit can operate outside the network of complexity demanded by contemporary living? Terry Gifford reminds us that 'retreat can also offer a temptation to disconnection, an escapism from complexity and contradiction'.[32] Instead of seeing the pastoral as a colluding, conservative force, it might be more apt to regard it as the comfort and the illusion of idealization. Such an understanding may account for the ambivalence of many towards the play itself.

PRAIRIE DOGS

McPherson's play does not offer some quixotic, quaint, unproblematic and homogenizing pastoral fifth province – a *Little [Public] House on the Prairie* – where disabling myths can be confronted and recalibrated. Instead what is foregrounded is the clash between the aspiration for connection and belonging of the pastoral and the disassociation and remoteness within the urbanized but not philistine world. The pastoral in *The Weir* is neither recuperative nor contestational of dominant ideo-logy, rather it is indicative of otherness, part dependent on its mysteriousness and on its transgressive tendency to undermine a material reality. Its relationship to the real is deeply suspect. Although it can be commodified by accelerated cultural transformations or by mutations that accumulate around it, the pastoral is, perversely, almost radically subversive in its conservatism. Given the fractured nature of modern society, Christopher Morash suggests that the monologue form suited McPherson. Since 'stories are no longer common property', what the characters in *The Weir*

> can share is the recognition that each is alone with a story of ghostly contact. These stories cut across the differences in class, gender and geography that in earlier Irish plays would have provided dramatic conflict. In a sense, the real ghost in *The Weir* is the ghost of an earlier, communal theatrical form.[33]

While *The Weir* is neither anti-pastoral nor 'post-pastoral', to use Gifford's phrase, it is a metapastoral, constructed around narrative and performance and dominated by the excesses of play, where lives and encounters are to be narrated, where stories manage to part explain, reconfigure and enact the past, offer it a coherence and delineate how one positions oneself within the narrative of living. Audiences must determine whether they are acted upon by narrative or propositioned by narrative, whether they are playing out narrative expectations and imperatives or shaping them. The peripheral position of the pastoral allied to its psychic viability ensures that the survival strategies, the ability to cope with major human diversions, the collapse of relationships or death are vital. The capacity to survive in a world marked by ordinariness rather than adventure is a trait of all of the play's characters. Within that, a cycle of recovery or integration can occur after a journey of darkness or a profound sense of disintegration has been experienced. What is vitally embedded is the sense of a core narrative that resists first-world living, where that self is constructed around a series of interlocking contradictions. The coherence of the self within the confines of the trauma of the pastoral is a great draw.

The impact of Valerie's story or potential fabrication is to ground the other characters into the realities of their own lives. Is that not the mystery of theatre itself; the fundamentally false illusion of the performance can bring the spectator to heightened awarenesses, perceptions and intuitions? In that sense, theatre is a confidence trick whereby pretence and contrivance can relate some sort of truth. *The Weir* is based on the illusion that sanctuary is possible within the frame of the pastoral. McPherson offers a space where the charade of authenticity is contested. Valerie, as a city person and as a woman, does so brilliantly as she is the one most alert to the need to contest dominant ideologies and modes of relating. Through its breakaway from wholeness and through its mishandling of authenticity, *The Weir* sanctions something altogether different. The characters tell stories that are deceptive and conceal deeper intent, yet, ironically, through acts of inauthenticity and malicious fabrication authenticities may be found. In *The Weir*, from dubious subjectivities, from gender objectification and from the paradox of pastoral liminality, the mischievous otherness of pastoral implausibility and mutability emerges.

MCDONAGH'S 'GOING NATIVE'

Martin McDonagh has had a very successful career in terms of box office and international awards, and his plays have been produced internationally, either using the original script as a starting point for productions or in translation, but, to date very few permissions have been given for adaptations of the work. Productions are obliged to work within the parameters of the published texts, and any serious deviations from the constraints and imperatives therein are discouraged or disallowed. As with all writing, it is possible to interrogate McDonagh's plays for dominant values, for repetitive or biased dramaturgical patterns and gender prejudices, as well as to test the work against current theatrical trends and traditions.

Evaluations of McDonagh's work to date have relied substantially on the complex relationship between theatre space, language, character and action, and more significantly, on the connections between the written and performed texts and the Irish contexts in which the majority of the plays are set. All the plays have been brushed by a range of critical analyses that relies on everything from Marxism to postcolonial theory, from feminist and gender evaluations to an interrogation of the postmodern imperatives and post-dramatic inclinations in the work.[34]

What interests me is how the conventions of a notional pastoralized naturalism informs but also limits the texts in unusual ways, and more substantially, how issues surrounding verisimilitude, mimetic realism and context, in political and socio-economic terms, seem to be the dominant but not the only frameworks through which critics and commentators take the plays to task, particularly for their transgressions of pastoral authenticity.[35]

Those who write what is considered to be realism/naturalism are tested by their ability to mimic the real world accurately, are measured by how appropriately the past is accommodated in the present, are checked to ensure that the relationship between cause and effect has some grounding in normality, verifiability and plausibility, analyzed to see if the physical utilization of the stage space is governed by the physical expectations of the real world, and, finally, are checked to affirm that language has some communicative coherence. (In production, gendered and age appropriate performances are deemed satisfactory if they are in tandem with expectation.[36]) Additionally, spectators seem to have in-built proxemic expectations surrounding the staging of intimacy and conflict between characters and around initiation, reflex and response rhythms in terms of actions and reactions of actors in performance, to comments, gestures and revelations. So, the expectations, assumptions and perceptions around realist staging are in part about credibility, in part about the suspension of belief, and in part about trusting the dramaturgy of the writer and the *mise-en-scène* of the production to harmonize or to at least find equivalence of stage action with perceptions of what constitutes the lived work. However, as Hanna Scolnicov rightly advises, 'It is only in the naturalistic theatre that the theatrical space tries to fool the audience into believing that it is essentially analogous to everyday space.'[37]

In McDonagh's work there are references to products like Complan, Kimberley biscuits, Tayto crisps, Frosties, published magazines, real television programmes and football championships, and there are references to real people and circumstances such as the Guildford Four, the Birmingham Six and the events of Bloody Sunday and other historical incidents, which suggest some brush with reality. There are always other trends and tendencies that suggest a deviation away from such realities.[38] Temporal cohesion and specificity are denied across the Leenane Trilogy, because no specific time period can be absolutely established from the facts of the play. McDonagh simplifies character motivation and deprivileges a depth model. Equally, his language is governed not by a naturalness that reflects people in normal living situations, but by the plasticity of language, by the deliberate heightening and extension of words and

Fig 1: Ensemble *Dancing at Lughnasa* (Photography courtesy of Abbey Theatre Archive)
(Photograph by Amelia Stein)

Fig 2: Brendan Conroy and Fiona McGeown in *Translations* (Abbey Theatre) (Photograph by
Paul McCarthy)

Fig 3: Stephen Rea in *Double Cross* (Photograph courtesy of Field Day Archive)

Fig 4: Ensemble *Observe the Sons of Ulster Marching Towards the Somme* (Abbey Theatre)
(Photograph courtesy of Abbey Theatre Archive)

Fig 5: Joan O'Hara and Olwen Fouéré in *By the Bog of Cats* (Abbey Theatre)
(Photograph courtesy of Abbey Theatre Archive)

Fig 6: Karl Shiels and Aidan Kelly in *Howie The Rookie* (Peacock Theatre) (Photography by Ross Kavanagh)

Fig 7: Ensemble *The Weir* (Royal Court) (Photograph by Ivan Kyncl)

Fig 8: Anna Manahan and Mick Lally in *A Skull in Connemara* (Druid Theatre) (Photograph by Ivan Kyncl)

Fig 9: Anna Manahan and Marie Mullen in *Beauty Queen of Leenane* (Druid Theatre)
(Photograph by Ivan Kyncl)

Fig 10: Frank McClusker and Lalor Roddy in *The Lonesome West* (Lyric Theatre/An Grianán
Theatre co-production)
(Photograph by Stanley Machett)

Fig 11: Don Wycherly and Catherine Walsh in *Eden* (Peacock Theatre)
Pauline Flanagan in *Bailegangaire* (Peacock Theatre) (Both photographs by Paul McCarthy)

Fig 12: David Tennant in *The Pillowman* (Royal National Theatre) (Photograph by Ivan Kyncl)

Fig 13: Ken Stott in *Faith Healer* (Almeida Theatre) (Photograph by Ivan Kyncl)

Fig 14: Denis Conway and Garrett Lombard in *The Walworth Farce* (Druid Theatre) (Photograph by Keith Pattison)

phrases, and delivered is a surface language that is ungrounded in sub-text, reliant on uncensored offence, blatancy, immediacy and naïvety, and is often completely not alert to the implications or effects of comments. These facts have huge implications for the staging of the work.

McDonagh is accused sometimes of inaccuracy in his representations of the west and he has been held to task for his approach.[39] What obligations does the writer have to the idea of authenticity? Some would argue that the writer is duty bound to reflect as accurately as possible the dealings and coercive dynamics of the 'real' world in which the play is set.[40] Others would argue that there is no requirement for any text to be either historically accurate or authentic, that texts, in this instance, written or performed, have no obligation to truth or integrity, yet when it comes to race, class or gender representations it is more difficult to sidestep the issue. If a writer does not query patriarchy, it might be argued that he/she is an agent of it, if the writer does not challenge prejudice, inequality and injustice, but simply reproduces it, distorts or adds to it, then he or she may be regarded as having racist leanings.

My argument will tease out the implications for the pastoral if space, language and character are unhinged from authenticity, and ask whether it is a reductive or liberating dramaturgy, or both? When it comes to McDonagh's work, few commentators and spectators seem guided by Scolnicov's thinking around the relationship between the real and the conventions of dramatic realism. Garry Hynes, as the director of the Leenane Trilogy, sees the work, as mentioned in my introduction, as an 'artifice': 'It's a complete creation, and in that sense it's fascinating.'[41]

PLASTIC FANTASTIC

Taking my cue from Hynes, the dramatic worlds as imagined by McDonagh are not defined by specificity, symbolic or abstract variables, but instead as spaces where not only are co-ordinates blurred but where associated meanings are amplified beyond almost all recognition and at the same time are bled dry of relevance. McDonagh's work seems to withhold the very notions of verisimilitude from the *mise-en-scène*, not so much by defamiliarizing it or estranging it, but by over-familiarizing it, by leaving the stage world in a decontextualized vacuum. In that way, pastoral realities evaporate; words both exceed their meaning and betray an absence of meaning and characterization veers away from a sensibility of roundedness or cohesion towards the grotesque.

McDonagh's first three plays, *The Beauty Queen of Leenane* (1996),

A Skull in Connemara (1997) and *The Lonesome West* (1997),[42] collectively known as the Leenane Trilogy,[43] all had Irish premières, even though they were co-produced by Druid Theatre, Galway and the Royal Court, London. The next two plays, *The Cripple of Inishmaan* (1998)[44] (Royal National Theatre) and *The Lieutenant of Inishmore* (2001)[45] (Royal Shakespeare Company), opened in London and Stratford-upon-Avon, respectively, and are the first two parts of an Aran Islands trilogy.[46] So, the first five of his performed plays, prior to *The Pillowman* (2003) (RNT) were set in notional west of Ireland locations, written by a young man reared in London who was deemed by many to be an Irish playwright by virtue of his parents hailing from Ireland.[47]

The five McDonagh plays under discussion here are set in mainly stereotypical cottage settings, in the west of Ireland, either in Leenane, County Galway, or the Aran Islands, and they apparently reproduce the dominant iconography of an old Ireland that would not have been out of place in any 1950s production at the Abbey Theatre. (Placed in these spaces are characters that use language that for many might appear to be consistent with the scenography and whose behaviour is stereotypically Irish, at its crudest, belligerent and drunken, those twin prongs long disparaged as the dominant drivers of the stereotype.) As there are so many of the trappings of a touristy Ireland, there is potential for detrimental and comforting expectations of audiences to be satisfied simplistically.

Theatrical space facilitates dramaturgical conventions and accommodates the collision of diverse signs, but space is almost always gendered, ideologically informed and perceived. Many traditional Irish dramatic spaces are constructed as pastoral, but also tabulated to signify values of innocence, backwardness, community and connection as mentioned in relation to *The Weir*. Yet, McDonagh seems not to embrace the symbolic or mythic possibilities of the west of Ireland spaces, instead he downplays, even disparages them.[48] Also Kiberd reminds his reader that many critics accuse McDonagh of being a 'plastic Paddy' from London

> who traduces rather than represents western people, exploiting them for purposes of caricature rather than expressing the pressure of a felt communal experience. Synge, as a gentleman from Dublin, faced similar charges, and answered by claiming to depict 'the psychic state of the locality rather than its actual sociology'.[49]

In that vein, the performance environment for *Beauty Queen* can be considered as being less about 'actual sociology' and far more about the 'psychic state of the locality', and if it is so, then it is a extremely harrowing one.

Beauty Queen is set in 'The living-room/kitchen of a rural cottage in the west of Ireland' (p.1). Identified is a 'long black range ... with a box of turf beside it' (p.1). Within this space there is a sink, rocking chair, dinner table and two chairs, a small TV, as well as 'a crucifix and a framed picture of John and Robert Kennedy' (p.1). Also of note is the fact that 'along the back wall' there is 'a touristy-looking embroidered tea-towel' which bears the inscription 'May you be half an hour in Heaven afore the Devil knows you're dead' (p.1). It is home to Mag and Maureen Folan, mother and daughter, who are locked into a destructive relationship, which by the end will lead to Mag's death at her daughter's hand, because she cruelly interfered in the blossoming relationship between Maureen and Pato and because she destroyed a letter from him to her, which asked her to go to America with him.

Immediately the physical stage environment is often perceived as attempting to establish a 'rustic' scenario that Michael Billington falls for.[50] The cooking range of *Beauty Queen* is substituted by a 'lit fireplace in the centre of the back wall, with an armchair either side of it' in *A Skull in Connemara* (p.63). These armchairs replace the 'two chairs' and the rocking chair in *Beauty Queen*. Again, a 'crucifix hangs on the back wall', and this is accompanied by 'an array of old farm tools, sickles, scythes and picks etc.'. It is home to Mick Dowd, who still stands as chief suspect in most people's eyes, in the death of his wife, Oona, some years past. He is also a grave-digger with responsibility for emptying graves to make space for new bodies. Soon he will be digging up the remains of his wife.

The Lonesome West is set in 'The kitchen/living-room of an old farmhouse in Leenane', where two brothers, Coleman and Valene reside (p.129). Their father has just been buried as the play opens. Coleman murdered him. Again on the surface it all seems too familiar – 'a table with two chairs downright, an old fireplace in the centre of the back wall, tattered armchairs to its right and left' (p.129). In addition, 'A long row of dusty, plastic Catholic figurines, each marked with a black "V", line a shelf on the back wall, above which hangs a double-barrelled shotgun and above that a large crucifix' and 'framed photo of a black dog' (p.129). *The Cripple of Inishmaan*, which quickly followed the Leenane Trilogy, is set on one of the Aran Islands, in 1934 or thereabouts, during and after the making of Robert Flaherty's *Man of Aran*. The play is about a young man, Cripple Billy, and his relationship with his community, how they handle his disability and his illnesses and maintain from him the secrets of his past and his parent's actions. Its stage environment is 'A small country shop' with a counter 'behind which hang shelves of canned goods, mostly peas. An old dusty cloth sack hangs to the right of these' (p.1). In addition, 'a mirror hangs on the left wall and a table and chair are situated a few yards away' (p.1).

The Lieutenant of Inishmore, like the previous play, is given an estimated time period – *circa* 1993. Again it is set in a 'cottage', with the usual trappings of 'a couple of armchairs' and a 'table' (p.1). A dead cat is on the table, and the wall displays a 'framed piece of embroidery reading "Home Sweet Home"'. The dead cat, it is assumed, belongs to Padraic, the madman of Aran, and this generates a need by Donny, his father, and Davey, a local teenager, to cover up the fact that the animal is dead.

Across the plays, it is the similarities rather than the differences that are apparent. All of these plays operate out of relatively fixed spaces. When there is occasional relocation, it is achieved often by not a substantial restructuring of the scenography, but by using the lighting to darken the dominant space, and the new location is framed by the narrowed focus of the lights and through the appearance of additional representative props, which are enough to suggest alternative locations.[51]

Scene 5 in *Beauty Queen* switches from Leenane to a 'bedsit in England', and to achieve this the stage is almost in darkness, 'apart from a spotlight' and a 'table' (p.34). If scene 5 shifts in *Beauty Queen* to London, *A Skull in Connemara* is relocated during scene 2 to a 'rocky cemetery at night, lit somewhat eerily by a few lamps dotted about'. Two gravestones are visible. The lighting here is like that in scene 8 of *Beauty Queen*, where 'the only light in the room emanates from the orange coals through the grill of the range, just illuminating the dark shape of Mag, sitting in her rocking-chair'. Mag is dead. The chair is moving of 'its own volition' (p.48). Lighting is used to suggest a sense of eeriness. In *The Lonesome West* the nature of the set is altered during scene 2 when Valene's new stove blocks out the 'fireplace' (p.140). Then, in *Lonesome West* the now customary external scene takes place beside 'a plain bench on a lakeside jetty', where Father Welsh and Girleen meet. The following scene has the 'stage in darkness' as Father Welsh recites his suicide note. This location is a liminal reality of sorts, between land and water, death and life.

In *The Cripple of Inishmaan* scene 3 shifts to 'a shore at night' (p.21), scene four is in the bedroom of 'Mammy O'Dougal' (p.30) and scenes 5 and 6 take place back in the shop. By scene 7, Cripple Billy has fled to Hollywood, and in this scene the 'sound of Billy's wheezing starts, as lights come up on him shivering alone on a chair in a squalid Hollywood hotel room' (p.52). It turns out that this is only a screen test, not the actuality of Cripple Billy's health and existence in America. Scene 8 is set in 'a church hall in semi-darkness', where many of the play's characters have gathered to watch a screening of *The Man of Aran*. The play's final scene is set back in the shop. In *The Lieutenant*, scene 2 shifts location to 'A desolate Northern Ireland Warehouse or some such'. James, a drug dealer, is hung upside down from the ceiling and 'two handguns are on the table stage left' (p.10), belonging to Padraic, who is in the process of torturing James. Scene 3 is set in 'A country lane'. Davey has his bike, and his sister Mairead is shooting at him with an air rifle. Scene 4 takes place back in Donny's house and scene 5 is another roadside location that operates as a temporary terrorist base (p.27). Scene 6 delivers one more 'roadside' location and scene 7 shifts back to Donny's house. 'A blood-soaked living-room is strewn with body parts ... Donny and Davey, blood-soaked also, hack away at sizeable chunks', is the location for scene 9 (p.55).

PRISON BREAK

There is greater location flexibility in these last mentioned two plays than in the earlier works, but the dominant interior settings are as before. Out of these early scenarios of homeliness and rustic subsistence, McDonagh generates carnage. In *Beauty Queen* the kitchen has been transformed into a space of torture, murder and madness. By the end the living-room is no more than a prison or asylum. The living-room in *The Lieutenant* becomes a slaughterhouse, a human abattoir, where bodies are shot and hacked up and where blood soils the entire floor. Donny and Davey set about mutilating bodies with an absent-minded casualness. The play ends with the return of Wee Thomas, the long-assumed dead, cat, whose re-entry is facilitated by him scrambling 'through the hole high in the wall stage left'. Davey remarks: 'so all this terror has been for absolutely nothing' (p.68). Donny and Davey initially contemplate killing Wee Thomas for prompting the carnage; instead the cat is offered some Frosties. The initial impulse to kill is overwritten, something most of the play's characters seldom can do. Instead, they are impulse-fixated.

By the end of *The Lonesome West*, Valene's latest batch of figurines is smashed by Coleman. Coleman uses the shotgun to blow up the new stove and to threaten Valene. The event that brings things to a crisis occurs when Coleman, who had cut off the ears of Valene's dog, takes them from a brown bag caked in blood and places them on the head of his brother. The murderous intensity of their brotherhood is brought to light by this incident, just after both had tried to make up by confessing past transgressions in order to satisfy the final wishes of the priest. However, even confession becomes competition, and it is not long before they begin to outdo each other.

During the final moments of the play Valene attempts to burn Father Welsh's letter, but a little through the process he 'blows out the flames' (p.196). He then pins the letter back on to the cross and combines it with the chain that Girleen had given to the priest. However, she would not take it back after the funeral. Valene 'attaches the chain to the cross, so the heart rests on the letter, which he gently smoothes out' (p.182). Girleen had cut the chain in two after she had delivered the suicide note from Welsh to the two brothers.

In *Beauty Queen* objects/props in space define the characters, or are an extension of their identities. The sink also functions as a way of emptying infected urine.[52] Complan, a nutrition supplement, is used by the daughter, Maureen, to force feed Mag, her mother, and cooking oil is used as an implement of torture by the daughter, and, ultimately, the poker is the final murder weapon used to slay her mother. Thus, domestic items transmogrify into something else. In *The Lonesome West* disputes over Tayto crisps become something that might lead to murder.[53] At one point, Valene's figurines of Christian saints are melted by Coleman in Valene's new oven, and Father Welsh plunges his hands into the hot concoction, having witnessed them brawl. For Father Welsh it is an act of despair, hinting at a Christian ritual of destructive self-sacrifice, which predates his final act of suicide that again has strongly sinister and perverted sacrificial overtones.

On the kitchen table, in *A Skull in Connemara*, are 'Three skulls and their sets of bones'. These remains have been taken from the graveyard, in order to make room for newer corpses. The skulls are getting smashed with a mallet, bits of which spray 'all over the room' (p.101). There is something taboo-breaking about this act. 'Mairtin: … Skulls do be more scary on your table than they do be in their coffin' (p.101). Later it is Mairtin's skull that is almost smashed, struck by a blow by Thomas.

In *The Cripple of Inishmaan* objects placed on stage will go on to have a major function in the work. The sack, for instance, has huge symbolic and material relevance. A 'sackful of stones tied between themselves, according to Helen, was how Cripple Billy's parents met their end. Billy believes 'they fell o'erboard in rough seas' (p.15). Johnnypateenmike tells Billy that his parents committed suicide, using a 'sack full of stones tied to the hands of them', so that insurance

money could be raised to get the treatment to save Billy (pp.73–74).
Kate tells Eileen the real story: 'it was poor Billy they tied in the sack
of stones, and Billy would be still at the bottom of the sea to this day,
if it hadn't been for Johnnypateen swimming out to save him. And
stealing his mammy's hundred pounds then to pay for Billy's hospital
treatment' (p.80). Of course, Billy gets to hear this revelation. His
response is to take 'the sack down from the wall, place inside it numerous
cans of peas until it's very heavy, then ties the cords at the top of the
bag tightly around one of his hands' (p.81). Before he gets a chance to
carry his actions further, Helen returns to the shop and agrees to go out
with him, having refused him earlier. Billy unties the sack and replaces
the tins. He has a reason now to live, but the TB that is in his body has
him coughing up blood. The only conclusion to be drawn is that he has
not long to live.[54] So whether it is skulls, sacks, Complan, pokers, cooking oil, figurines, dog ears or cats, McDonagh uses found objects and
animals for unusual purposes, partly to shock, partly to unnerve,
and partly to explore the fixed or reflexive meanings assigned to these
animals and to the spaces in which they are found.

GO FORTH AND MUTILATE

The use of a dialect in the plays seems to suggest something authentically
Irish as the language appears rooted in Hiberno-English. But an analysis
of the language reveals something more intricate and convoluted.
Nicholas Grene cites McDonagh from a 1998 article: 'In Connemara
and Galway, the natural dialogue style is to invert sentences and use
strange inflections. Of course, my stuff is a heightening of that, but
there is a core strangeness of speech, especially in Galway.'[55] Declan
Kiberd seems to substantiate this point, saying: 'In the use of language,
however, he remains utterly faithful to the people's speech.'[56] O'Toole
in his analysis of Garry Hynes's direction of *The Leenane Trilogy*,
suggests that she 'takes the elements of literary Western speech and
writes them out with the kind of fluorescent pens that Maryjohnny
Rafferty in *A Skull in Connemara* uses for doing bingo'.[57] O'Toole is
disassociating himself from a notion of linguistic accuracy, and seems
to support McDonagh's comment about a 'heightening' and 'core
strangeness' to words. Elsewhere, O'Toole is more expressive when he
claims that 'Gaelic is just a pale ghost behind the vernacular English of
the characters, its dead forms clinging on to an empty afterlife in the
baroque syntax of their speech'.[58] Nicholas Grene attests to the same
things but does not value them in the same way: 'where Synge put this

Hiberno-English strangeness to defamiliarizing poetic effect, in McDonagh it characteristically comes across as uncouth, ungainly and deflationary'.[59]

In her analysis of the use of Irish-English and its 'grammatical and lexicographic particularities', Lisa Fitzpatrick uses Loreto Todd's book *Green English* to argue that 'many of the key linguistic markers identified by Todd are strikingly absent' in McDonagh's work.[60] Fitzpatrick goes on to state that 'those quirks of dialogue construction that seem Irish, such as the repetition and inverted word-order, occur also in *The Pillowman*, suggesting that they are typical of the rhythmic cadences of McDonagh's plays, rather than attempts to recreate Irish speech patterns'.[61] Clearly, the language is neither authentic imitation nor fully appropriate to the settings, it is neither faithful nor a mutilation, more a mongrel hybrid form. Indeed, it could be argued that it has as much to do with how language is used in the work of David Mamet or Harold Pinter as it has to do with the Irish tradition of Hiberno-English or with English-Hiberno.

In terms of characterization, it is not so much that the characters do not sit easily in their pastoral environments; it is that many critics argue that they do not belong to or spring organically from those environments, giving rise to the accusations of implausibility and misrepresentation. On this matter, there is a great deal of dissent and opposition to the work. For Christopher Murray

> in general, McDonagh's characterization is unreliable. The characters are comic-book representations of an adult world from a child's perspective. This makes them two-dimensional, a frequently remarked point in discussion of his plays, but it also makes them inordinately cruel.[62]

John Waters argues that 'the characters do not have distinct personas or voice – all speak in the same patois of English words placed over the structure and syntax of the buried Irish. And yet, as characters they work because although lacking distincitive personalities, they do have distinct souls'.[63] Walter's final distinction is not clear to me.

For Victor Merriman the work is 'a kind of voyeuristic aperture on the antics of white trash whose reference point is more closely aligned to the barbarous conjurings of Jerry Springer than to the continuities of an indigenous tradition of dramatic writing'.[64] Merriman's argument elsewhere is that the characters are self-obsessed 'child-adults', resulting in 'the colonised simian' being reborn.[65] Mary Luckhurst, sustaining this argument, suggests that 'McDonagh is a thoroughly establishment figure who relies on monolithic, prejudicial constructs of rural Ireland to generate himself an income', and that his excesses are not radical and, further, that McDonagh's stereotypes do not undermine 'received ideas of "Ireland"'.[66]

Both male and female characters have extremely violent tendencies.[67] Maureen murders her mother, Girleen has a strong streak of violence, Mairead is hyper-aggressive, murderous and monstrous, and the brothers in *The Lonesome West* have uncontrollable violent tendencies. Coleman kills his father for insulting his hair. Padraic is sadism personified. Luckhurst believes that the characters in *Inishmore* are 'all psychopathic morons'.[68]

In relation to *The Lieutenant*, McDonagh claims that he was spurred on to write by the IRA atrocity in Warrington (26 February 1993), in which two boys, Jonathan Ball and Tim Parry, were killed. Despite the absence of justice and the destruction of innocence in the plays, McDonagh believes that the violence has a purpose:

> Having grown up Catholic and, to a certain degree, Republican, I thought I should tackle the problems on my own side, so to speak. I chose the INLA because they seemed so extreme and, to be honest, because I thought I'd be less at risk. I'm not being heroic or anything – it was just something I felt I had to write about. The play came from a position of what you might call pacifist rage. I mean, it's a violent play that is wholeheartedly anti-violence.[69]

Yet both John Peter and Michael Billington have different comments to make to Luckhurst. For Peter, when it comes to *The Lieutenant*, 'The violence is neither gratuitous nor self-admiring: it pays its way as drama because it is soaked in moral anger and lit up by the comedy of humane reason.'[70] Billington concurs: 'this is not simply a splatter play but a fierce attack on the double-standards of terrorist splinter groups'.[71]

Plays like *The Lieutenant* that deal with republican paramilitary activity are always going to be open to severe scrutiny. It could be argued that some people have for too long given resonance and depth to the motivations of terrorists. In this play, McDonagh takes out of such actions all mature reflection, personal responsibility and vision. But there are those, like Luckhurst, who believe that by so doing in *The Lieutenant* 'political substance is all but air-brushed away',[72] and 'air-brushed' for less than clear-cut reasons. Ironically, perhaps, for the Northern Irish Peace Process to move forward, in part, truth by necessity is 'air-brushed' away. The violence in the plays, as Luckhurst points out, also leaves itself open to the reaffirmation of stereotype in terms of Irishness, given the long pejorative association between Irishness and violence.

Whatever playwrights do with violence, it means that they are open to be confronted with a range of responses from irresponsibility to being puerile, even if they do, as McDonagh does, claim them to be 'anti-violence' and driven by a 'pacifist rage'. For Shaun Richards, 'what is most striking about the Leenane Trilogy's violence and depravity is the absence of any informing moral structure on which authority itself rests'.[73] The missing authoritative 'moral structure' is something that clearly irks many others as well. Fintan O'Toole's position on this is different, claiming that the world of the Leenane Trilogy is

> a version of one of the great mythic landscapes – the world before morality. It is the ancient Greece of *The Oresteia* – a cycle of death and revenge before the invention of justice. It is, perhaps more to the point, the Wild West of John Ford's westerns or Cormac McCarthy's novels, a raw frontier beyond civilization.[74]

Here, on the one hand, O'Toole is clustering the work along with those of high standing, and, on the other, he is subtly defending the plays from certain critical standpoints. In his programme note to *The Pillowman* O'Toole adds: 'His tricks and turns have a purpose. They are bridges over a deep pit of sympathy and sorrow, illuminated by a tragic vision of stunted and frustrated lives.'[75] *The Pillowman* reinforces my reading sensibilities of the earlier performed works. Whatever moral voice is harnessed in the plays, it often appears to be as perverse as it is absurd. In *The Lonesome West* Valene tries hard to emote as Father Welsh wishes him to do, because Tom Hanlon has just died, but Valene can only feign to 'bat a big eye' (p.150). Yet, in dealing with characters who struggle with empathy, morality and justice, McDonagh is prompted to express the following:

> There have to be moments when you glimpse something decent, something life-affirming even in the most twisted character. That's where the real art lies. See, I always suspect characters who are painted as lovely, decent human beings. I would always question where the darkness lies.[76]

How do the dramatic conventions of the notional real bear the weight of that 'darkness'? The dramaturgy of the plays demands some notional appropriation of the conventions of realism.

HASTY PREFIXES

In terms of realism the following words can serve as prefixes: rural, urban, middle-class and working-class, and to these one could add magic, neo-, anti-, and hyper-. The list can go on and on. Stephen Lacey argues, prompted by Raymond Williams, that a cornerstone of realism is 'defined primarily by the ambition not only to represent but also to interpret the world politically, "to show how things really are"'.[77] For McDonagh, there is no such motivation to reflect on how things were, are, or might be in his notionally pastoral, plastic environments.

McDonagh's notionally rural space is not there to mimic or to normalize behaviour but to amplify it, the props are present not so much as emblems of Irishness, but to take on an animation of their own, and language is not there to substantiate character but to show how character begins to melt at the edges, when any possible cohesion evaporates. At times, it seems as if mimesis makes way for the grotesque, and naturalized characterization moves towards archetype, stereotype and gargoyle-like representations, as John Lahr notes.[78] But as the frameworks of irony and subversion become so extensive, it becomes more and more difficult to place the work, more and more challenging to establish any dialectic or cross-current between the real and the world on stage. That way the expectations of the pastoral to be about refuge, recovery, belonging and community are deemed utterly suspect.

Regardless, Waters tussles with the concepts of reality and realism, arguing: 'It is a distorted reality, yes, but reality of a kind nonetheless.'[79] Later he adds: 'McDonagh's plays are not "real" in the sense of being naturalistic representations of reality. Rather they are impressions of reality, from a certain angle or vantage-point.'[80] O'Toole struggles in a similar way to define what is going on in the plays: he contends that the writing 'takes the conventions of kitchen sink drama and exaggerates them into a kind of dirty naturalism'.[81] Yet O'Toole evades the limits of this 'dirty naturalism' with another explanation, when he identifies the dramaturgical sensibility as the implications of two images superimposed:

> [one] is a black-and-white still from an Abbey play of the 1950s: West of Ireland virgins and London building sites, tyrannical mothers and returned Yanks ... But the other picture is a lurid Polaroid of a postmodern landscape, a disintegrating place somewhere between London and Boston, saturated in Irish rain and Australian soaps.[82]

And elsewhere again for O'Toole, 'the whole idea of theatrical realism becomes the biggest double-take of all'.[83] The disjunctions, the inappropriateness, the anomalies that O'Toole is attempting to highlight are apt indeed. Yet, that type of functionality is not unique to either McDonagh or to the Irish tradition. It is almost better to see it from another perspective.

McDonagh deals with things that have a very vague resemblance to the real, so it is not so much the superimposed photos that O'Toole mentions, rather it is the almost erased reality that frames the work – akin to the implications of unlit set, when the plays accommodate a change in location, which remains in the background, coming through in a spoiling fashion into the consciousness of the spectator, a constant reminder of its own constructed illusion. Traditionally, with realism, the real both frames drama or the interface between them, and the dialogue between both operated dialectically, with each informing perceptions of the other. With McDonagh, that too-ing and fro-ing is absent. In Samuel Beckett's work, Scolnicov argues that his

> space has no geography or topography, no within or without. Lacking co-ordinates in the theatrical space, all movement must be related to the stage, to the theatre space: characters enter from 'upstage right', not from next door or the street.[84]

Equally, McDonagh's stage scenarios may be notionally Leenane and the Aran Islands, but they lack the fundamental co-ordinates and the topography of the real, as well as the symbolic and myth resonators that accompany them. The plays operate almost totally within the co-ordinates of the dramatic spaces only, almost without reverberation. It is a space that feeds back in on itself, rather than reaching outwards. It is not a mirror up to nature or culture. In the main, it just reflects back on itself, exposing and exploring its own dramaturgical conventions, self-reflexively calling attention to itself as a construct, as all notions of a relationship with the real are siphoned indiscreetly away. If it can be accepted that the sociological dimensions are almost absent or deviant, then the usual ways of testing the ideologies of a text are stretched to their limits.

It relies as much on what the spectator offloads as meaning, as on what the plays themselves generate as meaning through performance. The spectator is very active in projecting on to performance. It is about the prejudices of perception. In McDonagh's work existential questions are not packaged through the anxieties, self-questioning, or self-recognition of the characters, more it is the responsibility of an audience to reflect on the minimal cognitive functioning of characters, their instinctive, unfiltered behaviours and the tokenistic narratives through which they structure their consciousnesses and justify or legitimize their behaviours, unlike Jack's or Valerie's narratives in *The Weir*. So the fitted-out space is almost decluttered of the real. Discussing Anton Chekhov, Michael Fryan argues that:

> The traditional function of literature in general, and of drama in particular, has always been to simplify and formalise the confused world of our experience; to isolate particular emotions and states of mind from the flux of feelings in which we live; to make our conflicts coherent; to illustrate values and to impose a moral (and therefore human) order upon a non-moral and inhuman universe; to make intention visible, to suggest the process by which it takes effect.[85]

However, for Fryan, Chekhov fails to follow that approach. Likewise, McDonagh refuses the ruse to put moral 'order' on his universe and by so doing, he centralizes 'flux' and the immorality of certain violent actions in particular. Like Chekhov, McDonagh imposes no system of justice; justice never gets in the way of anything. So viewing the work of McDonagh as having some uncomplicated relationship to the real and directly to the pastoral is indeed utterly futile and redundant.

HOW THE WEST WAS WON

Declan Hughes sees McDonagh as 'a Connemara Orton',[86] in effect Connemara and its pastoral subtext filtered through the attainments of Joe Orton's dramaturgy, suggesting something garish, fantastic, violent, parasitical and grotesque. The major missing ingredient is the sexual licence of Orton's work.

Yet, it is another Connemara that the critics seem to get hung up on most. McDonagh does not seem to be in the least interested in the romance of authenticity. Instead he offers semiotic indicators of a hollowed-out Irishness, one that has lost all significance beyond the replica, the caricature and the redundant.[87] Yet for all its absence, there is something energetically abundant and buoyant about the work. The conflicts are not simply universal, about mothers and daughters, brother battling with brother, fathers and sons pitted against each other. The relationship is not with the truth of things, but with the context. McDonagh brings the incongruous to everything, even to poverty and murder. Truth does not prevail. The good Samaritan Ray, Pato's brother, is almost murdered in *Beauty Queen* by Maureen. In *The Lieutenant* McDonagh makes relevant the spurious politics of morality, those who justify murder, who vest in themselves the authority to distinguish between 'legitimate targets' and not. Reality is the 'collateral damage' and integrity is the first victim of internal paramilitary 'friendly fire'. In *Lonesome West*, Father Welsh states that 'God has no jurisdiction in the town'; reality likewise has no jurisdiction. O'Toole is alert to the critical accusations against McDonagh (rather than against the work or both), and he argues that McDonagh is 'inauthentic, in the sense that his Ireland is, to them, unreal'.[88] O'Toole adds:

> Leaving aside the fact that comedy, however dark, does not aspire to realism, this seems to miss the point that he is in fact entirely true to his own place – that strange territory, half real and half dream world, known as exile. Pato Dooley in *The Beauty Queen of Leenane* sums up the convoluted ambivalence of a hyphenated identity: 'when it's there I am, it's here I wish I was, of course. Who wouldn't? But when it's here I am ... it isn't there I want to be, of course not. But I know it isn't here I want to be either.'

The imagination of McDonagh is not an occupied or usurped space, in the colonial sense. Instead, it is a hypenated space, a consciousness not brought about by exile, but by the existential condition of exile–home, margin–metropolis dichotomies. His works' relationship with reality is almost immaterial, as he disorientates and betrays any coherence. McDonagh seems to take a delight in inviting conventional naturalistic responses to the work but then twisting these conventions for another purpose. Further, he almost seems to take up the invitation to take the test of Irishness and Hiberno-English, knowing that he may fall short, more, desiring to fail and wanting to be accused of carelessness and ineptness. His provocative intuitions take him beyond language, character and illusionary space, towards a sensibility that queries motivation, sensitivities and embellishments to such an extent that all is found wanting, whether it be communication, commitment, terrorism, pacifism or social fidelity. McDonagh generates a reality that refuses to be bound up with old pastoral images of the west of Ireland. Indeed the plays become in part a plastic pastoral, a sort of replica pastoral, yet bizarrely and acutely alert to the poverty and implications of it on those living at subsistence levels.[89] Kiberd warns that the 'native quarter' in 'postcolonial literature and film is often a zone visited by touristic outsiders in search of a frisson'.[90] International audiences may hanker after that 'frisson', either unaware or uninterested in the fact that in McDonagh's work the west is a fiction, bled of its emblematic resonances, for myth is a curious anomaly and affliction, and symbolism is at best a stereotype and at worst a corrosive caricature of all that is deemed authentic. Because of the apparent roughness, inappropriateness, tactlessness and incompleteness of the plays, some critics lose no opportunity to confront them, but it is a bit like taking Pablo Picasso's later works to task because they are not especially accurate.

STONES IN HIS POCKETS: THE WRITERS STRIKE (BACK)

Marie Jones attempts to interrogate a pastoral west as envisaged by Hollywood film productions. A filming process provides the backdrop to *Stones in his Pockets*. Jones's well-worked point is that through the pastoralization of its Irish landscape, Hollywood, in the main, attempts to sell deranged versions of authenticity through the filtering of stereotypes that are convenient to audience expectations, representations that are not only carefully nurtured but also remain generally unchallenged. Gareth Griffiths is quoted by Colin Graham, who notes how 'an overdetermined narrative of authenticity and indigeneity characterizes rebirths of the old authenticities, whether these are used to sell or purchase the "authentic" once-colonised'.[91] Such a comment is not only pertinent to Jones's play, but to many others within the pastoral tradition. To the film crew, neither the local cows nor the film extras are Irish enough. For Jean Baudrillard, as Graham relates, in the 'midst of disintegration', 'authenticity here has ceased being a measurement of value (or even a proof of "true" existence) and becomes a sign of the need for such values'.[92]

GOING ETHNIC

In the performances that I have seen, there is a series of ads for a local hairdresser, jewellery shop and Chinese restaurant in some Irish town. The conceit is that the play the spectator is about to watch has been made into a film and that what you are about to witness, really is Jake and Charlie's movie, which has gained general release. There is also an advertisement for a forthcoming Hollywood movie – *The Quiet Valley*, the one central to the play itself. In the movie, the peasant Rory marries Maeve, the local landlord's daughter, during the Land League Wars in the 1870s–90s, and now that he is owner of the big house and the land, he is 'going to hand back the land to the people'.[93]

In the play itself the actors playing Charlie Conlon and Jake Quin share fifteen roles and the quality of the performances relies on the skills and dexterity of the characters and on the script itself to expose the values, ironies and contradictions of the film-making process itself. Of the four performances of the show I have seen, only Conleth Hill and Seán Campion collectively, the stars of the first production, displayed the necessary nuance, measured momentum and dexterity needed to keep the play focused.

The Hollywood star, Caroline Giovanni has great difficulty in getting her accent as authentic as possible, and of course that fixated ambition isolates the fact that nothing else is in any way authentic, particularly the movie they are making, which is full of basic historical inaccuracies and utterly ridiculous in sentiment, trying to exploit the injustices of land ownership, evictions and poverty.

The title of Jones's play is derived from the suicide of Sean Harkin, who after his first unsuccessful attempt to kill himself, re-enters a river laden down with stones in his pockets. The spectator has no real feel for Sean, despite how he is introduced to the play and despite the testimonies about him from others. Sean's suicide is well integrated in the second act, but as a plot device it is thin, as an audience has no real opportunity to generate empathy for him and really he never moves beyond the cliché of a disgruntled, angst-ridden, disillusioned, drug-taking 17-year-old male. Sean makes but a few brief and abrupt appearances during the first act. The cast will not be released for the funeral as fresh flowers are to be shipped from Holland and three catering companies are booked in for the film's wedding feast scene. The extras threaten to withdraw their services if they are not allowed to go to the funeral. Given that they are paid by the day, and given that many of the scenes have already been filmed, it would be necessary to reshoot the scenes again, so if the extras were to withdraw their services, a new power dynamic would come into play. The insensitive film producers are forced to relent to their demands, as a compromise is reached.

Moreover, if Hollywood exploits unspoilt backdrops, film extras and village communities in a disturbing manner, and if the locals in turn exploit what is available to them, then Jones's own narrative drive is partly based around the suicide of an extra (Sean Harkin), within the frame of her drama. He is a character whose trauma, because it is only primarily stipulated second hand through the sentiment of others or through flashback, is never given true presence, due weight or significance. Fundamentally, on a dramaturgical point, Jones is almost equally culpable of the type of exploitation and appropriation of which she accuses Hollywood. (Why not *Stones in her Pockets* and why not Charlene and/or Jackie as the main characters?) The urbanites of Dublin 4, Aisling and Simon are deemed almost non-Irish, and the locals fundamentally Irish. Hollywood is the enemy for destroying Sean's dreams and the world of drugs offering the only ecstasy that he can find. According to his friend Fin, Sean's 'virtual reality' comprises 'drugs and movies' (p.46). But it is not as simplistic as that.

Caroline romanticizes the west, seeing it as magical and mystical, the film producers want the input of the landscape at the expense of almost all else, and the locals in their need, greed and ambivalence co-operate until their rebellion in response to the demand to film during Sean's funeral. Jones's dramaturgy is not radical if it relies on the sentiment of native rebellion and subversion in the form of her two characters generating a script. The creative Irish extras win out, as they will make their own rival, dissident and authentic movie – telling it as it is – a sort of behind the scenes kiss-and-tell. In Charlie and Jake's movie, the blockbuster film extras will be the main characters and the main characters of the Hollywood film will have minor parts. This is not subversion that is pure, unsullied, Hollywood. Jones is susceptible to Hollywood's triumphal narratives, where the individual, through some act of will, overcomes impossible odds and succeeds, and she also commodifies such tenuous motivation needlessly. In the apparent victory of the weak (Jake and Charlie) over the strong (the Hollywood production team), the indigenous trumps the foreign imperial or the cultural colonization. Hollywood's hold on the representation of Irish pastoral is contested and accommodated by Jones.

For Joseph Grixti, according to Steve Neale, the horror genre 'propagates a sense of helplessness central to the maintenance of modern consumer culture'.[94] In terms of pastoral, that sense of helplessness must be investigated. The apparent absence of broader politics is significant in the pastoral context, in contrast to most Irish theatre writing in the 1980s that felt far more obligated to be addressing remorselessly issues of identity formation, history, subjectivity and nationhood.[95] Pastoral authenticity is an inappropriate framework for the plays under discussion here, and that ultimately generates interpretative confusions and misunderstandings. Inauthenticity can be seen as the fault line or fatal flaw, but it may also be its opposite. These plays take place in the gap between the 'gallous story' of postcolonialism and the 'dirty deed' of postmodernism, between the illusionary sanctuary of a rustic pastoral and a vengeful pastiche version of it, between the narrative focus of traditional Irish theatre and beyond truth or meaning in the sensation and perception focuses of the post-dramatic theatre.

NOTES

1. Terry Gifford, *Pastoral* (London: Routledge, 1999), p.7.
2. Ibid., pp.7–8.
3. Mária Kurdi, *Codes and Masks: Aspects of Identity in Contemporary Irish Plays* (Frankfurt on Main: Peter Lang, 2000), p.41.
4. Elizabeth Butler-Cullingford, *Ireland's Others: Gender and Ethnicity in Irish Literature and Popular Culture* (Cork: Cork University Press, 2001), p.9.
5. Shaun Richards, '"The Outpouring of a Morbid, Unhealthy Mind": The Critical Condition of Synge and McDonagh', *Irish University Review*, 33, Spring 2003, pp.201–14, p.202.
6. Colin Graham, *Deconstructing Ireland* (Edinburgh: Edinburgh University Press, 2001), p.140.
7. Ibid., p.139.
8. In his analysis of *The Quiet Man*, Colin Graham reminds us that Mary Flaherty, a designer, had created an 'authentic reproduction' of a Galway Shawl for Maureen O'Hara, who starred opposite John Wayne in the film. Graham claims that the 'shawl is typical of ... the inexhaustibility and centrality of the authentic in Irish Culture', *Deconstructing Ireland*, p.133.
9. Ibid., p.141.
10. Gareth Griffiths, 'The Myth of Authenticity' in *The Post-Colonial Studies Reader*, Bill Ashcroft, Gareth Griffiths and Helen Tiffin (eds) (London: Routledge, 1995), p.240.
11. Graham, *Deconstructing Ireland* p.132.
12. Luke Gibbons, *Transformations in Irish Culture* (Cork: Cork University Press, 1996), p.6.
13. Scott T. Cummings, 'Homo Fabulator: The Narrative Imperative in Conor McPherson's Plays', in E. Jordan (ed.), *Theatre Stuff: Critical Essays on Contemporary Irish Theatre* (Dublin: Carysfort Press, 2000), p.308.
14. Conor McPherson, *The Weir* (London: Nick Hern, 1997), p.3. (Hereafter, page references will appear in parentheses within the body of the text.)
15. In a newspaper article McPherson argues that Irish writing is 'mostly a bit scared' and 'if there's a message it is a simple one: I know you're afraid of dying alone in a ditch. I am too. Let's be together', and he adds: 'We all die alone. And we've been told that since we were babies. And it was beaten into us'. See 'Original Sin', *Guardian*, 7 February 2001.
16. Nicholas Grene, *The Politics of Irish Drama: Plays in Context from Boucicault to Friel* (Cambridge: Cambridge University Press, 1999), p.261.
17. Peter Stallybrass and Allon White offer an interesting but incomplete perspective, suggesting that 'the bourgeoisie ... is perpetually rediscovering the carnivalesque as a radical source of transcendence ... The carnivalesque was marked out as an intensely powerful semiotic realm precisely because bourgeois culture constructed its self-identity by rejecting it'. See *The Politics and the Poetics of Transgression* (London: Methuen, 1986), pp. 201–02.
18. Scott T. Cummings argues that the play is a 'characteristically cheeky response to the call for him to write characters who talk to each other instead of the audience. He has them tell stories'. See Jordan (ed.), *Theatre Stuff*, p.308.
19. By contrast, Artie in Billy Roche's *Belfry* (1991) rejoices in now having a story, despite the pain and trauma of a failed relationship.
20. Ciarán Benson, *The Cultural Psychology of Self: Place, Morality and Art in Human Worlds* (London: Routledge, 2001), p.225.
21. Ibid., p.239.
22. For an analysis of the Gothic in Irish literature, see W.J. McCormack, 'Irish Gothic and After 1820–1945' in *The Field Day Anthology of Irish Writing, Volume II*, edited by Seamus Deane *et al.* (Derry: Field Day, 1991), pp.831–54.
23. Margaret Llewellyn Jones argues that Jim is 'haunted both by the imminent death of his mother and his own buried sexual desires', that Jack's story is 'suggestive of opportunities he did not take up' and that Finbar's story reveals that he 'felt trapped by the community's close critical scrutiny, still persisting in the way he is judged even now'. Such restricted readings of the narratives, while insightful, are not helpful. See *Contemporary Irish Drama and Cultural Identity* (Bristol: Intellect, 2002), pp.98–99.
24. Dominic Strinati, *An Introduction to Studying Popular Culture* (London: Routledge, 2000), p.83.
25. Ibid., pp.83–86.
26. Sue Vice, *Introducing Bakhtin* (Manchester: Manchester University Press, 1997), p.175.
27. Lynda Henderson, 'Men, Women and the Life of the Spirit in Tom Murphy's Plays' in *Irish Writers and Their Creative Process*, edited by Jacqueline Genet and Wynne Hellegoarc'h (Gerrards Cross: Colin Smythe, 1996), pp.88–90.

28. Anne F. Kelly, 'Bodies and Spirits in Tom Murphy's Theatre', in Jordan, ed., *Theatre Stuff*, p.160.
29. While McPherson's screenplay *I Went Down* (1997) owes a good deal to *Midnight Run* (1988), *The Weir* is indebted to *The Usual Suspects* (1995): the former influence McPherson accepted, the latter he denied during a private conversation with me a number of years ago. In *The Usual Suspects* the lead character invents a story inspired by objects and items found in a police interrogation room.
30. Conor McPherson, *St Nicholas* and *The Weir* (Dublin/London: New Island/Nick Hern, 1997).
31. Dominic Strinati tells how film studios would pay 'fright victims' to feign collapse in terror at selected screenings of movies in order to boost ticket sales. See *An Introduction to Studying Popular Culture*, p.97.
32. Gifford, *Pastoral*, p.71.
33. Christopher Morash, *A History of Irish Theatre: 1601–2000* (Cambridge: Cambridge University Press, 2002), p.267.
34. See Hans-Thies Lehmann, *Postdramatic Theatre*, translated and introduced by Karen Jürs-Munby (London: Routledge, 2006).
35. Of course, the fact that a non-Irish-born playwright does so, seems part of the motivation, as does Ireland's colonial history, where there seems a recurring need to test representations for marginality, oppression, prejudice. The blatant, apparent simplicity of McDonagh's dramaturgy is for some an infringement, at worst it is deeply insulting, a continuation and a capitulation to old types and the worst excesses of colonial representations.
36. There is of course the issue of colour-blind casting as well.
37. Hanna Scolnicov, *Woman's Theatrical Space* (Cambridge: Cambridge University Press, 1994), pp.2–3.
38. There are also anomalies that may perhaps be casual carelessness. In *A Skull in Connemara*, for instance, there is mention of students taking Sociology as a single school subject. Within the Irish education system that is incorrect. Likewise, there is mention of the Central Office for statistics, rather than the Central statistics office – the latter is the Irish organization, the former is the British one.
39. While facts and drama have no direct connection, we still check for continuities and plausibility. If there is a movie set in Ireland, you expect the drivers to drive on the left-hand side, if it is continental Europe, on the right-hand side, for instance.
40. Alan Parker's film versions of *Angela's Ashes* (1999) by Frank McCourt, and Roddy Doyle's *The Commitments* (1991) were accused of overplaying the squalor of the circumstances of both texts in such a way as to facilitate a simultaneous negative and sentimental take on the world from which these texts emerge and in a way mirror. Likewise, audiences experiencing these works responded accordingly, and their own prejudices about Limerick in the 1930s and 1940s and Dublin in the 1940s respectively were indirectly facilitated. Famously, Neil Jordan's *Michael Collins* (1996) contained substantial inaccuracies.
41. Garry Hynes in an interview with Cathy Leeney, *Theatre Talk: Voices of Irish Theatre Practitioners*, edited by Lilian Chambers *et al.* (Dublin: Carysfort Press, 2001), p.204.
42. Martin McDonagh, *The Beauty Queen of Leenane, A Skull in Connemara* and *The Lonesome West* in *Plays 1* (London: Methuen, 1999). (Hereafter, page references will appear in parentheses within the body of the text.)
43. *The Trilogy* was initially directed by Garry Hynes and performed by Irish-born actors.
44. Martin McDonagh, *The Cripple of Inishmaan* (London: Methuen, 1997). (Hereafter, page references will appear in parentheses within the body of the text.)
45. Martin McDonagh, *The Lieutenant of Inishmore* (London: Metheun, 2001). (Hereafter, page references will appear in parentheses within the body of the text.)
46. Fintan O'Toole, 'A Mind in Connemara: The Savage World of Martin McDonagh', *New Yorker*, 6 March 2006, p.44. In this article McDonagh claims that he has only one piece of work, *The Banshees of Inisheer*, that remains unperformed, but the Rod Hall Agency listed a number of other plays on their website until very recently, namely, *The Retard is Out in the Cold* and *Dead Day at Coney*, while some previous articles on McDonagh mention a play titled *The Maamturk Rifleman*. See www.rodhallagency.com/index.php?art_id=000075
47. McDonagh was born in London on 26 March 1970 and was reared initially in Elephant and Castle, amongst a significant Irish immigrant community, and later in Camberwell. His parents were from Ireland originally, his father from Lettermullan, in county Galway and his mother hailed from Killeenduff, Easkey, in county Sligo. During his childhood, McDonagh regularly took holidays in Connemara and in Sligo.

48. *The Lieutenant* has an Aran Island location, according to McDonagh, simply because it is far enough from Belfast to delay the return of Padriac, so it is a logistical and structural decision. However, it is still part of an Aran trilogy, with one part of it yet to be performed. Elsewhere, he states that he wrote about the west of Ireland simply because he wanted to get away from the influence of writers like Harold Pinter, David Mamet and Joe Orton. But of course, the critic cannot trust his comments on these issues.

49. Declan Kiberd, 'The real Ireland, some think', *New York Times*, 25 April 1999.

50. Michael Billington regards the play as 'a model of rustic realism'. See 'New themes in Synge-song land: *The Beauty Queen of Leenane*, Royal Court Theatre Upstairs', *Guardian*, 8 March 1996. *A Skull in Connemara* is set in 'the fairly Spartan main room of a cottage in rural Galway' (63).

51. But these scenes often exist within the shadowy backdrop of the omnipresent unlit set. Not all productions do so, but if resources, material and financial, are available, then a more flexible staging environment is achievable; I am just taking my prompts from some of the productions I have seen or read about.

52. Letters appear as regularly as poteen. There is Pato's letter in *BQ*, Welsh's letter in *LW*, Billy forging the Doctor's letter in *CI*, and the illegal alcohol is either mentioned or consumed across all the plays.

53. In John B. Keane's play *The Field* (1965), it is reclaimed land and some elemental connection to it that gives rise to murderous vengeance.

54. Close to the end of the play, Bobby beats Billy with a 'length of lead piping', because Billy had lied to him about his illness, saying that he had TB and that he had three months to live.

55. Nicholas Grene, quoting from Joseph Feeney, 'Martin McDonagh: Dramatist of the West', *Studies*, 87, 1998, p.28, in 'Ireland in Two Minds: Martin McDonagh and Conor McPherson', *Yearbook of English Studies*, 35–1, January 2005, pp.298–311, p.307.

56. Declan Kiberd *New York Times*

57. Fintan O'Toole, '"Murderous Laughter" – "The Leenane Trilogy"', *Irish Times*, 24 June 1997.

58. Fintan O'Toole, 'Introduction' in Martin McDonagh, *Plays 1* (London: Methuen, 1999), p.xv.

59. Grene, 'Ireland in Two Minds', p.307.

60. Lisa Fitzpatrick, 'Language Games: *The Pillowman, A Skull in Connemara*, and Martin McDonagh's Hiberno-English' in *The Theatre of Martin McDonagh: A World of Savage Stories*, edited by L. Chambers and E. Jordan (Dublin: Carysfort Press, 2006), pp.141–54, p.145.

61. Ibid.

62. Christopher Murray 'The Cripple of Inishmaan Meets Lady Gregory' in *Theatre of McDonagh*, p.84.

63. John Waters, 'The Irish Mummy: The Plays and Purpose of Martin McDonagh' in Dermot Bolger (ed.), *Druids, Dudes and Beauty Queens: The Changing Face of Irish Theatre* (Dublin: New Island, 2001), p.50

64. Victor Merriman, 'Theatre of Tiger Trash', *Irish University Review*, 29–2, Autumn–Winter 1999, pp.305–17, p.312.

65. Victor Merriman, 'Heartsickness and Hopes Deferred' in *Twentieth-Century Irish Drama*, ed. Shaun Richards (Cambridge: Cambridge University Press, 2004), pp.255–56, p.253.

66. Mary Luckhurst, 'Martin McDonagh's *Lieutenant of Inishmore*: Selling (-Out) to the English', *Contemporary Theatre Review*, 14–4, 2004, pp.34–41, p.35.

67. He wrote '200 short stories that he planned to incorporate in a feature film called *57 Tales of Sex and Violence* … only one was actually about sex: "Anarcho-Feminists: Sex Machines in Outer Space", the remainder about violence'. Cited in 'The greatest playwright looks forward to Oscar night', (no journalist acknowledged) *Sunday Times*, 5 February 2006, p.19.

68. Luckhurst, 'Martin McDonagh's *Lieutenant of Inishmore*', p.36.

69. Quoted in Sean O'Hagan, 'The Wild West', *Guardian*, 24 March 2001, p.32. His account of the same creative impulse is rather different in the O'Toole *New Yorker* piece, where McDonagh claims: 'I was trying to write a play that would get me killed. I had no real fear that I would be, because paramilitaries never bothered with playwrights anyway, but if they were going to start I wanted to write something that would put me top of the list', p.45.

70. John Peter, *Sunday Times*, 20 May 2001.

71. Michael Billington, *The Guardian*, 12 May 2001.

72. Luckhurst, 'Martin McDonagh's *Lieutenant of Inishmore*', p.38.

73. Richards, '"Outpouring of a Morbid, Unhealthy Mind"', p.211.

74. O'Toole, 'Murderous Laughter', *Irish Times*, 24 June 1997.

75. Fintan O'Toole, 'The Pillowman Program Note', Cottesloe, Royal National Theatre, London, November 2003.

76. Sean O'Hagan, 'The Wild West'.
77. Stephen Lacey, *British Realist Theatre: The New Wave in Its Context 1956–1965* (London: Routledge, 1995), p.65.
78. John Lahr, 'Blood Simple', *New Yorker*, 13 March 2006, p.92.
79. Waters, 'Irish Mummy', p.40.
80. Ibid.
81. O'Toole, 'Murderous Laughter', *Irish Times*, 24 June 1997.
82. Fintan O'Toole, 'The Beauty Queen of Leenane', *Irish Times*, 6 February 1996.
83. Fintan O'Toole, 'Introduction', p.xii.
84. Scolnicov, *Woman's Theatrical Space*, p.147.
85. Michael Fryan's 'Introduction' to *The Seagull*, by Anton Chekhov, translated by Fryan (London: Methuen, 1986), p.xiv.
86. Mária Kurdi, 'American and Other International Impulses on the Contemporary Irish Stage: A Talk with Playwright Declan Hughes', *Hungarian Journal of English and American Studies*, 8–2, 2002, pp.76–77.
87. When asked by Sean O'Hagan as to how he responds to the inevitable accusations of cultural stereotyping, McDonagh responded by saying, 'I don't even enter into it. I mean, I don't feel I have to defend myself for being English or for being Irish, because, in a way, I don't feel either. And, in another way, of course, I'm both.' See Sean O'Hagan, 'The Wild West', *Guardian*, 24 March 2001, p.32.
88. O'Toole, *The Pillowman*, Program Note.
89. Nicholas Grene has coined the phrase 'Black Pastoral'. See 'Black Pastoral: 1990s Images of Ireland', *Litteraria Pragensia*, 20–10, 23 October 2004, www.komparatistika.ff.cuni.cz/litteraria/no20–10/grene.htm
90. Kiberd, *New York Times*
91. Gareth Griffiths, 'The Myth of Authenticity' in *The Post-colonial Studies Reader*, ed. Bill Ashcroft, Gareth Griffiths and Helen Tiffin (London: Routledge, 1995), p.240.
92. Graham, *Deconstructing Ireland*, p.139.
93. Marie Jones, *Stones in his Pockets* and *A Night in November* (London: Nick Hern, 2000), p.36. (Hereafter, all page details will be given in parentheses within the text.)
94. Steve Neale, *Genre and Hollywood* (London: Routledge, 2000), p.98.
95. Nicholas Grene quotes McPherson: 'I wasn't concerned with geography or politics … not from any need to address anything about my country'. See *Politics of Irish Drama*, p.261.

'Sounds from the Underground': Any Myth will Do?

RESTORED MYTHS

One of the significant tendencies in contemporary dramaturgy is the endeavour by writers to appropriate a range of myths, primarily, but not exclusively, from either the Irish or Greek traditions. What surprises, however, is the attempt to mythologize works across plays set in contemporary urban and rural settings.[1] It could be perceived that rural settings might be an easier space from which to springboard on the back of myth, given its connection to the history, land, ritual, traditions, superstitions and religion, whereas urban situations might appear to have less immediate access to these things, given particularly the late urbanization of Irish society. How so many texts of all kinds are sustained by myth or recycle the patterns of myth is remarkable from a dramaturgical point of view in the Irish tradition.

Helena Sheehan argues that myths are types of 'prototypical stories', where fundamental themes of existence are processed, through circumstances where characters or archetypes are tested, and by so doing 'basic curiosities, hopes, fears, desires, conflicts, choices and patterns of resolution' are tested.[2] Generally, then, there is a network of myths that intertwine, are reworked and recalibrated, presenting often quests for justice and making sense of revenge, violence and suffering, of loyalties, conflicts of duties, obligations and offering reflections on self-sacrifice and mortality. Sheehan identifies myths as 'synthesizing stories' that capture 'the *Zeitgeist* of a time and place, bringing to a focus what forces are at work, highlighting its problems, and crystallizing its values'.[3] Myths thus function as sort of organizational metanarrative. Richard Kearney raises Mircea Eliade's distinctions between sacred, holy time and profane time, and Kearney's own ideas on myth describe it as being outside time, relying on certain 'pieties', 'sacred prototypes', 'sacred precedents' and 'collective rootedness'.[4] The argument is based on the tension between the sacred and the profane, the spiritual and the secular, piety and plurality, remythologiz-ing and demythologizing and the need for a dialogue between myth and history, past and present.[5] However, Kearney warns that 'to demythol-ogise religion means therefore to demystify those mystic accretions of the Judeo-Christian heritage which derived from Hellenic, Orphic or Celtic paganism'.[6]

For Lisa Fitzpatrick, 'myths are built from individual acts, it is true: but for those acts to function at the level of myth, they must take on a wider significance; must tap into a shared symbology or system of meaning. If they fail to do so, they remain random meaningless deeds'.[7] Fitzpatrick argues for the broad scope of myths and how they must be collective if they are to maintain significance. Carl Gustav Jung's notion of the 'collective unconscious' situates a shared structure of knowing and is evident across dreams and myths, and I would argue dramaturgy. George Steiner, discussing 'mythical figures' and Jung's 'archetypes', argues that the mystical figure 'would be "a collective personification" giving bearable, joyous, explanatory forms to archaic collective fantasies and phases in the elaboration of the psyche'.[8] As civilization progresses and societies become more rational, this collec-tive figure degrades. But in art these figures survive as we 'revert to "the archetypal analogies", to the primal constellations of gesture and image in art, because the conscious mind, however emancipated and secularized, is both repelled and drawn towards its earliest stages of existence', suggests Steiner.[9]

Politically, Kearney raises the issue of Karl Marx's suspicion of 'ideological myths (superstructures) and the underlying realities of class domination' and exploitation.[10] This is something that is central to the work of Roland Barthes, who states:

> Myth does not deny things, on the contrary, its function is to talk about them; simply, it purifies them, it makes them innocent, it gives them a natural and eternal justification, it gives them clarity which is not that of an explanation but that of a statement of fact.[11]

That notion of making myths innocent is vital to our understanding of the social formations of myth and to the dramaturgical structuring of innocence in drama. Barthes adds that:

> In passing from history to Nature, myth acts economically: it abol-ishes the complexity of human acts, it gives them the simplicity of essences, it does away with all dialectics, with any going back beyond what is immediately visible, and it organizes a world

which is without contradiction because it is without depth, a world wide open and wallowing in the evident, it establishes a blissful clarity: things appear to mean something by themselves.[12]

The challenges facing the contemporary writer are whether or not older mythologies can be easily appropriated or consciously absorbed, if some type of dialectic structure is possible, despite Barthes's negative viewpoint, whether some validation of reality can be attested, without fulfilling the remit of the élite class, and what type of emerging or faux mythologies will be available to writers. Part of the additional difficulty with contemporary writing is the postmodern imperative to defer meaning, to collapse quests for justice and truth under the weight of irony or the postponement of significant meaning. Another challenge is to be found in the rejection of broad-based cultural and social mythologies.

BY THE BOG OF CATS: GOING GREEK

There is a specific tradition of Irish playwrights since the 1980s who draw on Greek myth in various forms, from Brian Friel with *Living Quarters* ('After *Hippolytus*') (1977), Tom Murphy with *The Sanctuary Lamp* (1975) (*Oresteia*) and Marina Carr with *By the Bog of Cats ...* (1998) (*Medea*), to the more blatant adaptations of Greek drama seen in Tom Paulin's *The Riot Act* (1984) and Seamus Heaney's *The Cure at Troy* (1990) and *The Burial at Thebes* (2004). Both Desmond Egan and Brendan Kennelly offered versions of *Medea*, and versions of *Antigone* are numerous.[13] Marina Carr's *Ariel* (2002) is based loosely on *The Oresteia*.

As a playwright, Marina Carr has the skills to manipulate many of the intricate realities of contemporary living, moving the spectator behind and beyond the facade of social norms, mores, conventions and expectations, locating the points of greatest contention and delivering moments of pure savagery and beauty, while still creating convincing dramas that are replete with intricate, maimed, destructive, wayward and marginal characters who are full of unrealizable longing. Carr started out writing in a Beckettian vein; *Ullaloo* was her first play to be written, but her third to be performed, in 1991, *Low in the Dark* was first performed in 1989 and *This Love Thing* in 1990. In these works there is a self-consciousness in operation and a reliance on the surreal or the absurd to generate incongruity and dramatic distance. Her dramaturgy changed utterly when she began to write plays set in the Midlands, the majority of which were set in the 'present' and in less clearly demarcated fantasy or transgressive spaces than her earlier work. This is where the Greek and classical influences are most in evidence. *The Mai* (1994) is loosely based on Sophocles' *Electra* and not on Euripides,[14] and *Portia Coughlan* (1996) owes a debt to the Egyptian myth of Isis and Osiris and to the story of Byblis and Caunus in Ovid's *Metamorphoses*. *By the Bog of Cats*[15] is fundamentally informed by Euripides' *Medea*. Oliver Taplin argues that when it comes to the impact of myth on Greek dramas, 'the constraint is minimal; the scope for artistry enormous'.[16]

In these Midlands plays, Carr takes desire, corruption, desperation and obsession to another level. Betrayal rather than compassion and savagery rather than empathy dominate. Little pretence is in operation, and little or no social codes are to be observed between the characters. Secrecy, shame and indignity run riot across the plays, thereby ensuring that there is not only an absence of morality but also an absence of reciprocal obligations. The characters are on different journeys and little compromise can be reached, unions between individuals are singularly intense and always fleeting. Yet an unrealizable faith exists in bonds, however irrational, corrupt and obsolete they may be, while violation and negativity can be as powerful a connection as positive communion. In her work the present cannot be a repetition of the past, even when characters are often desperate to make it so.

In Carr's work, myth and mask take precedence over the real or the psychological. Characters consistently identify with their persecutors and victims between themselves can become hostile rivals, vengeful towards each other and misdirect their anger. Carr does not set in stone clear-cut oppositions between male and female, nor does she reverse previous gender stereotypes where women were weak and ineffective in the shaping of dramatic action in so many plays written by men; instead, in her work the women characters determine and are shaped by the dramatic action. Portia in *Portia Coughlan* has her unquenchable belief in the bond that existed between herself and her twin and the consolation of the Belmont river, Hester in *By the Bog of Cats* has her daughter, her mother and her bog, the Mai in *The Mai* has her belief in the sanctuary of the Owl Lake (Lake of the Night Hag or Pool of the Dark Witch) and Sorrel has a purity of heart that her violation takes away in *On Raftery's Hill* (2000).

DON'T STOP ME NOW

In their quest for intensity, unity and connection, these characters push issues and incidents to their extremes, and when their desires are not realized, death enters the frame. The Mai kills herself rather than accommodate herself to her husband's infidelity and his unwillingness to bond; Portia commits suicide, unable to either let go or resolve the intensity of the bond she had constructed, imagined and experienced with her twin; and Hester destroys herself and her daughter rather than accommodate herself to the realities of the new relationship between Carthage Kilbride and Caroline Cassidy. Despite the fact that so many of Carr's characters commit suicide, 'their lucid perception of their own alienation, their evocation of mythical forces and their critique of the lack of accommodation of difference in small town or rural Ireland is powerfully articulated', according to Anna McMullan.[17]

Carr understands implicitly the self-destructive intent of her characters, but she does not wish for the spectator to wallow in such destruction, despite its almost unremitting relentlessness in performance. There is a critique of the self-destructive process that is built into the structures of the drama and into the actions of characters. In terms of Greek tragedy, Oliver Taplin summarizes the early plays of Euripides as follows:

> Noble figures struggle and endure in a world that gravitates towards destruction and waste. Sometimes they endure with dignity; sometimes they become savage, though none the less with a strength that gives them tragic stature.[18]

Carr's figures are not so much noble as outsiders, vagabonds, travellers and monstrosities in a variety of ways, existing in 'the dungeon of the fallen world' (p.219), as Portia describes it in *Portia Coughlan*, something which has cued Victor Merriman to read her work as 'representative and reprehensible in generating marginalized Celtic Tiger white trash characters for the delectation of middle class audiences'.[19] If death is the destiny of most of the characters in her plays, then the capacity to see what the future holds becomes all the more important. Many of her women characters have the power to prophesize, as prediction becomes a damnation of sorts and self-awareness a terrifying burden. In *By the Bog of Cats*, Catwoman predicts Hester's downfall, Hester's mother, Josie Swane, foretold that her daughter would only survive as long as the Black Swan lived. The myth of the Belmont river in *Portia Coughlan* is about the power of a woman to tell the future. When people looked into her eyes, they could see how they were going to die. Because everything that she predicted happened, the locals impaled her on a stake, leaving her to die a slow death. Bel, the God of the valley, was enraged by the community, so he flooded the whole place, churches, livestock and houses and took the girl down to the mouth of the Atlantic.[20]

In the classic Greek sense one cannot very easily draw distinctions between freedom and destiny. This is a recurring tension in Carr's drama. What is choice, what is destiny, what has action and wilful intervention to do with living, if consciousness has little impact on the instinctive compulsion to destroy, to cause chaos or to repeat cycles of dysfunction? Grandma Fraochlán exclaims in *The Mai*: 'We repeat and we repeat, the orchestration may be different but the tune is always the same' (p.123).

In that indeterminate space between choice and compulsion, where creativity and destruction blur, and where the community shuts itself away from the vision or trauma of the individual, this is the space within which Carr's work functions best. It is a dramatic world where emotions are utterly intense and scary, yet driven by a detailed, impulsive obligation to establish strong connections between cause and effect, where things are named for what they are. While there is a relationship between cause and effect across these Midlands plays, Carr blurs temporal and spatial continuity in *The Mai* and in *Portia Coughlan*. Witchcraft and evil seem to be the only way through which the locals can come to terms with Hester's power. (In Greek myth, Medea's mother died giving birth to her, so she was nursed by an elder sister. Her aunt, Circe, schooled her in the art of calling on the gods to aid her plans.)

As *By the Bog of Cats* opens, Hester Swane is told that she is going to die and the only way out of this is to risk leaving the bog and all that she holds dear. Like all great characters, she has the compulsion and the self-destructiveness to challenge and to face her own doom, with a reckless disregard for her own life and with regard to what she sees as her ineffable right. Hester's first encounter is with the Ghost Fancier (echoes of Ibsen's *Peer Gynt* (1867) here), who calls to take her away from the living world. The encounter takes place on a landscape of bog and ice and it symbolically captures the tensions of the play. As the performance begins, the Ghost Fancier gets his timing wrong, not knowing whether it is dusk or dawn, but he promises to return.

THE MASK OF MEDEA

Both Euripides' Medea and Carr's Hester resist banishment, fight rejection and love intensely the partner who has pushed them from their lives. Without following things through to their fullest, and given such activities can be a never-ending activity, it is still a worthwhile exercise to consider the parallels between both *Medea* and *By the Bog of Cats*, and to establish the direct similarity of character and story, such as the following parallels: Hester Swane/Medea, Carthage Kilbride/Jason, Xavier Cassidy/Creon, King of Corinth, Caroline Cassidy/Creon's daughter (Creusa or Glauke depending on the version). Medea's sons become the young Josie Swane. Indirect relationships are also significant, such as Xavier's son dying like Creon and his daughter by touching something laden with poison. The Greek choric function is taken over partially by Catwoman and Monica. In *By the Bog of Cats*, however, there is no Aegeus figure to offer alternatives and there will be no *deus ex machina* like one has in *Medea*.

In *Medea*, Jason, commander of the Argonauts, promises Medea everlasting love, if in return she will help him retrieve the golden fleece from her father, King of Colchis. Influenced by Aphrodite and Eros, she helps Jason. Regarded as a ruthless sorceress, with skills of magic and witchcraft, Medea wreaked destruction almost everywhere she went; whereas Hester's dominant skills are not so much destruction as impulsive survival. As the couple, Medea and Jason fled Colchis, Medea dismembered the body of Apsyrtus (Joseph) her half-brother, knowing that her father would pause to pick up the pieces, as it was essential, religiously, to bury the bodies of the dead whole. She also tricked the daughters of the King of Pelias into boiling him, for he had been responsible for the death of Jason's parents. Medea's love for Jason was a spell, whereas Hester's love for Carthage has more an earthly than otherworldly interference. Hester protected and built up Carthage Kilbride. When Jason was to take a second wife (as Carthage does in a way), Medea was to be banished, to be made stateless and without home, facing eviction from Corinth. Hester is to be shunted from her own home and her sense of rupture and unhomelessness disturbs her. Both women characters share an irresolvable anger at their rejection.

For Jason in *Medea*, the new relationship will be to his advantage, just as he had used Medea to acquire the Golden Fleece. So Jason marries for security, and Carthage marries Caroline for land. Medea kills her rival by giving her a poisoned crown and gown. But where Medea's destructive gifts were disguised as a peace offering, Hester's wedding gift is undisguised destruction and carnage. Yet Hester does not kill Caroline Cassidy. The rival woman appears on stage in the Carr text, but not in the Greek original. Carthage thinks that he is being reasonable. He buys Hester the house, gives her money and wants compromise of the type that most certainly benefits him. But Hester and Carthage have shared more than intense passion. Their bond is one of blood, of obligation and of promises. Hester had previously killed her brother, Joseph, witnessed by Carthage.

CALVARY

When Hester was 7 years of age her mother went away to live with her husband and her son, claiming that Hester was dead. Hester killed her brother out of this obsession for her mother. To be abandoned in that way, to await the return of the mother thirty-three years on, to fear the desertion of a lover and to fear the loss of her own child, more importantly her unwillingness to allow the cycle to continue, all ensure that this play ends in the most painful way. The wedding reception for Caroline and Carthage is a great example of a grotesque, carnivalized consciousness. Mrs Kilbride tells of how son and mother shared a bed and of how, in her honour, he prepared an imitation of Calvary in their own back garden. She turns up at the wedding in a white dress, and wonders how she was supposed to know that the bride would be wearing white. Josie also wears a white communion dress and Hester arrives at the wedding reception wearing a wedding dress. (In performance you have the incongruous situation of four women dressed in white on stage simultaneously.)

Hester burns down the house and sets fire to a shed with cattle locked inside. Because of her performance at the wedding, and because she has killed the animals, Carthage tells her he plans to take the child away from her. Hester invites her daughter to dance with her, in order that they might have their 'own weddin'' (p.327). It is significant that the dress that brings death to Creon's daughter in *Medea* re-emerges as the wedding dress. This particular symbol of femininity and union brings death across a range of Carr's plays. (Shalome wears one in *On Raftery's Hill*.)

While, many characters gather to indict Hester for killing Josie, Hester dances with the Ghost Fancier and plunges a knife into her heart, dying with the words 'Mam – Mam –', the same final words spoken by young Josie a little earlier (p.341). Hester knows her own pain and can articulate her mother's absence as the main source of it. Regardless, while she can stop one pattern that is Josie endlessly waiting for a mother's return, she cannot stop another, that of the destructive mother making decisions for parent and child, and in the best interests of the parent more than the child.

In Euripides' text, Medea kills her children to stop the King of Corinth avenging his daughter's death by killing her sons, to get at

Jason, and to avenge her rejection and his breach of his promises, before fleeing to Athens and being rescued by her grandfather, Helios. (Other variations on the myth suggest that Creon got revenge by killing thirteen of Medea's fourteen children and laid their bodies in the marketplace for all to see. [21])

According to Michael Walton, Euripides wrote about 'the power of the passions, the arbitrariness of fate, and the ambiguity of motive'.[22] Carr scans the same territory. Mystery never becomes mystification. Carr rejects the notional fatalism at the core of tragedy, so in many ways her work is a reimagining of the myth and so she delivers a revisionist myth. Tragedy's rhythmic unnaturalness seems to rule. It is not so much divine compulsion as the chaos impulse that besets Hester. The curse of the Swane family and its mythology are confrontationally exposed. Hester as woman, Traveller-woman and Bog-woman, is triply excluded and alienated. Medea had, however, betrayed her own father and killed her own brother, so she is no innocent. Hester had killed her own brother, so neither is she. Driven by the ecstasy of revenge, she becomes possessed. Revenge as blood sport is observable in many Greek texts and in Carr's work revenge is a central energy that takes the characters beyond rationality, beyond logic and beyond a moral framework. It is often the revenge of the dispossessed. Medea plots to kill Jason and his bride, Hester plots in a lesser way. Audiences may sympathize with the despair of Medea and Hester, but can they do so with the destruction of their children?

Oliver Taplin suggests that 'never, except in mad scenes, are the characters of Greek tragedy portrayed as automata or marionettes. Even when they are viewed as victims of the gods, they remain human and independent.'[23] If Carr's desire was to reinscribe women within the social arena, she does so not by creating positive images of woman, attesting to their humanity, but instead she has the tendency not so much to create gruesome female characters as ones so harmed and violated, and not necessarily only by patriarchy, but characters acutely alert to their own capacity to violate, hurt and inspire chaos and dread; women who are not ideal or responsible figures or placed on any pedestal. Hester's mother was cruel to Hester from the moment of her birth, first abandoning her child in the nest of a swan just after she was born and later chaining her child in the caravan, 'like a rabied pup' (p.273), according to the Catwoman.[24]

Hester seeks confirmation of her memories from all. Yet she was so young that things don't make sense and don't add up. Hester is desperate to ground the contradictions of her mother. She was cruel, she often left her child alone, neglected her, hurt her, but she could also sing and she could also love. Out of the hardness and the desperation, Josie was a formidable woman, strong, steely and rebelliously defiant. Her gift was song; her failure, her inability to be a caring mother. Yet Hester still sees the time until her seventeenth birthday as Edenic. Hester is in part only her mother's play thing. And that is the horror of the cycle. In Carr's world, parents are not people one outgrows; their stain and their spite, as well as their love, persist in their offspring and persevere in imposing pathways that are not of their own offspring's choosing. That way, agency is corrupted.

MOUNT RAFTERY

In Greek mythology, Zeus and Hera (Juno is her Roman counterpart) are brother and sister. She is queen of the gods, the daughter of the Titans, Cronus and Rhea. Hera is 'triple Goddess of the three stages of woman's life', the Child-Goddess, the Bride Goddess and the Widow Goddess.[25] For Adam Mclean, 'Hera sets the archetype for woman in relationship to man within a patriarchal social order, as ideal wife and companion … She is a Goddess of marriage … maternity and fidelity, a jealous guardian of the marriage vows and heredity.'[26] Zeus courted Hera unsuccessfully and then turned to magic, changing himself into a dishevelled cuckoo, for which she had sympathy, holding the bird to her breast. He then changed form, raped her and out of embarrassment she agreed to marry him, giving birth to six children. Zeus was renowned for his affairs and she avenged many of them.

In *On Raftery's Hill* Red Raftery is a serial abuser like Zeus, and he is also a victim of abuse. Dinah, his daughter and one of his victims, cannot fully explain her violation without drawing on the world of children's games, as cited before but worth repeating: 'Ud's just like children playin in a field ah some awful game, before rules was made.'[27] Here Carr links up a degraded infantilism or regression to a juvenile consciousness with the play's Greek precedents, through the evocation of an ancient time 'before rules was made'. The Raftery's neighbour from the valley, Isaac, explains the origins of the world:

> Isaac: … Zeus and Hera, sure they were brother and sister and they goh married and had chaps and young wans, and the chaps and the young wans done the job wud the mother and father and wud one another, and sure the whole loh a them was ah ud mornin, noon and nigh. I suppose they had to populahe the world someway. Is ud any wonder the stahe a the country and them for ancestry. (p.43)

Raftery's Hill cannot be Mount Olympus. A myth of origins that includes episodes of incest fails to help in this instance. There is a difference between a Greek myth of origins and of populating the world, and the reality of incest, so that the play never has the easy comfort of a mythological dimension. 'In her earliest appearance in myth', Hera 'is associated with the cow, showing her connection with fecundity and birth',[28] Mclean points out. Ded lives in the cowshed, Dinah gave birth there and not a maternity ward, and Red destroys the animals in his own fields, treating the place like an abattoir. Further, the linkage between the human world and the animal world is more pertinent than any ritualistic or dramatic precedent. Shalome's behaviour and madness is associated with the March hare by Dinah. In *By the Bog of Cats* Xavier threatens Hester, while brandishing a gun: 'Xavier: ... I ran your mother out of here and I'll run you too like a frightened hare' (p.328).

Dinah attempts to explain circumstances through the animal kingdom: 'Thah's whah we are, gorillas in clothes pretendin to be human' (p.30). Her internalization of Red's values is clear here, as Red's comprehension of the world draws on a similar sentiment: 'We were big loose monsters, Mother, hurlin through the air wud carnage in our hearts and blood under our nails, and no stupid laws houldin us down or back or in' (pp.31–32). And when Sorrel resorts to a similar perspective, stating 'We're a band a gorillas swingin from the trees' (p.56), the consolidation of a cycle of violation and internalization is almost complete. That tension between the human, the divine and the animal prompts the articulation of myth, and when the 'divine' is taken out of the equation, the relationship between the human and the animal comes to the fore.

This issue recurs in Carr's work. For example, after Portia's funeral in *Portia Coughlan*, her grandmother Blaize Scully again slanders her mother's family the Joyces, saying that when 'you breed animals with humans you can only bring forth poor haunted monsters who've no sense of God or man' (p.229). Of all the characters in *On Raftery's Hill*, only Isaac and Dara Mood have access to a different moral code. Dara attacks Brophy for his part in his daughter's death and Isaac, despite the quirks, still calls the world to order: for him 'Monsters make themselves. They were hopped into the world clane as the next' (p.43).

In Greek tragedy the humans were situated between the animals and the gods. The battles and the encounters were between woman and man and more than woman and man.[29] In Carr's work, the human in part becomes animal, and the animal becomes human as part of the blurring process, rather than the human being part divine. (Catwoman wears 'a coat of cat fur ... studded with cats' eyes and cats' paws' (p.271) and Hester in *By the Bog of Cats* states that she metaphorically refuses to be 'flung in a bog hole like a bag of newborn pups' (p.317). [30])

In *The Bacchae*, Dionysus demands worship from Pentheus. Pentheus refuses and is later dismembered by the intoxicated, bloodthirsty women (the Bacchae) who include his own mother Agauë. Michael Zelenak notes the appearance of 'Dionysian rituals of sparagmos (tearing apart the sacrificial animal) and omophagia (eating the animal's raw flesh)'.[31] In *On Raftery's Hill*, Sorrel is the sacrificial animal, hare-like and harmed. The switch from the concept of a destructive monstrosity to the vulnerability and symbolism of the hare is a constant strategy across the play. Red is a cruel hunter, killing a hare and then strangling the leverets in the lair. Sorrel's refusal to gut the hare becomes the mode of her own sexual violation, in a way that Sorrel becomes a hare of sorts, prior to her assault. Of course, as a Swane, Hester is directly connected symbolically as part of the perverse mythologizing with the swan, creatures that remain monogamous throughout their lives.

HOWIE THE ROOKIE: MARGINALIZED CITIES

In many of the plays the city is not so much commodified as a marker of deviance. Where the rural is aestheticized, sanitized, repressed and celebrated, a mythic sanctuary with the fantasy of intimacy, the city is under surveillance, hedonistic, transgressive, deviant and violent, with its criminal underworld feared, fethishized and equally mythologized. City plays are seldom about suburbanization, mortgages, schools, commuting, relationships, but about mainstreaming the underworld and its gangland economy. This is what Paul Chatterton and Robert Hollands call 'residual spaces', which are:

> traditional urban spaces inhabited by increasingly excluded sections of young people, including community bars, pubs, ale-houses, as well as the street, the neighbourhood ghetto or the council estate ... First and foremost, these spaces are defined against mainstream commercial development ... Unlike the bourgeois and middle-class appropriation of the traditional pub, residual spaces are viewed as 'down at heel' dilapidated reminders of a lurid era of poverty, vice and debauchery associated with the lumpenproletariat of Victorian times, now occupied by their twenty-first-century counterpart, the 'urban underclass'.[32]

They add, 'a second characteristic is that these spaces are inhabited, or perceived to be occupied at least, predominantly by the urban poor – the unemployed, welfare-dependent and shifty criminal classes'.[33] Finally, residual spaces are 'located either on the fringe of city cores, in poorer suburbs and council estates, or in marginal urban areas characterized as the "rough" and "down-market" parts of cities'.[34] In terms of city spaces, some contemporary playwrights felt the urge to rework Greek myths;[35] some turned to Irish mythology[36] and others to the myths of popular culture. When the circumstances of politics, society and culture were transformed, then new types of relationships emerged and new sorts of stories needed to be told. The fact is that most of these narratives take place in fragmented, disenfranchized and 'residual spaces'.

In relation to Mark O'Rowe's *Howie The Rookie* (1999), I want to look particularly at issues of masculinity, trauma, violence, working-class suburbia, and at how popular culture and its mythologies of sacrificial violence shape identities that have become increasingly performative. I will work with the frameworks or lenses offered by the martial arts figure of Bruce Lee, and the notion of fist fighting provided by Chuck Palahniuk's novel *Fight Club* (1997). For the characters, popular culture comes courtesy of Hollywood, the media, music and entertainment, video games and from the local store, Video Vendetta.[37] In an interview with Fiachra Gibbons, O'Rowe states that video came out when he was about 13:

> so he grew up on video nasties, cannibal movies and kung-fu flicks – *I Spit on Your Grave* and all that stuff. Really we only watched them for the goriness of the special effects. *Nightmare in a Damaged Brain* was so chopped to pieces by the censors that we would have to sit there and imagine what happened in the cut-out bits. I suppose they got our brains going.[38]

Initially, the link between The Howie Lee and The Rookie Lee in *Howie The Rookie* (and not *The Howie and The Rookie*) isn't inordinately complex, but the characters do form part of that tradition. Part 1 is narrated by The Howie, and part 2 by The Rookie – played brilliantly by Aidan Kelly and Karl Shiels, respectively, in the first production of the play, directed by Mike Bradwell and in the Peacock production (2006), directed by Jimmy Fay. Part 2 is a continuation of the first narrative, albeit from a different point of view. O'Rowe's characters do not share the same space. (It is interesting that the same actor didn't play the two roles and it would be interesting to consider the implications of it, if this were to happen.) The Howie Lee and The Rookie Lee are in

a sense doubles,[39] not in the sense of *doppelgänger* or fractured subjectivities, but in terms of layering and superimposition. The link is the
dead, mythologized film actor Bruce Lee, star of martial arts movies
–'You me an' The Bruce Lee' (p.18), as The Howie remarks to The
Rookie.[40]

In addition, in terms of popular culture, Palahniuk's *Fight Club* is a
great example of a text that highlights issues of split subjectivity, male
aggression and brutality, and of the imagined clarity that violence can
bring to a psyche in distress. I cannot confirm if this text has been influential or not on O'Rowe's work, but there are striking similarities with
it and O'Rowe's play. In this book, the narrator has a double – Tyler
Durden, an anarchic individual, who establishes a series of bare-fisted
fight clubs and promotes the concept of project mayhem. Fight clubs
spring up around the country by word of mouth. The novel is populated by men who supposedly discover meaning in acts of violence.
Initially, the novel's narrator finds consolation by attending support
groups for terminally ill patients. He fills his evenings moving from one
group to the other, without himself having any physical illness. His
falsehood is discovered by a woman, Marla, who herself takes pleasure
in the same routine. It is at that moment that the narrator springs Tyler
into being. In *Fight Club* the narrator and most of the other males in
the story metamorphose into Tyler Durden and the males in O'Rowe's
mutate into being Bruce Lee. Tyler Durden is the narrator's night state:
'This is a dream. Tyler is a projection. He's a disassociative personality
disorder. A psychogenic fugue state. Tyler Durden is my hallucination.'[41]

In some ways, The Rookie Lee is the Howie's hallucination. Not only
does the performativity of the monologues complicate the relationship
between space and time, but also The Howie Lee narrates initially
a story in the present tense, one which only The Rookie Lee can
complete. The Howie's later absence denies corporeality, and thus the
only realm of existence available is narrative – identity as a hypertext.
For many young men, violence is a form of self-validation and Bruce
Lee (famed as much for his ability to commingle different martial arts
styles as for the one-inch punch of immense power) is an heroic figure
amongst some young working-class men, in particular. In Lee's early
work, a teacher or a mother place restraints on vengeance. Here, in
Howie The Rookie, there is no figure of restraint. Lee's martial arts
movies emphasize self-defence as personal expression, but also combat as
a way of seeking justice. There are often vicious fights, exaggerated
by sound effects and unbelievable moves and blows. It is often a combat
situation with no holds barred. At the end of *The Big Boss* the police

arrive only to arrest Lee's character. He leaves the scene cuffed, having taken justice into his own hands after many members of his immediate family are murdered. In *Fist of Fury* the main character, Chen Shan, exits a building only to be met by armed police and military forces. He runs towards them as they shoot. So in the early Lee movies, at least, there is no sense of a happy ending or that the hero and the police are in alliance, as you would find with most Hollywood movies. In Lee's movies generally, there is not only an anti-authoritarian sentiment, but also an anti-police one. Further, there is a general denial of justice following on from normal police investigations into the murder of innocent parties. So, in a sense they become revenge dramas as they quest for justice that is not available to the dispossessed. The characters played by Lee step in to fight for somebody else, risking their own lives, but displaying self-sacrificing impulses that have mythic, religious and mystic resonances.

As Rookie gets ready for Dave's party, he tells himself that he 'looks like a warrior' (p.42). In this O'Rowe play it is a community of urban warriors, without a classical class grievance. Thus, the citation of Bruce Lee is not so much one of intertextual echo, as one of disassociative impersonation, the enactment of the sensation of supremacy through false allegiance. Really, it is less about dominance or patriarchal subjugation, rather more about acts of invisibility (non-entity), hiding behind the myth of the macho hyper-masculinity of Bruce. Also, the use of the Bruce Lee figure here, calls attention to the 'free floating' nature of identity, one without substance and one fundamentally grounded in artifice.[42]

Some critics suggest Tallaght, Dublin 24,[43] close to the Springfield area where O'Rowe grew up, as the locale for the play, but any close scrutiny makes it somewhat difficult to say that. Es Devlin's design for the first production was highly abstract.[44] Cathy Leeney describes Devlin's set as being 'sufficiently cold, unspecific and spatially open to communicate a sense of placelessness, of anomie'.[45] Dublin serves both as text and as symbolic landscape. The play's geography is intentionally suspect.[46] In *Intermission* (2003), written by O'Rowe and directed by John Crowley, the film is specifically located in the proximity of the Springfield area of Tallaght. A hand-drawn map of the neighbourhood, with distinct areas identified, forms part of the script.

In the 1980s and early 1990s parts of Tallaght were major unemployment black spots, and this pattern continues to a lesser extent to this very day, but Springfield *per se* is not one of them. Springfield, primarily an area of private home ownership, is, however, close to a great deal of social housing and many distinctly working-class communities.

Melissa Sihra raises the important issue of the 'conflictual resonances of the body and the "non-body"'[47] in the work of Marina Carr.
Here the play combines the ideal body of Bruce Lee and the 'non-body'
of the characters in a simultaneous way. Cathy Leeney's reflections,
cited earlier, on Marc Augé's notion of the 'non-place', links with the
notion of 'non-body', utilizing Sihra's phrase, and can be added to the
idea of non-space or non-Dublin. To these we can add the concept of
non-time or cultural timelessness, in order to understand how the figure
of Bruce Lee becomes a dominant, symbolic non-presence and instructive
and conscriptive inter-text.[48] O'Rowe blurs the co-ordinates of the
space, and specific references to Dublin are intentionally scattered,
something which in turn maps on to the disorientation of character.[49]

RAP(T) DUBLIN

As the play *Howie The Rookie* begins, Ollie and Peaches seek The
Rookie's help to beat someone up – they are 'after someone' (p.9), both
having gotten scabies from the mattress in Ollie's place. (The infestation
can be transmitted by either sexual contact or from shared bedding,
towels or clothing. It is also a disease associated with poverty.) Peaches
had to shave his body and was given cream which burned him up. His
trauma is added to when his father discovers him 'on the jacks floor in
his nip, bollox shaved to bits' (p.15). Rookie, by a process of elimination,
is regarded as the source of the contamination. The Ladyboy is also after
The Rookie because he stood on his Siamese fighting-fish – Betas. In
terms of illegality, while neither The Howie nor The Rookie Lee display any strong associations with criminal gangs or illegal activities –
apart from aggression and joy-riding of sorts, they do experience
violence in their everyday lives. (Some recent critics of the play over-
state their criminality, simply because they align working-class violence
with criminality in an all-pervading manner.)

The Howie volunteers to be part of the avenging party and The
Rookie is duly beaten up and 'Vengeance [is] extracted' (p.21). Up to this
point, The Howie Lee displays a great degree of arrogance and distance.
His desperation is only made conscious through the accidental death of
his brother, for which he is part responsible. The coins The Mousey Lee
died trying to retrieve had fallen from the Rookie's pockets earlier,
when he rejected (and fled) his mother's requests to stay at home and
take care of his younger brother.

The spectator gets a strong sense of The Howie's vulnerability after
he steps in to rescue The Rookie from Bernie's Down's Syndrome son.

The Howie cries after beating him up. He moves in a different emotional direction again when he asks The Rookie: 'Tell me your woes 'bout the fishes an' I will help you' (p.41). Further, he buys The Rookie some cream to ease the scabies itching. From here the play negotiates with a sort of innocent anarchic, redemptive heroism.

O'Rowe's characters communicate in very strange ways, often deploying slang, eloquent phrases, key words or action words as unfinished sentences. This is employed in order to reflect on a mindset that is blatant and focused in such a way that linguistic coherence is not necessarily beyond them, but that the characters are indifferent to it. (We get no sense of the occupations of most of the characters. In the main, money is in short supply. And the day after he is beaten up, The Rookie doesn't seem to have work commitments.) When they communicate in fragments, an audience must do the rest. The language is reminiscent of Anthony Burgess's *Clockwork Orange* and the destructive violence of that particular piece as much as the urban rhythms of contemporary rap music, something which codifies sexist, anti-law, macho and materially aspirational lyrics. (The actors in the first production of the play performed with distinctly working-class Dublin accents. But, apart from the local references, it would be interesting to consider the appropriateness of the play to any major urban centre, say, Detroit, USA.) Likewise, the naming of characters The Howie, The Rookie, The Mousey, The Peaches (only occasionally), and The Bruce adds something to the quest for distinctiveness and individuality within a social class, and something also done in the naming of real-life gangland figures.

CORPOREAL EXHILARATION

The changing connection between the two males is also significant, because the degree of violence also shifts, from a somewhat casual beating that The Rookie initially receives, through the brawl involving Bernie's son, to the more sinister fight in Dave McGee's gaff between the Ladyboy and The Howie Lee. This fight takes on the detail and sensibility of the final fight sequence to so many Kung Fu movies, a battle to the death between hero and villain –'Cos it's not normal fisticuffs any more, not Marquis of Queensberry. It's blood an' bone' p. (47). The Rookie states: 'Both cryin', I think, a weird kinda keenin' sound' (p.48). Leon Hunt argues that:

> Kung fu is a genre *of* bodies: extraordinary, expressive, spectacular, sometimes even grotesque bodies ... This ecstatic excess extends to

the aural dimension; Bruce Lee's panoply of shrieks and roars, rhythmically orchestrated thuds and swishes, the reverberative (orgasmic?) aftershocks that follow definitive strikes.[50]

He identifies in Kung Fu movies what he calls 'corporeal exhilaration'.[51]

The fight ends with The Howie being victorious, only for Peaches and Ollie to attack him. The Howie is thrown out of a window and is impaled on a railing. O'Rowe pushes things a bit further. The Hi-ace, with Flann Dingle driving and Ginger Boy surfing on the roof, pursued by the police, slams into the railing where The Howie is impaled – 'The Howie's body comes apart by itself, just before the two tons of metal slams into him, me mate, me new, me impaled mate, me namesake the name of Lee, me saviour' (p.51).

It is worthwhile considering the concept of impalement, because it can be argued that there is a strong sexual overtone to such an action. (This also calls to mind some paintings of the martyrdom of Christian saints, which can display a significant degree of sexual suggestivity.) Proof of this is to be found in O'Rowe's *Made in China* (2001) is full of references to same-sex sexual abuse, but the rape of Kilby – rectal penetration, by means of a pool cue – and the damage to bowel and organs that follow, become the means by which a policeman (Copper Dolan) and a gang leader (Puppacat) establish a binding agreement:

Paddy: They shook in your shite?!
Kilby: Shook symbolic, they did, all ceremonial, made the pact legit an' bindin' on the sufferin', the martyrdom of Kilby.[52]

Late in the play Kilby tries to re-enact his own assault, attempting to rape Hughie with an umbrella. Kilby describes his experience as that of being 'cue stick's whore' (p.79), but also sees the pain that he suffered during his violation as something that gives him the status and distancing of a Shaolin monk, practised in martial arts fighting. Further, when Kilby threatens Hughie, he speaks of 'impalin'' him (p.79). (Kilby's fantasy of revenge against Copper Dolan is to rape him.) *Made in China* offers a far darker vision of the perverted, retributive justice of street gangs with their rule of law, punishment beatings and twisted codes of honour. Instead of narrating the violence, as in *Howie The Rookie*, the spectator experiences sequences of violence on stage. (Ollie's homosexuality in *Howie The Rookie* is generally accepted, if a marker of difference, and makes it very different to the rampant homophobia throughout *Made in China*.[53])

If violence controls the dynamics of *Howie The Rookie*, its connection to sex is just as provocative. Throughout the drama there is an ongoing sense of sex without purpose or passion. If the scabies disease is the initial kickstart or the excuse for violence, then the death of The Howie comes about because of his rejection of Avalanche, Peaches' sister. She is referred to by Howie as being 16 stone weight (p.11), and that 'her grotesque arse [is] bet into a pair of ski pants … see her piss-flaps an' everything' (p.13). (On another occasion he describes her as a 'Dirty fat cunt' (p.27).) Peaches accuses The Rookie of 'Makin' her think someone loved her when she was unlovable? Givin' her hope' (p.49). There is nothing chivalrous about The Howie's behaviour towards either Bernie or Avalanche. O'Rowe shifts male relationships with the opposite sex towards indifference and rejection. Bernie is drawn to The Howie's 'machoness' (p.22), and she likes to watch 'blokes scrappin'' (p.23). Those gathered at the McGee party share a similar fascination. Sex and violence are fundamentally interconnected and nothing else seems to generate a value system. There is no alternative to that and nothing that could be equated with intimacy. Both sex and violence are just transactions. Ultimately, Howie's death is a form of self-destruction and not sacrificial, redemptive or heroic, as The Rookie would like it to be.

After The Howie's death The Rookie calls at his parents in order to 'Let them know he was good at the end' (p.51). On the television there is a video of the dead Mousey Lee being held steady in order to pose for the camera: 'The boy's face is grey. His eyes are on mine. His expression doesn't change' (p.51). The Rookie sits in the same seat from which the first recording was made, invited to do so by The Howie's father, because he is photogenic. In the double image of the living and the dead, an audience is challenged to consider the dynamics of violence and violation and the rupture from the tradition of the Irish wake. This scene captures the fundamental desensitization of a family to trauma. The family's pain is distanced and eschewed through a recording, in a way that violent films can manage to both satisfy a need to address an injustice and also ratify social immobility, without getting to its root cause, inequality.

The notion of empathy arises many times in O'Rowe's work. The Rookie gets a double whiskey for the price of a single from a barman, as he 'feels' for him, 'gives' him 'empathy' (p.32). But, like the defence of Avalanche's dignity, the empathy has little substance, because it is a society cut off substantially from its communal values and grief, not capable of acknowledging fully its own compromises, injustices, indoctrination and traumas. To be macho is not so much about expression, more about cultural compensation. Violence is a way of gaining respect and a way of marking out territory. The play is in part about men on the rampage, set loose on themselves.

URBAN GOTHIC

What the novel *Fight Club* and later the film version of it achieve is that they both reflect an anarchic sensibility along with a sheer desperation, for which contemporary consumer culture is, in part, accountable. *Fight Club* offers developmental phases of rebellion, unlike in O'Rowe's play, where the social system is just a given. It is Project Mayhem [with its mischief, arson, misinformation and assault committees] that is going to save the world in *Fight Club*, bringing with it 'A cultural ice age. A prematurely induced dark age. Project Mayhem will force humanity to go dormant or into remission long enough for the Earth to recover' (p.125). *Fight Club* deliberates on the notion of redemption through violence – 'There's the hysterical shouting in tongues like at church, and when you wake up Sunday afternoon you feel saved' (p.51).

American society offers the myth of progress and improvement, though here it is self-destruction that dominates O'Rowe's urban land-scape. The performance potential of this play is to escort an audience into the terrorism of a world where actions have no significance and are without resonance or connection. There is little or no honour to be found, even in self-sacrifice, and justice serves only a skewed function.[54] The anarchic tendencies of *Fight Club* become expressed publicly as attacks on social institutions, thus violation is more like spurious revenge, whereas O'Rowe's characters seem to have all but internalized such rage.

While the play is not in the territory of the romanticized working classes, which has a mythology all of its own, neither is it set in an under-class, with all the pejorative ideas and implications associated with the term. In this play there is none of the defiant intimacy of the working classes that is to be found in plays of a previous generation of writers. Likewise, the spectator experiences none of the communal supports and levels of care nominally associated with that social grouping. The play maps how disadvantage is perpetuated. The endeavour, commitment and strong work ethic as well as strong community spirit once associated with the working classes have shifted. For the characters, stoicism has become withdrawal; there is a huge absence of resistance and the levels of acceptance and tolerance are frightening. There is no protest and no political agitation. A true absence of connection and real impoverish-ment in terms of the imagination are visible. (Social and community groups in working-class areas would reject such an observation.)

What intrigues about this play is not the basic dysfunctionality that it creates; more, it is the misplaced emphasis on redemption. The play struggles with the status of virility, with testimony to little other than emasculation. Here the rehearsals of masculinity are off-key and thus the influence of popular culture is misappropriated at best. In this work of O'Rowe, emotion and pain are accessible only when they are routed through a habitual frame. The reality of the Lees is potentially one without tragic purpose; the discipline and self-defence of martial arts become self-destruction and carnage. It is a world that becomes locked into a 'performative hermeneutic' of sorts. Numbness abounds. The greatness of the play is in the fact that such numbness is uttered without voicing it simplistically. This is what Karl Shields and Aidan Kelly achieved so magnificently in their performances.

The Howie dies, like his hero, Bruce Lee, prematurely. Bruce Lee serves as both a cultural artefact and a motivating artifice. The artificiality of fiction condemns, more a *Game of Death* without reaching for the spectacle of nostalgia for the suburban working class. It is a world enveloping upon itself, as is the monologue – which has swapped metaphysical debate for the intertextuality of popular culture, martial arts movies and the metaphysicality or metro-corporeality of aggressively, narrated, doubled (and dubbed, perhaps) urbanized language. The characters are caught between the fabricated impersonality of suburbia and the impracticality of an increasingly performative, globalized, popular culture, wedged between the absence of physical amenities and the convenience and vicariousness of urban myth, and jammed between open spaces on the edge of the suburban sprawl and the partitioned and relatively immobile nature of socially ranked relationships. The generation and ingestion of popular culture, which is an urbanized phenomena in most respects, maps on to the production and consumption of a dystopic urban sprawl. Cities consume spaces, eating into the countryside, as Dublin and Tallaght have done. The overlaid personas of the two Lees are not only mobilized by popular culture and are repositories of it, but identities that are also mass-produced. It is no longer nation, rather, it is popular culture that is the more influential, and ideologically priming, in Benedict Anderson's words, the 'imagined community'.[55] Barthes comments:

> Thus every day and everywhere, man [*sic*] is stopped by myths, referred by them to this motionless prototype which lives in his place, stifles him in the manner of a huge internal parasite and assigns to his activity the narrow limits within which he is allowed to suffer without upsetting the world: bourgeois pseudo-physis is in the fullest sense a prohibition for man against inventing himself.[56]

These opinions are vital to an understanding of a play like *Howie The Rookie* as they explain how mythology stifles, prohibits, inhibits, stalls and deincentivizes working-class communities. The structuring of a counter-myth to that bourgeois one is faced down by many urban writers.

Stella Feehily's first play *Duck* (2003)[57] is set in suburban Dublin and it tells primarily the stories of the relationship between Cat and her friend Sophie, a first-year university student at University College Dublin who has had a Benylin addiction and who misuses laxatives, of Cat's relationships with two men, Mark, her wine-bar/club-owning (The Numero Uno), drug-dealing boyfriend,[58] and finally, Cat's casual affair with the ageing playwright, Jack. The play gives us a view of club culture and of family lives in disintegration, the violence and the money that drive a society, and the manner in which the main characters negotiate through these situations.

Mobile phone credit, video games and cable television connections are all dropped into the exchanges to make the text feel contemporary. What makes this play novel for audiences are the references to things that would have normally been excluded from plays of a previous generation. There are open and casual discussions about anal sex and bleeding, a scene where Sophie is seated on a toilet, leaving a phone message while she reads from a dictionary, with her underwear stretched around her knees, bath scenes between Cat and her two lovers, one of which turns savagely violent when Mark teaches her a lesson by persistently pushing Cat's head under water (ducking her), and a further bathroom scene where a naked Cat bathes and dries herself with a towel in the presence of Sophie.

The problem of course is how you bring together a rite-of-passage play about young adult females moving on and how you make that dramatic. The play opens with the two young women drunk; they are approached by 'two inner city lads', who try to assault them. When the males attack, Sophie strikes one with a Bacardi Breezer bottle and then uses the broken bottle to drive away the other, who is on top of Cat. Cat has problems with Mark. When he leaves her waiting for him in his car as he deals in an estate nicknamed 'Beirut' (p.5), she, in a fit of rage, places her purple cardigan in the fuel tank, sets the jumper alight and the vehicle explodes. The arson attack brings him to the attention of the police, who want to know how he can afford such a lavish lifestyle. They suspect drugs and the Criminal Assets Bureau (CAB) are waiting in the wings. She is only a convenience for him and it is not until she has the affair with the older man that he takes her seriously. During one scene, wearing balaclavas, he and a friend break into Jack's apartment and threaten to kill Cat. While the play is a rite of passage, key moments in it are worth considering. One is Cat's rejection of symbolism. Cat isn't Cat for Jack but 'Gina Lollobrigida' (p.39). While she controls the parameters of the affair initially, by the end Jack dictates. Mark calls her 'Duck', because of her big feet. Sophie's nickname is 'Gull'; she is only called it by her mother. Sophie's selection of definitions of 'Duck', 'Cunt', 'Wench' and 'Gull' from a dictionary is apposite, because it is about the definition of women within a highly formalized culture. One must question if they can be energized by definitions that set out to limit?

Sophie's college essay on women using arson historically as an act of revenge is a key attempt to mythologize defiance. And by the play's end the two women are moving on, Cat has stopped living with Mark, and Sophie is leaving home. The two women are on the roadside waiting for a taxi. Sophie has a broken arm because she fell out her bedroom window. Cat regards this as her first 'flight'. Both respond with 'chirp chirp', in an attempt to be playful but also out of a need to emphasize the symbolism of the piece. Duck and Gull flee their nests. In this instance, essentially myth is barely incidental and symbolism is a burden, unlike say Henrik Ibsen's *The Wild Duck* (1884).

DISINTEGRATED ENDINGS

Fiona Macintosh comments on and quotes György Lukác's idea that the tragic character is dead for a long time before he/she actually experiences death and that 'tragedy proper – begins' at the moment when the 'enigmatic forces have distilled the essence from a man, [and] have forced him to become essential'.[59] If there is no essence, can anything be essential? Carr's women characters are monstrous, frightening, intolerant, impetuous, cruel and injurious. They are content to wreck destructiveness and they leave behind annihilation. The characters cannot let go of pain or of primal obsessions; identity is consolidated out of pain, not pleasure, as pain is the reward on some level, pain is not a distraction, it is the validation. Hester murders her daughter not out of some irrational impulse but with the calculation and formality of myth that defies the accusation of hysteria or frenzy. In *Howie The Rookie* myths of sacrifice are offered not so much by Christian iconography, but by popular culture in the form of Kung Fu movies. The notion of sacrifice and bloodshed leading to renewal is challenged, as there is no formal renewal but paralysis and numbness towards the end of the play. In *Duck*, arson as an attack on male rule has little or no resonance and seeks no change of register.

Paul Makeham cites Jonathan Raban's notion of 'Soft City', which is 'The city as we imagine it, the soft city of illusion, myth, aspiration, nightmare, is as real, maybe more real, than the hard city one can locate on maps, in statistics, in monographs or urban sociology and demography and architecture.'[60] For Barthes, 'Myths are nothing but the ceaseless, untiring solicitation, this insidious and inflexible demand that all men recognize themselves in this image, eternal yet bearing a date, which was built of them one day as if for all time.'[61] While the writers are engaging with the repetition compulsion, they more than ever have wedged a gap between past and present, and have queried the eternalization of the real. Kearney sees myth as 'a potentially emancipator project',[62] and holds out for the recognition of a more 'liberating dimension of myth – the genuinely *utopian* – behind its negative *ideological* dimension. Supplementing the hermeneutics of suspicion with a hermeneutics of affirmation, we discern the potentiality of myth for a positive symbolizing project.'[63]

Myth liberates, or has the potential to do so. In Irish theatre, there is a sense of liberation in *The Gigli Concert*, less so in *Howie The Rookie* or *Duck*. Dublin city as a symbol of urbanization is increasingly a city that has no real myth of itself despite its history, apart from in the minds of refugees and economic migrants perhaps. The order of the world is not about origins, or about who you are, what you do or where you come from, but about how much you make and how you spend it. If the performance of wealth in the era of the Celtic Tiger was the 'mask' in the Jungian sense, Irish drama gives potential access also to the shadow.

The Celtic Tiger was temporarily the governing or foundation myth, placing responsibility internally and not collectively. The Irish Dream is transfigured almost into the American one, by a nation that has relinquished its postcolonial narrative. Our myths are no longer local bespoke, but internationalized and globalized on the back of first-world wealth. In contemporary culture, consumerism and consumption have come to the fore, or, as John Orr remarks, 'to consume is to perform ... To consume here means not merely to gratify but also to imitate'.[64] To consume is also an attempt to mythologize the Irish Dream, and as many critics remind us, wealth is the fundamental metanarrative, which motivates, sustains and explains material desire, while structuring class, gender and race inequalities. Consumption is anything but a new mythology as it has such a 'soft' underbelly. The current economic crisis has eaten away many of the economic gains hard won for many under the Celtic Tiger. The Celtic Tiger era seems increasingly less of a myth and more and more an hysterical mass delusion

A society existing between relative abundance and plenty and the new frugalities, between relatively healthy economy and toxicity, and a society 'between' myths may be a very difficult place to be, myths by which the nation of Ireland had lived, or the myths by which we construct our dramaturgy. Perhaps, we should not be too harsh on our playwrights for not addressing that new society as it emerged. It will take a new generation of writers and members of migrant communities to forge new narratives and perhaps intercultural mythologies, where they are refugees, pioneers, prisoners, actors, or agents of difference.

NOTES

1. Deborah Stevenson argues that at one point 'City life (as *gesellschaft*) was regarded as superficial and impersonal while life in the country (*gemeinschaft*) was celebrated as fostering positive and enduring relationships between close friends and kinship groups.' See *Cities and Urban Cultures* (Maidenhead: Open University Press, 2003), p.7.
2. See chapter 1, Helena Sheehan, *Irish Television Drama: A Society and Its Stories* (revised 2001) (Dublin: RTE, 1987) available at www.comms.dcu.ie/sheehanh/myth.htm [Accessed 20 May 2006]
3. Ibid.
4. Richard Kearney's 'Myth and Motherland' in *Ireland's Field Day* (London: Hutchinson, 1985), pp.62–80.
5. Also, for Freud, according to Kearney, religious myths were created to conceal 'libidinal drive-through mechanisms of inhibition and sublimation'. See *Navigations: Collected Irish Essays 1976–2006* (Dublin: Lilliput Press, 2006), p.393.
6. Kearney's 'Myth and Motherland', pp.64–65.
7. Lisa Fitzpatrick, 'Nation and Myth in the Age of the Celtic Tiger: Muide Éire?' in *Echoes Down the Corridor*, ed. P. Lonergan and R. O'Dwyer (Dublin: Carysfort Press, 2007), p.178.
8. George Steiner, *Antigones: The Antigone Myth in Western Literature, Art and Thought* (Oxford: Oxford University Press, 1984), p.126.
9. Ibid., pp.126–27.
10. Kearney, *Navigations*, p.393.
11. Roland Barthes, *A Roland Barthes Reader*, edited and introduced by Susan Sontag (London: Vintage, 1993), p.132.
12. Ibid.
13. See Marianne McDonald, 'Classics as Celtic Firebrand: Greek Tragedy, Irish Playwrights, and Colonialism' in *Theatre Stuff: Critical Essays on Contemporary Irish Theatre*, ed. E. Jordan (Dublin: Carysfort Press, 2000), pp.16–26.
14. Melissa Sihra, 'A Cautionary Tale: Marina Carr's *By the Bog of Cats*' in Jordan (ed.), *Theatre Stuff*, p.257.
15. Marina Carr, *The Mai* and *By the Bog of Cats* in *Plays One* (London: Faber & Faber, 1999). (Hereafter, all further references to the play will be in parentheses within the body of the text.)
16. Oliver Taplin, *Greek Tragedy in Action* (London: Methuen, 1978), p.164.
17. Anna McMullan, 'Gender, Authorship and Performance in Selected Plays by Contemporary Irish Women Playwrights: Mary Elizabeth Burke-Kennedy, Marie Jones, Marina Carr, Emma Donoghue' in Jordan (ed.), *Theatre Stuff*, p.41.
18. Taplin, *Greek Tragedy in Action*, p.27.
19. Victor Merriman, 'Theatre of Tiger Trash', *Irish University Review*, 29–2, Autumn–Winter 1999, pp. 305–17.
20. Marina Carr, *Portia Coughlan* in *The Dazzling Dark*, selected and introduced by Frank McGuinness (London: Faber & Faber, 1996), p.267. (References to this play come from this edition and not the *Plays One* published by Faber & Faber.)
21. For variations on the Medea myth, see Peter D. Arnott, *Public and Performance in the Greek Theatre* (London: Routledge, 1989).

22. Michael Walton, 'Introduction', *Euripides: Plays One* (Methuen: London, 2000), p.ix.
23. Taplin, *Greek Tragedy in Action*, p.165.
24. Mothers within the male writing tradition were often absent, and if absent, idealized, as in *Philadelphia, Here I Come!* (1964). *Portia Coughlan* contains a proliferation of destructive maternal figures. Portia cannot love her own children and when she dies she leaves them behind. The mother in *On Raftery's Hill* is dead, The Mai has died, as had her own mother, Ellen. Caroline Cassidy's mother (Olive) is dead.
25. Adam McLean, *The Triple Goddess: An Exploration of the Archetypal Feminine* (Grand Rapids, MI: Phanes Press, 1989), p.72.
26. Ibid., pp.71–72.
27. Marina Carr, *On Raftery's Hill* (Oldcastle: Gallery Press, 2000), p.56. (Hereafter, all page numbers will be given in parentheses within the main body of the text.)
28. McLean, *Triple Goddess*, p.72.
29. For the difficulties in theorizing the Aristotelian theatrical paradigm, see Ronald Vince in 'The Aristotelian Theatrical Paradigm as Cultural-Historical Construct', *Theatre Research International*, 22–1, 1997, pp.38–48.
30. The presence of swans and geese recur across *The Mai*, serving as symbols of intense love, innocence, and the black swan, specifically, as a sign of doom and death. And the story of Sam Brady and his cow, Billy the Black, in *The Mai*, serves as a tale of transgression. Sam was so enraged by Robert's infidelities that he initially let the cow loose in The Mai and Robert's garden and then, later, he took a gun and blew 'the head off the cob feeding innocently near the bank. It's true what they say: swans do keen their mates … It's a high haunting sound that sings the once-living out of this word', according to Millie, the Mai's daughter and the play's narrator (pp.157–58).
31. Michael X. Zelenak, 'The Troublesome Reign of King Oedipus: Civic Discourse and Civil Discord in Greek Tragedy', *Theatre Research International*, 23–1, 1998, pp.69–82, p.80.
32. Paul Chatterton and Robert Hollands, *Urban Nightscapes: Youth Cultures, Pleasure Spaces and Corporate Power* (London and New York: Routledge, 2003), p.177.
33. Ibid.
34. Ibid.
35. See Gavin Quin's *Oedipus Loves You* (2006) for Pan Pan Theatre Company.
36. The myth of Deirdre of the Sorrows and the Sons of Usna informs Vincent Woods's *A Cry From Heaven* (2005) and Paul Mercier's *Diarmuid and Gráinne* (2001), the former set in indeterminate historical space, the latter in contemporary Ireland and gangland. Further, Billy Roche's screenplay *Trojan Eddie* (1996) exploits the same myth. Dermot Bolger's attempts to map social squalor, drug addiction, money lending and poverty in a modern setting have been striking and unsettling in *The Lament for Arthur Cleary* (1989) (a version of *Caoineadh Airt Uí Laoghaire*, the eighteenth-century Gaelic elegy, written by Eileen O'Connell). See Martine Pelletier's discussion on both the origins of the piece and the relationship of the play to the old lament in 'Dermot Bolger's Drama' in Jordan (ed.), *Theatre Stuff*, pp.249–56. Paula Meehan's *Mrs Sweeney* (1997) is set in an inner-city flat complex in a world of AIDS, unemployment, drug dealing, petty crime and broken homes. When Mr Sweeney's pigeons are slaughtered, he responds with madness. Meanwhile the play's women characters find some resolution in a very conscious, exorbitant theatricality, as if this is the only way to promote serious social defiance. Meehan builds on the ancient Sweeney myth of exile and madness and him living amongst the birds.
37. Likewise, the ability of popular culture to permeate a consciousness is fastidiously articulated by mention of John Woo's *Last Hurrah for Chivalry* (1978), in the *Tarzan* movies, ('fuckin' *Weismulle*, p.20), and the athlete (The) Linford Christie, John Wayne, *Gladiators*, the television show, and *The High Chaparral*.
38. Fiachra Gibbons, 'The Dark Stuff', 24 November 2003, *Guardian*, see www.film.guardian. co.uk/interview/interviewpages/0,1091907,00.html [Accessed 8 January 2008]
39. Gar O'Donnell in Brian Friel's *Philadelphia, Here I Come!* (1964) is the obvious example, whose split subjectivity is the result of a repressive inability to give expression and release to a complex self and to the trauma surrounding the loss of his mother.
40. Bruce Lee was the San Francisco-born but Hong Kong-raised martial arts actor. He was well known for the TV series *The Green Hornet* (1966–67) and guest appearances in *Batman* (1966–67) before he went on to make a series of cult martial arts films comprising *The Big Boss* (1971), *Fist of Fury* (1972), *Way of the Dragon* (1972) and *Enter the Dragon* (1973). He died at 32 with a brain aneurysm on 20 July 1973, while working on *The Game of Death* (released 1978).

41. See Chuck Palahniuk's *Fight Club* (London: Vintage, 1997), p.168. (Hereafter, all page details will be given in parentheses within the text.)

42. Judith Butler argues that gender is a 'free floating artifice' and as a 'shifting and contextual phenomenon, gender does not denote a substantive being, but a relative point of convergence among culturally and historically specific relations'. See *Gender Trouble: Feminism and the Subversion of Identity* (New York: Routledge, 1990), p.6 and p.10, cited by Robin Roberts in 'Gendered Media Rivalry: Irish Drama and American Film' in B. Singleton and A. McMullan (eds), *Performing Ireland, Australasian Drama Studies Special Issue*, 43, October 2003, p.109.

43. Among many working-class communities, violent behaviour can be a reflex response to or caused by socio/political dynamics. Class differences in terms of health, crime (joy-riding, drug taking, burglary, etc.), school performance and employment success are blatantly palpable in contemporary Ireland, and the emergence of the Celtic Tiger (1993–2001 approx.) made that obvious and exacerbated disadvantage in many instances, despite the increasing participation of school leavers in Third Level education, for example, and fewer young men on the Dole. The recurrence of such high levels of economic activity in 2003/4 and until 2007 can be seen to have only added to the division. The impact of the current economic devastation cannot be predicted.

44. See slideshow at http://www.esdevlin.com/

45. Cathy Leeney, 'Men in No-Man's Land: Performing Urban Liminal Spaces in Two Plays by Mark O'Rowe', *Irish Review*, 35–1, Spring 2007, pp.108–16, p.111.

46. Dame Street is a well-known Dublin thoroughfare. Rowney Street named in the play doesn't exist in the capital, but it supposedly leads to Lime Street, which does exist, just off City Quay and close to Pearse Street and Windmill Lane. There are two Limekiln Lanes in Dublin, one in Harold's Cross and the other near Kimmage. Again, there are two Ashbrooks in the Dublin vicinity; one close to the Phoenix Park and the other in the Clontarf area. The 123 Bus, also mentioned in the play, serves the area between the Drimnagh area and Griffith Avenue. In the Springfield area of Tallaght there are a small number of shops that resemble the 'new shops', which are 'built in a circle, their backs face out to keep bandits at bay' (p.13).

47. Melissa Sihra, 'Renegotiating Landscapes of the Female: Voices, Topographies and Corporealities of Alterity in Marina Carr's *Portia Coughlan*' in *Performing Ireland*, p.24.

48. In *From Both Hips* (*Two Plays: From Both Hips* and *The Aspidistra Code* (London: Nick Hern, 1999), O' Rowe uses Don Johnson from the *Miami Vice* television series as a point of popular cultural connection, reference and identification and in *Made in China* it is action movie hero Chuck Norris, who also starred opposite Bruce Lee in *The Way of the Dragon*.

49. Gerry Smyth notes that 'the impression of space that emerges most strongly from postmodern geography is one of incompleteness, contingency and partiality. The sequentiality of time is always mitigated by the simultaneity of space', *Space and the Irish Cultural Imagination* (Basingstoke and New York: Palgrave, 2001), pp.14–15.

50. See Leon Hunt, *Kung Fu Cult Masters* (London and New York: Wallflower Press, 2004), p.2.

51. Ibid., p.3.

52. Mark O'Rowe, *Made in China* (London: Nick Hern, 2001), p.77. (Hereafter, all page details will be given in parentheses within the text.)

53. In Bruce Lee's films, *Fist of Fury* and *Enter the Dragon*, concluding or near final fight sequences offer impalements. In the latter, during a memorable hall of mirrors sequence, the evil leader, pierced by a spear coming through a mirror, dies impaled on a rotating, revolving panel, and in the former, one enemy is held in place while a sword falling from the air pierces through his body.

54. Gary Mitchell's *A Little World of Our Own* (1997) is set in Belfast, and it falls between two stools, between the representation of the embedded violence within a Loyalist working-class community and the macho celebration of the cathartic qualities of brutality and the myth of self-sacrifice. Mitchell wished to outline the extent of the violence; he also attempted to engage critically with its negative qualities and to state that there can be no distancing ambiguity, which preserves the spectator from the depths of the violence at the core of his theatrical community.

55. See Benedict Anderson, *Imagined Communities: Reflections on the Origins and Spread of Nationalism* (London: Verso, 1983).

56. Barthes, *Roland Barthes Reader*, p.145.

57. Stella Feehily, *Duck* (London: Nick Hern, 2003). (Hereafter, all page details will be given in parentheses within the text.)

58. Daragh Carville's *Observatory* (1999) is laudanum-motivated, and Bolger's *The Passion of Jerome* (1999) is cocaine-driven.

59. Fiona Macintosh, *Dying Acts: Death in Ancient Greek and Modern Irish Tragic Drama* (Cork: Cork University Press, 1994), p.78.
60. Paul Makeham, 'Performing the City', *Theatre Research International*, 32–2, 2005, pp.150–60, p.154, citing Jonathan Raban, *Soft City* (London: Hamish Hamilton, 1974) p.2.
61. Barthes, *Roland Barthes Reader*, pp.145–46.
62. Kearney, *Navigations*, p.390.
63. Ibid., p.393.
64. John Orr, *Tragicomedy and Popular Culture* (London: Macmillan, 1991), pp.6–7.

6

There's Something About Narrative

MASTERED NARRATIVES

During the 1980s and early 1990s, deeply troubled characters, during moments of isolated reflection or through extended narratives delivered in front of other characters, were afforded opportunities to express what could not be accommodated through inter-character exchanges of dialogue. In Tom Murphy's *Conversations on a Homecoming* (1985), through narrative Michael confirms his lack of success in New York and his attempted suicide. Frank McGuinness's character The Sinner Courtney in *The Breadman* (1990) suffers a nervous breakdown in response to the drowning of his brother and again it is during moments of reflective monologue that his traumas are given enhanced expression. Murphy's *The Gigli Concert* (1983) also deals with mental breakdown. The therapist, JPW King takes on the fantastical aspirations of his client, the unnamed Irish Man. Deluded and high on mandrax and alcohol, JPW sings like Beniamino Gigli, thus fulfilling the Irishman's fantasy transformation of being. Anne Devlin's main character Greta in *After Easter* (1994) initially straddles madness and mysticism, and ultimately finds expression through the subversive gesture of handing out communion wafers to people on the street and also through narrating a fairy-tale, which ends the play. Madness and trauma seem to find release through story and extreme gestures that have metaphoric and symbolic significances. Richard Kearney suggests that 'every human existence is a life in search of a narrative'.[1]

Language, particularly narrated language, is fundamentally linked to power, obedience, transgression, identity formation, citizenship, class, gender and race. In a colonial context the relative demise of the Irish language has had serious implications in terms of self-knowing and public expression. A nation evicted from its native language, despite the compromises and the complicities of its indigenous population, has untold consequences. Seamus Deane notes that 'Irish drama has been heavily populated by people for whom vagrancy and exile have become inescapable conditions about which they can do nothing but talk endlessly and eloquently to themselves', and in saying this he has in mind Friel's characters and 'the tramps of Yeats and Synge and Beckett, the stationless slum dwellers of O'Casey or Behan'.[2] That endless and eloquent talking, however, in much of the work under discussion here leads to change or transformation on some level, and therefore functions on a different level to what Deane has in mind.

For Kearney, 'From the word go, stories were invented to fill the gaping hole within us, to assuage our fear and dread, to try to give answers to the great unanswerable questions of existence: Who are we? Where do we come from? Are we animal, human or divine? Strangers, gods or monsters?'[3] But narrative is not only about dread: 'the great tales and legends gave not only relief from everyday darkness but also pleasure and enchantment'.[4] Fantasy gives distance and also the possibility of processing fears and anxieties from a distance, within a relatively safe and transactional space.

Kearney suggests that 'without this transition from nature to narrative, from time suffered to time enacted and enunciated, it is debatable whether a merely biological life (*zoe*) could ever be considered a truly human one (*bios*)'.[5] Further, Kearney offers that it is 'only when haphazard happenings are transformed into story, and thus made *memorable* over time, that we become full agents of our own history.'[6] While he is correct in his identification of the transformation of incident into narrative, the implications of such an action does not also lead to agency, especially when a narrative has a negative hold over individuals or characters, as is the case with most of the Irish tradition.

Kearney adds that 'when someone asks you *who* you are, you tell your story'.[7] However the veracity of that story is always questionable, given that people and characters shape their narrative with an audience in mind. Stories make sense of the circumstances of the characters, their impulses, action, inhibitions, repetitions and indulgence, and also the extent and the limits of their courage. Stories confront as much as conceal fears and desires. They deal with loss through distance, through frames that protect an audience. The subtle dramaturgy of that framing is crucial to the Irish theatrical tradition, at its best.

Ciarán Benson's work on the cultural psychology of self is extremely useful. What Benson has to say about identity applies almost equally to narrative formations and disclosures of characters in theatre. Characters, using either narratives or monologues, construct stories, out of which audiences make 'sense' of the theatrical world in which the character(s) operate(s). For Benson, 'The story or stories of myself

that I tell, that I hear others tell of me, that I am unable or unwilling
to tell, are not independent of the self that I am: they are constitutive
of *me*.'⁸ When directed towards people or characters, a story is often
delivered to affirm a point of view, as a way of seducing the listener(s)
or spectator(s), or as a way of postponing judgement. One can also take
people inside one's story, particularly through parable or fairy-tale. All
types of communications happen through that narrative process, values
are suggested both blatantly and indirectly, approval for certain ways
of viewing the world are attested and probably rounded down through
feedback, and propositions of connection are communicated through
tone, inflection, pause, hesitation or the lack of clarification.

Narrative becomes suggestive proposition, but also leaves itself
open to interpretation, misunderstanding, interrogation and ambivalence. Socially and culturally, the interrogation of another's narrative is
often vital to the establishment, as much as the mutual agreement or
vague challenges or quests for *faux* qualification, of non-contestation.
To test another's narrative or oblige individuals to account for themselves endlessly can bring destructive patterns to interpersonal or
intrapersonal relationships.

On a personal level, narratives are in some ways a form of self-talk
which are induced by not only self-taught mental responses or neural
pathways, but are also shaped by how one's environment contributes
to one's narrative, how it manipulates one's narrative, and how it
coerces through larger narratives. How narrative structures worldviews through master narratives proves more difficult to challenge. At
either extreme, one can be liberated by one's narrative or one can
be dispossessed by it, reduced by it or enabled by it. The characters in
dramas are shaped by the place in which they find themselves. That
recognition alone quite obviously theatricalizes the narrative, but also
complicates the processes of contextualization. The 'where'⁹ you are
that Benson works with is an endeavour to historicize and to contex-
tualize, but the space of performance is a found, contrived space,
where additional conventions dominate.

Tom Murphy's *Baileganagire* (1985), Frank McGuinness's *Someone
Who'll Watch Over Me* (1992) and Martin McDonagh's *The Pillowman*
(2003) all use narrative very deliberately and brilliantly, in order to
establish connections between identity formation and story, personal,
national and inter-national narratives, and while very different formally
to each other, in all three of these plays narrative, on the one hand,
offers the consolation of fiction, while on the other, it elaborates on the
way story-telling shapes socialization and indoctrinates, as the imprint

of ideological aspiration and restraint are everywhere. If a character's narrative breaks down, if he/she cannot 'locate' him/herself in the world, or if it is no longer possible to make sense of the world through narrative, as happens to Mary in *Bailegangaire*, the brothers in *The Pillowman* or the hostages in *Someone*, then a certain anxiety, distraughtness and trouble emerge. These plays dramatize the responses to such traumas.

BAILEGANGAIRE: TIME MACHINE

Tom Murphy's masterpiece *Bailegangaire* is an extremely complex play; in part, it is a family drama about how the past has formed the present, in part, it is about the retrieval and letting go of the narratives that shape and misalign individual consciousnesses and determine the relationships between characters, in part it is about the tradition of Irish story-telling itself, and, in part, it is about the hold of grief and trauma over not only the consciousnesses of the characters but also perhaps of communities and nations. An elderly woman, Mommo (Brigit) and her two granddaughters, Mary and Dolly, share a space in which the past and their individual histories (narratives) need to be exorcized. Central to the play is the grandmother's uncompleted story about her and her husband's return from a fair, when out of necessity they stopped off in a public house in the village of Boctán.

The tensions between the travellers and the locals gave rise to a laughing competition between the husband (The Stranger) and the local hero, Costello: Mommo's narrative then is about 'How the place called Bochtán – and its graund (grand) inhabitants – came by its new appellation, Bailegangaire, the place without laughter.'[10] That event and those that followed have shaped the consciousness of the village folk; for instance, the children laugh until the age of reason and not beyond, as 'Boctán forever is Bailegangaire', as Mommo suggests (p.76). (The story of the competition itself is something Murphy claims he overheard.[11])

Bailegangaire, of course, is part of a trilogy that includes *Brigit* (1988), a screenplay that deals with the frustrated relationship between Mommo and her husband, and *The Thief of a Christmas* (1985), which dramatizes the evening of the laughing competition itself. *Bailegangaire* is set in a traditional cottage in the old style, with a bed in the main living area. Anthony Roche argues, the 'image of the bed, the domestic centre, place of fertility, the nest, but now ... the place of decrepitude'.[12] The drama is located in a contemporaneous space that is infiltrated by events long past. The play begins at 8.10 p.m., which most likely coincides with the time a performance might start in the theatre. In *Bailegangaire*, the performance cosmos itself allows time and space to merge. In addition, Mommo's story starts and stops in such a way that it ties in with a feminine form of time and space, one that is circular and uneven and non-linear.

As the play begins the almost senile Mommo is about to kickstart her regular evening recital. For Dolly, it is all 'Seafóid, nonsense talk about forty years ago' (p.49), in contrast, for Mary it is Mommo's 'unfinished symphony' (p.56). Fintan O'Toole suggests that Mommo utilizes a 'baroque, highly stylized language, full of archaic syntax and remnants of Gaelic'.[13] As Nicholas Grene points out, she is indeed part of 'the early Irish peasantry' that playwrights like Murphy tried to forget.[14] Mommo is a *shanachie* in the traditional sense of the word. Usually in this tradition, the story-teller will tell his/her tale in the first person, 'pretending events actually happened to him/herself'.[15]

In contrast, Mommo sticks firmly to third-person narrative until almost the end of the piece. Of course, the suspicion is, from a spectator's perspective, that the story is a personal one, using the third-person narrative as a way of feigning distance. Interestingly, Mommo's self-interrogation contains many self-questions that are delivered in a 'childlike' fashion (p.45). Both senile and childlike, a type of adult-child, Mommo is a bit like the main character, Thomas Dunne, in Sebastian Barry's *The Steward of Christendom* (1995). Both of these plays transform the personal into the national through story-telling: 'Ireland's is a story told over and over again by a senile mind frozen in the past', as Nicholas Grene suggests.[16]

It appears as if a substantial part of Ireland's national narrative has been structured traditionally around issues of victimization, misfortune, hard luck, missed opportunity, and disasters, hunger, forced emigration and disease, families and communities shattered by loss. Yet, within that there has always been a persistent core of defiance, antagonism, and a dark resistance that often finds expression in black humour. Clearly, this national narrative has slowly shifted over the last number of decades, but what Murphy is doing is unearthing a basic narrative of trauma that has at its root inequality and injustice and a relative absence of agency on a broader social level. Clearly, on a personal level, there is some degree of agency, but there is impossibility of impacting on the larger social forces that gives rise to that general mode of subversion and derision, which black humour fosters.

Neither individuals nor nations can easily let go of the past for all kinds of complicated reasons, including grief, shock, anger, despair, particularly when such traumas are avoidable. While the past cannot be changed, its meaning, significance or its hold over the present can be contested or revised. Murphy seems to be challenging the darkest parts of the Irish national narrative through the frame of the laughing competition and the listing of disasters, natural, institutional, and man/woman-made.

ANOTHER BEDTIME STORY

During the play's opening moments the vital tensions between Mary and Mommo are established. Mary wants to celebrate their birthdays jointly, as if she intuits that not only a sharing of celebration interlocks them, but also that her future is tied in with that of Mommo. That they share more than their individual histories is of vital significance. This is Mary's perception, without her having access to the incidents or facts which bind them. Some profile can be put on the past that is currently beyond either the frame of coherence or confirmation, in that it has more to do with the resonance of the past in the present, the deliberateness of the past actions to invade behaviour.

Murphy is not arguing for some fundamental continuity between past and present, nor is he advocating a discontinuous present as the best mode of operation, more, he is proposing that in the collision between past and present direct connections cannot be easily articulated, but something larger looms, ghostlike, shapeless and haunting. The past bleeds into the present, palimpsest-like, with certain accretions and discolourations as inevitable consequences. Murphy complicates the personal histories of his characters and elaborates on the relationship between past and present, not in the sense of cause and effect, or of continuity, but more in the sense of contagion.

Through narrative, Mommo is communicating and obfuscating, hallucinating and fantasizing, and is denying and still desiring a different outcome to what happened on that fateful evening. From that blurred intense space some luminosity can emerge. From the off, Mommo offers to tell a 'nice story' (p.43) on a couple of occasions, but with wayward comments like 'incestuous drunkards and bastards' (p.43), the 'cursed paraffin' (p.43), and 'he has a big stick' (p.44), the spectator begins to expect more. In a way, the spectator is invited to begin his or her own speculations as to what actually has happened. From a spectator's/audience's perspective, this play can be very hard work, having to deal with the tedium of Mommo's memory structure, having to cope with his/her own impatience while Mommo stalls her story, and having to consider the way their own individual mindsets manage to structure, accommodate, revisit and revise personal and collective narratives.

Mommo begins her story at the marketplace in Tuam, just prior to Christmas. The trading has been good for some and bad for others. They have to bring back home with them 'eighteen snow-white geese' (p.45). Anticipated sales to fund Christmas spending have not been realized. It is a long trek back home. Before Mommo can progress her narrative, the arrival of Dolly changes the tension and triangularizes the dynamics within the play. What is at stake is more than the relationship between Mary and Mommo. Mary and Dolly have their own agendas; Mary is planning to leave if she cannot find peace and recognition at home, and Dolly wants Mary to take in her yet to be born baby, that is not Stephen's, her husband's, and for Mary to claim it as her own. (Previously, Mary had an affair with him, Stephen, in London.)

The first lengthy extract of Mommo's narrative introduces all of the characters in the bar, the owner, John Mah'ny, the strange Josie, the rabbit-rearing Costello with the big laugh, who can drive fear into kids with threats of the Bogey Man and Jack Frost. In the pub The Stranger sets the challenge, that he is a better laugher than Costello. As Mommo had insisted early on, what was to follow would concern the 'c'roner, civic guard and civilian on all that transpired in John Mah'ny's that night' (p.55).

Having aroused interest in her story, Mommo then falls asleep. Mary tentatively begins to tell that story in a mimicking of Mommo's style. Ultimately, this proves to be the playful subversive ingredient that Murphy uses to dislodge the hold that Mommo has over the story and that the story has over her. Play is also the component that prompts Mary's usurping of the power of the narrative itself. Interestingly, the part of the narrative that Mary takes over is Mommo's reflections on the greetings expressed by the couple as they enter the pub, and Mommo's conversations with her own father and he telling her that the Boctán's were 'ill bred', a 'band of amadáns an' oinseachs ... A low crew of illiterate plebs, drunkards and incestuous bastards' (p.56). Moreover, as Mary delivers these lines, she corrects herself to mimic or impersonate more exactly Mommo's narrative style. It is interesting that she does not feel comfortable straying from it, nor does she grotesquely undermine it. She wears, in a way, the mantle of Mommo, tests her own performance as Mommo. Although Mommo tries to sleep, Mary wakes her because she does not want to hear fragments of Mommo's story late into the night. But Mommo will not play along. However, Mary shifts gear: 'I won't just help you, I'll do it for you (*Progressively, she begins to dramatise the story more*)' (p.58).

Mommo begins to repeat what she had narrated previously, so the play's dramaturgy in a sense is indicative of the family frustration at the unfinished story. The ghastly topics that inspired the laughter that evening hint at something else: "'Twas the best night ever! – the impoverished an' hungry, eyes big as saucers, howlin' their defiance at the heavens through the ceilin'... inviting of what else might come or care to come!' (p.60).

Mary provides a detail that the locals are vexed by the strangers: that the villagers were 'strainin' towards the stranger like mastiffs on chains, fit to tear him asunder' (p.63), particulars which suggest a sort of primordial ritual sacrifice. This revelation unnerves Mommo, as she wonders how Mary knows about this and queries her in a 'suspiciously, but *childlike*' fashion (p.63; my italics). Two-thirds of the way into the drama, a sort of stalemate is reached. Mary has extended the narrative beyond the point where Mommo usually stops, so she challenges Mary with the statement 'Can yeh go on?' (p.63), to which Mary has to admit defeat. In a way, they are having their own competition.

Mommo then bequeaths a little more information. The laughing competition had reached a point where The Stranger wanted to withdraw, so did Costello, only for Mommo to lay down the supplementary challenge and trigger it off again. Now the drama is at a point where it might unfold into what was previously untold. Such a scenario is feared by Dolly, who wishes to put a stop to the momentum. The dramaturgy of the piece reflects the ways people respond to the pains of the past and how others stall or repress revelations.

At their grandad's funeral, Mommo never shed a tear, according to Dolly (p.66). Tom had been buried 'in that same hole in the ground a couple of days before. Not a tear, then or since' was displayed by Mommo (p.66). (Dolly also says that Mommo had to get married.) When Mommo falls into silence for some time, Dolly proffers a different kind of story, an alternative ending to their lives. Dolly offers to repair the roof, provide a video and remote control, and to sign over half the house, if Mary either stays or goes with a 'brand new one' (child) (p.66), which even can be returned after a year, for 'it'll be easy to make up a story' – to which Mary replies '*Another* story!' (p.67).

The tensions between the two sisters run deep. Dolly tells Mary that she is hated by Mommo and herself because she does not 'know terror', 'hatred' or 'desperation' (p.69) and Dolly is enraged by her own perceptions of Mary's relatively easy life, to such an extent that she is willing to 'show them what can happen in the dark of night in a field' and adds 'I'll finish another part of this family's history in grander style than any of the others' (p.69). Dolly: 'We filled half that graveyard'; she adds, 'I'll fill the other half' (p.69), meaning Mommo, Stephen and the foetus in her womb, perhaps.

RESTORED ENDINGS

Instead of running away again, having packed her bags, Mary increasingly realizes the deep need to end the story, but her choice of words is very curious – they are going to 'Live out the – story – finish it, move on to the place where, perhaps, we could make some kind of new start' (p.70). Earlier, Mary had offered to help Mommo remember the narrative, then she suggested that she would 'do it for' Mommo, and now it is living it out which is necessary. Mary knows only too well the connection between narrative and the restored enactments of being. In telling it there is revelation, in 'living' it there is the possibility of healing and transformation.

Mary understands the need that binds all three women. Although she admits that she is not the 'saint' that Dolly thinks she is, Dolly's response is to close down the revelation, while at the same time suggesting that that is not a burden worth carrying. That observation inspires her to say 'Wo ho ho, ho ho ho!' – an expression of mirth that triggers Mommo again (p.70). In such a manner, Dolly perversely provides Mommo, despite her drunkenness and despite her reticence, with the final prompt to finish her fable.

It emerges that Costello and The Stranger squared up to each other like 'two gladiators, circlin' the floor, eyes riveted together, silent in quietude to find the advantage' (p.70). Place is slandered by both men, with Costello calling their Ballindineside parishioners 'Hounds of rage and bitches of wickedness' (p.70). The trading of insults and the self-degeneration of the competitors around their occupations, geese farmer and breeder of rabbits, prompt both Dolly and Mary to laugh at Mommo's account and to 'forget themselves', and then for them to 'laugh at their own laughter' (p.70). These are part of an incredible series of stage directions through which Murphy is clearly signalling the trajectory and rhythmic intensity of the piece and how he imagines the play in performance.

Mommo recollects the atmosphere in the following way:

their heads threwn back abandoned in festivities of guffaws: the wretched and the neglected, dilapidated an' forlorn, the forgotten an' torments, the lonely an' despairing, ragged an' dirty, impoverished, hungry, emaciated and unhealthy, eyes big as saucers ridiculing an' defying of the low on earth below – glintin' their defiance, inviting of what else might come or *care* to come! – driving bellows of refusal at the sky through the roof … The nicest night ever. (p.75)

Then all three laugh together. It is as if by Mommo laughing at the event, at the sequence that she has refused to reveal up to now, there is the possibility of a new order: (Mary combs Dolly's hair, as Michael and Edward do in *Someone Who'll Watch Over Me*.) The two sisters laugh again at the protruding bulge that is Dolly's belly, and the stage direction reads 'Dolly [is] flaunting herself, clowning' (p.73). They laugh in an anarchic kind of way. Dolly: … (*To her stomach*) 'Good man Josie! … (*Uproariously*) Jesus, misfortunes!' (p.73).

Mommo is again triggered by the laughter and by the mention of 'Josie' and 'misfortunes', and she goes on to reveal some more: 'He who laughs last' is Mommo's measure of victory. It is no longer a laughing competition but a death match, despite the implications of the moments earlier when Mommo reconnected with her husband across the floor of the pub.

Early on Dolly had used the word 'misfortunes' (p.50) almost unconsciously perhaps, and this was the word that Mommo had offered the competitors to keep the competition alive: 'potatoes, the damnedable crop' (p.74), hay, oats, chickens, the injured, the dead – Her sons' deaths. 'Mommo: Oh she made a great contribution to the roll call of the dead' (p.74). Her sons, Jimmy and Michael, die in a flood trying to rescue an old ewe. The sisters' mother died in childbirth, leaving three children behind: 'nothing was sacred and nothing was secret. The unbaptized an' stillborn in shoeboxes', and 'pagan parcels in isolation forever' (p.74).

The exchanges were a mocking of trauma, life, existence, creation itself, which went on for five or six hours. Although the stranger throws in the towel, the locals would not have it. Costello reaches the realization that he is dying and raises a final laugh out of it all. He tells of not selling a single rabbit at the fair, and that he only flung them for fun at the front door of a local, Patch Curran. On Costello's death, the locals beat the stranger up. Josie takes his boots off to check if they were human feet and not cloven hoofs, and they were 'dragged off the cart and beaten, until the curate and the publican "prevailed again" the

Bolsheviks' (p.76). (At this point, Dolly has fallen asleep as the play heads towards its end. Mary undresses and joins the two of them in bed.)

Mary tells her side of the story, ending in Tom's death, who had thrown paraffin on a fading fire. She speaks in a voice akin to Mommo's, using sentence structures, turns of phrase and cadences similar to her grandmother, for it is only in this voice that she can account for the death of her brother. Two days after Tom dies, later 'didn't granddad, the stranger, go down too' (p.76). Mary uses the double terminology to define him.

In the final minutes of the play, dialogue is interspersed with the prayer, 'Hail Holy Queen (*Salve Regina*)', and the long-awaited naming of Mary by Mommo occurs. Mary again adopts Mommo's voice: the 'fambly … of strangers [are given] another chance, and a brand new baby to gladden their home' (76). (Her final speech is accompanied by Schubert's *Notturno*.) So they are not just strangers, but reconstituted as a family, and one with a new sense of home. (The acceptance of Dolly's baby is regarded by O'Toole as a 'symbolic resurrection of the dead'.[17] On that, I think he goes a little too far.)

So at the play's core is both the laughing competition itself and the dark topics that drove it, and the release that laughter brings to the characters. Laughter is seen as an emancipation, as a way of overcoming obstacles and tensions that exist between tribes. It is not so much a laughing cure, rather, laughter is regarded as a way of renewing bonds, as a way of recalibrating social connections. Division makes way for intimacy, tension for a bond that reflects some type of formal re-inclusion. Laughter ensures that the characters engage on the level of play. Laughter is the carnivalesque darkness that is both transgressive and celebratory, where all that is sacred is mocked and where all that is profane is celebrated. (Carnival is additionally connected to the winter solstice – the time when the play is set.) The play is also about how the ritual of carnivalesque laughter is turned on its head, because with the death of Costello, Tom and the Grandfather, it leaves the frame of performance and play. It is as if the laughter, which became motivated more and more by distress, unleashed something altogether more dangerous. In a way the ferocity and the extreme of play demands a sacrifice. Play, instead of liberating, lacerates.

Roche points out that 'at the abstract mythic level, Mommo suggests the traditional feminine personification of Ireland as the Sean Bhean Bhocht or Poor old woman'.[18] Anne O'Reilly points out that 'Generations of Irish women have lived stories that have been authored by men.'[19] In an extended criticism of Murphy's work, Lynda

Henderson argues something that I have already mentioned in relation to *The Weir*, that women characters in Murphy's work have 'nothing to offer the metaphysical debate' and that the women characters are 'excluded from the abstract, spiritual dimension'.[20] While such criticism may stand up in relation to some of his plays, it is inappropriate when it comes to *Bailegangaire*. Roche is right in that Mommo has that symbolic dimension, but she also has the metaphysical one that Henderson sees as absent. However, Anne O'Reilly's comment that 'Women are both contained and constrained within Irish drama which is largely located within patriarchal narratives',[21] leaves the play open to a different type of scrutiny and raises questions about agency. Although Mommo was not an active competitor in the laughing competition, hers is the role of trickstress, mistress of misrule, encouraging and initiating, setting the stakes and calling the odds. Ultimately, through death, there is some possibility: this is something that McGuinness also realizes in *Someone* and McDonagh in *The Pillowman*: it could be argued that this is the fundamental fantasy of patriarchy.

SOMEONE WHO'LL WATCH OVER ME: SENSORY DEPRIVATION

Someone Who'll Watch Over Me is partly inspired by the experiences of Brian Keenan,[22] John McCarthy and Terry Waite, amongst others, all of whom were held hostage during the late 1980s and early 1990s in Beirut, Lebanon. McGuinness heard the mother of Brian Keenan on the radio pleading for his release, and that broadcast was the initial spark for the drama. During the 1980s Lebanon experienced not only a civil war, but also a partial invasion by Israel. A peace-keeping force was deployed in the area. Many Lebanese disliked the American backing of Israel and the overall undue influence of the West. From the early 1980s, many extremist groups used hostage-taking as a way of advancing their own agendas.[23]

Many people were kidnapped, some were held captive for short spells and others for extended periods of time, some were executed and two died in captivity.[24] By the end of 1991 the crisis had come to an end with the release of the last hostages. The likes of Brian Keenan, Terry Waite, John McCarthy and Tom Sutherland published accounts of their ordeals.[25] On one level the play is not a factual but an imaginative account of the pressures, strains and responses of characters to a hostage-taking experience, and on another level, it addresses the needs of England and Ireland to renegotiate a new relationship, to give up biases and prejudices and to be to a lesser extent prisoners to the circumstances of history.

Dramaturgically, the play is structured notionally around the scenario of a joke; Paddy Englishman (Michael Watters), Paddy Irishman (Edward Sheridan) and Paddy American (Adam Canning) are held in the one space, chained to the walls in a cell. McGuinness keeps the captors off stage,[26] in part to avoid explaining or interrogating their causes, in part to keep the violence and intimidation at bay, and in part as a way of keeping invisible the actual horrors of torture and psychological intimidation the real captors faced during this time. It is not a failure of nerve on McGuinness's part; more, it is an attempt to insulate an audience on one level from such physical horrors, which might hinder the necessary engagement on another level. Each charactor has to work out who and what they are, and each has to find ways of accommodating, even temporarily, each others' peculiarities and idiosyncrasies. Tolerance, patience and negotiation are offset by insecurity, rage and intractability.

The drama is also a kind of grotesque laboratory experiment, where other types of confinement, in terms of history, culture and stereotype, are tested. Ultimately the play is about surrendering moral high ground, about re-evaluating the Irish–English relationship,[27] (with the generous assistance of the American, Adam, as honest broker), about short-circuiting instinctive and unconscious national responses and about undermining expectations. This is achieved primarily through dialogue, but more substantially, through the notion of narrative compositions and improvisations. Edward's hostility towards the English is blatant in the litany of clichéd accusations made against Michael (Mick), who is regarded as a war-obsessed British person: 'Tell us all about the war.'[28]

The notion that they are innocents abroad, caught up in something outside of their control, is carefully deconstructed by McGuinness. Edward accuses Adam of exploitation for research purposes: 'You want them disturbed, don't you, doctor?' (p.5). Edward disregards the working methods of some Italian who reported on the 'Troubles' in Northern Ireland, who wanted 'Kids crying, kids cut to pieces, preferably dead kids' (p.5). Yet, as a journalist, Edward is also exploiting the suffering of others. Edward waved his Irish passport when he was taken hostage, but Irishness means nothing to the captors.

Michael's wife has just died, and having lost his job, he goes to Beirut to take up a job at the university. And while he is the most naïve, his nationality hints at the imperial role the British traditionally played in the Middle East. During the play's prologue Adam is alone and he hums 'Someone to Watch Over Me'. Scene 1 is two months later and

Adam is joined by Edward. Immediately the spectator gets a sense of the complex emotions that intertwine them. On the one hand they need to pass the time and support each other, on the other there is an intense sense of boredom and dread. They are comfortable discussing sex, masturbation and sexual fantasies.

WAITING FOR ENDINGS

However, the relative agreeableness and harmony between Adam and Edward, after some months together, is shattered by the arrival of Michael. Michael is initially berated by Edward, but during the following scene Michael's presence and later participation in a game called 'Shoot the movie' leads to all kinds of unease.[29] Adam's movie is inspired by Alfred Hitchcock, but is implicitly about Michael, the Englishman who comes to the Lebanon. Edward's narrative takes its inspiration from the sensibility and register of Sam Peckinpah's notoriously violent movies, and into the mix he adds a touch of magic realism. It is a tale of a singing nun who comes to Beirut on a mercy mission. (Adam suggests the character should be played by Madonna.) The nun (echoes here of *The Sound of Music*) miraculously prompts local children to learn English, and along the way the whole nation is converted to the notion of loving one's neighbour. The missionary zeal of the nun of course echoes the professional zeal of the doctor and journalist, and this combines with the confusion central to Adam's Hitchcockian tale. Everything seems to blur into something else; guests invited to dinner become shadow figures, and the missionary nun, despite her message of humanity and community, is murdered.

Michael takes a risk by participating in the game; he builds on Edward's story, by including a figure of peace and tolerance – Mahatma Gandhi. Adam interjects: 'a Richard Fucking Attenborough movie' (p.16) – meaning his *Gandhi* (1982). Simultaneously, Edward ironizes both the Merchant Ivory-type movie that emerged in England in the 1980s and the international successes of the Irish Film sector, with movies like Jim Sheridan's *My Left Foot* (1989).

Edward dampens Michael's attempts to play, and also expresses his frustration with what he regards as Michael's naïve optimism, a belief in progress and individual success against the odds. It is the 'live happily ever after' (p.16) scenario that frustrates Edward. Instead Edward's perspective is that they are doomed. While the narratives are playful and suggestive, there is also opportunity for the implicit and explicit hostilities between the captives to be voiced. Also through the frame of narrative, admissions and emotions can be articulated that would normally remain undisclosed.

Fiction allows them to communicate in a different register, while at the same time affording them the opportunity to test scenarios and perspectives and also to challenge each other's take on their given circumstances. In the lines 'Come on, give us a dose of the stiff upper lip. Raise our morale, old boy. Tell us about the war. So many chappies went through what we're going through' (p.16), the spectator can grasp Edward's bias, aggression, vulnerability and fear. What he refuses to accept is the solidity of defiance and the consolation of precedents that Englishness/Britishness can offer. In a way, Edward and Adam are projecting on to Michael their own fears. They wish him to be intensely afraid so that their own fears will not seem so extreme. Together, all three movies reflect on the complex situation in which they find themselves. The imaginative, playful, metatheatrical space offers the captives a space of working out, of negotiation, or consolidation, where they can articulate both consciously and unconsciously their concerns.

HOSTILE TAKEOVERS

The tension and the aggression between them prompts another movie scenario. It takes the format of a joke, 'three bollocks in a cell' (p.17). Now we have a co-operative narrative, unlike the earlier ones where the interventions were marked more by subversive intent. In this moment of intercommunication, a willingness to acknowledge and accept that fiction is the energy that binds them, that sustains them and that bears the weight of revelation.

The scene heads towards its conclusion with discussions of the structure of Richard Attenborough's *Gandhi*, where during the opening scene the main character is shot, through to a moment when

> Adam: Michael, I am Sam Pekinpah. This is a gun. (*He points his finger at Michael.*) You are dead. (*He shoots Michael.*)
> Edward: What a senseless waste of human life. (p.19)

The mock execution reveals so many things. It raises the fear of death, the vulnerability of life, a sense of play, but also the fact that in the real hostage-taking scenarios, many captives faced moments of mock execution.

And just as the movie *Gandhi* was too long for Adam's liking, he fears that they will be held for a long time in Beruit. So it is very clear how the moments of scenario-making allow the characters to jump backwards and forwards between fiction and reality, how fiction offers sustenance and assurances, affords the chance to articulate indirectly governing anxieties and how story allows them to form a tighter bond. How long that might last, of course, is anybody's guess.

RECEIVED ENUNCIATION

Edward and Michael debate the nature of Hiberno-English and the causes of the Irish Famine. Michael sees Hiberno-English as a mere dialect to which Edward responds:

> We've taken it from you. We've made it our own. And now, we've bettered you at it. You thought you had our tongues cut out, sitting crying in a corner, lamenting. Listen. The lament's over. We took you and your language on, and we won. (p.30)

The issue of language and imperialism is glossed over by Michael, as is the root causes of the Famine, which he prefers to see as a dietary issue, an over-dependence on the potato, and not a political or economic one. But if Edward scores the points here, his sense of being 'one generation removed from the dispossessed' (p.30) is ruthlessly challenged. Adam reminds him of his university education, large salary and comfortable home. While Michael rightly refuses any personal responsibility for the Irish Famine, his casualness and unwillingness to think through the implications of imperialism are exposed. Both characters find reasons to apologize for their carelessness and stupidity and this leads to impressive moments of imaginary drinking, communal sharing and the rendition of songs/narratives.

Scene 4 reintroduces the song 'Someone To Watch Over Me'. Adam switches from the song to his parents and comments on his own successes, which are delivered in their voices. He is confusing reality and dream, past and present, haunted as he is by snippets of dialogue, songs and perspectives on the world, to which he responds aggressively and confusedly. Captivity is having an increasingly disorientating effect on him. He wants to destroy an Arab. Adam begins to 'feel like a hunted animal, even though I am caught in this cage' (p.26). He concedes that he may be on borrowed time as they are going to 'Fuck' him 'dead' (p.26).

CHAINED MELODIES

As scene 6 begins the spectator knows that Adam is missing, assumed dead. Adam's chain is empty. Edward is refusing to speak and eat. He is on hunger strike. One of the captors wept and this is seen as evidence that they have killed Adam. In some brutal exchanges, Edward accuses Michael of wanting him dead, of taking comfort from his death in that it increases his own chances of survival, as there will be outcries and greater pressure brought to bear from the international community, as it was the practice to hand over the bodies of those who had died.

Michael forces Edward to state that Adam is dead, as he knows enough about grieving and mourning, about admission and acceptance. Denial is not useful. Then Michael encourages a sort of memorial service for Adam. Edward expresses his affection for Adam. In response Michael recites the poem *Love (III)* by George Herbert. As the play heads towards a conclusion, Edward and Michael function more and more from a textualized reality, where story and memory dominate as a way of keeping at bay the reality of their circumstances.

Previously, Edward had sung 'The Water is Wide', and Michael offered his 'Sir Orfeo', from Old English, which is inspired by Ovid's Orpheus myth, as a positive perspective on the world. Both are serious and very emotional. Orfeo lived a living death after the departure of Herod, his lover, who was taken by the King of the Underworld. He enters the underworld, plays music and the beauty of the sound prompts her release. Both the song and the story are about intimacy, love and togetherness, rescue and redemption. (Adam changes register with the song 'Amazing Grace', which ultimately becomes his funeral song.)

The energy alters in a variety of ways in the final few scenes. Michael and Edward re-enact the 1977 Wimbledon Ladies' final between Virginia Wade and Betty Stove. Edward gets to play Betty Stove, the loser of the match, and the Queen. Virginia's victory gives them both hope and now it is not Dawn Run at Cheltenham or Glasgow Celtic's victory in the European Cup but an English victory that offers consolation. In celebrating an English success, Edward is letting go of the Irish mindset, which is that any nation but the English is usually supported in all things. Michael re-enacts a childhood favourite in 'Run, Rabbit, run, Rabbit, Run, run, run'.[30] Nothing can take them too far away from their unease. Slowly, Edward is beginning to fall apart, very vulnerable to thoughts of his family and home.

THE STOCKHOLM EFFECT

During the second to last scene Edward is close to breaking point. Michael and Edward conspire to imaginatively escape in a flying car, prompted by the children's film *Chitty Chitty Bang Bang* (1968) (which was conceived of by Ian Fleming and with a screenplay by Roald Dahl and Ken Hughes). This scene contrasts very much with the earlier movie sequences. The more adult-type of critical, almost self-consciously cynical thinking that informs the earlier narratives, makes way for a more childlike type of consciousness. It is a regression back to a mindset of childishness, in some ways. It also links to the notion of trauma that they experience, which is at the level of violation that prompts regression. The car brings Edward on a flying visit back home to communicate with the ghost of his dead father.

To witness in performance two adult characters, Stephen Rea and Alec McCowen, in the first production and in the many subsequent productions of this play that I have seen, indulge in such a re-enactment of a children's movie, is to experience their pain and despair, which no level of articulacy could generate. Imagination, regardless, is still key to their humble defiance. Eric Morris and Alan Hoe suggest that hostages regress 'to an almost childlike state referred to as "traumatic psychological infantilism"'.[31] This ties in with many of the studies of victims' responses to hostage-taking that are modelled on the theories of rape trauma. (This is substantiated in the play by Adam's comment 'they got my ass over a barrel, and I ain't wearing no jockey shorts. I smell oil ... they're going to fuck me dead' (p.26).)

Eventually, Edward does break down and attempts to communicate with the ghost of his dead father, pleading with his father to 'tell' him a 'story' (p.55). This fixation on story and the need for story means that play persists in building on the possibilities of narrative. In the final scene there is an integration of gesture and narrative. Michael enacts the Spartan story told by his father, and combs Edward's hair. The only way Michael's father can get in any way close to describing his experiences as a prisoner of war during World War Two was by describing what the Spartans did before they went into battle. They combed each other's hair: 'The bravest men sometimes behave like women' (p.50). What goes unmentioned is the notion of routine, almost pre-scribed homosexuality amongst this group of men. The gesture in the play is not reduced to some form of sexual intimacy, but that of simply touch in each of the five productions of the play that I have seen.

If audiences wonder about Michael's sexual orientation given the many details of his effeminacy, then sexual orientation is directly raised when Michael asks Edward if he slept with Adam. Edward denies it and states: 'I would like another child. I want another child' (p.49). (In McGuinness's work there is often a codification of homosexuality in the plays and, apart from the reference to the Spartans, this approach is supported by mention of Virginia Wade and Betty Stove, as both players are known to be lesbian.) Michael bids farewell to Edward, and then is left alone, as Adam was during the prologue. He cites again from the poem *The Wanderer*, whose words remind him of his father, his love of his country, his sense of belonging and connection, but also a sense of mercy and self-fortification.

Michael's final lines are a repeat of the two lines cited previously in the Old English. However, he only translates one, 'A man who is alone may at times feel mercy, mercy towards himself' (p.51). Michael does not deliver the line that is the equivalent of 'Fate is fate'. That responsibility is left to the audience to provide. Michael's nationality sustains him as much as his father's strength to survive his war experiences. Now like his father, he faces potentially periods of sustained silence. At the play's end, Michael also rattles his chains. Terry Waite states, in his foreword to his book on his hostage experiences: 'Your spirit can never be chained.'[32] Keenan in his preface claims: 'in the circumstances in which we found ourselves physically chained together we both realized an extraordinary capacity to unchain ourselves from what we had known and been.'[33] So even in the face of such brutality and captivity, a sense of freedom and unrestraint can be maintained. Dignity comes from communication and connection, and these are often negotiated through gesture and primarily through narrative in the instance of this play. Narrative breaches the space between the characters that are chained to the wall of the cell, and thus kept apart.

In this play narrative is a space of avoidance and fantasy, but it is also one of contestation and liberation, where ideas and emotions can be tested and worked at, exchanged and negotiated. The hostages have to work through their own biases and prejudices. At the outset, Edward and Adam can negotiate a position of mature exchange by stating that they will tolerate the worst that can be thrown at each other and will forgive it. However, the arrival of Michael complicates it all. Edward loses all mature perspective. Each character stereotypes the other according to nationality, and each behaves in a way that affirms national stereotypes for both each other and for audiences alike. McGuinness creates a more complex perspective. Michael takes on some of Edward's characteristics and thoughts, particularly around the notion of laughter as the best means of expressing defiance. Edward has to let go of his ideas of dispossession, and Adam of the belief that global capitalism implicitly assigns him as an American with sufficient value to keep him alive. In terms of the English and Irish relationship, it is not the same old story, although it starts out that way. By the play's end Edward is set free and Michael held captive alone, finding succour in old texts, in mercy and companionship, in his belief that he remains free in his dreams and that by rattling his chains he can give expression to and maintain his defiance.

THE PILLOWMAN: WAR ON NARRATIVE

The Pillowman, set in an unspecified totalitarian state, shows considerable tonal and dramaturgical consistency with much of McDonagh's other work, but at the same time it was to be a surprise in a way, given that his five previously performed plays had Irish settings. While the earlier McDonagh plays contained a great deal of brutality and cruelty, the challenges *The Pillowman* sets in terms of violence and staging are a good deal more confrontational and testing and the play has more in common with the work of contemporary British[34] writers, like Mark Ravenhill[35] and Sarah Kane.[36] (The curious irony, of course, is that *The Pillowman* was substantially drafted in 1993–94, before any of his Irish plays were produced.)[37] What is remarkable is the number of international performances that *The Pillowman* has received since 2003.

And of course, even if *The Pillowman* denies any specific context, it must be kept in mind that it was first performed in late 2003 as the war in Iraq (the War on Terror) was ongoing, with democracy supposedly as one of its key motivations. Indeed, the interrogation techniques, notionally in the name of democracy, deployed by American army forces in the Abu Ghraib prison in Iraq find many parallels with the McDonagh play.[38] For some, democracy is the prize and not a weapon in a war on terror. McDonagh is entering indirectly this contemporary debate, not as some political theorist, but as someone who is reflecting on the fabrication of narratives of enablement, forgery and disruption and the justification of state terror.

The Pillowman maps the interrogation of Katurian Katurian Katurian (KKK), a writer whose stories seem to be the templates for a series of gruesome murders involving children. He is the chief suspect, and has been detained along with his brain-damaged brother, Michal. It is not so much that tactics of the totalitarian state are taboo to democracies, but that the play focuses on brutal interrogation techniques and on the murder of children and not adults, as is the usual methodology of most narratives, especially Hollywood's, which remain for the most part wary of serial child killers.

The McDonagh play considers the circulation of ideology in an unnamed totalitarian state. The drama establishes the regimes through which citizens are recruited, indoctrinated and interpellated by systems and structures of governance. It considers how institutions, totalitarian and democratic, through narratives socialize, discipline and induce re-enactment, most especially within the boundaries of family life. It is not so much that families simply imitate the configurations of the state, more-over, it is the difficulties of those units to evade the distinctive practices of the state, which ultimately foist positive aspirations and false realities and illusions before the populace. Such citizens become most likely both misguided and beguiled agents of the state. For Ciarán Benson:

> Family is the crucible in which self is forged. Whether directly by incorporating or indirectly by rebellion, the family and its associates (the church to which the family belongs, the schools it chooses for its children, its various loyalties in politics and play) supply and edit the self-constituting narratives available to its offspring, and powerfully influence the structuring of their identities.[39]

The parents of the Katurian family decide on totally different child-hood realities for two brothers: Katurian gets the privileged lifestyle, full of love, encouragement and admiration, and Michal is gifted all of the negative experiences, whereby he is ritually tortured and abused, as part of some grotesque artistic experiment.

STAGING TOTALITARIANISM

Unlike totalitarian states, democracies are based notionally on the enti-tlement of their citizens to certain freedoms, equalities and rights.[40] Anthony Giddens proposes that 'democracy is the most significant inno-vation in the twentieth century' and he highlights the fact that in this century 'there is not just a gradual expansion of democracy; something has happened that is radically pushing forward the democratization of political systems across the world' as people have 'discovered that communism and a command economy doesn't work'.[41]

Unnatural, fundamentally restraining or inhibiting socio/political structural dynamics are not truly acknowledged within this democratic model, and such forces are associated only with undemocratic societies. However, democracies function, in part, by means of ranked relation-ships and they normalize inequitable distributions of wealth and social inequality by disguising certain injustices, social immobility and repression, in terms of gender, race and class, all in the guise of a freedom to choose and to exercise human will.

Giddens presses for an increasing process of 'democratizing democracy' and envisages great progress due to the procedures of 'transnational democratization'.[42] And it is this 'transnational democratization' which fuels globalization and of course a war on terror. Indeed, the unnamed totalitarian state of *The Pillowman* offers on the surface the ultimate point of contrast with contemporary democracies.

Clearly, non-identical formations such as Italian Fascism under Mussolini, Hitler's national socialism in Germany, Russia under Stalinist rule, Mao's China after the communist victory in 1949, and Fidel Castro's rule in Cuba since 1959 have all been equated with totalitarianism, as have either single-person dictatorships or a 'dictatorship of the proletariat'[43] – the rule of the people in another guise. Associated with either extreme right- or left-wing ideologies, and far more potent than either absolutism or autocracy, citizenship within totalitarian states is generally equated with powerlessness, unerring regimentation, fragmentation, centralized rule and with the ideological control of culture, education and judicial, religious, political and interpersonal relationships. The mass media, art, pedagogy and technology are tools of subordination and regimentation, as is popular culture.

In this notional unitary state, there is no truly oppositional voice countenanced, and it is thus seen in pejorative terms by most, especially those who espouse liberal democratic values. Karl Dietrick Bracher calls it 'plebiscitary acclamation' because it 'manipulates assent to the exercise of power by a leader or a monopolistic party'.[44] There is not only the promoted sense of benign rule, but that any violation of human rights serves a higher order, thus a lack of accountability permeates the system. A higher, evolving freedom beyond democracy is hailed as a sort of Utopian fantasy of equality. Thus the elimination of personal freedoms is a normalized price and worthwhile sacrifice of such activities, resulting in what Bracher describes as 'exalted submission'.[45] Such a state certainly debilitates and reduces self-confidence, whereas, for example, Hollywood movies typically promote heroic individuality that finds individual and not collective solutions, where justice is realized. Within democracies, individuality is not perceived as corrupt *per se*, but as a natural unit of recognition, whereas within totalitarian states there is the obvious overriding of individuality for the benefit of the greater good. Risk and the taking of initiative would not be necessarily encouraged. Totalitarian coercion is even more sophisticated than monarchic, dictatorial or imperial rule. Bracher summarizes it as

> an absolute and exclusive ideology; legalized terror legitimized by chiliastic promises; through control of political and social life by means of pressure and threats, fear and coercion; the creation of the 'new man' to fit the new and perfect totalitarian order; the preclusion of future conflict by means of suppression of all opposition in favour of ideological political cohesion and effective technological function; lastly, as the basis for a legitimisation of this unprecedentedly brutal extermination of individual freedom, the identification of oligarchic dictatorial leadership with the interests of the 'whole', the 'community of the people' (*volksgemeinschaft*) or the 'class of workers and peasants', an identification as fundamental as it is fictitious.[46]

The town where the play is set, Kamenice, has no specific geographic location (towns by that name can be found in Northern Albania and in the Czech Republic). There is of course mention of a Jewish quarter (Lamence, whose dictionary meaning is in 'layman's terms'), but that is more a matter of ethnicity than nationality. Likewise the play is not set within any specific time frame.

It is more the spirit of totalitarianism that McDonagh is after, and not the preciseness of the socio/political parameters, which some London critics found lacking. The totalitarian state has dramaturgical, metaphorical as well as symbolic significances.[47] McDonagh offers a truncated totalitarianism writ small,[48] where totalitarianism symbolizes anything from imperialism, state oppression, repressions, even perhaps academic/critical interrogation of theatre itself. The flexibility, even portability of the concept is hugely significant. Of course, McDonagh grew up in London and has no direct experience of totalitarianism, however writers can extrapolate and make sense of oppression and violence in different ways. I am less interested in the factual content and pervasiveness of totalitarianism and more concerned with the contextual subjugations and the fantasy of the writer/child oppressed by institutional restraint.

McDonagh pursues the legal processes, police interrogation and the creativity of a specific writer, in order to reflect upon the fears and anxieties and lack of freedom therein. Katurian's tales are parables or fables that warn about the dangers of interpersonal encounter and are full of negative experiences and foreboding, partly about the threat to individuality in the face of apparent state or parental omnipotence.[49] It is persuasive to suggest that the oppressive totalitarian state is the springboard for Katurian's negative imaginings, but to restrict McDonagh's play to such a worldview is to miss the point, as his work is more playful and elusive than that. The general political interrogation is full of recurrent ironies that cannot be sidestepped by critical interpretation. Likewise, the role of the writer in the totalitarian state has been romanticized and McDonagh ironizes that fact a great deal.

In order to give further substance to the sensibility of the play in performance, I would like to briefly identify some of the staging choices made for the original Royal National Theatre, Cottesloe production. The music composed by Paddy Cunneen is dominated by eerie Eastern European tones,[50] and the scenography by Scott Pask brought the play into alternative territory. (The production relied on distinctly English accents in the London performance, and not voices with some Eastern European inflection.) John Crowley directed the piece in the spirit of a carnivalesque Grand Guignol, which ultimately, is about destabilizing the gaze, perspective and presence of the spectator. Mikhail Bakhtin in two books *Rabelais and his World* and in the *Problems of Dostoevsky's Poetics* explains the concept of Carnival. Carnival is of course about the festivalization of the real, while making space for difference, desire and the imagined. The underworld space itself is liminal, and 'paintoverable', transgressive and other. (The feast of the pig.) The body is fundamental to its tradition, as is the notion of both the violated and the reproducing body. Likewise, mock trials, mock kings (The Pillowman character) and mock deaths (the survival of the little mute girl) are substantial components.

Sue Vice articulates the parameters of Bakhtin's thinking on *mésalliances*, which leads to strange combinations, 'lofty with the low, the great with the insignificant, the wise with the stupid'.[51] This is the world of McDonagh. The playwright instead of presenting an audience with the innocence and pure body of a child, gives us the abject body of the violated child and dead children. As Vice argues, 'the abject confronts us … with those fragile states where man strays on the territories of animal'.[52] Reverence or empathy for a child's suffering is not so much contested as moved into an alternative space. It is the figures of violated and mutilated children and the crucified child in *The Pillowman*, however distanced and theatricalized, which potentially shocks most.[53] This is the space where unease is generated, where the darkness begins to glow. In addition, corpses in McDonagh are carnivalized through the notion of dark play.

The past and the acting out of narratives are accommodated in *The*

Pillowman through a sort of monstrous and transgressive performance that casts aside any notion of verisimilitude in favour of the grotesque, inhumane cartoon-heightened style. In the play's first production, these scenes of excess and torture initially took place on elevated platforms, backstage left and right, with the bedroom spaces opening up from behind screens. The audience witnessed the electrocution sequences, with the grotesque as the main reference point. (The actor performing as Michal played the teenage Katurian in the flashback/narrative sequences and a young boy played the young Michal.) However, the play's dramatic present was played out within a relatively realistic representation of a prison cell, with the exception of the 'Little Jesus' narrative re-enactment.

As Katurian presented his first re-enacted narrative he delivered the voices of the parents, while the actors playing the parts enacted the gestures. As Katurian destroyed his best story, there was the burning of the story in both spaces. For the 'Little Jesus' story, the re-enactment happened, not up high as in the previous acting out of a narrative, but mid-stage towards the back of the performance area. A screen rotated behind the actors' illustrating key scenarios. Both the nice parents and the cruel foster-parents in the 'Little Jesus' story were played by the actors who initially played the Katurian parents, and the character shifts were indicated only by a 'slight costume' change (p.67), as the script suggests. The little girl in this story believes that she is the 'second coming of the Lord Jesus Christ' (p.68) and thus wore an exaggerated false beard. No beating sounds were heard; only blows were visible, which again was an attempt to break the notion of verisimilitude.

The text suggests that the Blind man should be performed by the actor playing Katurian, while in performance it was the actor playing Michal who took the role. The little girl in the 'Little Jesus' story was resurrected as the girl in the 'Little Green Pig' tale. For the final moments of the production, the set was altered. The light that hung over the interrogation table was whisked away, altering the interrogation space and making free a space for the imagination.[54] (The written text also suggests that the actor playing Katurian sits on a bed in 'an approximation of a child's room' and he 'narrates the short story which he and the mother, in diamonds, and father, in a goatee and glasses, enact' (p.31). That production choice changes the meaning of this scene, moving it from participative re-enactment to something more distant.)

So this dominant theatrical space was governed by the conventions of naturalism, whereas the alternative spaces were guided by a very different stylistic approach. It is the melding of both realities that seriously skews the co-ordinates of the real, as the relationship between cause and effect begins to break down.

RE-ENACTMENT

As the play opens, Katurian is hooded and duly disorientated, awaiting the arrival of his interrogators/ torturers. The catalogue of strategies, emotional, psychological and physical, used to extract 'the truth' during cross-examination is similar to those listed in any Amnesty International report on prisoner mistreatment. Katurian cannot understand why he has been arrested, believing that he only tells stories and that he has 'no axe to grind, no anything to grind. No social anything whatsoever' (p.7). However, Katurian is fearful the text may have unintentional political allegory and if so, he is more than willing to remove it.

Despite all that Katurian has to say about his own innocence, Andrea Jovacovic has been killed, recovered on a heath with blades down her mouth, and Aaron Goldberg is dead, found in a dump behind the Jewish quarter, while his toes were discovered in the Katurian home. A third child, a little mute girl, is now missing. Katurian is invited to tell a story, not knowing why he has been asked to recount it. The hope is that through interrogation, narrative intelligence can lead someone to 'actionable intelligence', to use a phrase from US military parlance.

At the basis of Katurian's stories is the idea that a child is treated badly, according to Tupolski. Ariel's whole justification for torture is premised on the exact same thing: 'I may not always be right, but I stand on the right side. The child's side' (p.78). The perversity of it all is that totalitarian states are never on the 'child's side'. Moreover, Katurian's actions, in killing his parents, are about the 'child's side'. However, the re-enactments carried out by Michal are not from the 'child's side'.

Katurian's 'The Tale of the Town on the River', which was published in *The Libertad*, is set in Hamelin. A boy's toes are cut off by a stranger, despite the child's act of kindness. The injury saves him later, when he is unable to keep pace with all of the other children as they are lured away by the Pied Piper of Hamelin, who was chasing the children all along. The non-payment for the removal of an infestation of rats was just an excuse to take the children away. Again innocence is violated, but the initial act of brutality brings with it perverse redemption.

On a broader scale, while the patriarchal family is a perverse and perverted agent of the state, it cannot be a simplistic representative of the state. The child's revenge on the destructive, gluttonous father in 'The Little Apple Men', who is tempted into eating the razor blades hidden inside hand-carved pieces of apple in the shape of men, cannot be read simply as an anarchic or subversive gesture of violation, directly either towards a character or towards the state. However, it can be indicative of it. (Ariel's murder of his own abusing father can add perspective to all of this.) The 'comeuppance' for the father in the above story is followed by another act of sadistic revenge. The little girl is also forced to swallow razor blades. This stylistic twist shifts the usual register of fairy-tales, making destruction not just interpersonal but indicative of a pattern of repeated, cyclical violation.

While Katurian, under interrogation, spurns any deconstruction of his own writing for inherent values or as reflections on justice, in reality, to a considerable extent, he is writing out of the horrors of his past. Moreover, his refusal to read into his own stories is strategic in the face of his interrogators, but disingenuous in terms of his own psyche. The relentless and morbid content of his stories, and the violation of children at the core of almost all of his work, cannot be evaded. This is Katurian's particular fantasy:

> Well ... I kind of hate any kind of writing that's even vaguely auto-biographical. I think people who only write about what they know only write about what they know because they're too fucking stupid to make anything up. (p.76)

Writing needs the imagination more than personal experience, Katurian argues, but attempts by writers, in general, to deny contexts and the potential of experiences even as indirect influences or to hide behind the fiction of purely imaginatively driven work are clearly false in most instances. Katurian may deny any direct influence that his personal past has had on his writing, but what he cannot rebuff is its impact of the actions on himself and his brother. Katurian brutally kills both parents. Katurian acts out the fantasy of the Pillowman, the core narrative about a figure who can bring a graceful ending to the suffering of children, and Michal acts out the stories of his brother, narratives that are filtered through the trauma of their growing up.[55]

At 14, Katurian discovered the body of his brother, who was still alive despite the torture. Katurian murdered his parents that evening, exhibiting the core violence of his parents, but unlike them, he takes care of the abused Michal. No comfort can erase Michal's trauma. His re-enactment of his own violation, and his use of his brother's stories as prompting narratives, confirm this. When Michal confesses his deeds to Katurian, the sheer perversion of re-enactment is fully realized. For Michal, 'The little boy was just like you (Katurian) said it'd be' (p.48). Michal claims that he was 'just doing' (p.55) Katurian's stories to test 'how far-fetched' they are (p.50). It takes the meaning of narrative to a different level. Re-enactment is not agency, but perversion.

LEGACY

Michal had told Katurian earlier that the latest missing girl, Maria, had been crucified like the main character in the 'Little Jesus' story (Snow White meets the young Jesus of the New Testament). Instead, as his last hurrah, as a serial killer of children, Michal re-enacts the 'Little Green Pig' story and the rescued girl appears on stage, covered in green paint. In the initial rendition of this story, the little green pig is pink and very different from all the other pigs on the farm that happen to be green.[56] The farmers (society) repaint the pink pig with green indelible ink, so that he will not be different. However, one evening after a heavy shower, perhaps divine intervention, all the green pigs turn pink, except of course the once pink pig, whose permanent green colour cannot be erased. His uniqueness is reaffirmed. It also suggests that individuality cannot be obscured, despite the broad strokes of an ideologically repressive society.

Despite the girl's survival and the fact that Katurian had nothing to do with the deaths of the other children, he is still executed. And while Katurian's stories may have an impulse towards 'fashionable downbeat' endings, they still retain some innate sense of fundamental legitimacy that moves way beyond either natural or poetic justice. 'The Pillowman' tale is a redemptive fantasy, something that ensures that little children don't die alone, for he is a 'soft person' to hold the hand of a child close to death. (Tupolski's own child drowned while fishing alone.) The Pillowman urges the child to commit suicide in order to avoid pain in the future. If they agree, the Pillowman would stage 'tragic accidents'. However, the Pillowman's job makes him unhappy, so he decides to visit his younger self and to end his suffering. The little Pillowboy sets fire to himself.

Michal identifies with the Pillowman, regarding him as something of a hero: 'He reminds me a lot of me' (p.52). When Katurian tells 'The Pillowman' story, he impersonates the description of the Pillowman. Katurian slays both his parents, covering their faces with a pillow, and he sees his suffocation of his brother as a mercy killing.[57]

(Ariel also killed his father with a pillow, in an act of self-defence.) Neither life nor death matters; 'it is about what you leave behind', according to Katurian (p.60). He reflects further: 'They're not going to kill my stories. They're all I've got' (p.60). Katurian wants his stories to survive. That is why he agrees to confess to the crimes.

McDonagh gives Katurian an alternative ending, bringing him back from the dead, and allows him to rewrite the finale of the drama. This time Ariel puts out the flames that envelop the output of the writer, placing the work in the case file where it will remain unopened for fifty years. In the final narrative, Michal, as a child, is visited by the Pillowman and given the chance to die, but Michal opts for life, and the degradation and suffering it entails, so that his brother can live his dream and be a writer. Michal sacrifices his sanity and agrees to bear the burden of nightly torture out of kindness and love. Instead of offering one of his usual downbeat endings, Katurian tenders an unfashionably optimistic one. Katurian's final narrative, from the realm of death, is a fundamental plea to grant meaning to the pain and suffering of his brother and, of course, to himself.

AGENCY

Can literature perform a subversive activity that confronts with subtlety or otherwise the imposed order, or does most writing serve as a means of perpetuating values, and of subliminally and aggressively conditioning the citizen? Either way, literature as text or state rule delivers suggestive and counterfeit narratives that cannot be without ideological imperatives and inhibitions. What at first may seem like a futile opposition between democratic freedom and the compulsion and control of totalitarianism is not so clear-cut. Under the banner of freedom all kinds of discord are negated, legitimate queries invalidated and different needs other than material ones subordinated. The redemptive entrepreneurial and cultural narratives of Willy Loman in Arthur Miller's *Death of a Salesman* (1949) and the justice-driven literary ones of Katurian have their own pathologies. Like the salesman, a writer has 'got to dream', as 'it comes with the territory'. Miller understands Willy's need to leave some mark on the world, describing it as a 'need for immortality, and by admitting it, then knowing that one has carefully inscribed one's name on a cake of ice on a hot July day'.[58] Katurian's fantasy is that his work will one day be unearthed from an archive and perhaps revered, as a work of genius or at least merit in its own time, which is conceivably the fantasy of every failed writer.

In *The Pillowman* totalitarianism becomes both grotesque and perverse in the spirit of Grand Guignol. *The Pillowman* brings about cycles of abuse and a legacy of violation. If it is the figure of the writer who contests the reality of the totalitarian state, and such a state symbolizes the corruption of patriarchy and familial authority, then the sacrosanct nature of the family unit within democracy is just another enabling fairy-tale. It is the series of indoctrinating parables and serial narratives of democracies that shape, motivate and inhibit its citizenship. Ultimately, however, to be told that story at bedtime doesn't always guarantee that the citizen will be 'good' in not so much the prison-house of the real, but the haunted house of moral ambivalence. Narrative is a battlefield, given the globalization of the media and its communication of terror through images of laceration, carnage, trauma and death. If terrorism is, in part, the fate of first-world countries, child murder is framed as the ultimate depravity. The relative security and sanctuary that democracies offer is often just a fairy-tale, when greater things are at stake, like political stability, national security, institutional, party and individual reputations. Democracy can be at times just a demotic freak show – a pathology of innocence. Today, in its war on terror, some first-world democracies have devised their own theatres of cruelty, with its black prisons and phantom states.

Michal's self-sacrifice in his willingness to live in order that his writer brother can fulfil his potential, which is Katurian's ultimate fantasy, gives ultimate merit to suffering, which has strong Christian overtones. Yet, Katurian's resurrection and the irony of the 'Little Jesus Story' capture McDonagh's contestation, dismissal or at least perversion of Christianity myth and iconography.

Through narrative, each of the three plays discussed here elevates the works on to another, fantastical register, where there are dialogical tensions evident between fact and fiction, freedom and restraint, and despair and redemption. *Bailegangaire* considers how grief takes on the shape of narrative and how an inability to resolve is captured by the play's feminine form of circular healing. Yet its focus is on what might be regarded as a patriarchal laughing competition and of women's relationships defined in relation to men, the grandfather, Costello, Dolly's husband Stephen, Mommo's sons and Tom, her grandson. That complex and ambiguous tension between the feminine and the masculine is present throughout the text. By the play's end, Mary promises to take care of Dolly's baby, and offers another story; here we have the consolation of narrative, the strength derived from convictions in beliefs and values. Fintan O'Toole notes that Mary is 'at the mercy of a story being told'.[59]

The sense of being at the mercy of a society or a story is evident throughout the tradition of narrative theatre.

On *Bailegangaire*, Fintan O'Toole states: 'Folk tales are a programme for survival, not a fantasy of escape.'[60] Indeed he believes these capture 'archetypal folk tale heroes, struggling for home against ferocious obstacles' to get back to the family.[61] All three plays are struggles for home, the fantasy of home and the need to get back to a place that is no longer accessible. The brothers in *The Pillowman* want the impossible comfort of family, the hostages in *Someone* want to get back home, to return to the past prior to their captivity and the women in *Bailegangaire* want to experience the world as a collective family unit, bonded and unbroken.

To name something in order to articulate it even in a blurred way, is not the same thing as demanding a coherent perspective on the world. Subjectivity is suspect, dispersed, but it does not mean that there can be no halting space, no perspective and no continuities on offer. Fundamentally, as Ben Brantley states in relation to *The Pillowman*, 'McDonagh is not preaching the power of stories to redeem or cleanse or to find a core of solid truth hidden among life's illusions.' He adds, it is 'about, above all, storytelling and the thrilling narrative potential of theater itself'.[62] In a world dismissing the continuities of narrative and in a world challenging the coherence of story, these plays, part of the Irish and Anglo-Irish traditions, are more than adequate responses: each is exemplary.

NOTES

1. Richard Kearney, *On Stories* (London and New York: Routledge, 2002), p.129.
2. Seamus Deane, 'Introduction' in *Brian Friel: Selected Plays* (London: Faber & Faber, 1984), pp.14–15.
3. Kearney, *On Stories*, pp.6–7.
4. Ibid., p.7.
5. Ibid., p.3.
6. Ibid.
7. Ibid., p.4.
8. Ciarán Benson, *The Cultural Psychology of Self: Place, Morality and Art in Human Worlds* (London: Routledge, 2001), p.45.
9. Ibid., p.4.
10. Tom Murphy, *Bailegangaire* in *After Tragedy* (London: Methuen, 1988), p.43. (All further references will be given in parentheses within the text.)
11. Fintan O'Toole, *Tom Murphy: The Politics of Magic* (Dublin/London: New Island/Nick Hern,1994, revised edition), p.231.
12. Anthony Roche, *Contemporary Irish Drama: From Beckett to McGuinness* (Dublin: Gill & Macmillan, 1994), p.161.
13. O'Toole, *Tom Murphy*, p.191.
14. Nicholas Grene, *The Politics of Irish Drama: Plays in Context from Boucicault to Friel* (Cambridge: Cambridge University Press, 1999), p.219.
15. Ibid., p.222.
16. Ibid., p.229.
17. O'Toole, *Tom Murphy*, p.194.

18. Roche, *Contemporary Irish Drama*, p.147.
19. Anne O'Reilly (Kelly), *Sacred Play: Soul Journeys in Contemporary Irish Theatre* (Dublin: Carysfort Press, 2004), p.32.
20. Lynda Henderson, 'Men, Women and the Life of the Spirit in Tom Murphy's Plays' in *Irish Writers and Their Creative Process*, ed. Jacqueline Genet and Wynne Hellegoarc'h (Gerrards Cross: Colin Smythe, 1996), pp.87–99, p.90.
21. O'Reilly (Kelly), *Sacred Play*, p.21.
22. Brian Keenan was taken hostage on 11 April 1986 and was freed on 23 August 1990. (Leigh Douglas and Philip Padfield, kidnapped ten days before Keenan, were later murdered.) Keenan was held initially in solitary confinement, and later with John McCarthy, before ending up with McCarthy and three Americans Frank Reed, Tom Sutherland and Terry Anderson. Keenan recollects the monotony, hostages teaching captors English, the beatings, blindfolding, lack of exercise, almost continual absence of natural light, the savagery, the terror, unsanitary conditions, the lack of privacy and the physical illnesses, including 'Beirut Belly'. He also documents how he went on hunger strike after one bad beating. On one occasion Keenan and McCarthy imagined an absurd conversation between Margaret Thatcher and Charles Haughey, their respective heads of state at that time.
23. Across the Middle East the most notable hostage-taking situations were the Tehran American Embassy hostage event in 1980, the Iranian situation in 1981 and the Libyan hostage situation in 1984. The Beirut hostage crisis was to be the most prolonged. The Pro-Iranian group, Islamic Jihad was the main group associated with the kidnappings. Libya, Syria and Iran had some influence over the hostage takers.
24. Formally and officially, governments refused to negotiate with hostage takers, but behind the scenes numerous deals were done. The deal that got greatest public profile was the arms-for-hostages deal brokered by the American Army Officer Oliver North, called the Iran–Contra affair, discovered after North was arrested in Iran. Iran needed weapons for its war against Iraq. America promised to sell them arms in exchange for help in releasing the hostages. The money raised from the sale was then passed on to Contra rebels in Nicaragua, who were trying to bring down a Socialist government. Korean, German, French, American, British and Irish hostages were held during this period. See for further details Eamonn Jordan, *Someone Who'll Watch Over Me: A Critical Commentary* (Dublin: C.J. Fallon, 2000), pp.49–53.
25. See John McCarthy and Jill Morrell, *Some Other Rainbow* (London: Bantham Press, 1993), Tom and Jean Sutherland, *At Your Own Risk: An American Chronicle of Crisis and Captivity in the Middle East* (Colorado: Fulcrum, 1996) and Terry Waite, *Taken on Trust* (London: Hodder & Stoughton, 1993) and Brian Keenan's *An Evil Cradling* (London: Vintage, 1992). Despite the relative similarities of incidents and circumstances in which the captives were held, the exceptionally different responses of the individuals to those events provide a fascinating comparative read, apart from the related horror of their captivities and the inspiration to be found in their courage and tenacity to survive.
26. Brian Keenan saw his captors as pawns in a large reality: 'Imagine a man aged twenty to thirty, but with the maturity and intelligence of a thirteen-year-old, a mind steeped in fundamentalist and medieval suspicion, a mind propagandized into a set of beliefs and values which was not informed enough to understand, but weak and fearful enough to accept unquestioningly. The natural and healthy instincts of youth are twisted and repressed by a religious and moral code that belongs more to the days of the Inquisition.' See Keenan, *Evil Cradling*, pp.137–38.
27. This play is, of course, part of a broader trilogy on the British and Irish relationship that includes *Mutabilitie* (1996), set in Cork in 1598, during the Munster Wars, which mimics the Shakespearian five-act form, and *Mary and Lizzie* (1989), a wild, mobile, fantasia about two sisters, Mary and Lizzie Burns, who live with Frederick Engels, successful businessman, writer and friend and financial supporter of Karl Marx, and is inspired by Ibsen's *Peer Gynt* (1867).
28. Frank McGuinness, *Someone Who'll Watch Over Me* (London: Faber & Faber, 2002), p.16. (Hereafter, all further references will be given in parentheses within the text.)
29. Some of the most inspiring details emerge from the inventiveness of the captives, in the games they invited, the speculation and omens they identified, the industriousness of their planning and scheming and in the collaborative attempts to communicate with the other captives held in the same buildings, using notes written on small pieces of paper and messages written on silver cigarette paper with a match. They also devised their own version of a deaf and dumb language to communicate across a corridor. On occasion, Terry Waite was next to McCarthy and Keenan and Waite used Morse code to tap out a message. Waite in his book tells of his

frequent coded conversations between himself and one of the Americans, from one cell to the next. Attempts to communicate and the sharing of information were vital.

30. Terry Waite in his book records his first memory – what he calls the 'dawning of conscious life'. He hears 'Run rabbit, run, run, run' played on a gramophone. He had scarlet fever and as his mother was pregnant, he was moved into an 'isolation hospital for some weeks'. See *Taken on Trust*, pp.9–10. The pain of separation is recalled during his time of captivity. Later in Waite's book, he returns to the same song, 'Run rabbit, run rabbit, run, run, run': 'Why have you been running so fast, Waite? Where to? For what? One thing seems clear. You're certainly not going to be able to run for a long time to come. Not, I suspect, for a long, long time.' See p. 256.

31. Eric Morris and Alan Hoe, *Terrorism: Threat and Response* (New York: St Martin's Press, 1988), pp.46–8.

32. Waite, *Foreword*.

33. Keenan, *Evil Cradling*, p.xvi.

34. Aleks Sierz identifies offences, sensation and shock tactics as part of a new style of theatre in 1990s Britain. See *In-Yer-Face Theatre: British Drama Today* (London: Faber & Faber, 2001).

35. Mark Ravenhill claims that in hindsight, the murder of Jamie Bolger, almost 3 years old, by the young boys Robert Thompson and Jon Venables, both 10 at the time, in February 1993 was the incident that prompted him to write plays. He describes it as 'somehow something had shifted, that a tear in the fabric had happened ... Shop, videos, children killed by children. It wasn't a project I set out to write. But it became one.' Such a tragedy motivated Ravenhill, and he speculates on how others of his generation, including McDonagh, were moved by the same incident. See Mark Ravenhill, 'Tforum: A Tear in the Fabric', *Theatre Forum*, 26–9, Winter/Spring 2005, pp.85–92, p.90.

36. Sarah Kane's *Blasted* (1995) achieved a certain notoriety because of a scene where a character eats a child, and of course Edward Bond's *Saved* (1965) contains a scene where a child is stoned in a pram by a group of youths, which is one of the crucial moments in British theatre.

37. Fintan O'Toole in his Program Note to the Royal National Theatre production suggests that '*The Pillowman* reminds us that he has an English ear as well as an Irish one. In his dialogue, Harold Pinter and Joe Orton blend seamlessly with Tom Murphy and John B. Keane to create a vibrantly original mixture of absurd comedy and cruel melodrama.'

38. Most recently, shocking revelations were made about so-called Black sites, covert CIA-run prisons where human rights violations and torture are deployed in order to gain intelligence.

39. Benson, *Cultural Psychology of Self*, p.212.

40. Constitutional democracies stress majority rule, the rights to fair elections and public representatives, the presumption of innocence within the legal system, morality, the absence of terror, the rights to privacy, free speech, freedom of assembly and association, and legitimate the capacity to dissent. An emphasis on freedom, ranging from individual choices, through free speech and the freedom of the press are notional prerequisites. These are all the variables that are supposedly absent under totalitarian rule.

41. Anthony Giddens, *Reith Lectures* 1999, www.lse.ac.uk/Depts/global/publreithlectures.htm [assessed 10 March 2009]

42. Ibid.

43. Karl Dietrick Bracher, 'The Disputed Concept of Totalitarianism: Experience and Actuality' in *Totalitarianism Reconsidered*, ed. Ernest A. Menze (New York and London: Kennikat Press, 1981), p.16.

44. Ibid., p.15.

45. Ibid., p.17.

46. Ibid., p.20.

47. In theatre, all too often police/militaristic states are a simplistic shorthand for totalitarianism, especially in adaptations of Greek classics.

48. The map is not the territory. The socio/political realities or totalitarianism are not the substantial ingredients; it is the psychic territory of threat, mayhem, absence of cause and effect and due process, and the individual vulnerability of all concerned.

49. Caryn James in her article on the New York production relates the descriptions of John Crowley, the director of the London and New York productions, of how McDonagh 'had actually written the stories that became Katurian's before tackling the play (he created them for possible screen versions that never materialized) and in its first incarnation *The Pillowman* resembled "stories strung together" ... In its revised form, those same stories "keep looping

back on themselves," as a detail dropped here later pops up there, to create "a wilderness of stories"'. 'Critic's Notebook: A haunting play resounds far beyond the stage', *New York Times*, 15 April 2005, www.theater2.nytimes.com/mem/theater/treview.html?res= 9E06E1DC103EF936A25757C0A9639C8B63&fta=y [assessed 10 March 2009]

50. See Paula Rego's *The Pillowman Triptych*, www.tate.org.uk/britain/exhibitions/rego/pillowman. shtm [assessed 10 March 2009]

51. Sue Vice, *Introducing Bakhtin* (Manchester: Manchester University Press, 1997), p.152.

52. Ibid., p.174.

53. London audiences in 2003, especially, experienced the play, perhaps sensitive to the trial of Ian Huntley, who was found guilty of the murders in 2002 of the young girls, Holly Wells and Jessica Chapman, in Soham. The Soham murders gave rise to a frenzied sensibility around the safety of children in a culture. The Moors murders carried out in 1960s by Myra Hindley and Ian Brady carried a similar type of focus.

54. Christine Madden notes, commenting on the production of *The Pillowman* at the Deutsches Theater, Berlin, during the Heidelberger Stüchkemarkt festival, that 'Far from being presented naturalistically, everything in the play converged on the idea of a world gone wonky, from the ingenious set – an Irish drawing room, complete with typical doors and wall mouldings, tilted 90 degrees to the left – to the cartoon like yet sinister presence of the actors. In its sharp absurdity the production felt like Flann O'Brien on cocaine.' *Irish Times*, 24 May 2004, www.irishtimes.com/newspaper/features/2004/0524/index.html [assessed 10 March 2009]

55. According to Caryn James, 'For two preview performances in London, Mr Crowley also had an actor in a pink Pillowman costume onstage. "I thought it would be quite spooky and scary, but it wasn't," he said of that experiment. For one thing, that Pillowman too closely resembled an English cartoon character called Mr Blobby. For another, people said it looked nothing like *The Pillowman* of their imaginations, even though the costume had faithfully reproduced Katurian's description.'

56. The colour green has also a fundamental association with Irishness, and, secondly, classical British stereotypes have long associated the Irish with pigs. Victorian representations of Ireland used illustrations of Irish families sharing living spaces with pigs, as indications of the lack of civilization amongst the Irish, rather than reading the fact of shared accommodation as having more to do with grave economic lack. (The little green pig 'really liked being green … liked being a little bit different, a little bit peculiar' (65), and is 'peculiar' whether it is green or pink.) When asked to describe the little Jewish boy, Katurian states that he had 'browny-black' hair. However, the boy was half-Irish – 'It's a shame his mum was fucking Irish, and her son closely resembled a red fucking setter', according to Tupolski (97).

57. See Marina Carr's *By the Bog of Cats* in *Plays 1* (London: Faber & Faber, 1999) and John Steinbeck's *Of Mice and Men* (Harmondsworth: Penguin, 2000, originally published 1937); both texts include mercy killings of sorts.

58. See *The Theatre Essays of Arthur Miller*, ed. Robert A. Martin (New York: Viking Press, 1978), p.142.

59. O'Toole, *Tom Murphy*, p.152.

60. Ibid., p.189.

61. Ibid.

62. Ben Brantley, 'A Storytelling Instinct Revels in Horror's Fun', *New York Times*, 11 April 2005, www.theater2.nytimes.com/2005/04/11/theater/reviews/11pill.html [accessed 10 March 2009]

7

The Glut of Monologues:
Look Who's Talking, Too

EACH STORY HAS SEVEN FACES

For a time in the 1990s, monologues became increasingly a staple of Irish drama, or more accurately, monologues written mainly, but not all, by men, for male characters, with female characters all too noticeable by their frequent absence, with some loose references to the feminine serving the type of symbolic function that many commentators have traditionally resisted or found utterly distasteful and prejudicial. If one was to categorize loosely these monologues, then one could identify four broad strands.

The first cluster comprises single character interior monologues, with the actor on stage telling a story, without too much embellishment, as Conor McPherson's *Rum and Vodka* (1994), *The Good Thief* (1994) and *St Nicholas* (1997) exemplify: the first play is about a male hitting emotional and social turbulence, the second about a character out of his depth in a criminal underworld, and the third play about a theatre critic and his encounters with vampires. In a similar fashion, Jennifer Johnston's *Christine* (1989) (also known as *Ananias, Azarias and Miseal*), its companion *Mustn't Forget High Noon* (1989) and *Twinkletoes* (1993) are single character monologues that deal with violence and its implications for Northern Ireland, prior to the establishment of the peace process.

The second group also involves a single actor on stage, except that on this occasion there is a great deal more re-enactment, with the performer impersonating a range of characters, dexterously switching between roles, and perhaps using the props within the space for very specific and imaginative purposes – fundamentally, more a one-person show than anything else. Examples of this cluster would include Donal O'Kelly's *Catalpa* (1994), which is a re-enactment by Matthew Kidd, in his bedsit, of his rejected screenplay about the rescue of Fenian prisoners from Australia by the whaling ship Catalpa, and Conall

Morrison's *Hard to Believe* (1995), which is set in an attic space and is about a spin doctor for military intelligence in Northern Ireland, who is about to commit suicide.[1] Finally, Richard Dormer's *Hurricane* (2002) is based loosely on the life of the snooker player, Alex Higgins.

The third discernible cluster of monologues consists of two or more characters narrating a sequence of events from their own perspectives, where they may or may not interact with each other, the latter being the more likely scenario. Subdivisions exist within this broad grouping and they are dependent on the degree to which either the narratives substantiate or contradict each other. These are inter-digitated narratives. Brian Friel's *Faith Healer* (1979) seems to have initiated that tradition and he followed it up stylistically with *Molly Sweeney* (1994); in the former, three characters reflect on the faith-healing ability of Frank Hardy, the joy and the havoc he brought to the lives of his mistress/wife Grace and his manager, Teddy. In the latter, detailed is the interference in the life of the visually impaired Molly Sweeney by two males, her partner Frank, and her surgeon Mr Rice. With Friel's *Faith Healer*, there is so much contradiction and so many anomalies in the diverse accounts that it is difficult to decide what to believe, indeed, disbelief may be the unprompted response, the natural condition.

In McPherson's *This Lime Tree Bower* (1995) the three male characters extend the narrative by brief turns, and each from their own perspective on the substantial incidents of a robbery and a rape. Eugene O'Brien's *Eden* (2001) has a couple, Billy and Breda, who relate, again by short turns, different perspectives on their relationship over a weekend. The physical theatrical space between characters in *Faith Healer* or *Eden* is either the void of death or an inability to communicate. In the former, each character has their own designated stage space, but there remains no contact, while in *Eden* (2001) the actors share seating on stage, which was well apart,[2] but do not engage with each other, apart from one poignant occasion in the Peacock Theatre production, directed by Conor McPherson.

O'Rowe's *Crestfall* (2003) has three female characters, Alison, Olive and Tilly, who in turn reflect on a life in a midlands town, where all kinds of butchery and savagery take place over an evening. Each story interlocks. The second narrative builds on the first and the third on the previous two. The final node within this cluster of intermeshing monologues is when the characters, on the surface, have relatively tenuous or autonomous relationships with each other. Paul Mercier's *We Ourselves* (2000)[3] is a series of monologues, which follows the lives over a number of years of seven characters who had previously worked

together in a vegetable factory in Germany. Each narrative is stylistically different. In McPherson's *Port Authority* (2001)[4] the connections
between the three characters initially appear incidental at best.
However, it is the layering of the monologues that offers a complicated
perspective on things, rather than the impact of individual stories in
isolation, in the instance of these last two mentioned plays.

The fourth and final strand is evidenced by Michelle Read's *Play
About My Dad* (2006),[5] which is literally about the death of her father
at a particular time in her own career, and Gerard Mannix Flynn's
James X (2003), a testimony of brutality and violation that Flynn's
character James O'Neill experienced at the hands of agents of church
and state, which is rooted in Flynn's own testimony to the High Court
in his claim for compensation against the state. Overall, the monologue
range runs from single monologues, whether dramatic or testimonial to
layered monologues, from interlocking, if contesting, monologues to a
series of loosely related monologues whose connections are often
notionally tenuous. McPherson points out that his monologues are 'set
in the theatre' (p.132),[6] so the identifiable parameters of the notionally
real world are in abeyance. (In contrast, Dermot Bolger's *In High
Germany* is set on 'platform 4 of Altona railway station, Hamburg,
Germany'.[7])

Many explanations and theories abound as to why there is such a
glut of monologues. Might monologues be the 'easy wipe formula',[8] as
Michael Colgan, director of the Gate Theatre suggests, or is it the
'restoration of the lost art of narrative',[9] as Michael Billington claims
of McPherson's *The Weir*. Or are monologues saying something about
relationships in crisis? For Brian Singleton the monologue formats
'reveal an anxiety about theatre as a medium for communication'.[10]
Karen Fricker argues that 'Irish drama is an ongoing chronicle of male
weakness, frailty, failure, reflecting a culture in which representations of
masculinity and femininity have been historically, and problematically,
linked to national identity.'[11] She adds, 'With guilt comes paralysis.'[12]
Marina Carr's comments sum up, in some ways, many of the resist-
ances that people have towards monologues:

> I can write monologues very easily ... There is something intrin-
> sically un-dramatic about the monologue ... They are easy to
> write and you can get all the information that you want across.
> You can indulge your 'literary sensibility', you can show 'I can
> write beautiful sentences', but finally, that is not what theatre is
> about. It is about the spoken word and conflict. It is about people
> bouncing off of one another.[13]

Those critics alert to Ireland's religious background will of course connect narrative to the confessional space/sacrament of Roman Catholicism, the purging and retributive process where absolution is available. Further, many see no merit in the monologue, because nothing obliges the plays from being little more than static therapeutic transactions, with no change earned. If, previously, Irish theatre from the 1960s to the 1980s was jammed in the processes of memory retrieval and the primary use of the history play was a means of making sense of the past, and more indirectly the present, the monologue, while often grounded in narrative memory, is less of an immediate disguise or denial of the present.

ABSURD PERSON SINGULAR

It might also be said of the monologue that it is more suggestive of the type of single identity that is regularly absent from the Irish theatrical tradition, a healing of the rupture brought about by colonialism, where split subjectivities were the inevitable consequence of oppressive rule.[14] Of course Mark O'Rowe's *Howie The Rookie* bucks that trend, as the two characters are co-joined by the play's title, and it pushes the tradition of Irish dramatic doubles in a new direction, with Bruce Lee, the martial arts figure, the mythic point of origin/convergence/cohesion. (Such a move could be read as a switch from postcolonialism to the colonization of popular culture, by way of Hollywood or the Californication[15] of identity.)

Clearly, one cannot divorce monologues from their cultural moment.[16] Contemporary plays have emerged from a youth population in the 1980s and early 1990s that was more likely to spend less time in contact with its families, friends or communities than previous generations. Smaller family units, single siblings to rooms, a high incidence of chat/confessional radio show formats, access to television, music and video games in the rooms of teenagers led to a sort of headphone/headset, room-alone, media-saturated generation. Second-level students in Ireland were also increasing the time spent doing homework, exam revision and preparation, as if they were professional students, thanks to a highly competitive points system, furthering isolation, and, of course, this was before the Internet, chat rooms, social sites, mobile phones and texting. Furthermore, there was increasing exposure to what Gerry Smyth calls the 'Oprahfication'[17] of society, that strange mix of confession, the naming of upset or hurt in a very public domain of television broadcasts, and collective celebration of success, defiance and recovery.

The rise in monologues also parallels the early emergence of the Celtic Tiger, and as Robert Putman warned,[18] the more society serves economic and financial capital requirements and imperatives, the more social and interpersonal capital decreases (however uncomfortable one might be with the emphasis on 'capital' used in this way), or higher incidences of individualism, self-reliance and self-focus emerge. In theatre, monologues seemed to set aside interpersonal spaces to a significant degree, meaning there was less of an immediate contestational reality. If these monologues set aside the interpersonal, they also often set aside context, and it is here where some of the benefits and complications emerge. Further, given the strong connection between monologues and suicide, the internalization of play leads to death, so the monologue form has a strong alliance with suicide, and the especially frightening incidences of suicide amongst young males, with the inability of males to communicate, to talk, to seek help, or to be unhinged by despair. Aloneness proves to be the revised cultural norm, as well as a form of sanctuary.

McPherson's *Rum and Vodka* is in part about inappropriate attempts to validate the self – the masculinity astray model. The character loses his job, but he has been spending and drinking and acting irresponsibly for some time. He is casually and serially unfaithful to his partner, with whom he attempts to have sex while she sleeps. He remarks: 'I saw myself in the mirror. I looked like I was dead. Like I'd been beaten to death. I scrubbed myself from top to bottom. I was pissed out of my head. I felt okay' (p.32). This pattern of acknowledgement and almost simultaneous denial is evident in many monologues. His *faux* paranoia is evident in the lines 'I often think the world gets together behind my back while I'm on the jacks or in bed and makes hasty decisions about new ways to get me to leave the planet' (p.9). *Port Authority* continues that pattern of male insecurity and ungroundedness. Joe states: 'I've no idea about myself! I don't even know if I'm happy or sad'! (p.151). Dermot admits that he 'was generally a bit of a disaster' (p.156) and Kevin adds, 'And I was thinking maybe there isn't a soul for every person in the world. Maybe there's just two. One for the people who go with the flow, and one for all the people who fight. Maybe lots of us just share a soul' (p.179). Male characters display an absence of awareness, a lack of internal composure, an inability to construct an inner dialogue rather than an inner monologue. Reflection seems endlessly postponed, not because of indifference *per se*, but because of an inability to validate or substantiate; the world is all just out there, at a distance, detached and never close enough to engage with.

In Conall Morrison's *Hard to Believe* the central character John Foster is on stage, in an attic space surrounded by the costumes of previous generations. He is a spin doctor for military intelligence. The play opens with John listening to Schubert and he exclaims, 'music to top yourself to'.[19] He has just come back from the funeral of his mother and is about to electrocute himself. Before he does so, John wears his mother's dress, his brother's sports jacket and his grandfather's religious robe, so as to suggest the different layers of accumulated identity and the distinct values and imperatives that each has transmitted to him. His brother died eight years previously in a booby-trap placed under John's car. John was the intended target. He, himself, has no religious beliefs. Key to his success at work comes about when he establishes the inexpensive 'Four, Square, Laundry, Service' (p.319) and gets to inspect, literally, the dirty linen of the local community for evidence of paramilitary activity. His ex-girlfriend, Monica had a termination, from which he gets the idea of listening in on confidential help lines and stopping women on their way back from England following abortions, in order that he can blackmail them (p.332). Monica left him when she heard of his deeds. Now he is in a 'stable relationship with two pieces of liver and a jam jar'[20] (p.332).

Jennifer Johnston's *Twinkletoes* (1993)[21] is a story of 37-year-old Karen, who lives alone now that her teenage daughter has just got married and her husband, Declan, remains in prison for republican paramilitary activity, having spent nine years already behind bars. She has returned home from a night in the pub and reflects on the pressures and controls around her. A local man, Danny McCartney, is interested in her, she perhaps in him, but word would get around. Her aloneness, her abandonment, and her sense of betrayal come across: 'I want to have more kids. I want love. Not just on Thursdays. Aye, Declan, I love you. I lie well' (p.29).

Johnston's *Christine* and its companion piece *Mustn't Forget High Noon* accounts for the relationship between Christine and Billy Maltseed. In *Christine* Billy has been shot and the news of his murder leads to the death of his father due to shock. After his friend Sammy was shot, Billy joined the Regiment, a loyalist group. Karen in *Twinkletoes* bemoans the absence of other children, and Billy and Christine can't have any. Fundamentally, there is the need to have faith, however hard it is to believe. For the characters, believing is the key to survival, whether it is a belief in God, community, humanity, self or the future. John Foster's remarks on fabrication are pertinent:

And when I realized it was *all* fabricated, that everybody was peddling their stories to prove their points of view, that there were no facts, nothing you could really believe in ... then I decided the only way to keep that fact clearly in front of my eyes was to become one of the people who was helping to make it all up, one of the fabricators, see it from inside the machine. (p.335)

In *Twinkletoes* Karen's comment on her deception is also apt: 'On Thursday, I'll tell him ... everything and nothing' (p.30), and it is that tension between 'everything' and 'nothing' which is central to the monologue.

Up to this point the discussion has focused primarily on single-character monologues. I now wish to broaden the focus. Set in Edenderry, *Eden* is the story of Billy and Breda's failing relationship. He spends his weekends on pub crawls, is impotent, yet has vivid sexual fantasies about a younger woman, Imelda Egan. Breda is hankering after a return to the earlier romance of their relationship.[22] Breda, once called 'Pigarse', has had a weight problem and has dieted for some time. She is more confident and hopes that a special evening out will lead to some type of reconciliation. For his part, he doesn't want that. (Details of infidelity and casual sex are prominent in the drama. Billy's friend, Tony, is a local stud, and Ernie Egan's wife, Evonne, has threesomes with 'the two Boylans'.)[23] Male casual conversation is called 'talkin' shorthand,' 'ol' shorthand' or 'talkin' shite' (p.3), and later is described as 'fierce shorthand, load of me hole rigmarole' (p.4) and 'eegoty shorthand' (p.25). Yet the monologue preserves an audience from the indulgences of such 'shorthand' conversations. If Billy's sexual fantasies, inspired by a painting in his bedroom of a harvesting scene, are of him having sex behind a tree with Imelda while people watch, Breda's sexual focus is on solo sex, prompted by accessing weekly a book of sexual fantasies. The scenario to which she returns again and again is one of a harem and group sex, and that inspires her own fantasy, which starts off with her being prepared for the Sultan, with Billy bound, but he can't be restrained, so breaks free of his binds, joining the action as she indulges in wild sex and where they all 'come together in one huge amazin' orgasm' (p.7). (There are certain fantasies that Breda is not so keen on, involving 'bondage, and rape and Alsatians' (p.8), which are detailed in the book.)

By the play's end Billy has made a fool of himself with Imelda, and Breda has gone home from the pub alone, initially, finding herself beside the canal with Eoghan, the putting green salesman. As she has sex with Eoghan, he blurs into the Sultan. In a way her sexual infidelity has as much to do with sexual frustration and emotional despondency, as it does with desire (or is this a male playwright's take on female desire?): 'Billy is behind us in the tent, tied up in the tent, forced to watch us, and I'm laughin' because he can do his thing and me, I can do my thing. I grab hold of the sultan's hair and it's over now, beautifully over, heavy with breath, both of us, and we kiss' (p.36). She can laugh all the way 'up the town', whereas Billy after his night out slips despondently into the bedroom with his children. In a way, it is hard to see her actions as a victory, other than one for dysfunctionality, desperation and disappointment.

PURE MULE

The different individual perspectives on their relationship keeps an audience working to stabilize the contradictions and obviously toiling to anticipate where all of it will lead. Neither counselling nor talking long-hand or 'shorthand' will resolve their differences. Male impotency has its root in many different areas, emotional, physical or psycho-sexual, but none of these is teased through in the drama. The impotence of a society to support such problems shines through, as does the dysfunctional dynamics of an alcohol-focused community. Everything is 'pure mule', a phrase Breda and her friend Eilish use to describe 'anythin'' from a night out, to a long queue, to shite beer, to a bad snog, but it always meant that the thing was desperate, or disappointin'' (p.14).

With Eoghan by the canal, Breda states: 'I'm tellin' this total stranger about me marriage, and the more I'm goin' on the better I'm feelin'', but the audience is only told of the satisfaction of telling (p.35). The audience never gets to hear that opinion of her marriage, perhaps luckily. Harvey O'Brien describes the one moment of possible contact in performance between them: 'As Wycherley's character struggles with an inner conflict where he suspects he may be attracted to his own wife [Catherine Walshe] and resists it (because that would interfere with his self-image as a freewheeling stud), the actor casts sidelong glances at his silent co-star, who sits frozen in a pose of intense concentration.'[24]

In McPherson's *Come on Over* (2001) imposed isolation is transgressed and the characters on two occasions interact. It is a moment between a Catholic theologian, Matthew, and a woman, Margaret, his former girlfriend from years back.

> Matthew (*to Margaret*): I was lost.
> Margaret (*to Matthew*): Stop. Keep going, I'm sorry.[25]

Later Margaret takes off her hood and he tells her to put it back on.

Eventually she puts it back on. The play ends with Margaret embracing him and he leaning against her. Likewise, in *This Lime Tree Bower* there is a consistent failure to acknowledge the constant, if unlit, presence of other actors on stage. Yet, again, there is one moment when the characters interact. Ray is telling about him puking over a visiting academic, and Frank responds by saying to him 'I never heard that.' Ray replies, 'I've been saving it.'[26] (Johnston's *Christine* ends with the only character saying 'I hope I haven't taken up too much of your time' to the audience (p.55).) Singleton argues that monologues like these 'use the onstage presence of the other silent and seemingly un-present characters to act poignantly as referents to the spoken text'.[27] In McPherson's *St Nicholas* the actor addresses the audience directly, acknowledging consciously its presence, while in most other plays this does not occur.

Clearly, Billy and Breda have great difficulty in relating to each other. Each character delivers their own take on the world – their individual 'talk time'. As characters they need to talk together, yet dramatically, if they did talk, the potential dialogue between them would probably not take off, as it would lack resonance, accuracy and intensity of the type that might shift the destructive dynamics of their relationship to something more resourceful – evidence of which is found in their recollections of dialogue between each other. It would be uninteresting to stage,[28] yet in the monologue, with each offering a perspective on the world, alone, uninterrupted, unchallenged, it seems to bring an audience further into the mindset of the character, to comprehend the structures of intention and denial, of desire and destructiveness at the centre of each narrative formation. In the above plays, the characters display yearning and a need for comfort, but seem to refuse regularly the mantle of agency. Each has some reflections on violence, but the next cluster of plays to be evaluated zooms in on brutality and abuse in very different ways.

Of O'Rowe's *Crestfall*, Fintan O'Toole argues that if the play 'was indeed a movie, it would probably be banned … [having a] climax of such extreme violence that it makes *Reservoir Dogs* seem like a Hallmark Mother's Day card'.[29] Heroin abuse (the scourge), bestiality, forced abortions ('Mine taken foetal, scraped out fatal' (p.28)),[30] animal mutilation, incest, paedophilia, human violation and six murders are documented by the narratives. All three stories offer individual perspectives on this 'savage quarter, this perpetual crestfall', without either the playfulness or the indiscretion of the two narratives delivered in *Howie The Rookie*. The violence in *Crestfall* is a brutal search for extremes that seems to be validated by the authenticity of a female voice. In *Howie The Rookie* the violence is described more like street fighting or arcade game style. What O'Rowe's work seems to consider is that neither pain/pleasure nor joy/despair offers the coherence and the assurance of identity. The lenses of performance and irony introduce casualness and a sort of defiant flippancy, when characters refuse to accept that they will be hurt by interaction. So it is almost a childish defiance, the two fingers to the trauma of existence and a closing of the senses to darker realities.

In contrast, the violence in Gerard Mannix Flynn's *James X* (2003),[31] which builds on his previous novel *Nothing to Say* (1983), is altogether different and the elements of bravado and boisterous defiance are really a confidence trick. In the introduction to the play, Flynn believes that the character 'begins a quest to rescue his own story' and that 'The truth will set you free.'[32] And while Flynn talks about his character James O'Neill, the narrative reflects many of the extreme incidents from his own life. It is predominantly Flynn's story, with Flynn performing, under the guise of O'Neill. The connection between Flynn and his character is not like that of any other work under discussion here. James is in the High Court before a tribunal 'giving testimony about the events of his life at the hands of the agents of church and state' (p.6). James, 'a man in his forties', carries 'a file containing State documents relating to himself and at various times throughout the play he reads reports from this file' (p.11). Brought up in a family of thirteen, in Connolly House, Dublin, his is a notional history of delinquency, deviancy and anti-social behaviour. At the age of 11 he is sent to St Joseph's Industrial School, Letterfrack, Connemara (no pastoral idyll here), from there to a Reformatory School in St Conleth's Daingean, to mental institutions in Portlaoise Hospital and Central Mental Hospital Dundrum for the 'criminally insane' (p.39). Then at 16 he is sent to St Patrick's Institution – a prison for young offenders, so that by his early twenties his life has been scarred by interacting with the agents of Church and State, including a short stay at Goldenbridge, while his mother went into hospital to give birth and during her recovery period, where he remembers a great deal of physical and psychological violence. Initially, as an aggressive response to the judiciary, James insists that he will tell 'it my way, to myself. I won't delay. I won't abandon myself. I'll reclaim myself, myself' (p.14).

The narrative recounts, his early years, including his birth. An audience gets a feel for the circumstances – the poverty, the trouble-making, the delinquency, the violence at industrial school – after two days at home for his holidays he had to have two operations to repair damage from beatings dished out by the Brothers. To this list is added the psychological diagnoses by the institutions of the state and time in jail for a larceny he did not commit. All of this revelation is framed and presented in the language of defiance, aggression and a perceived sense of injustice.

STATE DELINQUENCY

In prison, he had near insanity experiences, which he calls 'an orgy of madness' (p.42). Out from prison, at 21, he hits the streets of Dublin, forms some bands, gigging at the 'Frozen Arts Centre' (p.50), and then spends a great deal of his time fighting, arguing and getting drunk and high, generally eking out trouble. There is evident rage, maliciousness, numbness, disbelief, despondency and above all denial in his narrative. Now in therapy, somehow the objective of James's therapist is to move from positions of 'relapse' to 'release'. Then, close to the play's end, James gets his day in court and the opportunity to make a 'statement'. What the audience has heard up to now is the abridged version certainly, but more importantly, the fabrication, composed partially in denial. Also it serves to give an audience a (foot)hold on the story, without being bludgeoned by the burden of the deeper trauma. It is a false story, a 'grandiose' cover-up. Another voice emerges, as a new sense of purpose and calculation filter through:

> So here goes. See that story I just told you. That's the same story I told to myself all my life. That's my grandiose story, my euphoric recalling of the events of my life. If I hadn't gotten that version I wouldn't have survived … I didn't discover my birdy (penis) myself at the industrial school … That's my sideshow story, my Jewish humour. (p.52)

Later he adds, 'But now it is time to tell the truth. The honest truth. This is my statement. My truth. The real story. The story I came to tell' (p.52). He goes on to document beatings, physical and sexual assaults, and the emotional tortures that he experienced in these institutions: the brother who 'orally raped' him on his way to Letterfrack, and the anal rape at the hands of a caretaker at the same institution. Persistent beatings were meted out there and also at the reformatory school. In prison he was raped by another inmate and nothing was done when it was reported. Nobody would either listen to or accept his story, each time he tried to relate it to an agent of the state. It was professionals, and professions in denial at best, utterly negligent at worst, conspiring with a society which could not countenance the abuse deriving from agents of church and state, who could not accept that they tacitly facilitated such violation. (How much easier is it to be in denial about another's abuse?) 'I never spoke those words till now, never had the voice, only the fear. I thought it was all my fault and drinking my bollix off numbed the pain away,' he claims (pp.53–54). The shame he felt falls away. He hands back to the state his file, because the documents are really their belongings, their accounts, their narratives, their judgements, the state's evidence against itself, the state's 'shame' and the state's delinquency (p.54).

A truth narrative and its brutality give the meaning necessary to sustain a life. The play ends with little emotion in the lines spoken. But behind the facts there is the subtext, the hidden content that reflects the trauma, and the burden of denial and isolation. Truth potentially brings freedom from shame. His female therapist said that he 'was only as sick' as his 'secrets' and that the 'truth would set' him 'free' (p.52). Testimony tests that sentiment. Testimony queries the value of telling, the validating of secrets and the disregard for the lies of the state. There is, of course, the 'life-lie', the narrative needed to make sense of despair and to frame survival.

That he is a survivor of such horror in a democracy is almost beyond belief. It is hard to take in that the state and its agents, when '*in loco parentis*', would do such wrong but in such cases would hanker after 'no-fault settlements' (p.54). This was not the Dark Ages; this was 1973, when Ireland joined the European Community. If this was documentation sourced from times of colonial rule, there would be outrage.[33] For O'Toole, 'The story they [the official documents] tell is not really about the boy who is the subject of all the official reports. James X is the torch that illuminates the institutions and gives form to the official mentality, and Flynn is right to use him as a buffer between himself and us. The rawness and ferocity of the story need to be controlled and shaped, so that Flynn, calm and composed, can be all the more devastating.'[34] The composure and generosity of the actor[35] is vital here, and is rightly picked up by O'Toole, when he notes: 'Flynn has performed an act of astonishing generosity.'[36] Truth is about the unburdening of shame, the doling out of responsibility, about the reclamation of dignity, being in this instance blatantly non-performative. Flynn stands before an audience as evidence of the violated body. Flynn is neither actor nor truth-teller/informer, witness nor narrator. He is a survivor. Performance can only celebrate that heroic bravery. And of course, Flynn's role gets us into the functions of the performer, and what an actor brings to a performance, and the complex relationship between actor and audience reception, which I will examine through the lens of naïvety.

THE SPECTACLE OF NAÏVETY

For individuals, narrative functions as a statement of implicit and explicit experiences and perspectives of the world in such a way that there is an almost synonymous relationship between narrative and the narrated self, veiling the false sense of unity and cohesiveness that narrative purportedly brings. Often, for a human being the public narrative and the need to impress, manage to betray the private narrative, which is often a more complex accumulation of needs, desires, fear, beliefs, sensations, reflections, actions, failures, hesitations and rewards. The expressivity of the body often betrays the intent and consistency of personal narratives expressed in public, and the obligation on the actor is to do likewise, to find the necessary physicality and expressivity that contest the relative cohesion of scripted character narratives.

In single-person monologues the actor is often standing relatively still; there is little by way of sweeping physicality, in that the composition of the visual image is relatively static, especially when working within unaltered physical scenographic environments, apart from lighting. The act of performance is one of delivery and one of leakage, of revelation and self-betrayal, through subtext and physicality, through mindsets, assumptions and values revealed implicitly and explicitly in a monologue. The audience is obliged to rely more on the nuances of language and story structure as much as on the visual, with far more emphasis on verbal codifications than is the norm in contemporary cultures, where the visual dominates. Playwrights afford their characters inner-constructed narratives that audiences will buy into, or from which the characters themselves can salvage something, whether it is by way of dignity, non-accountability and irresponsibility, fuelled by unconscious need, imperatives to procreate, drugs or alcohol addiction, or by a supreme hatred of the innocuousness of the ordinary.

Jim Norton, who played Jack in the first production of *The Weir*, noted that after performances, audiences kept coming up to him, wishing to tell their stories.[37] Monologues and/or narrative disclosures seem like an invitation to share, to reaffirm community. In an *Irish Times* interview with Eileen Battersby, O'Rowe notes: 'When I heard the actors I realized they spoke to the audience, they make the audience complicit.'[38] In a way he is attempting to reflect on how audiences respond to such a type of opening up. While there may be non-contested narratives, audiences can fulfil a dialogical, adversarial function by grasping the unsaid and reconfiguring the narrative. How might an audience be positioned thus? I suppose by being more aware than the character, by viewing characters as somewhat in denial, too openly naïve, which may of course have something to do with class, with most of the characters in monologues, male and female, coming from the working classes.[39]

Naïvety is established in a number of ways, initially through the illusion of progress, the belief that something can be done to initiate change. In *Eden*, Breda loses weight, hoping that it will make a difference to her marriage, and Billy believes that sex with Imelda will resolve his impotency. In O'Rowe's *Howie The Rookie*, the males think, fancifully, that they can somehow inhabit the combative spirit of Bruce Lee. After The Howie is ejected from a window, The Rookie responds 'me impaled mate, me namesake the name of Lee, me saviour', and he will go home to The Rookie's family to 'Let them know he was good at the end'.[40] The redemptive tones clearly suggest naivety, as does the filtering of violence through the lens of irony, false heroics and masquerade.

The feminine across so many of the plays is romanticized. In *Rum and Vodka* the narrator states: 'If I could be with that girl (Myfanwy) she could cure my life' (p.25). In *Port Authority*, Kevin's, Dermot's and Joe's[41] relationships with themselves and with the women in their lives are deeply suspect. There is this tension between the real and unrealizable partner. For Kevin it is his flatmate, Clare, about whom he fantasizes, but he settles for Trish. For Joe, it is his neighbour Marion, and not his wife Liz. In contrast, Dermot's wife states that she is with him, 'because I knew you'd always need someone to look after you. And I always will' (p.182). Singleton suggests, 'Abetted by the monologue form, Woman, with whom these characters are preoccupied, is rendered mute and denied self-determination.'[42] On the relative 'muteness' I can agree, not so on the 'self-determination', as neither gender seems to have access to that. While women did serve a symbolic function traditionally in Irish theatre, in the monologues it has little resonance beyond the personal and the immediate, because it has no metaphoric or mythic aspiration in terms of composition, just the literal.

In many of the plays, male impotency is an issue. Billy and Christine in *Christine* and *Mustn't Forget High Noon* cannot have children. Billy accuses her of being 'barren' (p.48) in his piece, and in her monologue she says that he was incapable of having children – 'I never had the heart to tell Billy what they said at the hospital ... I just let him think it was my fault ... You know the way some men are ... they get very hurt about that sort of thing, ashamed' (p.55). In *Eden*, Billy is impotent and in Dermot Bolger's *Tramway End* (1990) Monica's husband is impotent and this ruined their relationship to such an extent that when he died, she admits to poisoning him, even though she is not held accountable:

> I tried to pray but nothing would come. You've stolen my youth and left me barren, you've stolen my gaiety and gave me shame, and when I die I will die unmourned. But I could forgive you, Swifty, everything except that ... seated there at the right hand of God, you have stolen my Christ away from me.[43]

In *Eden* the vulnerability associated with children takes the form of Breda telling of a woman on the chat show *Kenny Live*, whose child was murdered by Myra Hindley and who is pleading for no parole for the killer of her child. At times of frailty, Billy remembers the little boy he 'pulled outta the sea', but he never found out if the child ever lived or died, preferring the ambivalence (p.6). The death of The Mousey Lee in *Howie The Rookie* is the source of monumental trauma, and is in stark contrast to the survival of the child in *Crestfall*, which smacks of naïve redemption. In Bolger's *In High Germany*, after the defeat to Holland in the European championship, Eoin still has things to believe in: 'I saw thirteen thousand pairs of hands moving as one, united by pride. I knew Frieda will still be waiting up, with my child, my future, a tiny pearl inside her.'[44] In McPherson's *Come on Over*, Matthew is back in Ireland to investigate the remains of a child that has not decomposed, who had been buried possibly four hundred years ago, as he hides a secret of his rape of a young 11-year-old girl, Patience, who had stabbed him in the face. He is going to say that the preservation of the corpse is a miracle, despite the fact that a corpse once moved begins to decompose. It is a miracle because he wants to see it as evidence of the will of God, and as a sign of God's forgiveness: 'Not trusting God was my greatest sin. But he sent me this little girl. Preserved for hundreds of years. To forgive me' (p.204).

So many playwrights use the notion of dead or violated children, or the inability to have children as a way of calibrating meanings that may not be available through any other device. It is a type of dramaturgical 'shorthand'. In *Hard to Believe* there is a pair of children's boots, backstage on a case, as if to represent the aborted child from John's relationship with his girlfriend. Differently, in the case of *James X*, it is the child from the age of 3 branded delinquent by agents of the state that haunts an audience. Richard Kearney argues that:

> The narrated action of a drama, for example, solicits a mode of sympathy more extensive and resonant than that experienced in ordinary life. And it does so not simply because it enjoys the poetic licence to suspend our normal protective reflexes (which guard us from pain) but also because it amplifies the range of those we might empathize with.[45]

But I think the monologues work in a more complicated fashion. Clearly, innocence or the violation of innocence, as I have argued elsewhere, is the default setting for much of Irish dramaturgy, and it also takes audiences into a position of naïvety. In addition, it is the naïvety of adults in relation to their dealing with children, or in grasping after a level of symbolism that is not earned, which also smacks of naïvety. In a way, like so many plays, the excesses real or the imagined of the male are tamed. They are punished in childlike ways. In *Eden*, Billy is infantilized, going to sleep in the children's room, just as the character in *Rum and Vodka* does after his binge of waywardness. Both men voluntarily exile themselves to the child's world. Progress, uncontested violence, identification, the feminine, impotency, innocence, redemption and infantization are all part and parcel of the same processes of naïvety.

Peter Brooker identifies the concept of '*Haltung*', which runs through Bertolt Brecht's vocabulary. It means 'learning, critiques, pleasure or productivity, and in his very last years ... "naivety"'.[46] Brooker adds the naïve:

> therefore fittingly joined together contraries; it was a look, a posture, an attitude of mind: it implied an intelligent simplicity, innocence and shrewdness, joining the conceptual and concrete, the popular and the philosophical. A naïve attitude would estrange the familiar, and problematize the self-evident, signalling a dialectical movement from the ordinary and everyday to the original and innovatory.[47]

This estrangement is added to by the ideas of 'trickster' and 'dreamer'.[48] The subversive part of the Irish story-telling tradition does that; the monologue at its best does likewise, positioning itself somewhere on a continuum between dreaming and trickery. Helen Gilbert and Joanne Tompkins argue that story-telling can disperse 'the viewer's focus'.[49]

For Stephen Di Benedetto, the group of thirty-something Irish male playwrights is not:

> going far enough to make their point clear to audiences, they rely

on our understanding and empathising with their predicaments, rather than suggesting an alternative course of action to try and come to a solution. Their worlds inevitably explode or fail, without negotiating a path that might avoid destruction.[50]

Brian Singleton states the monologue 'traps characters in the past tense and keeps them frozen in unenlightened isolation'.[51] In some instances both critics are correct, in others inaccurate. Kristin Morrison notes 'evasion itself is often the main action' of narrative.[52] Audiences become a sort of spurious community, feeding back into the process, by individually and collectively either embracing or being repelled by revelations and by all the variations in between, but also by engaging and joining 'together contraries'. Audiences, in this dynamic, have more power, more responsibility, because it is the naïvety that characterizes monologue performance best of all.

According to Benson, 'A story is an answer to a question.'[53] A story is also the answer an individual or character wishes to give, it can be an alibi, selective, fictive, imaginative, exaggerated, and can contain all sorts of self-deception. Unravelling the contradictions, the anomalies, 'unenlightened isolation', false justifications undermining the self-aggrandisement, and empathizing with either the person's or character's journey, or the inequity of an encounter, are all part of the process. Most monologues are about making a story stick. Yet it is the contestation of that narrative from within or from without which is often the defining attribute: from within, through acts of self-betrayal, belated acknowledgement or revision, and from without, by engaging dialogically with a plausible alternative or by the upgrading of one's narratives, myths, symbols and metaphors with the aid of another. In theatre, contestation is also possible through an actor's interpretation of his/her role, or through the provision of rival non-complementary disclosures, as with *Faith Healer*, if not from other characters, at least from an audience.

Alternative stories allow revision, reconstruction, the remaking, upgrading and recalibrating of narratives. Further, both culturally and interpersonally, the meshing of narratives is often fundamental to relationships, if communities can agree an evolving narrative, however fanciful or insecure the partners are with it, motivated by it or dedicated to it. Since monologues are delivered in isolation, often without layering, there are less immediate possibilities of this dialogical process.

Thankfully, dark nights of the soul are not going to drive people out of the theatre, because the composition of the monologue does something unusual, through the convergence of pain/pleasure and play, voyeurism and exaggeration, the 'ordinary' and the 'original'. It is the absence of either mature reflections or serious existential interiority that is foremost. It is the unknowingness that filters through. There is a strong sense that narrative emotion is only feasible when it is marked/enhanced by performance. The greatest confidence trick, of course, is that through the displacement that play brings about the characters do not feel anything too deeply. That is the essential pleasure of naïvety that audiences work with. Delivering a solo narrative, one assumes that the actor is hyper-alert to the feedback and forms a bond with an audience, as there is no other character on stage to focus on or to interact with. This self-consciousness almost equally applies to an audience, thus the spectator receives the energy of the performer and the narrative ambivalence – as Richard Schechner notes, 'performance is the domain of the audience', thus in the transmission of the mono-logue, potentially naïvety is also positioned within the 'domain of the audience'.[54] So, in a Brechtian sense, there is both a conscious dramaturgical naïvety implicit in the performance narrative as well as in the potential reception of the piece.

MONOMANIA/MONOPHOBIA

Nicholas Grene rightly argues that for an older generation of Irish play-wrights the 'stories told … betoken the layered nature of Irish culture as palimpsest of past and present, with the mythic buried within it',[55] whereas with McPherson's work, Grene claims, narratives 'are truths of ordinary experience, spoken without any amplifying echo-chamber of myth or archetype'.[56] He goes on to suggest that 'What we are given are stories in shallow space: deeper structures, echoes and resonances are deliberately denied.'[57] For me, that depth is not so much 'deliber-ately denied' as significantly inaccessible to contemporary dramaturgy. In *St Nicholas* (1997) the male theatre critic, without a name, states 'I had my health. I had resolve. But most important. Over everything else. I had a story.'[58] If a society offers no resonating myth, the final authority might be the myth of self through having a 'story'.[59] Ciarán Benson, as already pointed out, argues that 'who' and 'what' you are is a function of 'where' you are.[60] Maybe the 'who' and 'what' you are is not a 'function' but a fiction of 'where' you are, the illusion of placing oneself within a myth, within a narrative, within a specific space. Fundamentally, such a narrative is about negotiations between inno-cence and guilt, making sense and non-sense, self and non-self, space and non-space, narrative and non-narrative, and between authenticity and inauthenticity. Many public myths are stabilizing narratives, modes of reaching and yearning, yet there is often an inability to make sense of desire and shame, and guilt is often the profoundest trauma. If so, the myth of self is an elemental contestation of the demise of metanarratives or master narratives; it is a struggle to constitute a defiance of the post-modern impulse to unhinge subjectivity against an identity in free fall.

Traditionally, dominant practices of Irish theatre dramaturgy emphasized collective communal spaces where people interacted, in conflict, where connections and intimacies had a history and depth, however negative these might be. The recent trend is for people to have at best tenuous associations. Now disconnection is normalized, whether it is Corn Exchange's *Everyday* (2006) by Michael West or Paul Mercier's *Homeland* (2006). The monologues seem to have been a mid-point on that journey between old and new, mythologizing identity and through the brief recognition of connection between characters, reflecting back on to an audience the communicative structures of contemporary culture itself, the novelty and naïvety of newness. Maybe, then, that dramaturgical gesture is not so naïve after all. Maybe it is about accountability and not complicity, about resilience, about expressivity, and maybe that myth, however it might be downplayed, is worth talking about? If you can't 'bounce' characters off each other, as Marina Carr suggests, then you can perhaps bounce them and their duplicitousness and notional naïvety off an audience, which might be called not so much the haunting spectre of naïvety as the spectacle of naïvety.

NOTES

1. In chapter 3 I looked at Marie Jones's *A Night in November* (1994), set in an unspecified location, which is about the journey of the bigoted working-class Ulster Protestant, Kenneth McCallister, from tribal prejudice to the following of the Republic of Ireland's football team to the 1994 World Cup.
2. The design, by Bláithín Sheerin for the Peacock production, had brownish patterned carpet on all surfaces.
3. Thanks to Passion Machine for providing me with the unpublished script.
4. Conor McPherson, *Port Authority* in *Plays Two* (London: Nick Hern, 2004), p.132. (Hereafter, all page details given in parentheses within the text for this and all other plays.)
5. Fintan O'Toole argues that 'In recent years we have seen the emergence of what might be called reality theatre: shows in which the actor writes and presents his or her own experiences. Hitherto, the form has been used to explore extraordinary events with an urgent public dimension. George Seremba's *Come Good Rain* was about his own kidnap, torture and near-murder by the Obote regime in Uganda.' O'Toole goes on to say, 'But all of this seems to substitute a personal for an artistic intimacy. Instead of making us care about herself and her father through language, insight, and expression, she seeks to make us care through friendship. Because we like Michelle, we will like her Dad, and because we like him we will be as moved by his death as she is. This isn't art, though, it's emotional blackmail.' O'Toole finds that it is only when the political and the personal merge that such projects work. Fintan O'Toole, 'Review, *Play About My Dad*' at the Project Arts Centre, Dublin, *Irish Times*, 4 February 2006, www. ireland. com/newspaper/features/2006/0204/pf1164158910HM2REVIEW.html[accessed26/10/ 2006]
6. In his Author's Note to *Three Plays*, McPherson says, 'The first problem for the actor

performing these pieces is probably "Where am I?" "Where is the play set?" I've made up my mind about this. These plays are set "in a theatre". Why mess about? The character is on stage, perfectly aware that he is talking to a group of people … The temptation may be to launch not a one man "performance", to "act things out". But such a performance will never be as interesting as one where the actor trusts the story to do the work.' Conor McPherson, *This Lime Tree Bower, Three Plays* (London: Nick Hern, 1996).

7. Dermot Bolger, *In High Germany* in *A Dublin Quartet* (Harmondsworth: Penguin, 1992), p.73.

8. Michael Colgan, *South Bank Show*, special episode on Conor McPherson, London Weekend Television, 18 May 2003.

9. Michael Billington, *South Bank Show*.

10. Brian Singleton, 'Am I talking to myself?', *Irish Times*, 19 April 2001, www.ireland.com/newspaper/features/2001/0419/pfarchive.01041900070.html [accessed 10 October 2006]

11. Karen Fricker, 'Same Old Show: The Performance of Masculinity in Conor McPherson's *Port Authority* and Mark O'Rowe's *Made in China*', *Irish Review*, 29, 2002, pp.84–94, p.85.

12. Ibid., p.87.

13. Marina Carr in interview with Melissa Shira, *Theatre Talk*, eds L. Chambers, G FitzGibbon and E. Jordan (Dublin: Carysfort Press, 2001), pp.60–61.

14. Helen Gilbert and Joanne Tompkins, *Post-colonial Drama: Theory, Practice, Politics* (London: Routledge, 1996), p.129.

15. See Red Hot Chili Peppers album by this name.

16. There are also arts policy contexts. There is probably a direct relationship between funding revenue declines, not even so in terms of amounts, but in terms of true costs, and a decrease in the number of actors per production. Monologues can be low risk financially, and if the texts and performances are of a high standard, the production becomes all the more rewarding, because audiences are drawn by the high quality of the performances, which are regarded as memorable. The monologue also makes touring easier. And when monologues seemed to win the hearts of audiences, it set a template. Irish monologues internationally were also an issue, in that Irish theatre could not export large-scale productions, but it could small-scale ones. Finally, the Irish plays by the younger generation of playwrights that got breaks in London were initially monologues.

17. Gerry Smyth, *Space and the Irish Cultural Imagination* (Basingstoke: Palgrave, 2001), p.98.

18. Robert Putman, *Bowling Alone: The Collapse and Revival of American Community* (London and New York: Simon & Schuster, 2000).

19. Conall Morrison, *Hard To Believe* in *Far From The Land*, edited by John Fairleigh (London: Methuen, 1998), p.311. (Hereafter, page details will be given in parentheses within the text.)

20. If Irish monologues end in death and are thus suicide notes, then, American ones, it seems, by young writers tend to be about masturbatory sex. As always, Irish theatre is better with death than sex.

21. Jennifer Johnston, *Twinkletoes, Mustn't Forget High Noon, Christine* (also known as *Ananias, Azarias and Miseal*) in *Three Monologues* (Belfast: Lagan Press, 1995). (Hereafter all page details will be given in parentheses within the text.)

22. Mic Moroney suggests of *Eden* that 'Like recent work from Enda Walsh, Ken Harmon and Mark O'Rowe, this slots into an Irish idiom of monologue-driven, dialect-intoxicated, only part-feminised lad's theatre full of adrenalised Hiberno-English, rhyming slang and florid nick-names painting a vivid portrait of pub-drenched machos and their foolish sexual rivalries'. *Guardian*, 27 January 2001, www.arts.guardian.co.uk/print/0,4125707–110430,00. html [accessed 10/10/2006]

23. Eugene O'Brien, *Eden* (London: Methuen, 2001), p.3. (Hereafter, all page details given in parentheses within the text.)

24. Harvey O'Brien, Review of *Eden*, www.culturevulture.net/Theater/Eden.htm [accessed 30/09/2006]

25. Conor McPherson, *Come On Over* in *Plays Two* (London: Nick Hern, 2004), p.198. (Hereafter all references will be given in parentheses within the text.)

26. Conor McPherson, *This Lime Tree Bower* in *Three Plays* (London: Nick Hern, 1996), p.118.

27. Singleton, 'Am I talking to myself?'

28. See the film version of *Eden* released in 2007.

29. Fintan O'Toole, Review *Crestfall*, *Irish Times*, 22 May 2003.

30. Unpublished text.

31. First performed at Project Arts Centre in 2003, the revived production a year later included 'Flynn's multimedia exhibition Safe House, Safe Place, on three levels of Liberty Hall'. See

Fintan O'Toole's *'Review of James X'*, Liberty Hall, *Irish Times*, 2 October 2004, www.ireland.com/newspaper/features/2004/1002/3800189922HM2SATREVS.html [accessed 10/10/2006]

32. Gerard Mannix Flynn, 'Introduction', *James X* (Dublin: Lilliput Press, 2003), p.7.
33. The documentation published alongside the performance script is appalling in the views and attitudes taken. In 1970 a Doctor's Note to the Juvenile Courts tells of James's claims of physical abuse at Letterfrack. Dr Stevens's (not real name) assessment of James X for the Eastern Health Board notes 'possession and control by little men', 'homicidal fantasies', 'evidence of severe neurosis', but states he was not 'psychotic' (79).
34. O'Toole, *'Review of James X'*.
35. Frank McGuinness's *Baglady* (1985) deals with violence, abuse and the drowning of a child, and he moves his story forward using a very complex format, but ultimately the violated body plays a key role in the revelation of a story that pieces together the past using all kinds of devices, where the shame, guilt, hurt, denial, the self-monitoring and self-accusations all reveal themselves.
36. O'Toole *'Review of James X'*.
37. Jim Norton, *South Bank Show*, special episode on Conor McPherson, London Weekend Television, 18 May 2003.
38. Eileen Battersby, 'The Eloquence of Rage and Fear', *Irish Times*, 18 March 1999.
39. John Banville's novel *The Book of Evidence* (2002) is very interesting, in that audiences seemed to resist the arrogance and articulateness of the character on stage, in a way that a reader of the novel would not be afforded the same defiance. Articulation in the hands of the upper or middle classes has always been something resisted by theatre audiences, who prefer articulacy, in general, to remain with the notionally dispossessed and the working classes.
40. Mark O'Rowe, *Howie the Rookie* (London: Nick Hern, 1999), p.51.
41. Joe is Kevin's grandfather. Dermot's boss, O'Hagan, it is suggested, is the son of the neighbour that Kevin fancied. O'Hagan sends Kevin a photo of Marion, after she passes away.
42. Singleton, 'Am I talking to myself?'
43. Dermot Bolger, *Tramway End* in *A Dublin Quartet*, p.142.
44. Dermot Bolger, *In High Germany* in *A Dublin Quartet*, p.108.
45. Richard Kearney, *On Stories* (London and New York: Routledge, 2002), p.138.
46. Peter Brooker, 'Key Words in Brecht's Theory and Practice of Theatre' in Peter Thomson and Glendyr Sacks (eds), *The Cambridge Companion to Brecht* (Cambridge: Cambridge University Press, 1994), pp.185–200, p.198.
47. Ibid., p.199.
48. In post-colonial literatures, Gilbert and Tompkins raise the notion of the 'trickster', who is capable of disrupting 'all conventional categories, including corporeal hierarchies upon which various forms of discrimination are based', and the latter through 'transformations'. See *Postcolonial Drama*, p.235.
49. Ibid., p.129.
50. Stephen Di Benedetto, 'Shattering Images of Sex Acts and Other Obscene Stage Transgressions in Contemporary Irish Plays by Men' in *'Performing Ireland': Australasian Drama Studies Special Issue*, 43, October 2003, ed. B. Singleton and A. McMullan, pp.46–65, p.63.
51. Singleton, 'Am I talking to myself?'
52. Kristin Morrison, *Canters and Chronicles: The Use of Narrative in the Plays of Samuel Beckett and Harold Pinter* (Chicago: University of Chicago Press, 1983), p.8.
53. Ciarán Benson, *The Cultural Psychology of Self: Place, Morality and Art in Human Worlds* (London: Routledge, 2001), p.45.
54. Richard Schechner, *Performance Theory* (London and New York: Routledge, 2003, revised edition).
55. Nicholas Grene, 'Stories in Shallow Space: *Port Authority*', *Irish Review*, 29, 2002, pp.70–83, p.75.
56. Ibid., p.80.
57. Ibid., p.82.
58. Conor McPherson, *St Nicholas* in *Four Plays* (London: Nick Hern Books, 1999), p.177.
59. Monologues in Irish theatre tend to be about urban characters. As Fintan O'Toole notes, 'No one has ever mythologized this housing estate, this footbridge over the motorway, that video rental shop. It is, for the writer, virgin territory'. See 'Introduction' to Dermot Bolger's *Dublin Quartet*, p.2.
60. Benson, *Cultural Psychology*, p.ix.

Conclusion

MORAL HAZARD – CT[2]

The Celtic Tiger period exposed, in a general sense, Ireland's formidable ambitions and creativity, its optimism, adventurousness, a genuinely open intercultural awareness, as well as the darker sides, its competitiveness, off-putting self-assurance, unconcealed greed, smugness and its capacity to be deluded by the new Irish Dream, a consciousness spawned not only by some media outlets, spin doctors, bankers, estate agents and believers in a low tax economy, but also by those convinced by the merits of free market forces. The only thing different about this economic cycle to most others was that the bubble was bigger than on almost any other occasion in first-world economies, and the fact that so many individuals had themselves invested in that bubble, politically, financially, intellectually, emotionally and socially. It was not only the nation's élite and the cash rich that speculated through investment mainly in property and indirectly in the financial markets through pension funds, but also many civil servants, tradespeople and the middle and lower middle classes and many members of the new migrant communities also borrowed and invested.

The ridiculous notion of a soft landing at the expense of the truth of economic cycles of boom and bust was pedalled by a majority of commentators, most with vested interests. That most of the population bought into the notion of a soft-landing corrective had as much to do with self-delusion as with a false sense of uniqueness, for the economic warning signs were present; the declines in export and manufacturing activities, losses in productivity, unregulated inflation, increases in the purchases of services, luxury spending, much of which was funded by easy credit and with very little put aside for the rainy day. Major governments internationally were doing the same thing.

Today, as I write, the current political system is virtually obsolete and is not appropriate to the present circumstances, and in truth, it has not been for some time. The inability to achieve radical reform in the health sector is but one example of many as to how it is not policies of best practice that drive initiatives, but a mode of cobbling together overly compromised agreements between vested interests.

Improvised, ad-hoc and inappropriate macro-economic policies were and are formulated without vision, as political leaders play to the circumstances and the pressures of lobby groups. It isn't just about the economy; it is about individuals and communities, about the safety and future of the country just as much as it is about important things such as money. Through recent political decisions, the future of the country is tied in with the stabilization of the banking system. The recently established National Asset Management Agency will handle the toxic assets of the major banks. The nation is facing exponential increases in national debt, and long-term indebtedness, even bankruptcy, after years of reducing national debt as a percentage of Gross National Product.

Some have used the analogy of the perfect storm to explain the economic downturn. Eventually, yes, recession will pass like all storms do; however, what it will leave in its wake may well be a great deal of devastation, while any recovery plan must be driven by a different set of aspirations to the previous ones, with equality, justice and a fairer distribution of wealth as central platforms and not concerns that are paid lip service. And as for the markets, regulation is a fundamental. The markets have proved fundamentally that it should not decide on price, on risk or on its own standards. Other types of interventions must exist beyond soft-touch regulation. Nations cannot just place unjustified trust in markets and in 'competition' as they set out principles of citizenship. Quantitative easing might be one solution of many to current global problems, but a different type of qualitative easing has to be fundamental to social change.

A relatively healthy, expanding economy did bring with it pluses and minuses, as should be the case, but ultimately the nation failed collectively to prepare as adequately as possible for the fact that many economic variables were always going to be beyond a small nation like Ireland's control. The expectation exists that many of our playwrights should have dealt more convincingly with that era, in all its immediacy. The relative failure to do so probably was always a good thing. I also think that our playwrights would not have been capable of mapping that reality successfully, because much of it was an artifice, but also much of that global reality was illusionary and misapprehension, and not easily accessible to the writers, in terms of knowledge, understanding or interest, but more importantly, probably impossible to grasp or dramatize successfully, if one is to insist on some palpable relationship between text, performance and context.

During times of change in particular, the relationships between societies, texts and performances are not so easily marked, as sometimes texts and performances anticipate changes or are slow to react to those modifications; sometimes anticipation and unawareness can be happening simultaneously in the one piece. Further, many contemporary texts seem to have disengaged from embracing that simplistic text–society interface, either in terms of form or content. There are so many ways of making theatre and many different types of imaginative interventions possible that do not function as if there is some innate relationship between text and performance and current national or international contexts. Edward Bond's comment that 'modern society does not own imagination, it only exploits it',[1] serves as a serious warning. Under this dispensation, the imagination does not point towards alternatives – it is not available as a position of difference or dissent, for it takes the shape of deviance and aberration only. But we cannot just take a single perspective on this. It needs to be made more complicated.

For these reasons, my approach has been about reading with and against the grain of the dramaturgy, explicating the dominant features, highlighting the contradictions and exposing the anomalies and biases therein. Analysis of dramaturgical practices has both textual relevance and performance imperatives, but also implicitly a political obligation, not only in the sense of broader politics but in the collusion of cultures to pedal and substantiate consciously and unconsciously the ideologies of the dominant classes and thus normalize hierarchical power relationships, justify injustices and gender and class objectifications. From the impetus and impact of these individual chapters, I have been alert to what is similar, obsessive, recycled, self-consciously acknowledged veiled reference or appropriation. I have pulled together the continuities and discontinuities, the shorthands, the elaborations, the borrowings, the piggy-backings of a tradition's approach to dramaturgy and what is encrypted. I have not argued for a national house style. The tensions between text and context, public and private discourses, real and imagined are ongoing.

'[M]ythologically', the village 'doesn't resonate any more', Declan Hughes declares.[2] Hughes believes that too much contemporary playwriting focuses on the village, which 'is no longer the objective correlative for Ireland: the city is, or to be more precise, *between* cities is'.[3] Despite Hughes's assertion, some contemporary writers have continued to look towards the village for resonance, or for different sorts of resonances to the ones Hughes had in mind. Space and place still tend to evoke rural perspectives, while urban spaces have altered as well, as both attempt to cater for some sort of resonating myth.

Dealing with issues of innocence is something that brings together myth, the pastoral and narrative through issues of justice, sacrifice, origins. Carr's *On Raftery's Hill* exemplifies that. While many contemporary plays may lack the resonance of myth, others can be viewed as offering a more narrow focus, a more self-conscious, inward and self-absorbed disposition, which fundamentally is about establishing, consolidating and imagining a myth of self. Clare Wallace argues, discussing McPherson's 'penchant for the small-scale story', that his narratives 'are tales which lay claim to no monumental significance, mythic references or universal applicability'.[4] That switch in emphasis from the collective to the individual, from the heroic to the lower-key character is just one of the many trends in contemporary dramaturgy that can be traced across the chapters in this book. Textual practices construct identities, values, objectifications, prejudices and normalize inequalities, stress the survival of the fittest and affirm how dissent is either absorbed or eliminated, or how protest challenges hierarchies, then often ends up reinforcing them. Story-telling facilitates those types of transactions.

The metatheatrical however is the overarching feature from my perspective, as it can be dark or light, seditious or dissenting. In McGuinness's *Carthaginians* (1988) the characters turn on Dido at the end of the performance of his script, *The Burning Balaclava*, and they all shoot him. After *The Burning Balaclava* the characters can begin to bury the dead of Bloody Sunday and when the characters eventually name the dead of Bloody Sunday, it is done within the context of all that has transpired before the incident. In performance, this is a deeply moving and harrowing moment. At the end, Dido addresses the sleeping figures and the spectators:

> Dido: What happened? Everything happened, nothing happened, whatever you want to believe, I suppose ... How's Derry? Surviving. Carthage has not been destroyed. Watch Yourself ... Play.[5]

Dido's final word is 'play', as if play is the invitation, the obligation and an alternative.

That invitation to 'play' is picked up brilliantly in Enda Walsh's *The Walworth Farce* (2006), where a father and two sons, in a London flat on the Walworth Road, enact a farce around the day they left Ireland, never to return. The family remains almost totally sealed off in their own world. One son, Sean, gets out on a daily basis to do some shopping for props/provisions, and on this occasion, comes home with the wrong bag of shopping. Like all good farce, all it takes is an accident, rather than some decisive action, to kick-start the drama. The father, Dinny, is the actor/manager, director, scenographer, stage manager, critic, adjudicator and spectator. The sons are playing to and for him, and less for each other. It is a measure of their commitment to their father that is being tested throughout the performance. Blake and Sean share between them multiple roles. The set is part prison, sanctuary and acting place, to use Tom Kilroy's terminology from chapter 2, but re-enactment is not about enablement or contestation. It is about repressing the real memory of why they left Cork and it is an endlessly rehashed, farcical myth of exile, with appropriate ditzy music. The truth of the matter is that they fled because Dinny had killed his brother, Paddy and sister-in-law, Vera on the day of his mother's funeral. (The farce as performed is about wills, sex, money, murder and death. There are two funerals on the one day, which cross over. The deaths are brought about because of an accident involving an elderly man being glued into a speed boat, a horse that is struck by the boat which has left the water, and a woman passing by who is killed by the horse.)

The arrival of the Tesco's employee, Hayley with the correct bag of shopping brings the curtain down indirectly, so to speak, on the re-enactment in its usual form. Blake kills his father and sets himself up to be killed by Sean. Sean is left alone on stage and endeavours, as an act of desperate consolation and consolidation, to enact a farce of the day that was in it – doing what he knows best. Sean locks the door, redresses the stage, and he reprises the main scenes from the farce's first act. Sean then gets Hayley's coat, handbag and Tesco plastic bag, puts some brown shoe polish on his own face, so that he can make 'Hayley's entrance'.[6] It ends, as the stage direction suggests, 'as we watch him carefully lose himself in a new story' (p.85). There is a fundamental terror in the thought of someone reprising a scenario in such a way. For Walsh, however, the characters 'are not Irish builders, they are Irish theatre makers in a council flat on the Walworth Road. I kept having to remind myself that they are actors, a director and a writer in a play ... as opposed to deranged, feral ... beings.'[7] Richard Schechner's work on the idea of dark play is very appropriate here. He argues that

> Dark play occurs when contradictory realities coexist, each seemingly capable of cancelling the other out, as in the double cross ... Dark play subverts order, dissolves frames, breaks its own rules, so that playing itself is in danger of being destroyed ... Unlike the

inversions of carnivals, ritual clowns, and so on (whose agendas are public), dark play inversions are not declared or resolved: its end is not integration but disruption, deceit, excess, and gratification.[8]

The violence that farce in general can sustain is captured so well by Walsh. It is a world of dominance, violence and intimidation from start to finish that can only end with one conclusion. There is 'disruption' and 'deceit', but little 'gratification' in the furtherance of performance by Sean. Despite the location, the world of this drama cannot so easily piggyback on the myth of exile and the trauma of diasporic experiences. As a consequence, it is not farcical irony but something different, which the macabre darkness of play facilitates. Walsh is contesting the tradition of say Tom Murphy's *A Whistle in the Dark* (1961). While Walsh has said that he is 'not self-consciously stamping that into the ground',[9] he effectively is. He is contesting the very sensibility of the world of Murphy's drama, deeming it to bear no resemblance to the reality of Ireland in a new millennium. Walsh tells Colin Murphy, 'I knew I wanted to write the play that every Irish playwright has to write – the old Irish people in London – but (I knew) I have to explode that kind of play and bring it somewhere else.'[10] There is a sinister tone to much of Dinny's oppressions, as the three actors in his script carry coffins made from cornflake boxes, don costumes and fake moustaches, and run between characterizations in a hyper-real fashion. It is an insane world of coerced performance.

Metatheatricality is the opportunistic assertion of dysfunction gaps, absences, omissions, transgressions and opportunities. Play is about make-believe, about release and about the establishment of a space of transition, of working out and of recognition, most of all a protective and insulating strategy. How play and violence meet is indeed what Walsh does best in *The Walworth Farce*. Sabine Dargent's excellent design concept for the Druid production and Mikel Murfi's direction drew brilliantly energetic performances from the cast in the Druid production.[11] In *The Walworth Farce* despite the darkness, the oppression and the repression, the dexterity and vivacity of the actors in performance ensure that a positive disposition towards the mayhem is brought into operation.

DEVOLVED VIOLENCE

Violence is one of the lenses that raises substantial issues for dramaturgy and representation and which works across a number of the chapters in this book. While danger, violence, madness and murder have always prevailed in theatre generally, and in Irish plays specifically, something very different is happening with violence currently and thus conflict is treated in a very different way. Traditionally, playwrights historicized violence, whereas today through sensation and irony, violence is reconceptualized and reframed. Today, it is frequently a violence of the margins, of gangland, of the dispossessed or the mad or insane. Organized crime, money laundering and contract killing are often the staple diet. The problems seem to be that the more guns, the more beatings and mass shootouts you have on stage, the less likely one is to take it seriously.

In Declan Hughes's *Twenty Grand* (1998) the nature of the family business has changed, from small-time village shopkeeper of traditional Irish theatre to big-time drug dealer. Somewhat differently, Gary Mitchell's *A Little World of Our Own* (1997) deals with a loyalist working-class community and the macho, deluded self-destructiveness therein. Most of his other work considers the same terrain of post-ceasefire violence. I have earlier dealt with a series of plays that deal with sexual violence in the chapter on innocence. Stella Feehily's female characters in *Duck* (2003) experience gangland, as do O'Rowe's characters in *Made in China* (2001) and his *Crestfall* (2003). The work of Martin McDonagh in particular has been berated because of its inability to challenge the imperatives of violence.

EXQUISITE PAIN

In much of the contemporary dramaturgy globally, there are increasing levels of violence and mutilation, with an escalating smudging of pleasure and pain through a fetishistic eroticization of violence.[12] Irish playwrights are engaged with a similar type of hazing. What is recent, however, is that the distinction between pleasure and pain has been blurred, so neither pain nor pleasure proves to be any provisional point of reference. The dialectical tensions of truth and deception, freedom and constraint, tyrant and justice cannot be played out so easily. A distinction between pain and pleasure seems to be the more realizable mode. Yet although pain is rightly decontextualized in many modern texts, given a spectator's immunity to it, it also tends to be sanitized, whereas previously play offered a deliberate and dialogical process that subtly underlined the pain and at times saw it as enabling: Patricia Burke Brogan's play *Eclipsed* (1992) achieves something like this.

In general the decontextualization of pain/pleasure plus the commodification of both are increasingly the mainstay of the contemporary dramaturgy, which has as much to do with irony, as it has led to a lack of empathy available to an audience when it comes to contemporary work. Pain is alienated to such an extent that its impact is often utterly emptied of meaning beyond the frame of performance.

In McDonagh's work the characters seem to have internalized a sense of self that lacks awareness and is almost without empathy, and there is no restraint on either their revenge fantasies or on the limits to which they will wound. In *The Lieutenant of Inishmore* Donny and Davey are forced to hack up bodies, and they do so with the playful indifference of boys playing in a sand box. Of course, the body parts are fake, and in performance there is no attempt at authenticity; still some spectators found such scenes offensive. *The Pillowman* (2003) contains scenes of murder and torture, and hints at all kinds of other violations though the lens of Grand Guignol. McDonagh's dramaturgy in its excess and provocation does not oblige his characters to bring a mode of reflection to their realities; that onus is on the spectator.

Historically, the trauma of identity was associated with imperial rule and the need to confront oppression. The pain aligned with a generated empathy for the disenfranchised, the romanticized and dispossessed.[13] It is little wonder that the majority of successes of Irish theatre since 1980 are dominated by history/memory plays and audiences are engaged by an understanding of historical, sometimes nostalgized, injustice. Contemporary injustices are less palatable perhaps to spectators. On the other hand, under postmodernism, subjectivity supposedly has mutated into commodified individuality or into something that is not fixed but circulating and volatile. Postmodernism has prompted the idea that all activities and responses are merely imitative, simulated and ungrounded activities that are marked by a complete disacknowledgement of presence and by a dangerous refusal to champion any value system or prioritize any judgements. In effect, the postmodern retort can be fetishistically internal and graphically demonstrative only in terms of performance, really play for play's sake. That way violence gets caught up in the loop of play that only the best work can contest. Walsh's work is a great example of this.

IMPERIAL PERFORMATIVES

It could be argued that representations of Ireland and Irish characters in an international arena in particular, always become 'other', 'other' as fetish, stereotype or deviant. On that basis, one could argue that the violence and drunkenness associated with the Irish monologue plays out the colonial mindset and global stereotype, and the presence of the adult child in so many plays does the same thing. Jen Harvie in her discussions on 'the imperial metropolis' raises the idea of 'imperial performatives – repeated presumptions that they know different cultures better than those cultures know themselves'.[14] While not agreeing that this comment can apply more to Irish plays produced in London and New York, more than elsewhere, it does raise significant issues around performance imperatives and assumptions of understanding.

What is often attractive to this sense of Irishness are the modes of sociability, subjugation and split subjectivities, the relative lack of agency, flickers of authenticity amid the subversive defiance of play, and emancipatory energies, in the face of denial, limitation, alienation and repression. In Irish dramaturgy generally, an easy egalitarianism is possible, when the enemy is blatant and when one has access to few provisions or opportunities; however, when power and material disparities are far more visible within a framework of plenty, then collective aspiration often seems sentimental, even delusional because the precise nature of inequality is no longer obscured. It becomes more complicated when victimhood is naturalized or inequality normalized within the frame of Irishness.

I would also argue that the serious number of productions of McPherson, Carr, McDonagh, McGuinness and Friel abroad are not driven by their perceived foreignness, primitiveness, quaintness or isolationism, because something beyond a limited, regressive, prejudicial spectacle or voyeurism is needed for audiences to come back for more. A capacity to resonate or vibrate beyond either the genre specifics of the work, its locale and its socio/historic constructiveness is so important. It is far more about an emphasis on relationality, about the committed energies that can be generated within constructed scenographic environments between performers themselves and performers and audiences. In that way the work is not simply corralled by Irishness or whiteness or by a vague non-Englishness, but translated, transposed and transformed in unique ways. There can be a welcome commitment and supplementary indigenous inputs, even at times a contestation, appropriation or erasure of a supplementary and ineffable Irishness. Moreover, they are not grounded in futile attempts at authenticity. Authenticity is the fault line for so many of these performances, as such an obsession can weaken the intense theatricality of the work and obscure other performance potentials. Ondřej Pilný argues that 'The mystique of Irishness' (Seamus Deane's phrase) once 'affirmed by an older tradition of writing and criticism, makes way for an ironic tabulation of Irishness'.[15]

Irishness is as much 'ironic' as iconic, real and surreal, manipulated to be whatever one wants it to mean. Diasporic communities are only one part of target audiences, who all bring their own experiences and are willing to attribute and project values and perceptions with a mix of prejudice and anticipation, sentiment and denial. I suppose it is when Irishness is deemed as softly sentimental, less civil, more easily readable or codeable, and more open than most other nations, that many have great difficulties with production and reception.

And while UK-based directors such as Michael Attenborough, Nicholas Hytner, Robin Lefèvre, Adrian Noble, Trevor Nunn, Ian Rickson, Max Stafford Clark or the American Wilson Malam have worked very successfully with the text-based tradition, it is my hope that directors such as Anne Bogart, Robert Lepage, Katie Mitchell, Thomas Ostermeier and Robert Wilson will take up the challenges of classic and new Irish writing produced by residents and citizens home and abroad and performed and designed by professionals of exemplary standing. That way the conventions, convictions and dramaturgies will be truly tested for consensus, conspiracy, complicitness, dissonance and dissidence.

In the work of an older generation there is an anxiety or concern in the writing to be inclusive, to provide the overview and to deliver the critical frameworks necessary to engage with the world. There is a sense of explanation, even if it is privileged and prejudiced. Incompleteness, rather than an all-embracing overview, drives the contemporary dramaturgy – stories partially tell what is, and characters display limited and fractional awareness to the worlds in which they live and construct. The more contemporary writing seems confident in its incompleteness, in its unrepresentableness. New dramaturgies have been fermenting and many have been practised by a range of innovative performances and non-text-based devised practices.

The greatest dilemma for all writing, however, lies within the dramaturgy itself; it is not necessarily one of articulation or imagination, but of the increasing challenge to find dramatic situations or circumstances into which to pitch characters/performers in a collective space, where there is something substantial and uncertain at stake. Dramaturgically, when there is something at stake then urgency, necessity and recognition are consequences of it. As societies evolve, new dramaturgies emerge; there is very evident a switch from a narrative-based tradition towards devised work that is more body, image and movement aware, operating with a distrust of language and the causality or sequentiality of text, and a greater impatience with the older ways of telling stories.

Despite spurious claims as to its insularity, and despite the gross inability to reflect on contemporary circumstances, Irish theatre offers a dramaturgy of 'excess', evoking Pilkington's comments from the earlier section of this book, and it is equally about absence, it is one of celebration of defiance as much as it is conservative, it is tangential rather than representative, it is vocal in its ambivalence as well as hushed in its diffidence, it is manipulative in its ideological leanings as much as it is dissenting of injustices, even when framing it conservatively or inappropriately. Above all, at its best the dramaturgy of Irish theatre takes itself as seriously as it needs to, while being imaginative in its dissidence.

NOTES

1. Edward Bond, 'Modern and Postmodern Theatres' in an interview with Ulrich Koppen, *New Theatre Quarterly*, 50, May 1997, p.103.
2. Declan Hughes, 'Reflections on Irish Theatre and Identity' in *Theatre Stuff: Critical Essays on Contemporary Irish Theatre*, ed. E. Jordan (Dublin: Carysfort Press, 2000), p.12.
3. Ibid.
4. Clare Wallace, *Suspect Cultures: Narrative, Identity and Citation in 1990s New Drama* (Prague: Litteraria Pragensia, 2006), pp.58–9.
5. Frank McGuinness, *Carthaginians* in *Plays 1* (London: Faber & Faber, 1996), p.379.
6. Enda Walsh, *The Walworth Farce* (London: Nick Hern, 2006), p.85. (Hereafter, all further references to this play will be given in parentheses within the text.)
7. Enda Walsh in an interview, www.stannswarehouse.org/enda_interview.html [accessed 10/01/2009]
8. Richard Schechner, *The Future of Ritual: Writings on Culture and Performance* (London and New York: Routledge, 1993), p.36.
9. See Peter Cawley, 'I Hate Farce', *Irish Times*, Ticket Section, 17/03/2006, www.ireland.com/theticket/articles/2006/0317/3308369510TK1703WALWORTH.html [accessed 01/05/2006]
10. Enda Walsh cited in 'An Irish farce in London', Colin Murphy, *Village Magazine*, 30 March 2006, www.villagemagazine.ie/article.asp?sid=2&sud=55&aid=1530 [accessed 01/05/2006]
11. Garrett Lombard played Blake, Denis Conway took the role of the father of the family, Dinny, Aaron Monaghan performed as Sean, and in its current run, Tadhg Murphy replaced Monaghan and Hayley was originally played by Syan Blake and in 2008 by Mercy Ojelade and in between both by Natalie Best.
12. David Cronenberg's film *Crash* (1996), based on the novel (1973) by J.G. Ballard, offers additional, alternative perspectives and points to other emerging patterns. After an almost fatal accident, the characters re-enact (as part of their sexual fantasy) the gruesome details of a fatal car crash. Others restage, for an audience, the car crash which killed James Dean; while attempting to replicate the death of the actress Jayne Mansfield: they die in the process, fulfilling in part some underlying death wish and in part some postmodernistic impulse, by essentially refusing to distinguish between the world of play and the real. In effect, there is no overlap from one world to the next, there is no sense of retrieval; play has lost its purpose. At one point the performance artist/stunt man comes across the crash scene where his friends have been injured or just died and he proceeds to take photographs. Cronenberg's desire may have been to insist that increasingly there is no distinction between fact and fiction and that the characters are locked into a cycle of obsessional re-enactment.
13. In our modern world, power has become very problematic, to such an extent that one cannot immediately name it, and if one can, one cannot dramatize it with any sense of persuasion. Discernible power in a dramatic frame becomes, ironically by the very nature of its usual sub-

tle reality, stereotypical, primarily because it loses its invisibility, diluting in most instances the dramatic effect.

14. Jen Harvie, *Staging the UK* (Manchester: Manchester University Press, 2005), pp.196–7.
15. Ondřej Pilný, *Irony and Identity in Modern Irish Drama* (Prague: Litteraria Pragensia, 2006), p.110.

Primary Bibliography

Barry, Sebastian, *The Steward of Christendom* (London: Methuen, 1995).
—— *Hinterland* (London: Methuen, 2002).
Bolger, Dermot, *The Lament for Arthur Cleary* and *In High Germany* in *A Dublin Quartet* (Harmondsworth: Penguin, 1992).
—— *The Passion of Jerome* (London: Methuen, 1999).
Breen, John, *Alone it Stands* (unpublished text, 1999).
Burke-Brogan, Patricia, *Eclipsed* (Galway: Salmon Press, 1994).
Carr, Marina, *Portia Coughlan* in *The Dazzling Dark: New Irish Plays*, selected and introduced by Frank McGuinness (London: Faber & Faber, 1996).
—— *Low in the Dark, The Mai, Portia Coughlan* and *By the Bog of Cats* in *Plays One* (London: Faber & Faber, 1999).
—— *On Raftery's Hill* (Oldcastle: Gallery Press, 2000).
Feehily, Stella, *Duck* (London: Nick Hern, 2003).
Flynn, Gerard Mannix, *James X* (Dublin: Lilliput Press, 2003).
Friel, Brian, *Living Quarters, Philadelphia, Here I Come!* and *Translations* in *Selected Plays* (London: Faber & Faber, 1984).
—— *Dancing at Lughnasa* in *Plays 2* (London: Faber & Faber, 1997).
—— *Give Me Your Answer, Do!* (Harmondsworth: Penguin, 1997).
Hartigan, Anne, *Jersey Lillies* (unpublished text, 1996).
Hughes, Declan, *Shiver* (London: Methuen, 2003).
Johnston, Jennifer, *Twinkletoes, Mustn't Forget High Noon, Christine* (also known as *Ananias, Azarias and Miseal*) in *Three Monologues* (Belfast: Lagan Press, 1995).
Jones, Marie, *Stones in his Pockets* and *A Night in November* (London: Nick Hern, 2000).
Kane, Sarah, *Blasted* (London: Methuen, 1996).
Keane, J. B., *Sive, The Field* and *Big Maggie* (revised texts) in *Three Plays*, ed. Ben Barnes (Cork: Mercier Press, 1990).
Kilroy, Tom, *Talbot's Box* (Oldcastle: Gallery Press, 1979).
—— *Double Cross* (London: Faber & Faber, 1986).
—— *Double Cross* (Oldcastle: Gallery Press, 1994).
—— *The Secret Fall of Constance Wilde* (Oldcastle: Gallery Press, 1997).

McDonagh, Martin, *The Beauty Queen of Leenane, A Skull in Connemara* and *The Lonesome West* in *Plays 1* (London: Methuen, 1999).
—— *The Cripple of Inishmaan* (London: Methuen, 1997).
—— *The Lieutenant of Inishmore* (London: Methuen, 2001).
—— *The Pillowman* (London: Faber & Faber, 2003).
McGuinness, Frank, *Borderlands* in *Three TEAM plays*, ed. Martin Drury (Dublin: Wolfhound Press, 1988).
—— *Plays 1, The Factory Girls, Observe the Sons of Ulster Marching Towards the Somme, Innocence, Carthaginians, Baglady* (London: Faber & Faber, 1997).
—— *The Dazzling Dark: New Irish Plays*, selected and introduced by Frank McGuinness (London: Faber & Faber, 1996).
—— *Mutabilitie* (London: Faber & Faber, 1997).
—— *Plays 2, Mary and Lizzie, Someone Who'll Watch Over Me, Dolly West's Kitchen* (London: Faber & Faber, 2002).
—— *The Bird Sanctuary* (London: Faber & Faber, 2002).
—— *Gates of Gold* (London: Faber & Faber, 2002).
—— *Speaking Like Magpies* (London: Faber & Faber, 2005).
—— *There Came a Gypsy Riding* (London: Faber & Faber, 2007).
McPherson, Conor, *Rum and Vodka, The Good Thief* and *This Lime Tree Bower* in *Three Plays* (London: Nick Hern, 1996).
—— *The Weir* (London: Nick Hern, 1997).
—— *St Nicholas* in *Four Plays* (London: Nick Hern, 1999).
—— *Come On Over* in *Plays Two* (London: Nick Hern, 2004).
—— *Port Authority* in *Plays Two* (London: Nick Hern, 2004).
Mercier, Paul, *Studs* (unpublished text, 1989).
Mitchell, Gary, *A Little World of Our Own* in *Two Plays* (London: Nick Hern, 1997).
Morrison, Conall, *Hard To Believe* in *Far From The Land*, edited by John Fairleigh (London: Methuen, 1998).
Murphy, Thomas, *The Sanctuary Lamp* (Oldcastle: Gallery Press, 1976; revised edns 1984, 1994).
—— *A Crucial Week in the Life of a Grocer's Assistant* in *A Whistle in the Dark and Other Plays* (London: Methuen, 1989).
—— *Bailegangaire, Conversations on a Homecoming* and *The Gigli Concert* in *After Tragedy* (London: Methuen, 1988).
O'Brien, Eugene, *Eden* (London: Methuen, 2001).
O'Kelly, Donal, *Catalpa* (Dublin/London: New Island/Nick Hern, 1997).
O'Rowe, Mark, *From Both Hips* (*Two Plays: From Both Hips* and *The Aspidistra Code* (London: Nick Hern, 1999)).

—— *Howie The Rookie,* (London: Nick Hern, 1999).

—— *Made in China* (London: Nick Hern, 2001).

Paulin, Tom, *The Riot Act: A Version of Sophocles's Antigone* (London: Faber & Faber, 1985).

Ravenhill, Mark, *Shopping and F***ing* (London: Methuen, 1996).

Roche, Billy, *The Wexford Trilogy* (London; Nick Hern, 2000).

—— *Cavalcaders* in *Two Plays* (London: Nick Hern, 2001).

Walsh, Enda, *Disco Pigs* and *Sucking Dublin* (London: Nick Hern, 1997).

—— *The Walworth Farce* (London: Nick Hern, 2006).

Wilde, Oscar, *The Importance of Being Earnest* in *The Importance of Being Earnest and Related Writings*, ed. Joseph Bristow (London: Routledge, 1992).

Select Bibliography

Anderson, Benedict, *Imagined Communities: Reflections on the Origins and Spread of Nationalism* (London: Verso, 1983).

Arnott, Peter, D., *Public and Performance in the Greek Theatre* (London: Routledge, 1989).

Ashcroft, Bill, Gareth Griffiths and Helen Tiffin, *Post-colonial Studies Reader* (London: Routledge, 1995).

Bagley, Christopher and Kathleen King, *Child Abuse: The Search for Healing* (London and New York: Tavistock/Routledge, 1990).

Barba, Eugenio, 'The Deep Order Called Turbulence: The Three Faces of Dramaturgy', *Drama Review*, 44–4, Winter 2000, pp.56–66.

Barry, Kevin 'Making Space For Theatre', *Irish Times*, 17 October 1992, Weekend Section, p.3.

Barthes, Roland, *A Roland Barthes Reader*, edited and introduced by Susan Sontag (London: Vintage, 1993).

Benson, Ciarán, *The Cultural Psychology of Self: Place, Morality and Art in Human Worlds* (London: Routledge, 2001).

Bertha, Csilla, '"They Raigne ouer Change, and Doe Their States Maintaine": Change, Stasis, and Postcoloniality in Frank McGuinness's *Mutabilitie*', *Irish University Review: A Journal of Irish Studies*, 33–2, Autumn–Winter 2003, pp.307–21.

Blyth, Eric and Judith Milner (The Violence against Children Study Group), *Taking Child Abuse Seriously* (London: Hyman 1990; reprinted Routledge, 1993).

Boal, Augosto, *The Rainbow of Desire* (London: Routledge, 1995).

Bolger, Dermot, ed., *Druids, Dudes and Beauty Queens: The Changing Face of Irish Theatre* (Dublin: New Island, 2001).

Bracher, Karl Dietrick, 'The Disputed Concept of Totalitarianism: Experience and Actuality' in *Totalitarianism Reconsidered*, ed. Ernest A. Menze (New York and London: Kennikat Press, 1981).

Briere, John, N., *Child Abuse Trauma: Theory and Treatment of the Lasting Effects* (London: Sage Publications, 1992).

Butler-Cullingford, Elizabeth, *Ireland's Others: Gender and Ethnicity in Irish Literature and Popular Culture* (Cork: Cork University Press, 2001).

Carr, Marina, 'Dealing with the Dead', *Irish University Review*, 28–1, Spring 1998, pp.190–97.

Cave, Richard Allen, 'Questing for Ritual and Ceremony in a Godforsaken World: *Dancing at Lughnasa* and *Wonderful Tennessee*', *Hungarian Journal of English and American Studies*, 5–1, 1999, pp.109–27.

—— 'The Abbey Tours in England' in *Irish Theatre on Tour*, ed. Nicholas Grene and Christopher Morash (Dublin: Carysfort Press, 2005), pp.9–34.

Cave, Richard and Ben Levitas, eds, *Irish Theatre in England* (Dublin: Carysfort Press, 2007).

Chambers, Lilian, Gerald FitzGibbon and Eamonn Jordan, eds, *Theatre Talk: Voices of Irish Theatre Practitioners* (Dublin: Carysfort Press, 2001).

Chambers, Lilian and Eamonn Jordan, eds, *The Theatre of Martin McDonagh: A World of Savage Stories* (Dublin: Carysfort Press, 2006).

Chatterton, Paul and Robert Hollands, *Urban Nightscapes: Youth Cultures, Pleasure Spaces and Corporate Power* (London and New York: Routledge, 2003).

Clarke, Brenna Katz, *The Emergence of the Irish Peasant Play at the Abbey Theatre* (Ann Arbor: University of Michigan Press, 1982).

Cleary, Joe, *Outrageous Fortune: Capital and Culture in Modern Ireland* (Dublin: Field Day Publications, 2007).

Cregan, David, '"There's something queer here": Modern Ireland and the Plays of Frank McGuinness' in *Performing Ireland*, eds Brian Singleton and Anna McMullan, *Australasian Drama Studies*, *Special Issue*, 43, October 2003, pp.66–75.

Dean, Joan FitzPatrick, 'Tales Told by Martin McDonagh', *Nua: Studies in Contemporary Irish Writing*, 3.1–2, 2002, pp.57–68.

Deane, Seamus, 'Introduction', *Brian Friel: Selected Plays* (London: Faber & Faber, 1984).

De Marinis, Marco, 'Dramaturgy of the Spectator', trans. Paul Dwyer, *Drama Review*, 31–2, Summer 1987, pp.100–14.

Dromgoole, Dominic, *The Full Room: An A–Z of Contemporary Playwriting* (London: Methuen, 2000).

FitzGibbon, Gerald, 'Interpreting Between Privacies: Brian Friel and the Boundaries of Language', *Hungarian Journal of English and American Studies*, 5–1, 1999, pp.71–84.

Fitzpatrick, Lisa, 'Language Games: *The Pillowman, A Skull in Connemara*, and Martin McDonagh's Hiberno-English' in *The*

Theatre of Martin McDonagh: A World of Savage Stories (Dublin: Carysfort Press, 2006), pp.141–54.

—— 'Nation and Myth in the Age of the Celtic Tiger: Muide Éire?' in *Echoes down the Corridor*, eds Patrick Lonergan and Riana O'Dwyer (Dublin: Carysfort Press, 2006), pp.169–80.

Foley, Imelda, *The Girls in the Big Picture: Gender in Contemporary Ulster Theatre* (Belfast: Blackstaff Press, 2003).

Foster, R.F., *Luck and the Irish: A Brief History of Change, 1970–2000* (Harmondsworth: Penguin, 2007).

Fryan, Michael, 'Introduction', *The Seagull*, by Anton Chekhov, trans. Michael Fryan (London: Methuen, 1986).

Furay, Julia and Redmond O'Hanlon, eds, *Critical Moments: Fintan O'Toole on Modern Irish Theatre* (Dublin: Carysfort Press, 2003).

Furniss, Tilman, *The Multi-professional Handbook of Child Sexual Abuse: Integrated Management, Therapy and Legal Intervention* (London: Routledge, 1991).

Gibbons, Luke, *Transformations in Irish Culture* (Cork: Cork University Press, 1996).

Gifford, Terry, *Pastoral* (London: Routledge, 1999).

Gilbert, Helen and Joanne Tompkins, *Post-colonial Drama: Theory, Practice, Politics* (London: Routledge, 1996).

Graham, Colin, *Deconstructing Ireland: Identity, Theory, Culture* (Edinburgh: Edinburgh University Press, 2001).

Grant, David, 'Breaking the Circle, Transcending the Taboo' in Eric Weitz ed., *The Power of Laughter: Comedy and Contemporary Irish Theatre* (Dublin: Carysfort Press, 2004), pp.41–50.

Grene, Nicholas, *The Politics of Irish Drama: Plays in Context from Boucicault to Friel* (Cambridge: Cambridge University Press, 1999).

—— 'Person and Persona', *Irish University Review: A Journal of Irish Studies*, 32–1, Spring–Summer 2002, pp.70–82.

—— 'Black Pastoral: 1990s Images of Ireland.', *Litteraria Pragensia* 20–10–23, October 2004, www.komparatistika.ff.cuni.cz/litteraria/no20-10/grene.htm

—— 'Ireland in Two Minds: Martin McDonagh and Conor McPherson', *Yearbook of English Studies*, 35–1, 2005, pp.298–311.

Grene, Nicholas and Christopher Morash, eds, *Irish Theatre on Tour* (Dublin: Carysfort Press, 2005).

Harris, Susan Cannon, *Gender and Modern Irish Drama* (Indianapolis: Indiana University Press, 2002)

Harvie, Jen, *Staging the UK* (Manchester: Manchester University Press, 2005).

Harrington, John P. and Elizabeth J. Mitchell, eds, *Politics and Performance in Contemporary Northern Ireland* (Andover: University of Massachusetts Press, 1999).

Henderson, Lynda, 'Men, Women and the Life of the Spirit in Tom Murphy's Plays' in *Irish Writers and their Creative Process*, ed. Jacqueline Genet and Wynne Hellegoarc'h (Gerrards Cross: Colin Smythe, 1996), pp.87–99.

Hoyles, John, *The Literary Underground: Writers and The Totalitarian Experience, 1900–1950* (Toronto: Harvester Wheatsheaf, 1991).

Hunt, Leon, *Kung Fu Cult Masters* (London and New York: Wallflower Press, 2004).

Hynes, Garry, interview with Cathy Leeney, *Theatre Talk: Voices of Irish Theatre Practitioners*, eds Lilian Chambers, G. FitzGibbon and E. Jordan (Dublin: Carysfort Press, 2001), pp.195–213.

James, Caryn, 'Critic's Notebook: A Haunting Play Resounds Far Beyond the Stage', *New York Times*, 15 April 2005.

Janko, Susan, *Vulnerable Children, Vulnerable Families: The Social Construction of Child Abuse* (New York: Teacher's College Press, Columbia University, 1994).

Jenkyns, Marina, *The Play's the Thing: Exploring Text in Drama and Therapy* (London and New York: Routledge, 1996).

Jordan, Eamonn, *The Feast of Famine: The Plays of Frank McGuinness* (Berne, London and New York: Peter Lang, 1997).

—— ed., *Theatre Stuff: Critical Essays on Contemporary Irish Theatre* (Dublin: Carysfort Press, 2000).

—— *Someone Who'll Watch Over Me: A Critical Commentary* (Dublin: C.J. Fallon, 2000).

Kearney, Richard, 'Myth and Motherland' in *Ireland's Field Day* (London: Hutchinson, 1985).

—— *Transitions: Narratives in Modern Irish Culture* (Dublin: Wolfhound Press, 1988).

—— *On Stories* (London and New York: Routledge, 2002).

—— *Navigations: Collected Irish Essays 1976–2006* (Dublin: Lilliput Press, 2006).

Keenan, Brian, *An Evil Cradling* (London: Vintage, 1992).

—— 'Out Of The Shadows', *Irish Times*, Weekend Section, 8 May 1993.

Kerwin, William, ed., *Brian Friel: A Casebook* (New York and London: Garland, 1997).

Kiberd, Declan, *Inventing Ireland: The Literature of the Modern Nation* (London: Vintage, 1996).

—— 'The Real Ireland, Some Think', *New York Times*, 25 April 1999.

Kilroy, Tom, 'A Generation of Playwrights', *Irish University Review*, 22-1-2, Spring–Summer 1992, pp.135–41.

Kurdi, Mária, *Codes and Masks: Aspects of Identity in Contemporary Irish Plays in an Intercultural Context* (Berne: Peter Lang, 2000).

—— 'American and Other International Impulses on the Contemporary Irish Stage: A Talk with Playwright Declan Hughes', *Hungarian Journal of English and American Studies*, 8-2, 2002, pp.76–77.

—— '"Teenagers," "Gender Trouble," and Trickster Aesthetics in Gina Moxley's *Danti Dan*', *ABEI Journal*, 4, 2002, pp.67–82.

—— 'An Interview with Frank McGuinness', *Nua: Studies in Contemporary Irish Writing*, 4-1-2, 2003, pp.113–32.

Lacey, Stephen, *British Realist Theatre: The New Wave in its Context 1956–1965* (London: Routledge, 1995).

Lahr, John, 'Blood Simple', *New Yorker*, 13 March 2006, pp.92–4.

Leeney, Cathy and Anna McMullan, eds, *The Theatre of Marina Carr: Before Rules Was Made* (Dublin: Caryfort Press, 2003).

—— 'Hard Wired/Tender Bodies: Power, Loneliness, the Machine and the Person in the Work of Desperate Optimists', *Performing Ireland, Australasian Drama Studies Special Issue*, 43, October 2003, pp.76–88.

—— 'Ireland's "Exiled" Women Playwrights: Teresa Deevy and Marina Carr' in *The Cambridge Companion to Twentieth-century Irish Drama*, ed. Shaun Richards (Cambridge: Cambridge University Press, 2004), pp.150–63.

—— 'Men in No-Man's Land: Performing Urban Liminal Spaces in Two Plays by Mark O'Rowe', *Irish Review*, 35-1, Spring 2007, pp.108–16.

Lehmann, Hans-Thies, *Postdramatic Theatre*, translated and introduced by Karen Jürs-Munby (London: Routledge, 2006).

Liddy, James, 'Voices in the Irish Cities of the Dead: Melodrama and Dissent in Frank McGuinness's *Carthaginians*', *Irish University Review: A Journal of Irish Studies*, 25-2, Autumn–Winter 1995, pp.278–83.

Llewellyn Jones, Margaret, *Contemporary Irish Drama and Cultural Identity* (Bristol: Intellect, 2002).

Lojek, Helen, *The Theatre of Frank McGuinness: Stages of Mutability* (Dublin: Carysfort Press, 2002).

—— *Contexts for Frank McGuinness's Drama* (Washington, DC: Catholic University of America Press, 2004).

Lonergan, Patrick, *Theatre and Globalization: Irish Drama in the Celtic*

Tiger Era (Basingstoke: Palgrave, 2008).

Lonergan, Patrick and Riana O'Dwyer, eds, *Echoes Down the Corridor: Irish Theatre – Past, Present, and Future* (Dublin: Carysfort Press, 2007).

Long, Joseph, 'Frank McGuinness in Conversation with Joseph Long' in Lilian Chambers, G. FitzGibbon and E. Jordan, eds, *Theatre Talk: Voices of Irish Theatre Practitioners* (Dublin: Carysfort Press, 2001), pp.298–307.

Loomba, Ania, *Colonialism/Postcolonialism* (London and New York: Routledge, 1998).

Luckhurst, Mary, 'Martin McDonagh's *Lieutenant of Inishmore*: Selling (-Out) to the English', *Contemporary Theatre Review*, 14–4, 2004, pp.34–41.

—— *Dramaturgy: A Revolution in Theatre* (Cambridge: Cambridge University Press, 2006).

Lyotard, Jean-François, *The Postmodern Condition: A Report on Knowledge* (Minneapolis: University of Minnesota Press, 1986).

Macintosh, Fiona, *Dying Acts: Death in Ancient Greek and Modern Irish Tragic Drama* (Cork: Cork University Press, 1994).

Maguire, Tom, *Making Theatre in Northern Ireland: Through and Beyond the Troubles* (Exeter: University of Exeter Press, 2006).

Makeham, Paul, 'Performing the City', *Theatre Research International*, 32–2, 2005, pp.150–60.

McCarthy, John and Jill Morrell, *Some Other Rainbow* (London: Bantham Press, 1993).

McCormack, W.J., 'Irish Gothic and After (1820–1945)' in *The Field Day Anthology of Irish Writing Volume II*, ed. Seamus Deane (Derry: Field Day, 1991), pp.831–54.

McDonald, Marianne, *Ancient Sun, Modern Light: Greek Drama on the Modern Stage* (New York: Columbia University Press, 1992).

—— 'Classics as Celtic Firebrand: Greek Tragedy, Irish Playwrights, and Colonialism', in *Theatre Stuff: Critical Essays on Contemporary Irish Theatre*, ed. E. Jordan (Dublin: Carysfort Press, 2000), pp.16–26.

McDonald, Marianne and J. Michael Walton, *Amid our Troubles: Irish Versions of Greek Tragedy* (London: Methuen, 2002).

McGuinness, Frank, 'I am not confident for my country's future', *Irish Times*, 25, 26, 27 December 1989,p.8.

McLean, Adam, *The Triple Goddess: An Exploration of the Archetypal Feminine* (Grand Rapids, IL: Phanes Press, 1989).

McMullan, Anna, 'Gender, Authorship and Performance in Selected

Plays by Contemporary Irish Women Playwrights: Mary Elizabeth Burke-Kennedy, Marie Jones, Marina Carr, Emma Donoghue' in *Theatre Stuff: Critical Essays on Contemporary Irish Theatre*, ed. E. Jordan (Dublin: Carysfort Press, 2000), pp.34–46.

—— 'Unhomely Stages: Women Taking (a) Place in Irish Theatre' in *Druids, Dudes and Beauty Queens: The Changing Face of Irish Theatre*, ed. Dermot Bolger (Dublin: New Island, 2001), pp.72–90.

—— 'Masculinity and Masquerade in Thomas Kilroy's *Double Cross* and *The Secret Fall of Constance Wilde*', *Irish University Review: A Journal of Irish Studies*, 32–1, Spring–Summer 2002, pp.126–36.

McPherson, Conor, 'Original sin', *Guardian*, 7 February 2001.

Merriman, Victor, 'Theatre of Tiger Trash', *Irish University Review*, 29–2, Summer 1999, pp.305–17.

—— 'Heartsickness and Hopes Deferred' in *Twentieth-century Irish Drama*, ed. Shaun Richards (Cambridge: Cambridge University Press, 2004), pp.255–56.

Mikami, Hiroko, *Frank McGuinness and his Theatre of Paradox* (Gerrards Cross: Colin Smythe, 2002).

—— 'Kilroy's Vision of Doubleness', *Irish University Review: A Journal of Irish Studies*, 32–1, Spring–Summer 2002, pp.100–09.

Moore, Thomas, *The Soul of Sex* (New York: HarperCollins, 1998).

Morash, Christopher, *A History of Irish Theatre 1601–2000* (Cambridge: Cambridge University Press, 2002).

Morris, Eric and Alan Hoe, *Terrorism: Threat and Response* (New York: St Martin's Press, 1988).

Morse, Donald E., Csilla Bertha and Mária Kurdi, eds, *Brian Friel's Dramatic Artistry: 'The Work has Value'* (Dublin: Carysfort Press, 2006).

Murray, Christopher, *Twentieth-century Irish Drama: Mirror up to Nation* (Manchester: Manchester University Press, 1997).

—— 'The History Play Today' in *Cultural Contexts and Literary Idioms in Contemporary Irish Literature*, ed. Michael Kenneally (Gerrards Cross: Colin Smythe, 1998), pp.89–122.

—— '*The Cripple of Inishmaan* Meets Lady Gregory' in *The Theatre of Martin McDonagh: A World of Savage Stories* (Dublin: Carysfort Press, 2006), pp.97–115.

Morrison, Kristin, *Canters and Chronicles: The Use of Narrative in the Plays of Samuel Beckett and Harold Pinter* (Chicago, IL: University of Chicago Press, 1983).

Neale, Steve, *Genre and Hollywood* (London: Routledge, 2000).

O'Dwyer, Riana, 'Dancing in the Borderlands: The Plays of Frank

McGuinness' in *The Crows Behind the Plough: History and Violence in Anglo-Irish Poetry and Drama*, ed. Geert Lernout (Amsterdam: Rodopi, 1991), pp.99–115.

—— 'The Imagination of Women's Reality: Christina Reid and Marina Carr' in *Theatre Stuff: Critical Essays on Contemporary Irish Theatre*, ed. E. Jordan (Dublin: Carysfort Press, 2000), pp.236–48.

O'Hagan, Sean, 'The Wild West', *Guardian*, 24 March 2001, p.32.

O'Reilly (Kelly), Anne F., *Sacred Play: Soul Journeys in Contemporary Irish Theatre* (Dublin: Carysfort Press, 2004).

O'Toole, Fintan, *Tom Murphy: The Politics of Magic* (Dublin/London: New Island/Nick Hern, 1994, revised edition).

—— 'Introduction' in *Martin McDonagh, Plays One* (London: Methuen, 1999).

—— *Critical Moments: Fintan O'Toole on Modern Irish Theatre*, eds Julia Furay and Redmond O'Hanlon (Dublin: Carysfort Press, 2003).

—— 'A mind in Connemara: the savage world of Martin McDonagh', *New Yorker*, 6 March 2006, pp.40–47.

Orr, John, *Tragicomedy and Popular Culture* (London: Macmillan, 1991).

Orr, John and Dragan Klaic, eds, 'Introduction' in *Terrorism and Modern Drama* (Edinburgh: Edinburgh University Press, 1990).

Palahniuk, Chuck, *Fight Club* (London: Vintage, 1997).

Pavis, Patrice, *Theatre at the Crossroads of Culture*, trans. Loren Kruger (London and New York: Routledge, 1992).

—— *Analyzing Performance: Theatre, Dance, and Film*, trans. David Williams (Ann Arbor: University of Michigan Press, 2004).

Peacock, Alan, ed., *The Achievement of Brian Friel* (Gerrards Cross: Colin Smythe, 1993).

Phelan, Mark, 'The Fantasy of Post-nationalism in Northern Irish Theatre: *Caught Red Handed* Transplanting the Planter', *Performing Ireland, Australasian Drama Studies Special Issue*, 43, October 2003, pp.89–107.

Pilkington, Lionel, *Theatre and the State in Twentieth-century Ireland: Cultivating the People* (London and New York: Routledge, 2001).

Pilný, Ondřej, *Irony and Identity in Modern Irish Drama* (Prague: Litteraria Pragensia, 2006).

Pine, Richard, *The Diviner: The Art of Brian Friel* (Dublin: University College Dublin Press, 1998).

Putman, Robert, *Bowling Alone: The Collapse and Revival of American Community* (London and New York: Simon & Schuster, 2000).

Raphael, Frederic and Kenneth McLeish, trans., *Medea* (London: Nick Hern, 1994).

Ravenhill, Mark, 'Tforum: A Tear in the Fabric', *Theatre Forum*, 26, Winter–Spring 2005, pp.85–92.

Renvoize, Jean, *Innocence Destroyed: A Study of Child Sexual Abuse* (London: Routledge, 1993).

Richards, Shaun, '"The Outpouring of a Morbid, Unhealthy Mind": The Critical Condition of Synge and McDonagh', *Irish University Review*, 33–1, Spring–Summer 2003, pp.201–14.

—— ed., *The Cambridge Companion to Twentieth-century Irish Drama* (Cambridge: Cambridge University Press, 2004).

Roche, Anthony, *Contemporary Irish Drama: From Beckett to McGuinness* (Dublin: Gill & Macmillan, 1994).

—— 'Women on the Threshold: J.M. Synge's *The Shadow of the Glen*, Teresa Deevy's *Katie Roche* and Marina Carr's *The Mai*', *Irish University Review*, 25–1, Spring 1995, pp.143–62.

—— 'Re-Working *The Workhouse Ward*: McDonagh, Beckett, and Gregory', *Irish University Review: Special Issue: Lady Gregory*, 34–1, 2004, pp.171–84.

Rokem, Freddie, 'Antigone Remembers: Dramaturgical Analysis and Oedipus Tyrannos', *Theatre Research International*, 31–3, pp.260–69.

Schapiro, Leonard, *Totalitarianism* (London: Pall Mall, 1972).

Schechner, Richard, *The Future of Ritual: Writings on Culture and Performance* (London and New York: Routledge, 1993).

—— *Performance Studies: An Introduction* (London and New York: Routledge, 2002, second edition).

—— *Performance Theory* (London and New York: Routledge, 2003, revised edition).

Scolnicov, Hanna, *Woman's Theatrical Space* (Cambridge: Cambridge University Press, 1994).

Sierz, Aleks, *In-Yer-Face Theatre: British Drama Today* (London: Faber & Faber, 2001).

Sihra, Melissa, 'A Cautionary Tale: Marina Carr's *By the Bog of Cats*' in *Theatre Stuff: Critical Essays on Contemporary Irish Theatre*, ed. E. Jordan (Dublin: Carysfort Press, 2000), pp.257–68.

—— ed., *Women in Irish Drama: A Century of Authorship and Representation* (London: Palgrave, 2007).

Singleton, Brian, 'Sick, Dying, Dead, Dispersed: The Evanescence of Patriarchy in Contemporary Women's Theatre' in Sihra, M. ed., *Women in Irish Drama: A Century of Authorship and Representation* (Basingstoke: Palgrave Macmillan, 2007), pp.186–200.

Singleton, Brian and Anna McMullan, eds, *'Performing Ireland': Australasian Drama Studies Special Issue*, 43, October 2003.

Smyth, Gerry, *Decolonisation and Irish Criticism: The Construction of Irish Literature* (London: Pluto Press, 1998).

—— *Space and the Irish Cultural Imagination* (Basingstoke and New York: Palgrave, 2001).

Soja, Edward W., *Postmetropolis: Critical Studies of Cities and Regions* (London: Blackwell Publishers, 2000).

Stallybrass, Peter and Allon White, *The Politics and the Poetics of Transgression* (London: Methuen, 1986).

Steiner, George, *Antigones: The Antigone Myth in Western Literature, Art and Thought* (Oxford: Oxford University Press, 1984).

Stevenson, Deborah, *Cities and Urban Cultures* (Maidenhead: Open University Press, 2003).

Strinati, Dominic, *An Introduction to Studying Popular Culture* (London: Routledge, 2000).

Sutherland, Tom and Jean, *At Your Own Risk: An American Chronicle of Crisis and Captivity in the Middle East* (Colorado: Fulcrum, 1996).

Sweeney, Bernadette, *Performing the Body in Irish Theatre* (Basingstoke: Palgrave, 2008).

Szabó, Carmen, *'Clearing the Ground': The Field Day Theatre Company and the Construction of Irish Identities* (Newcastle: Cambridge Scholars Publishing, 2007).

Taggart, Ashley, 'Theatre of War? Contemporary Drama in Northern Ireland', in *Theatre Stuff: Critical Essays on Contemporary Irish Theatre*, ed. E. Jordan (Dublin: Carysfort Press, 2000), pp.67–83.

Taplin, Oliver, *Greek Tragedy in Action* (London: Methuen, 1978).

Thomson, Peter and Glendyr Sacks, eds, *The Cambridge Companion to Brecht* (Cambridge: Cambridge University Press, 1994), pp.185–200.

Trotter, Mary, 'Translating Women into Irish Theatre History' in *A Century of Irish Drama: Widening the Stage*, ed. S. Watt, E. Morgan and S. Mustafa (Bloomington: Indiana University Press, 2000), pp.163–79.

Turner, Cathy and Synne Behrndt, *Dramaturgy and Performance* (London: Palgrave, 2007).

Vanek, Joe, 'In Conversation with Derek West', *Theatre Ireland*, 29, Autumn 1992, p.26.

Vice, Sue, *Introducing Bakhtin* (Manchester: Manchester University Press, 1997).

Waite, Terry, *Taken on Trust* (London: Hodder & Stoughton, 1993).

Wallace, Clare, *Suspect Cultures: Narrative, Identity and Citation in*

1990s New Drama (Prague: Litteraria Pragensia, 2006).

Walton, Michael, 'Introduction', *Euripides: Plays One* (Methuen: London, 2000).

Waters, John, 'The Irish Mummy: The Plays and Purpose of Martin McDonagh' in *Druids, Dudes and Beauty Queens: The Changing Face of Irish Theatre*, ed. Dermot Bolger (Dublin: New Island, 2001), pp.30–54.

Watt, Stephen, Eileen Morgan and Shakir Mustafa, eds, *A Century of Irish Drama: Widening the Stage* (Bloomington: Indiana University Press, 2000).

Weitz, Eric, *The Power of Laughter: Comedy and Contemporary Irish Theatre* (Dublin: Carysfort Press, 2004).

Williamson, Margaret, 'A Woman's Place in Euripides' *Medea*' in *Euripides, Women, and Sexuality*, ed. Anton Powell (London: Routledge, 1990).

Wilson, Rebecca, 'Macabre Merriment in McDonagh's Melodrama *The Beauty Queen of Leenane*' in *The Power of Laughter: Comedy and Contemporary Irish Theatre* (Dublin: Carysfort Press, 2004), pp.129–44.

Zelenak, Michael, X., 'The Troublesome Reign of King Oedipus: Civic Discourse and Civil Discord in Greek Tragedy', *Theatre Research International*, 23–1, 1998, pp.69–82.

Index